The Improbable Existence of Life After Divorce

A COMEDY

R.M. SNIDER

ISBN 978-1-7360380-1-7

Cover and interior design (and all the things) by R.M. Snider

Fonts:
Berlin Sans FB Demi (by David Berlow, Desktop License)
Calibri (Microsoft Business License)
Cardenio Modern (by Nils Cordes, free for commercial use)

Chapter 1

"Valentine's Day . . . bummer."
—Dr. Peter Venkman

Russ wasn't sure why he'd asked Stem to drive. In all the years they'd known each other, he'd never seen the Australian behind the wheel. Russ didn't even know if his friend had an American driver's license. Yet, at the moment, he reasoned Stem's questionable driving skills might be of great benefit to him. He hoped the man might accidentally turn into oncoming traffic—a semi, if luck would have it—that would careen into the passenger side of the Prius at such a high speed that Russ' airbag would not have time to deploy before his forehead collided with the dashboard, thus ending his pitiful existence. If anyone was most likely to continue on with their life without permanent, debilitating emotional scars as a result of causing such a tragedy, Russ believed Stem would be it—with the exception of Katie, of course, who, by this moment, had probably fantasized at least half a dozen times about his unfortunate and particularly gruesome death.

The Prius turned onto Walnut Street in the cozy college town. To Russ' disappointment, the hybrid bore not a scratch nor blemish from Stem's driving. But just as they pulled into Meemaw's driveway, the driver turned to look at his friend, to say something unusually touching and sensitive—and the car jolted as the front passenger fender grazed the side of Meemaw's brick mailbox.

Though Stem had passed his driver's exam some twenty years

earlier, he wasn't used to driving on the right side of the road. "Sorry about that," he quickly apologized.

Russ shrugged. A scraped fender was just as well. Not the gruesome death he had wished for, but a small penance, he supposed, for his grievous sin, a mark on the silver paint like the scarlet letter itself. Perhaps he'd touch it up with a streak of crimson nail polish as further punishment for his transgressions.

The driver hopped out, but as he reached a gangly arm into the back seat to retrieve a bag of Wavy Lays, he questioned, "You coming, mate?"

The look of absolute dejection was an apropos accessory to the dispirited shrug Russ offered as his response.

Stem, whose memory was as reliable as a digital currency chain, found himself strangely at a loss to recall what sentiment he had been about to share with his dejected friend just the moment before he struck the mailbox. But suddenly, it returned. Satisfied, his lips parted in a crooked-toothed grin and he chirped, "Things are looking up."

Through hollow eyes, Russ questioned, "In what way is that statement true?"

"With your recent termination of employment, effective 8:03 this morning, and, since Katie wants nothing more to do with you, you've become a free man with no obligations or tie downs. And now that you're living at Meemaw's house, you're only one kilometer from *my* house." He wasn't sure this was sun-up enough, so he added for good measure, "And only seven hundred meters from the new Dairy Queen."

Stem waited for a positive response from his friend, but when none was given, he grabbed his chips and headed into Meemaw's to say hello and rummage her pantry for ramen noodles.

Russ occupied the passenger seat for an interminable length of time. He knew how he got there—how it came about that he should be moving back into his childhood home—but he wasn't sure *how* he got there. He'd committed a vexing act of indiscretion which had irreversibly impacted his life, catapulting it in precisely the direction he had no desire of going. And now, what could he do but move back in with Meemaw and return to a childlike state, in a sense, relearning his steps, figuring out where he'd gone wrong and growing up again so that, eventually (he hoped, although sometimes he didn't) he would go back out into the world and do it better a second time.

Russ rolled out of the passenger door, trudged across the lawn of dead weeds, and was hit with the familiar odor of days past as he pulled open the screen door. He was sure he would never get over (and secretly, he never *wanted* to get over) that shag carpet which occupied every room of the house (including both bathrooms, though mercifully not the kitchen). The burnt orange rug complemented the yellowish macramé artwork and the dark brown paneling. He was almost sure he'd seen a photo taken some time in the early 1970s revealing that the macramé had, in fact, once been white—but he knew you could never trust the colors in photos of that decade. Enhancing the décor was the smell of cigarettes which never seemed to go away although Meemaw claimed she stopped smoking in 2003.

This was his home once, the place where he changed from a boy into a man. And what man was he today? A thirty-eight-year-old soon-to-be divorcee. A fired college history professor. A bloke who'd gathered up his dignity in a trash bag and tossed it over an abysmal cliff.

Russ felt shame wash over him. Perhaps if he was quiet enough, Meemaw would never know he'd moved back in.

"Rusty!" she hollered over the sound of both televisions—the one in the living room and the one in her bedroom. Even in her stage 4 metastatic cancerous state, her lungs could project.

He stalked down the hallway and stopped at her door.

"Stem said she kicked you out," she rasped. "And on Valentine's, of all days. And he said you cheated on her. That was a derned foolish thing to do and I didn't raise no fool of a grandson. Come here and kiss me and tell my why you did that. And did I know her? It was a her, wasn't it? You didn't go queer, did you?"

He was so mortified that his eighty-four-year-old grandma knew he'd had an affair that he just shook his head and said, "No, ma'am. It was a girl."

"A girl? Lawd, you ain't on the sex registry are you?"

"No, ma'am. She was a sophomore at the university."

"Your student? I thought all them was Christians! Christian University, after all," she trailed off.

Meemaw would've been easier to read if she hadn't lost her eyebrows to the chemo treatments. She always spoke through her eyebrows, and, now, he saw how terribly difficult it was to know what she was thinking.

"Well, give me a kiss, then," she demanded. "I still love you. Always will, even if you went and done a fool thing like that. Why you did it, I just don't understand. Don't care how pretty that college girl was. Katie was the best thing that happened to you since I took you in myself, even if I was raisin' three other of my grands. Lawd knows no one else 'round here would've taken you in, seein' as you're half Eastern Indian. This is Arkansas and they don't call this White County for nothin'! So, why'd you do it? Tell me why you broke my Katie's heart, not that I mind you movin' back in with me."

She muted the tv, a sure sign he must speak for what he did.

But how could he explain it? He knew, two months ago when it began, there had been a reason—maybe several—a driving force that had compelled him to forsake his marriage vows to the most amazing woman he'd ever met but, for the life of him, he could not recall any of those motives now.

He shrugged. "Guess I thought it was a good idea at the time."

"And now?"

"Now . . ." He wanted to say something unreasonable like, "I wish I had a time machine to go back and *not* do it," but what came out was more realistically an option. "I wish I'd just wake up dead."

She snapped her fingers and he sensed her eyebrows shot up so high they would've kissed her blue curls had she not lost them too. "You can't wake up dead, and you know that. You'll either wake up alive—on this earth—or you'll wake up alive in Heaven. I didn't raise no fool of a grandson. You say it again and I'm calling that helpline. 1-800-SUICIDE. I'll have them lock your butt up or whatever they do for people who say dumb things like that."

He felt her chastisement like he was twelve again and had called his cousin Lance stupid. "Sorry, Meemaw. I won't say it again."

"Now you done broke up with that girl, didn't ya?"

He nodded, too ashamed to admit it had technically been her who had initiated the demise of their pseudo-relationship.

Meemaw barked, "Stem said *she* dumped *you*!"

Again, he nodded.

"Good. You deserved that. You know I'd spank you if I was feelin' up to it. But I still love you. I always will."

She crossed her arms, closed her tired eyes, and sighed. Then, without opening her eyes, she cast a net of instructions. "You gonna hafta wash them sheets on that bed before ya sleep on it. Lance's two littlests stopped over last weekend and I'm just sure one of 'em peed the bed, but I ain't had the strength to check up on it. And unload the dishwasher, would ya, sweetie? Now Stem says you ain't workin', so you gonna be doin' your part 'round here, ya hear?"

He felt even more twelve than he'd felt two minutes ago and dutifully replied, "Yes, ma'am."

Stem was actively involved in slurping his second bowl of ramen noodles when Russ entered the kitchen and turned on the light. In response to the glow, the Aussie wore a bewildered expression, as though Genesis had just begun. "What the bloody heck is going on?" he demanded to know.

"What?"

Gaping, he gestured to the light switch. "You can't do that, mate. It'll run up Meemaw's electric bill. She's on a fixed income, you know."

"You're eating up her food and you're going to lecture me about the electric bill?"

"Meemaw knows I must have sustenance," his friend protested. Assuming he'd won the argument, he reached up with his long, thin fingers and shut off the light.

The sky was the color of ashes and the small window above the sink let in scant gray light. Russ felt his way around the pantry-sized kitchen as he unloaded the dishes, shuffling past Stem who had planted himself on the step ladder in the middle of the floor. However, after less than a minute of enduring his slurping noises, Russ offered the man a fresh spoon.

"No, thank you," Stem said, rejecting the utensil.

Russ insisted. "So you'll quit slurping."

As if Russ had suggested he use a garden hose to rinse out his sinuses, Stem argued, "I can't very well use a spoon. It's too dark to see the noodles."

Though he was a loyal friend, his presence was sometimes exasperating. For twenty-five long seconds, Russ endured the lingering sound of ramen noodles ungracefully finding their way past the man's lips, but then, he laid his foot down. As the lights switched on, he plunged the spoon into his friend's bowl. "There!"

The bowl was, however, empty.

Irritated, Russ retrieved the utensil and tossed it into the appropriate drawer. As he returned to the sink to scrub dishes, Stem thrust his skeletal hand into the drawer and retrieved a handful of mismatched flatware before dropping them in the sink.

"What are you doing?" Russ roared.

"Well, they're dirty now," insisted Stem.

"No, they're not—you just took them out of the drawer!"

"Don't you know how germs transfer? One of these spoons touched the inside of my bowl—which I had eaten out of—and then *you* put it back in the drawer with the others, so now they're all contaminated."

"I don't care!" Russ said stubbornly.

Stem stomped his foot, his brown curls shuddering from the impact. "Meemaw is immuno-bloody-compromised! You can't allow her to use spoons with my germs on them. What if I'm sick?"

"You *are* sick," growled Russ as he jammed a pot on the bottom rack of the dishwasher.

Stem laid his bowl in the sink, and, as he headed for the door, called, "I've got a classful of future physicists waiting on me and I don't have time for your nonsense!"

"Oh, no!" yelled his mate. "You've got plenty of time before your class starts. Come back here and clean your dishes!"

Stem guffawed. "Meemaw says guests don't have to wash their own dishes. You, on the other hand, live here."

It had taken nearly two weeks for Russ to get another job. Unremarkably, none of the nearby state universities were interested in hiring a tenured history professor who had recently been fired for having an affair with a sophomore (and in the middle of February, to boot). But the retailer American GadgetTech in Cabot didn't mind, as long as he could work nights, weekends, and holidays.

And he could. And he did. For a month, Russ immersed himself into the mindless work of selling cheap electronics to people who wished they were cheaper. And he did what he could for Meemaw, which he'd never felt like was enough—and even more so now that she was dying.

On March 23rd, Russ took a bowl of chicken broth into her bedroom. She was sleeping like a bag of bones hidden under a mound of blankets.

"Meemaw?" he called softly.

"Oh, there's no reason to knock," she crowed before falling into a coughing fit.

Russ wasn't sure when it was customary to call hospice in, but he had already suggested it a number of times. "Absolutely not!" Meemaw had objected. "And if you call them I'll crawl out of this bed and whip your hide!"

He waited patiently for her coughing spell to ease up, and, though she recovered slightly, she never did completely.

"Sit down," she ordered, taking the bowl from him. She sat it on her nightstand amidst an array of mugs and cups half-full of other food and drink items she'd been offered. He always meant to clear them but never remembered to before she fell asleep again, and he worried the clanking of dishes might awaken her.

"I need to tell ya somethin'," she began. "Now, I know I'm dyin' and I know, soon as I do, your cousins will be upon this place like maggots on a carcass. So, what I'm fixin' to tell ya is very important. So, listen, sweetie. I ain't got the breath to say it again. Now, over there in my closet on the far-left side behind my church dresses—oh, by the way, bury me in the blue one—there's some—oh, and my pearls—other items which are of utmost importance. I'm sorry to say, but it's your entire inheritance and I want you to have it. It ain't for Lance or Becky or JoAnne or none of the others. It's just for you. Now, go on. Go get it."

Meemaw had never spoken of inheritance or wealth, except to say they didn't have any and wouldn't be getting any, so Russ' interest was piqued. Not that he wanted to dwell on her death, but he was a reasonable fellow and knew it was inevitable.

"Back here?" he asked, pulling her dresses out of the way.

"Yes," she nodded. "Back there in that corner."

He reached in, felt a fang, and screamed.

"Oh, don't be a baby," she chided. "It's only a bobcat. Here, I'll get it—" which they both knew was impossible with her constant coughing and sputtering.

With the help of his phone flashlight, he retrieved said bobcat—which was thankfully very dead and stuffed and conveniently mounted to a platform—along with a cookie jar shaped like a rooster, a wooden easel contraption, and a shoe box of assorted trinkets.

"Now, bring those here," she ordered.

As soon as he laid them beside her on the bed, she all but snuggled the bobcat.

"You never met my sweet Jasper baby," she said as she stroked his fur. "Used to be my pet when I was a little girl. Daddy had him stuffed when he died and told everyone who came to the house that he shot and kilt himself a bobcat. Truth is, we just found her as a kitten and I raised her up and tamed her. Anyway, I never had her out when y'all was growin' up 'cause y'all were so mighty wild, and, by the time I'd raised y'all, your older cousins was already havin' babies and they were twice as children from hell as the rest of you, so Jasper just got stuffed away in my closet. But turns out, these things are worth some money. So, I want you to hide him from your cousins—hide all this stuff—'cause they'll be upon this place lookin' for treasures of every kind, which, to their disappointment, they won't find." Tossing him a wink, she grinned and whispered, "And then, once they all leave, you can sell it. Would probably fetch a thousand dollars on eBay."

Everything she had just told him—save for the part about his cousins, which was entirely true—he found preposterous, and he owed that to the oxycontin/fentanyl concoction she was throwing back every few hours. However, he listened straight-faced and *yes ma'amed* his grandmother when appropriate.

"And this here is a cookbook stand. I had hoped it'd be my sweet Katie's and she'd get all my recipes—you'll have to go snag those from the kitchen shelf, the one below Peepaw's old cheese grater. And that rooster cookie jar was my grandma's, so I figured it'd be worth something. And those are just old things in that box. You can sell them if you want, but they all mean something to me. I'll write it down for you, not that you're likely to care."

Russ realized he hated this conversation. Not because there was anything unpleasant about Meemaw, but because she was giving her things away which meant she really was dying. With all his recent loss, he found it impossible to hold in his tears.

"Oh, don't start that up," she snapped, waving her hand as though swatting a fly. "You know how I can't stand to see a boy cry. Well, come here, sweetie."

She pulled him close, which he allowed, and he'd expected to feel the squishiness of her bosom like he always had as a boy, only now her chest was as welcoming as a cadaver.

"Now, now," she said, almost belittlingly as she pushed him into the chair beside her bed. She never could stand boys crying, but worse, she didn't like feeling culpable for it. "You're the executor of my estate. So, when I'm gone, whatever the cousins don't take, which'll probably be everything, will be yours to sell and do whatever ya want with. Don't keep nothing for my sake. Sell it all, I say, and make yourself a little money. Lawd, I know you ain't makin' much at that pitiful job you got. And make sure my sweet Katie knows I love her and always will. You'd better tell her that *or I'll skin you*. I want her there at the funeral—I want you *both* there. I wished y'all'd get back together before I die so I could see y'all together one last time. But anyway."

She crossed her arms and rested her head and eyes. But just as quickly, they popped back open.

"Now, hide that stuff I just gave ya," she instructed. "You won't have any time once I die. Your cousins will be upon this place, like I said. Locusts on Egypt."

He had nowhere particularly to "hide" a bobcat, rooster cookie jar, cookbook stand, and shoe box of trinkets except for the back of his car, so he hauled them out and laid them to rest there, shutting the hatch as one throws dirt on a grave. He also remembered to grab her recipes, although he doubted they would ever find their way to Katie. He needed to rush to get to work in time, but after the conversation they'd just had, he couldn't bear to leave without kissing her again. He tiptoed into her bedroom, making note that he needed to clear her nightstand of the untouched food elements—and also call in hospice, despite her protests. Her cheek felt unusually thin, like the old sheets which had been on the bed in the extra room when he had come to live with her at age nine, so he kissed her forehead instead.

"Rusty?" she said, her voice groggy yet, somehow, peaceful.

"Yes, ma'am?"

"I forgot to tell ya. Peepaw had some storage shed over in . . ."

He waited, feeling the pressure of his one o'clock work schedule combined with the very little time he still had to enjoy her presence. After a minute, he whispered, "Meemaw?"

"Hmm?"

"You were saying something about Peepaw's storage shed."

"Rose Bud is where it is. Mermaid Lane. The end of it. All the way to the end. Key's in that box of knickknacks I gave ya. He always kept one with him—left this duplicate here in case he lost the other'n. He practically lived there, it seemed. You know, I never went there, not after he disappeared anyway. Didn't even tell the police to look there. Didn't even think about it. Figured he'd run off and left me with all these wild kids to raise, which he did."

Her coughing spell lasted so long that Russ knew without a doubt he would be late to work. Oh, well. With any luck, he'd get fired and could live off the sale of the bobcat carcass for a month or so before having to reenter the job market.

It also struck him, though, that he hadn't heard Meemaw talk about Peepaw for years. The man had disappeared when Russ was twelve. It was Searcy's oldest unsolved missing person's case. Oddly, at the time, it almost seemed like the most natural thing for him to have done.

Yes, Peepaw was here a few days ago, but he never came back. That's fine, I think. Yes, just fine. Peepaw was hardly ever around anyway.

And now that Meemaw mentioned it, Russ did vaguely remember Peepaw's storage shed. Strange, how that memory just came right back. Peepaw used to go there for days at a time. It didn't seem odd when Russ was a kid that his grandfather would disappear for such long stretches, but now, as a man himself, it did seem very peculiar.

"Meemaw? I've gotta go to work now."

"I love you, Rusty, and I always will. The spare key's in that box. He must've tooken the original."

"I'll take care of it," he promised, hurrying to the door before another revelation of inheritance seized her.

Russ drove to work, remembering only as he sat in his car for his thirty-minute meal break that a large, stuffed predator lingered somewhere behind his seat. When he got home at 10:50 that night, he went in to check on Meemaw. She lay there cold, with her arms still crossed and the same expression upon her face—dead.

Chapter 2

Katie came to the funeral.

Russ had seen her from a distance, but she had not sat with the family nor joined their procession, nor had she greeted any family members after the funeral. But she had been there and Russ realized it was the first time he'd been in the same room—same building—as her since she'd been at that 8:00am meeting in the dean's office. She'd had to find out from Dean Scarborough that morning that her husband had screwed around with a sophomore named Caydee, of all names. The hurt look in her eyes as he admitted yes, he had done that, had been crushing. He had taken Katie—*his* Katie—his precious, sweet, humble, loyal, trusting Katie—and he had crushed her soul like a mean-hearted boy stomps a frog. For reasons he still could not work out, he had done the very thing he knew would hurt her the most. And yet, she was the last person he'd wanted to hurt in all the world. If everyone was lined up and, for some extraordinary cosmic reason, he had to crush all of their souls one by one, he'd put her at the end of the line. And when he reached her . . . he'd never willingly crush her. Never. But yet, he had. He saw it in her eyes.

"It was like the terminator," he'd told Stem.

"Ah," said his friend, nodding.

"In the first movie when Sarah Connor crushes his head and his red eyes go out."

They just sat on his bed in his room at Meemaw's like two schoolboys pining over the loss of one of their loves. Only Russ wasn't in high school—he was a thirty-eight-year-old ex-college professor, and Katie wasn't just some junior school crush. She was his only love. His wife of eight plus years. The one he'd waited twenty-nine years to find. He was her protector. She was his fawn. He didn't deserve her—that he knew from the first day she noticed him. It was something about her spirit, the one inside her. It had spoken to his in a supernatural way, and said, "You matter. You're important." He had never felt that way with anyone except for Meemaw. Even with Stem, his best friend, he sometimes believed he could be forgotten, second-tiered to a box of Fruity Pebbles or a frozen supreme pizza. But Katie had given him something he'd yearned for, something he needed in a wife. He knew she loved him and was devoted wholly to him.

And he'd crushed her.

"I spoke to her," Stem whispered as they hoisted Meemaw's casket into the hearse.

"What did she say?" Russ asked, a slight strain in his voice. How did his short, one-hundred-and-twenty-pound grandma weigh this much?

"She said, 'Tell him I said I'm sorry about Meemaw. I'll miss her too.'"

Those words were to Russ like a fourteen-year-old boy receiving a folded piece of paper with *yes* nestled in a heart. Suddenly, Meemaw's casket wasn't so heavy and that black suit he'd forgotten to take to the dry cleaners after Marco Cavillo's wedding reception last summer didn't feel so sweaty.

"Did she say anything else?" he asked, hoping his friend would convey good news.

"Not about you."

It was cold water on a fire. "Wait—what does that mean?"

"It means what I said. She didn't say anything else about *you*."

Russ had not forgotten about the cookbook stand and recipes.

Maybe he should call her about them? Or maybe just mail them to her? Or maybe just hang onto them for another time. He couldn't decide, but every time the dilemma popped into his mind, there came Jasper, poised in the trunk, ready to pounce on something.

How in the world does one tame a bobcat? Or keep a taxidermized creature in their closet for over thirty-eight years without their grandson knowing about it?

But Jasper came in handy when they reached the graveside.

"Pop the boot, would ya?" asked Stem. "I've got to lose this blazer."

A moment later, his scream murdered the somber silence. "What the bloody—"

"It's stuffed," Russ said, doing his best to hide the smirk he knew was fighting to be worn like a victory medal. "I thought you grew up in the outback."

"Well," he said, somewhat affronted. "When we found something like that hanging out in the boot, we didn't stick around and exchange names."

"Well, meet Jasper. Meemaw gave it to me. Says it's worth a thousand dollars."

Stem's expression might've suggested Russ had said a million dollars. "What? And you're just driving everywhere with it, bumping it around back there with that other junk, dinging it up beyond recognition? A prize like that should be on display. Did she kill it herself?"

"It was her childhood pet, apparently."

"Meemaw is the coolest."

As they somberly walked to the graveside service, Russ looked around in the crowd like a man searching for his crush. Several times, he feigned to look over his shoulder and smiled at a cousin's baby who was sitting behind him just so he could spy for Katie. This did not work for two reasons. One: Katie was not there. Two: His cousin mistook his intentions and handed him the baby, who promptly spit up all over his suit.

The cousins had propped the screen door open with a potted plant that had died last winter. For several seconds, Russ stood there staring at it, feeling somehow supernaturally connected to it. At one point, they had both been vivacious creatures—now, both were lifeless lumps of carbon. He was complacent to stay outside with the withered vine, but the smell of food coming from inside pulled Stem along who, subsequently, pulled Russ into the house.

"Cuz!" exclaimed Russ' cousin Keplin. Shifting his cigarette from his right hand to his left, which was holding his beer, the guy threw his open palm up in a gesture of invitation as one might to a one-year-old who was learning to give a high five. "Rusty, my man, how's life treating you?"

Prior to Meemaw's funeral, Russ had not seen Keplin since the latter's high school graduation seventeen years earlier. Following it, the younger cousin had promptly disappeared, and, though his mother, Cindy, claimed he had joined the Army, this declaration was disputed on several occasions by Keplin's sister, Kirstin, who said he'd moved to California to work in a gluten-free sourdough bakery. Consequently, at the moment Russ entered the house just now, Kirstin was removing the macramé from the wall.

"I always wanted this," she cooed as she clutched it to her chest, out the open door.

"Seriously, bruh," continued Keplin. "What's been up with you?"

Russ nodded slowly, taking in a deep breath. "Got fired. My wife is divorcing me. Meemaw died last week."

"Bruh," Keplin replied, dragging the syllable out for a solid seven seconds. "Too heavy, man."

With that, the prodigal cousin turned to someone else and engaged in a conversation about the Razorbacks' horrible spring training.

Russ drooped to the couch. However, within a handful of seconds, as he felt the seat of his pants soaked through, he leapt to his feet.

"Tater peed there," explained his cousin JoAnne as she

crouched on the shag carpet, diapering a half-naked baby. "But it's all right—Bobby said we'd just take the couch. We'll clean it later. He's goin' right now to pick up the rental trailer."

"Shoot!" hollered her sister Becky as she spit out a mouthful of Dr. Pepper. "You're takin' that, JoAnne?"

"Yeah."

"Well, I done already told Walker to go get his truck 'cause I was takin' it."

"Nuh-uh," said JoAnne. "I am. Dogs tore up ours and we been sittin' on the ground for too long. Hurts Bobby's back to play his video games."

"Well, I need one 'cause I'm movin' to Hot Springs with Walker."

JoAnne threw her baby up on her shoulder and pursed her lips. "Well, we'll see who gets it loaded first."

Becky shot a look of icy blades at her sister and stormed off.

In addition to the two sisters, Russ had grown up in the house alongside their older brother, Lance. The bully, who was Russ' older cousin by twelve days and larger cousin by seven vertical inches and one hundred and twenty pounds, appeared in the kitchen doorway. "There you are," he said, pointing a crooked finger at Russ. "Get your skinny butt in here and square this away."

Before he could do anything about it, Russ found himself in the kitchen and, worse, between Lance and their cousin Gemini. Had he realized he was being summoned to referee an argument between the two alpha-sexes of their generation, he'd have run the other way. Lance might've had muscle on Russ, but Gemini had crazy.

As unbelievable as it was now, Gemini had been a shy high schooler who wore her hair long and straight, thought Jncos were a sin, captained the academic team, and was voted most likely to succeed. However, her junior year of college she dropped out and shacked up with a tattoo artist named Beast. Soon thereafter, the pair opened a business together which specialized in body alterations. Gemini's upgrades included fanged canine teeth with red tips, black titanium fingernails implanted in her nail beds, and four spiky silver studs imbedded into her skull. She'd done a stint in The Women's Professional Wrestling circuit and had become well-known for her signature move, the vag ripper, but she was disqualified due to a recent stipulation regarding body alterations. Last Russ heard, her lawsuit against the WPW was still pending.

"Rusty?" she barked at Lance. The veins in her forehead made the studs pulse with each heartbeat. "Why'd you drag *him* in here?"

Lance put his arm around his smaller cousin and grinned. "'Cause you're the executor of Meemaw's estate, ain't that right, Rusty?"

Gemini cocked her head and glared at Russ as she took a step closer. "Is that right? Meemaw put you in charge?"

"She . . ." he wavered. "She said you all can take whatever you want."

Gemini slapped the counter, her metal nails half an inch away from maiming the icing on a triple-layer chocolate cake an elderly lady from Meemaw's church had baked for the grieving family. "Well, I'm takin' what I want, and make no bones about it—that matching bedroom set is mine!"

"Oh, no you ain't gonna take Meemaw's furniture!" hollered Lance. "That's gonna be my weddin' gift to Courtney!"

As Lance moved in to slug Gemini, Russ ducked out of the kitchen.

"Them two still fightin'?" asked JoAnne as she poked a breast into her baby's open mouth.

Russ had no comments to make, but one of his younger cousins did.

"Sounds like that time we stuck that ol' raccoon and alley cat in that trash can," said Haley as he nudged Keplin. "Remember that, cuz? That was before you moved away."

"Ah, yeah, bruh!" laughed Keplin. "That was sick!"

"Yeah, it was. That raccoon licked that cat's tail!"

"Was that totally Megan Colley's cat, dude?"

"Yeah, it was!"

Just then, Lance exited the kitchen, cupping a bloodied cheek in one hand, making a beeline for the bathroom. On his heels, Gemini darkened the doorway and growled, “Who’s gonna help me load that furniture onto my diesel?” Her glare at Keplin and Haley informed them they’d been selected for the task. They nodded dutifully and raised their hands for good measure.

Russ didn’t especially want to stay in the same room as JoAnne, who felt no need to cover her breasts as her baby guzzled his dinner, so he retreated to his bedroom. On the way there in the hallway he crossed paths with Kirstin’s son, Kendrick, who was just pulling on a familiar Nirvana t-shirt.

“Hey, that’s mine,” said Russ, pointing at it.

“Whatever, loser,” snorted the disrespectful kid, adjusting the shirt over his hoodie. “My mom said I could have anything I wanted.”

Russ gaped. “Dude, that’s *my* bedroom. That room right there. I *live* in there. You got that from *my* room.”

The teen flashed him a half-smile. “Finders keepers, ya know?”

Having taught college history classes for thirteen years, Russ had had his fair share of disrespectful teens, but for whatever reason, he’d never felt so affronted than when a fifteen-year-old boy walked away in his prized Nirvana t-shirt.

“Did you see that?” Russ asked Stem when he reached his bedroom.

“What?”

“My cousin’s punk kid just stole my Nirvana shirt.”

“That sucks, mate.”

“Got my first kiss in it.”

Noticing his bed, dresser, Meemaw’s ancient, caned chair—and every other scrap of furniture or accessory—had been snatched from his bedroom, Russ sat on the floor across the room from Stem and leaned his head back against the wood paneling.

“You want any cheese balls?” asked the Aussie.

Russ shook his head.

Peering into a cardboard box, Stem said, “Your cousins cleaned out the pantry, but Meemaw always kept a secret stash just for me. I managed to get to it before anyone else found it. Looks like she left me fruit chews, gummy bears, beef jerky, Star Crunches—"

"She bought you Star Crunches?" Russ gaped. "She *used* to buy me those, but then she said Little Debbie got too expensive, so she switched to the gross store brand."

"Have one, mate," said his pal, tossing one across the room.

The sticky crunch of that chocolate cookie brought back memories of his childhood. Pushing JoAnne on the tire swing out back. Sneaking out after bedtime with Lance to go buy fireworks. Shooting them off in the backyard after Meemaw left for work at the pastry tart factory.

Good times.

"Hey, Rusty!" came a voice.

Peering at him from the doorway was a slender woman with Birkenstocks peeping out the ends of her Patagonia trousers and a shapeless knitted crossbody purse slung across her pink linen blouse.

Russ blinked. *Granola cruncher*. But as she siphoned off the rest of her kombucha tea, recognition struck.

"AnnaLyn?" he gasped and jumped up and gave her a warm hug. It wasn't as good as hugging Katie or Meemaw, but it relieved a fraction of his heartache.

Gesturing across the room, he said, "This is my friend, Stem. Stem, this is my cousin, AnnaLyn."

The strangers shook hands and exchanged greetings.

"You here for the carnage?" jested Russ, though he knew she probably wasn't.

"No, I don't need anything," she laughed. "Just came to say hi to everyone—knew you'd all be here."

Somehow being lumped together with the rest of his cousins made him feel mournful.

Looking around the room, he apologized. "I had a chair you could sit in but someone's taken it."

"Oh, the floor's good," assured the woman. "We sit on it all the time at home."

They plopped down together and she accepted a package of fruit chews from Stem.

"So, how you been, cuz?" she asked as she popped one into her mouth. "I haven't seen you since, gosh, your wedding?"

"Lance's second," corrected Russ.

"That's right," she chuckled. "The beer garden wedding."

"Which soon migrated next door to the stripper club before Lance was arrested for disorderly conduct."

They shared a mutual laugh.

"Gosh, it's good to see you," she said.

"You too," he agreed as he felt a sharp stab of guilt. He had been in charge of contacting the family and, clearly, AnnaLyn had slipped through the cracks. "I'm glad you got the news."

"Yeah, me too. I got a message from Jessica."

"Hosley?"

"Yeah, you know we were friends back in high school, and we reconnected on Facebook a few years back. She said she saw Meemaw's obit on the newsfeed. I wanted to make it for the funeral, but I couldn't work out the flight details."

"I'm sorry," he apologized. "I forgot to contact you and—"

She brushed it off. "No big deal. Out of sight, out of mind."

A few times over the years, he thought he ought to reach out to her, but he hadn't. But now was as good a time as any to begin rebuilding that bridge which had laid in disrepair for so long.

"So, your husband and kids?"

"At home. Yeah, had to leave them behind. Just too expensive to fly us all here from South Carolina. Plus, I'd be so distracted with the kids—just wouldn't be worth it. So, Bennett stayed with them. He gave me some business about trying to do their homeschooling with them while I was gone, but that'll be a hoot, I'm sure. But they're all doing well. Healthy and happy. And what about Katie? Is she around? I was hoping to get to hug her."

The stinging hurt more than he could bear to admit.

"No, she . . . well she kicked me out."

He tried to hide the pain in his eyes, but the strength it took caused them to fill like a tub.

"Oh, I'm sorry," she said, hugging his shoulders.

He realized, at that moment, how much he longed for and desired the touch of a woman.

"I deserved it, to be honest. Can't blame her for a thing."

"No," she said, but nothing more. Just a hug—a long squeeze—and it was more than she could've spoken.

"Well, how's the university?" she asked at length.

"Lost my job, as well."

"Rusty," she said, but not in the same reproachful tone his other cousins used. This was more an endearing, an *I'm-a-safe-person-you-can-be-honest-with* tone. "What's happened?"

His sigh caused his cheeks to puff out, but he pressed onward. "I had an affair with one of my students."

Enough said. Everything was now explained.

Well, almost everything.

"What about your church?" she asked. "How are they handling this?"

To be honest, he didn't know. It wasn't *his* church—setting aside the fact that it was actually God's church, it belonged to both he *and* Katie. It was a jointly shared entity like a banking account or a movie store membership.

"I haven't been back since it all came out," he confessed.

Genuine concern filled his cousin. "Have they reached out to you at all?"

"A few times," he said, downplaying the fact that he could no longer count all the friends' messages and phone calls which he'd ignored out of guilt. "But it's touchy for them, I know, considering how the church and university are entwined. Also, Katie recently started working part-time for the church, so that makes it . . ."

"More complicated," she finished, giving his knee a gentle pat.

He agreed with a nod.

She looked into his eyes, sending tenderness and compassion along telepathic waves. "Is there any hope for mending this?"

"I wish there was, but . . ."

In a gesture of love, she took his hand and prayed right then and there for him. "And you will always be in my prayers, as you always have been," she added after the amen.

"I like her," Stem said, pointing a finger at the woman. "Can we be Facebook friends? What's your last name? Are you on Instagram?"

Moments later, Russ was summoned into the living room where he was shocked (but not really) to see that almost every scrap of furniture, decoration, trinket, and knickknack had made its flight out the open front door like the Israelites from Egypt. To his further surprise, even the dead plant was gone. AnnaLyn joined him, and, eager to watch the family drama play out, Stem tagged along, two bags of gummies in his hand.

Poised in the living room were Russ' nine cousins (and more if you counted their significant others). While some wrestled their little ones on the floor, most stood with arms crossed and feet spread shoulder-width apart. The mood was ominous, as though the Grim Reaper had come for his, only to discover that Gemini had already claimed the bedroom set.

"Listen up, y'all," announced Lance, the unofficial spokesperson for the group. Upon his left cheek he bore three blood-streaked marks. "Meemaw left Rusty in charge of her estate, seein' as he's a highfalutin college teacher or whatever he does. So, now, let's hear from him."

Russ opened his mouth to speak, but Lance cut him off.

"Rusty, tell us what other, uh, things of value—"

"Assets," Walker piped.

"*Assets*," stated Lance, as if he'd invented the word himself, "Meemaw had. We cleared out this place, and, to tell the truth—" he leaned in and lowered his voice, as if this message was at risk of reaching enemy ears "—I'll be derned if this was all she left us."

The others heartily agreed.

Once again, Russ opened his mouth only to be interrupted by his boisterous cousin.

"So, come on. Tell us what else she had, Rusty."

Russ cleared his throat and waited a moment to make certain no one else was about to speak.

It was Kendrick, the punk kid in the Nirvana tee, who interrupted him this time.

"Mom, can I just go hang out with my friends or what? I don't care 'bout nunnuh this bullcrap."

"That's my shirt," said Russ, but not before the boy had hustled out the front door. His remark, however, had not gone unnoticed, and everyone stared at him as though he'd spoken the dumbest words ever to cross mankind's lips. Holding out for their sympathy, he pouted, "He stole my Nirvana shirt."

"This is about Meemaw's estate," Lance growled. "Not some lame shirt. Now, you've kept us waitin' long enough, so get on with it."

Russ began with a long sigh. "So, this is it. This is Meemaw's estate. You're looking at it. The house and everything in it—or what *was* in it."

AnnaLyn's younger brother Haley raised his hand and waited for Russ to call on him. Then, after dutifully spitting his tobacco juice into his Wendy's cup via the straw, he questioned, "When're we gettin' our share for the sale of this here house?"

"It'll need a lot of work first," Russ explained. "Meemaw saved up enough to replace the living room window unit, and the insurance should replace the roof from the hail damage it got last spring. But it could use several more repairs which'll cost money, if anyone wants to help with that."

The only person to volunteer support of any kind was Stem. "I'll help, mate. Anything for Meemaw."

Russ patted his friend on the back. "So, after the repairs, I'll list the house."

"But how much money we gonna get?" asked Walker, who, technically, was only engaged to a cousin.

Russ shook his head. "I don't know what it'll appraise or sell for. Won't know until the repairs have been completed."

"You gonna get right on that, boy?" Lance said in a tone that stated more than questioned. "Some of us got bills to pay, ya know? That money'd come in handy, the sooner the better."

"I'll get it done as quickly as I can," promised their cousin. "If anyone would like to come over sometime and help paint, I'd—" He could see it was pointless to finish that sentence.

"So, Rusty," said Gemini. "You're telling us that Meemaw didn't have a banking account or a checking account? She had no stocks or bonds? No IRAs or 401k?"

"She didn't have *anything*." Oddly, when Russ heard himself say this, he felt he spoke with more conviction than he had all evening.

"So, you spoke with her financial adviser, then?" Gemini challenged.

He tried turning her question back at her, but the words "Financial adviser?" rolled off his tongue with a laugh. "Look, we can all quit pretending she was rich. We all know she was an elderly woman who lived on a fixed income."

Their blank stares left room for doubt, and Russ could feel his blood pressure soar.

"Come on—she was *not* a wealthy woman," he argued. "Most days, she ate raviolis straight from the can, or when I came to visit, frozen pizzas, which she considered a real treat. And to celebrate special occasions, she'd treat me to McDonald's. She'd always get a kid's meal just so she could give me the toy."

Several pairs of eyebrows rose, no doubt a genetic trait they'd inherited from their grandmother.

"I didn't play with it," he clarified. "She was just a very giving woman. She tithed twelve percent of her social security check to church each week and another three percent to Children's Hospital and said she did that because she didn't think waiters should get more tips than God. I didn't bother telling her the standard for waiters got upped to twenty percent."

The longer he had to justify to his greedy cousins how their grandma spent her fixed income, the angrier he got.

"The rest of the money she had, if she ever had any leftover, she used to buy diapers for JoAnne's babies, for Lance's bail bonds, for Becky's grocery money when Walker was in between jobs—" his face felt hot "—and for sending each and every one of you five dollars on your birthday! And I bet nunnuh y'all ever bothered sendin' 'er a thank you card, did ya?"

He was thankful his complexion wasn't pale like Becky's or else they'd both look like tomato soup, but he did regret that anger often made his natural Arkansas-brewed accent come forth. With judgmental eyes, he scanned the crowd who now avoided sharing a direct gaze with the furious man.

"Oh, sorry, I forgot," he interjected. "Peepaw's old storage unit. It needs to be cleaned out. Anybody wanna volunteer to help with that?" He allowed enough time for everyone to check their watches or examine their fingernails or stare at the shag carpet. "I didn't think so! Now, y'all get on back to your own houses!"

As the place cleared out, Stem whispered to his friend, "That is only the second time I've ever heard you say y'all. And the other time was in your sleep."

An hour later, AnnaLyn knocked on the door of Russ' bedroom.

"I'm the last one out," she announced. "Got to talking in the driveway with Gemini. Gosh, she's changed. Anyway, thought I'd say goodbye. I'm headed out for the night but wondered if you'd like to have breakfast tomorrow."

Smiling, Russ replied, "I'd like that."

"Honestly, I'm sorry I can't stay longer and help you fix up the house and clean out Peepaw's storage shed. Gosh, I'd forgotten all about that old thing."

"Me too," he chuckled.

"Seems like he was always there working on something or other, I guess. Anyway, I'll swing by in the morning. Gotta be to the airport by noon, so maybe get here around eight?"

Even though he'd forgotten about her until an hour and a half ago, Russ knew he'd miss AnnaLyn, and he promised himself he'd remember he liked her and he'd keep in touch.

Chapter 3

"Did you know the only thing your blood-sucking cousins left in Meemaw's pantry is a jar of expired peanut butter?" griped Stem. He cradled it in his palms and stared at it like a precious stillborn kitten. "If only I'd known this was here before May of last year, this would *not* have happened."

Mournfully, he gently laid the jar to rest in the trash can.

The kitchen linoleum felt cool to Russ' calves, and the cabinet knobs behind his back weren't unbearable as long as he kept them positioned on either side of his spine.

Stem checked the time on his cell phone. "I've got to leave for class in approximately twelve minutes. But before I leave, let's line out what *you* are going to do today."

Russ shrugged. Lately, sitting on the floor had seemed as good a thing as any.

"You should go to the shops," suggested Stem. "Pick up some, let's see, frozen lasagna, Hot Pockets, chips, lollies. You writing this down? No? All right, I'll make a note on my phone and text it to you."

His friend sat motionless.

Stem nudged his foot with his own. "The grocery list, mate. What else you need?"

Russ shrugged. "I don't have any money."

"There's the food bank."

Stone-faced, Russ stared ahead, his jaw sagging behind his pursed lips.

"All right," said Stem conceding that his friend appeared as eager to grocery shop as have his yearly colonoscopy. "You wanna call the insurance about this roof instead? Supposed to rain tonight."

Russ stared ahead.

"How about the air conditioner company?"

"It's only March," Russ said flatly.

"Actually, we are ten days into April, mate." Stem knew his friend's mood had been slipping down into a dangerous level of darkness ever since the double whammy of losing the two most important women in his life—and it worried him. "Okay, how about we start small? You haven't showered since last month, so why don't you go take one."

"Cousins stole my soap."

"We'll add that to your shopping list."

"And shampoo."

"Got it."

Russ huffed. "And towels. And shaving cream. A razor. Toothpaste. Toothbrush."

"They took your bloody toothbrush? Gross."

"And deodorant. And clothes to put on once I'm clean. Oh, and laundry detergent. And how about a washer and dryer, while you're at it?" In an uncommon move, the dejected man cursed and kicked a cabinet door, leaving a scuff mark upon the orangey-colored woodgrain.

Stem sank down next to his friend and offered him his last four Pringles, which the dejected man refused.

"You have to get up and do something, you bludger. You can't sit on the floor for-bloody-ever. You've got to get up and get moving."

"I see Katie's attorney on Friday," Russ offered. "She wants the house, my car, and alimony."

Stem smiled at the news. "Well, that takes care of Friday. Things are looking up again. And what will you do today?"

Sitting on the floor or, better yet, napping on it sounded like a good option, but Russ knew his friend wouldn't let him get away with it.

"Your schedule, mate?" Stem said, placing a hand on his shoulder. "What'll be on today's agenda?"

Leaning his head back and shutting his eyes, Russ conceded. "I could go clean out Peepaw's old storage unit, I guess. Bet it's full of rats and spiders and moldy crap." With a sigh, he added, "Probably'll take weeks to clear out."

Stem beamed. "That's wonderful!"

Much to Russ' surprise, the end of Mermaid Lane in Rose Bud turned out to be extremely rural. Like the hair of its namesake, the surface of the road slowly faded from pavement to gravel to dirt which quickly turned into mud due to the pelting rain. The Prius braved the rugged terrain like a little tugboat in the open ocean. For all the rain, Russ could hardly make out the road, and making out the trees which lined it on either side was impossible.

Since the inheritor of Peepaw's and Meemaw's estate had not gone to the storage shed the day before (or the day prior to that), Stem insisted they go together. *Today.*

"Well, this place is in the back o' Bourke," observed Russ' traveling companion as he laid doom to a bag of licorice bites. "Suppose Peepaw just wanted to get away from it all, yeah?"

Russ hardly heard the man.

A question swam in the ponderings of his mind for the past several weeks, and now he found the drone of the rain on the roof of the Prius the perfect background music to precipitate a venture into the water to explore it.

Where did I go wrong?

Until the morning he stepped into his 8am meeting with Dean Scarborough—and discovered Katie there too—Russ had managed to keep this thought out of his mind. In fact, he'd not even allowed himself to dwell on what he'd done with the other Caydee. Hadn't they only been together a few times? Four at most. Anything less than six isn't a pattern—just a series of incidents. At least, Stem had once said that, and, although Russ knew he was referring to science at the time, it did not invalidate the fact that what had happened with Caydee had been merely incidents. Right?

And what about Meemaw? He knew, if he hadn't been so consumed with his affair and the special care *his* Katie required, he would've had time to tend to his grandmother's needs more. Perhaps, if he had, she'd still be alive.

"There," said Stem, pointing ahead.

Russ saw nothing but Meemaw's fragile body lying in her bed, her once strong voice now a raspy imitation of itself like a sickly ghost. She had depended on him to help her but he'd been so distracted, especially since Caydee had come into his life, that he hadn't—

Stem hollered something. *Stop*, was it?

Suddenly, the steering wheel became impossible to turn. Had the tires jammed into a rut?

"Brakes, mate! Hit the brakes!"

At once, everything registered. Russ' heart sped up. Both feet went for the brake. His hands gripped the wheel, although Stem was now manning it. The small hatchback fishtailed, slinging mud at a cattle gate like presidential candidates. It was ugly and ungraceful, but the car managed to slide to a stop about two inches shy of getting a barb wire tattoo.

For seconds, the friends sat stunned with nothing but the wailing rain to disturb their stupor. When Russ felt his left leg cramp up, it dawned on him that his feet were still smashing the brake. He released it only to realize the car wasn't in park. Panicking, he stomped the pedal, mistaking the gas for the brake. The Prius made a mediocre attempt to intimidate the barb wire fence, however, said fence retaliated by scratching six inches of the paint. Somehow or other, the emergency brake was engaged.

Quickly pressing the button to shut off the ignition, Stem declared, "We'll let the engine cool down a bit, mate."

Still in a daze, Russ' head rocked up and down slowly.

No one could say whether they were waiting for the rain to stop or their heart rates to cool down or Stem to finish his licorice bites. But it was that, a few minutes later, Stem broke their silence by asserting, "It's wet enough to bog a duck out there, mate. We should've brought some proper footwear."

"Cousins took my rain boots," Russ murmured.

Upon hearing this, his friend, mid-bite, exclaimed, "Crikey! First the ramen noodles. Then your toothbrush. And now your bloody gumboots? Is nothing sacred to your kin!"

Russ shrugged and muttered, "Least they didn't get Jasper."

Disgusted with humanity, Stem jammed the last of the lollies into his mouth. As he chewed, he sensed the hum of the rain being slowly overtaken by a strange noise which reminded him of a flock of clowning kookaburras upon a telephone wire. Turning his head slowly, he discovered the sound was the laughter emanating from the man behind the wheel, and it was so forceful and neurotic that it jerked the Prius with each lurch of his body. As Stem waited for the peculiar scene to play out, he felt both strangely amused as well as overcome with thankfulness that he had shut off the engine when he'd had the chance.

There was nothing funny about his situation, but Russ could not make the chortling subside. The more he tried to control it, the more uproarious it grew. And why contain it anyway? He'd not felt like laughing in weeks, maybe months. But his stomach, which he had recently neglected to both fill and tone, grew sore from the spasms. Tears rose in his eyes, and, soon, the sounds coming from his chest were no longer happy ones. He'd not grieved Meemaw's death or his upcoming divorce—and he wasn't even certain that it was mournfulness which initiated the bizarreness which was overtaking him right at that moment—but he knew he was helpless to stop the wave of emotions.

When at last his wailing ceased, Stem rested a gentle hand on the man's shoulder, and Russ was grateful that, even amidst the recent uprooting of the two most important people in his life, he still had his faithful friend by his side offering comfort.

"Mate," Stem said softly. "Have you seen my box of animal crackers? I think I left it in here."

Russ stared at him blankly through reddened eyes.

"It was small—" he demonstrated with two fingers "—with jungle creatures on the side and a little handle on top." Taking his friend's eye drying on his jacket sleeve for disinterest in the subject, he muttered, "All right, but if you find it, it's mine."

The rain soon eased up, allowing them to study their surroundings. Mermaid Lane had abruptly ended at a metal cattle gate beyond which a structure, like a small, ancient prairie-home-turned-toolshed, idled in a field. But there was no storage facility or sign of civilization in any direction, save for the muddy thoroughfare which had led them there.

Glancing around, Russ tossed up his hands and sighed in defeat. "Well, we tried."

"Oh, come on, mate." Pointing to the lone building in the valley, Stem begged, "Let's go explore the place."

Gesturing to the waterlogged field, Russ argued, "But it's soaking wet."

"You got something better to do, yeah? Rather go sit at home and feel sorry for yourself?"

Though they had not worn the proper gear to battle untamed prairie grass and mud, they climbed over the stout metal gate, and, by the time they reached the building, the rain had completely stopped, which really made no difference since Russ was soaked from his tennis shoes up to his belt. He cursed his luck and circumstances, although he secretly admitted to himself that this little adventure through the mud and rain was the most fun he'd had in weeks.

There was no door lock nor was a light switch to be seen, and their phone lights were poor heroes against the darkness outside and the layers of grime on the unwashed windows. But it was illumination enough for Russ' meager excitement to diminish to disappointment as he surveyed the empty space. In one corner, a random pile of old, rotting boards laid upon the dirt floor like a football pile-up, and in a windowsill sat an ashtray (butts and all), but there was nothing else worth mentioning.

"Well, this wasn't worth a trek through a swamp," grouched Russ. "And this certainly isn't Peepaw's storage unit."

"How do you know? This den's as good as any for a bloke to take a reprieve from his duties."

Russ frowned as he took one last look around. Shrugging, he offered, "Maybe you're right. Maybe he cleared the place out before he skipped town."

"Or he's a pharaoh."

"What's that mean?"

"You know. An ancient ruler of Egypt."

"Yes, I'm a history professor—"

"Former," Stem called him out.

Rolling his eyes, Russ corrected, "*Former* history professor—I know what a pharaoh is. But what do you mean Peepaw's one?"

"Archaeologists. You know, they get all excited to explore a pyramid and find treasure but when they get in there, bam! The place has been robbed by tomb raiders—just like this shed."

Something about that statement hit Russ off guard like a southpaw. Whatever he thought he might find during this adventure on Mermaid Lane, the prospect of never finding it filled him with disappointment verging on grief. Tears sprang to his eyes, and, suddenly, the zeal of venturing across a wet field to inspect a pioneer-days relic dissipated like dew at sunrise. He kicked at the wood pile and sighed, "It's not like I expected to find treasure."

"What *did* you expect?"

He headed for the door. "I don't know. Maybe to figure out what happened to him. Or why he always came here, or there, or wherever he went."

"Never know what you'll find in old places like this, mate. Sometimes hidden treasures. More often . . ."

"Nothing," sighed Russ, finishing his friend's sentence. Standing in the doorway, peering at his car which was pinned to the fence (quite literally), he remarked, "I hope those barbs didn't puncture the radiator or anything important. Let's go see if it starts and check for leaks. We may need a tow truck."

His friend's voice came out of the darkness. "What do you think this is?"

Turning, he squinted. "That pile of boards? I think the roof started to cave in right there. This place is probably condemned."

"Turn on your torch. Come here and have a look, mate."

Under the dim light of the iPhone, Russ observed, "Nothing but a decaying mound of lumber."

"No, look at this," Stem insisted with a trace of excitement in his voice. Lifting some of the pile, he remarked, "Underneath these. Looks like a door laying on its side, yeah?"

"It's probably just the old one to this place and some farmer tossed it there and left it behind just like everyone else in his life."

But when they had dug and shifted boards for a minute and the item in question was at last freed from its load, the two friends felt chills run up their spine. It was not just an old, rotten piece of wood—rather, they beheld a very solid and ancient door which was firmly hinged to the floor. Upon its face was attached a regal brass plate embossed with the title: 42B.

Spying the deadbolt, Russ quickly fished from his pocket the only key which he had found in the box of Meemaw's trinkets. Pointing at the emblem imprinted on the worn leather tag, he gasped, "It's got the same number."

Triumphantly, Stem declared, "This *is* Peepaw's shed!"

"And that door leads somewhere."

Dropping to his knees, Russ said a short, silent prayer and thrust the key into the hole (albeit the wrong direction on his first attempt but he righted the mistake on his second). With some wiggling and sweet talking, it finally turned, and the satisfying click of the lock filled the air.

Neither man said a word, but as one mind, they reached down

and lifted the stout door. It was remarkably heavy for its size, as though lead was hidden between the woodgrain like a stowaway. Carefully and slowly, they lowered it onto its face. At their feet, like a grave, lay a darkened rectangular hole. Both reached for their phones, but as Russ fumbled to turn on his flashlight, he dropped it into the black abyss.

Chapter 4

The men stared down into the hole, neither daring to make any moves for fear of disturbing the darkness beneath their feet.

"There's steps," Russ whispered, pointing down surreptitiously as though they were being spied upon.

Stem shook his head. "I don't do scary stairs that lead down into dark holes."

"I thought you grew up in the outback and wrestled alligators."

"First off, Australia has crocodiles not alligators. Secondly, I'm technically from the city."

"Yeah, but didn't you have poisonous snakes—"

"Venomous."

"—and funnel spiders?"

"Which is why I don't go into holes in the ground," he hissed.

"All right. There's a flashlight in my car. Katie put it in an emergency kit she made for me. Let's go get it."

"Wait," Stem objected. "Let me call it."

"My phone? No."

"Yes, it'll light up and we'll be able to see down there."

Holding his phone firmly so it didn't also disappear into the dark hole, Stem dialed Russ' number. The sound of a slow, repetitive dong rose up from the mysterious cavern beneath them like an eerie song from the dead.

"Bugger!"

Russ jumped at the exclamation. "Crap! What is it? What do you see?"

"You changed my ringtone!"

Holding his hand over his pounding heart, Russ chastised, "You scared the daylights out of me!"

"What is this anyway? It sounds like the call to some feast of cannibals in the underworld."

"It's 'Hell's Bells' by AC/DC."

"Acca Dacca," Stem smiled. "I recognize the guitar now." Then narrowing his eyebrows, he pouted, "But I liked the 'Shimmie Shake.'"

"Well, I didn't," Russ objected. "People were giving me stupid looks every time The Wiggles started singing in my pocket."

Judging from the glow below, they surmised the place where it had landed was about eight to ten feet beneath them.

"Let's go get that flashlight," repeated Russ. "Then we'll come back for my phone."

"You'll go sus it out first, yeah?"

Russ had been plagued on and off the past month with a death wish. It had led him to do rash things like leave all the doors unlocked at night and drive without his seatbelt. However, a warning from a cop the week prior reminded him that he could not afford to pay a traffic fine. But he was still secretly on the lookout for a way to accidentally be killed and end his misery, and the suspicious steps into blackness seemed like as good an opportunity as any.

The call to the tow truck was forgotten, and, with both flashlight and Stem's iPhone light in hand, Russ descended the stairs. It was when he got halfway down and realized there was an open wooden rail to one side of him leaving him vulnerable to whatever lay in the darkness beyond that his life flashed before his eyes and he decided he'd rather live. Snatching up the wayward phone off the concrete floor, he hustled up the stairs.

"Oh, man," Russ griped as he caught his breath. "My screen's cracked!"

"Should've paid extra for the insurance."

"You said it was a scam."

"Well, it was . . . until you screwed up, lost your job, and began a life of destitution."

As Russ checked to make sure he could still log into the device, Stem quizzed, "What was it like down there?"

"Dark. A little cooler, like a cave."

"What did you see?"

"Not much. I was trying to just focus on my phone so I didn't see something weird and freak out." When Stem hesitated, Russ felt himself fill with bravery. "Come on. We'll go down together."

"Okay, but you first."

Russ descended the steps a second time, Stem's hand on his shoulder all the way down. However, almost as soon as their feet hit the concrete, Stem rushed into the darkness.

"Look!" the man exclaimed.

"What is it?"

Before he could get a good look in Stem's direction, the man appeared with a rifle.

Russ quickly jumped out of the way of the barrel. "Crap! What the heck? Don't point that at me. Where'd you find it?"

"Over there." When they reached the appointed spot which had at once caught Stem's attention, the pair admired a shelf which was loaded with weaponry—guns, swords, maces, and even cannon balls.

Excited, Stem exclaimed, "Just look at all these! Peepaw was a Y2Ker!"

Russ turned a dagger over in his hand. "I don't think he even knew about that. He disappeared when I was like twelve."

Stem dismissed Russ' assumption of Peepaw's knowledge. "Y2K was first mentioned in 1985 and popularized beginning the summer of 1995."

"Still, I don't think he kept up with things like that. He'd never used a computer as far as I know."

While Stem ogled the weapons, Russ turned to examine the rest of the basement.

"Hey, I need that torch," Stem said, reaching for it.

Acquiescing, Russ handed over the flashlight and moved about on the light from his phone. Dim as it was, exploring the darkness made him feel like a tomb raider from days past.

From what he could see, the basement was massive—the size of a modest warehouse—and it was comprised of twenty or more rows of identical metal shelves which appeared to be sturdy but of a more handmade variety than store bought. The most curious thing of all, though, was not the size of the space or quantity of shelves but, rather, the variety of items which this place housed. Metal objects—urns, masks, sculptures, jewelry, household items, and more—rested beneath a layer of dust, undisturbed for over a quarter of a century.

Stopping at one spot, Russ swiped a finger across the delicate etchings on a lady's mirror and brush set. The golden color of the metal revealed beneath the layer of grime reminded him of his wedding band.

"Hey, come here!" hollered Stem.

Russ found him rummaging through a shelf loaded with pipes, tobacco spittoons, and other smoking implements.

Shoving a long-stemmed pipe into his mouth, Stem asked between clenched teeth, "How do I look?"

"Like you're thirty years away from lung cancer."

"Haha," the man chuckled, though only half-heartedly. Like a kid in a toy store, he zoomed off to examine items on the next row. "This is incredible. Where did he get all this stuff?"

The question jogged Russ' mind, dusting cobwebs off memories from the past. "He was a welder in a machine shop. So, I wonder if he made all this. I think he used to do that, craft little things. Seems like he gave me a pin to wear on my collar or something like that. I don't know what happened to it."

Stem popped his head down the row where Russ was looking at a tiny metal menagerie. "Well, look at it this way—now you've got gobs of his creations. But honestly, I find it difficult to believe he made all of these objects. The diversity is incredible—shape, style, design, not to mention the superb grasp of metallurgy required for their production. And a lot of these appear vintage, as if they're the real deal."

"I doubt that," Russ scoffed. "If these were then some of them might be worth some money. Peepaw wouldn't have had any way to buy them, and why would he store valuable treasures in a dusty basement underneath a field anyway?"

"To keep them hidden, maybe?"

The argument seemed plausible but Russ quickly dismissed it. "No. These are just his own little knockoffs, something he piddled around with when he should've been home with his family." Frowning, he set a pair of miniature giraffes back on the shelf, aligning their tiny feet up with the holes left in the dust where they had stood at attention for years.

Stem appeared with a samurai sword whose beauty was veiled beneath layers of dust. "It's bloody heavy."

"Looks like a piece of junk."

"You're gonna sell it on eBay."

Russ' eyebrows dove into a perfect V-shape as he backed away slowly, shaking his head.

"You need money, mate, and this'll fetch forty or fifty dollars easily. Peepaw's contributions to the Russell bailout fund. Besides, you promised Meemaw you'd clean this place out, so you're obligated."

Russ sighed, knowing his friend would do it with or without his support. "All right, but don't expect me to babysit the bidding."

"That'll practically take care of itself. Just grab some more things to take with us."

"Why take them anywhere? Can't we just leave them here?"

"No, we've got to take photos of them for the listings."

Picking a brass contraption off a shelf, Russ held it up. "Here. Take a pic."

Stem was incredulous. "No one's going to buy that brick-a-brack with your bloody scary mug soiling the background. We must take them back to Meemaw's and get proper photos." In response to Russ' frown, he added, "Buyers will pay more if they're quality snapshots."

Russ didn't want to bother with what was destined to be a fruitless and time-wasting endeavor. "We can't take all of this home."

"Well, not in one trip, but consider this your funding for the future. If you play your cards right, you might not have to worry about work for another decade."

That was laughable. "Who'd want this old junk anyway?"

Stem didn't appreciate his friend's obstinance. "Oh, plenty of people with nothing better to do than bid on items they don't bloody need. That's what keeps eBay in business. Now grab something."

Russ sighed in resistance to the demand.

"That goldish Mayan-looking mask," Stem suggested. "Should fetch some double digits."

The divorcee made one last attempt to object to the endeavor of commerce. "Seems like a lot of work for a few bucks."

His friend's indignance filled the cellar. "So, you'd rather be taking orders from a nineteen-year-old who thinks he's smarter than you just because he can program a new laptop, yeah?"

Russ pursed his lips. He would've liked to object, but in truth, the thought of going into one more day of work at American GadgetTech made him want to gouge out his eyeballs with that dusty sword.

Knowing he'd won that argument, Stem smirked. "Then be your own boss, mate. Monitor your eBay items in the comfort of your underwear from the convenience of your kitchen table."

"Gemini took the 8-piece dining set."

"Well, now you can afford one from the resale shop."

Russ awoke from his nap on the shaggy carpet (he had loved

those as a kid). Standing over him, holding the samurai sword, was his eccentric friend.

"Now, here's what I've done," explained Stem as though they were already in the middle of a conversation.

The groggy man wiped his eyes and glanced at the time on his phone. It was just after seven o'clock in the morning.

"This is how the Chinese do it," Stem explained. "You list the item for $0.99 so the bidding starts low. But you charge a few dollars extra for shipping and handling. But see, eBay gives a discount for sellers who buy their postage through *them* versus buying it directly from the shipping company, so you're pocketing a little bit of what the buyer's paying you for it. And in addition to this, you pay a smaller fee on the transaction itself because of the lower sales price."

"So, I'm scamming eBay over a few dollars?"

"Hey, dollars add up, mate," Stem stated with indignance. "Taking into consideration what the comps are selling for, the eBay and Paypal fees you'll have to pay, and the cost of shipping, it's my estimation you'll earn between $87 and $102."

Russ yawned and stretched. "I literally can't believe you stayed up all night just to make $87. You could earn that in 2 hours at the university—or probably in minutes counting cards at some casino."

"Let me correct your erroneous assumptions," asserted his friend as he held up a hand to silence the man. "First of all, I slept from 12:37am until 6:43am, so I did *not* stay up all bloody night working on this. Secondly, I will not be visiting any casinos. But those facts are beside the point. This isn't my money anyway—it's *yours*, and you're a very poor man now that you've gone and made decisions with the wrong head."

"Cheap shot," he groused.

"But well earned."

A shrug was Russ' only defense.

"And it takes you approximately seven point nine hours to earn $87, unless you count taxes, in which case you'd have to work more like nine point one. Now, I've already listed this sword and the wicked heavy gilded lead mask. And I'm just about to get to the jewelry."

"What about the bobcat?"

His friend took a step back and wrapped a protective arm around the stuffed feline. "You can't bloody sell Jasper!" he protested. "He's been in your family longer than you have!"

There were rare moments when Russ witnessed the humanity in his friend, shiny glimpses which revealed a deep inner connection to something meaningful on this earth other than food, to a living and breathing entity (even if it was now stuffed). And Russ happily seized these moments as opportunities to vex his friend's nerves.

Grinning, Russ lowered his voice. "That stiff has been in Meemaw's closet for going on forty years. I'll sell him for bottom dollar."

Stem's expression hardened and he glared at the man. "You've gone troppo, mate! The stress—the grief—it's got to your head. Now, lay back down, you bludger, and let me take care of this!"

Russ knew he had already found the checkmate for his friend's rare display of humanity. Narrowing his eyebrows, he stated, "Selling Jasper was Meemaw's dying wish."

Red streaks of anger coursed across Stem's neck and face, and his buggy eyes looked as though they might pop out of his skull.

"Her dying wish," Russ slowly repeated.

Checkmate.

As Stem opened his mouth to spew out his objection, his crooked teeth gleamed in the morning's light. "Well, the least you could do is bloody stock your pantry! A man will die without sustenance!"

With that, he stormed off to rummage through the empty cabinets, hoping to find a scrap of food somehow hidden miraculously from the former pantry raiders. Russ took the opportunity to examine what his friend had done on eBay.

It had been years since he'd visited the website. In truth, he didn't even know people still utilized the platform. In his early college years, he had found it useful for buying and selling textbooks. That is, until he discovered Amazon. When that revelation had come, he switched allegiance and never looked back. Staring at the screen now, he was surprised at how much the vendor platform had not changed in the past twenty years.

A memory from his childhood passed through his mind. After Peepaw disappeared, Meemaw had to get creative with her moneymaking endeavors. She opened her own eBay shop and stuffed the hall coat closet to the brim with boxes and bubble wrap and Beanie Babies. And there had been her handwritten threat taped to the door: “Stay out or else!” Of course, Russ did not dare trespass into the former coat closet. In fact, even years after her four grandchildren had left her home and she’d closed her eBay store and all traces of it had been removed from the premises, he was leery of violating the sacred ground for fear of her reprimand.

Stem returned with empty hands and a frown. “Not a bloody scrap of food. You’ve got to go to the shops this morning, mate.” The disdain in his stare was palpable. After casting one final glance at Jasper, he barked, “I must freshen up before my nine o’clock physics class. The university holds their profs to standards, you know!”

Chapter 5

Repairing electronic devices had never been a strength of Russ', and nothing had changed since he'd been hired at American GadgetTech. According to the YouTube video he'd consulted, replacing the laptop's battery should be a quick ten-minute fix. At this point, however, he was clocking two hours and counting, and every second drew out new frustrations.

Ten feet down the counter, his boss Dirk, a young man not even old enough to legally purchase alcohol, leaned against the glass display top, scrolling through TikTok. As Russ set the screwdriver down with a sigh (again), the kid snickered and muttered something under his breath. Hearing it, Russ barked, "What was that?"

"Nothing, bruh," said the twerp.

"Oh, so you can stand there and insult me but you're not man enough to say it to my face?"

"You're just jealous that I can totally do a simple thing like that in, like, five minutes."

Through gritted teeth, Russ grumbled, "Well, maybe if you'd show me how to do this then it wouldn't be difficult for me."

The kid shook his head and plucked his jacket off a hook on the wall. "It's my lunch break."

As his manager exited out the back door, Russ gripped the

screwdriver handle and squeezed with all his might. “Ahhhh!” he yelled. Then, as he was the only one in the strip mall store, he impulsively hurled the tool across the narrow room. As though tossed by a professional knife thrower, the point lodged into the stiff plastic front of a box containing a helicopter drone. Bending forward, he dropped his elbows to the countertop and hung his head.

“God, get me out of here,” he prayed. “Or just kill me.”

At the sound of a chime on the front door, his head bobbed up.

“What’s up, mate?” chirped Stem.

A loud sigh was pushed out of his friend’s lungs. “Nothing. What’re you doing here?”

“Caught a ride with a student. I’m tutoring him for free and he’s driving me places.”

“Ah,” Russ replied with a nod.

“Yeah, I thought I’d hang out here ’til you were done and then we’d go grab some grub.”

Russ glanced at his phone. “I don’t get off for, like, five more hours.”

“Cool,” said Stem. “What’re ya working on there? Anything I’d like?”

“Supposed to be switching out this battery for a new one but I have no idea what I’m doing.”

“I can do that for you, mate.”

“Great. Grab that screwdriver.”

Following where his finger was pointing, Stem caught sight of the tool. The annoying, shrilling screech of metal tightly rubbing stiff plastic filled the airspace for a moment as he withdrew it. “Have it out for that toy, did ya, yeah?”

“I’ve always hated the thing,” Russ joked. “No, I’m just so frustrated. When that twerp hired me, he didn’t bother to tell me that I’d be repairing broken electronics.”

“This is a gadget store, mate. Electronics are their specialty.”

“I know, but I just assumed I’d be ringing up customers and putting boxes on the shelves. But he assumed, because of my ethnicity, that I'd be some kind of expert."

"First off, you're assuming his assumption. And, besides that, science has proved that ethnicity is not a predictor for an individual's comprehension of mechanical processes. Just look at me. My grandmother was a native of Australasia—you know, indigenous Polynesian descent—and my great-grandfather was from Malaysia."

"And you look like a white guy."

Stem offered a crooked smile. "Yeah, and I'm a wiz at computers. So get out of my seat, you mechanically impaired drongo."

With gladness, Russ vacated the repair station, leaving the task to his friend. Plopping down in the chair behind the cash register, he sighed. "I just hope I can find a way out of this place. I can't work at GadgetTech for the rest of my life."

"Mate, you won't work here for-bloody-ever. After all, given the rise in online commerce and the throw-away society we live in, this store is likely to cease existence within five years."

"So, you're predicting I'll lose my job and live off unemployment?"

"Actually, the future of American GadgetTech is a moot point. I'm predicting that, come summer, there will be plenty of collegiate job vacancies, one of which you'll procure."

While Russ hoped that was true, it hardly eased his current job vexations. That was weeks down the road, and, in a way, he almost dreaded it.

Searcy, which boasted less than 25,000 full-time citizens, was basically a social oasis in a sparsely populated desert. For nine months of the year, the city teemed with life bolstered by the scores of energetic young adults who called Harding University home, while the surrounding micro-communities experienced a superfluity of land in contrast to the sparsity of their population. This resulted in geographical insulation, keeping Searcy no less than forty-five minutes from any other sizable metroplex. As Russ' chances of resecuring a job at Harding were about as high as

Peepaw magically appearing out of thin air, that left only one higher education facility in the area at which he could seek employment—and given they currently offered no bachelor degree programs in history, he doubted very much they would be interested in hiring him (and he was certain he could not earn enough money there to support himself even if they did). Thus, to regain a teaching position, he would have to relocate.

As much of an outsider as he felt at times, he hated the thought of leaving the community he grew up in. Everything was familiar there. And besides, a large part of him still hoped there could be reconciliation for him and Katie. If he moved . . . the chances of mending their relationship were nonexistent. Of course, he was scheduled to sign his divorce papers in the morning and that alone nearly petrified him beyond rational thought.

As the front door of the store chimed, Russ looked up, eager for something to distract his mind. Through it entered a man clad in a camouflage hunting jacket and matching ballcap upon which was embroidered in orange thread "Trump 2024." To Russ' forced smile, the shopper tossed a gruff reply. "Great. Any of y'all speak American 'round here?"

A quick glance was exchanged between the two men behind the counter before Stem piped up, "I speak English."

Into a Styrofoam coffee cup, the man evacuated a stream of tobacco juice. "Guess that'll hafta do."

Despite Stem's helpfulness and knowledge about his electronic issue, the man headed to the exit a minute later, just as disgruntled as when he had entered. In a faux Indian accent which he'd perfected in high school, Russ called, "Have a very nice day, sir."

As he pushed out the door, the man muttered something insinuating the "American owned business" sign on the front door was a sham.

Following the battery replacement, Stem began on a lengthy list of repairs which were backlogged for nearly two weeks. In less than an hour, he'd whittled the punch list down to eight items. Dirk returned with a half-emptied Sonic drink in hand only to announce minutes later that he had to run to the bank and complete some other errands, which Russ suspected was really just a cover for something else he'd rather be doing like playing video games at his girlfriend's house. However, given that the store was loads more tolerable when his boss was out, Russ welcomed Dirk's aversion to work.

Business was slow so Stem got some music going.

"How'd you do that?" asked his buddy.

"It's just Spotify."

Pointing to the ceiling where the sound of Mozart's Eine Klein Nachtmusik filtered out, he clarified, "Yeah, but how'd you get it to play through the speakers?"

"Bluetooth, mate."

The classical music lulled Russ into a mindful state, and, soon, his mind was running with regrets and guilt. "Do you think there's hope for us?"

"For you and me? Sure. We're mates."

"No, I mean for me and Katie. Do you think she'd ever take me back?"

Tapping his chin with the screwdriver, Stem spent a moment contemplating the question. Then, he shook his head. "No, she was pretty adamant that she was moving on."

"When did she say that?"

"The other day."

"Wait, you've spoken with her?"

"Yeah, I talk to her often. We were, after all, friends too, yeah?"

"Yeah," Russ said, his voice trailing off. "Wait, what's she said about me?"

"I can't tell you that. That's confidential information."

"But has she mentioned if she'd like to maybe reconcile? Or give me a second chance? Or, like, if we could maybe date again?"

"Mate, like I said, I can't tell you exactly what she's said to me."

"But wait, do you tell her what I say to you? Could you let her know that I'm sorry and want to . . . redo this, start over?"

"First of all, you know her phone number, same as I do. You can just give her a ring if you want to say something to her."

Russ recoiled at the idea. "No, I can't call her. What would I say?"

"All those things you just asked me to tell her—that you're sorry and want to redo this, start over. But you might think your words through a little more before you call her so you don't sound like a bogan. She's smart, you know. You're not gonna impress her if you're dripping with bumbling idiocy."

"But you said she said she was moving on."

"Yeah."

"So why would she listen to me?"

"Mate, if she won't listen to you then she sure won't listen to me. You're her husband, after all."

Only for the next seventeen hours, Russ silently fretted.

While he was deep in thought, the door chimed. Through it came a teenage boy, still small in stature, flaunting a quarter inch of peach fuzz on his upper lip. Behind him trailed his mother who looked like she'd just stepped out of Sunday school. Russ did his best to muster a smile—one thing Meemaw had impressed upon him was to look like you're up to the job. Without making eye contact, the boy approached the counter with a small device in his hand which Russ didn't recognize. Before the GadgetTech employee could say a word, the boy dove into his issue.

"I bought this refurbed Elgato HD60 S+ because I'm boosting my streaming. Yeah, I'm like always cheesing and the other players are like, 'You're stomping us. Tell us your secrets,' so I'm gonna stream my easter eggs and stuff on my YouTube channel. Anyway, this POS is like totally not streaming at 1080P. I've got the HDR set up on my computer and I've got my Twitch all set up, but I bought this from this sketch website and I think it's a fake. Can you check it out for me?"

The boy might as well have been speaking a foreign language. Russ had never been a gamer nor had he kept up with the latest technology. Gaping, he pointed to Stem, who had already taken notice of the situation and was motioning for the boy to come speak with him.

As the boy opened his mouth to repeat his question, the scientist questioned, “You have your OBS account linked, yeah?”

“Well, no, not yet because I was gonna—”

“Unplug the system. Set that up and do a test check with the HDR video capture first. Then, if that’s a go, link the device up. If it’s still not working then you may have to change the FPS on your computer.”

“I’ve already checked that.”

Stem glared at the boy. “I’ve already checked that, *sir*.”

The boy squirmed and looked up at his mother who silently urged him to show respect. Giving in, he murmured, “I’ve already checked that, sir.”

Pleased with the boy’s response, the prof continued. “In that case, do what I said and, if it’s still a dud, get a refund.”

“But they won’t give me my money back. I already asked.”

Exasperated, Stem griped, “Then quit buying cheap components from shonky websites! You’ll get ripped every time if you keep that up.”

“Yes, sir,” the boy hastily replied.

“And get off your butt and go for a walk every now and then, yeah?”

“Yes, sir.”

Staring the kid in the eye, Stem ordered, “And make sure you respect your mother and do your chores first, yeah?”

With a look of abject terror, the kid nodded. “Yes, I will, sir.” Then gazing up at his mother, the boy begged, “Mom, can we leave now?”

Pleased, she thanked Stem for his help and led her son to the door.

When they’d gone, Russ observed, “You’d make a good dad.”

“Yeah?” said Stem, smiling at the notion. “Well, maybe I’ll be one someday.”

Chapter 6

Prior to his meeting with Katie's attorney, Russ had worked on his responses to various questions he thought likely would be asked.

When did your relationship with Caydee begin?

Where did your first act of infidelity take place?

Do you still love Katie?

Dutifully, he'd planned each answer, even recording helpful notes on his phone in case his mind went blank.

Truth be told, the meeting had been much less personal than he had anticipated, which left him feeling a little let down for reasons he could not determine. It had seemed the only thing the attorney was very concerned about was making sure she got a copy of Russ' driver's license and had the man sign on the seller's line on the title to Katie's van as well as on the deed to their house. Since he felt entirely guilty for the dissolution of the marriage, he offered up his John Hancock on all requested documents without complaint (though, secretly, his heart ached so much he worried he might be experiencing a coronary).

As he drove back to Meemaw's, he was overwhelmed with the urge to visit the coffee shop on the north edge of campus. It only seemed right, since he and Katie had made countless fond memories there over the years. However, the university had legally banned him from stepping foot on campus again, and, though Midnight Oil Coffee was technically not on Harding property, given its proximity to the university, he made the wise decision to park across the street and simply stare at the place that had served so long as his second home.

He had made so many memories on that campus but the one which, at that moment, took forefront in his mind was that last day there. Like a criminal, he'd been escorted out of Dean Scarborough's office between two security officers (Chad and Frank, two Cowboys fans he liked to tease when their team stunk up a game). In shame, he'd hung his head as he walked between them, avoiding eye contact with anyone he encountered, students and fellow profs alike. Stem, whom he had texted in a panic, had met him at his car, taken his keys as though Russ was leaving a frat party at 4am, and driven him to Meemaw's. The dismissed professor had not even been allowed to clean out his office before vacating the premises, but he had received a text days later which stated that everything of his had been delivered to his home, that is, the one he had formerly shared with Katie. He wasn't sure he'd ever see any of it again.

Now, sitting in a vacant parking lot in the cool shade of a walnut tree across from the Heritage building, Russ felt grief wash over him. It wasn't delirium like before when he'd lost it in the car with Stem because of lack of sleep and nutrition. No, this time he intensely felt taken over by all he'd lost.

Katie.

Meemaw.

His church family, a group of endearing friends and companions.

Everything he'd worked for in his career, the safety and security that it brought, his status as a college professor—the familiarity of belonging somewhere . . .

All gone.

He suddenly felt as if he had died and was looking up from the grave, grieving a life that was no more. Somewhere along the way to getting here, he'd lost himself. The fact was, he'd been dead for quite a while—it had just taken everyone else a little longer to realize it.

And now, what kind of life did he have?

He was penniless. An orphan. A lousy electronics repairman. A shamed adulterer.

Grief bowled him over like a wave to a sandcastle, and, in the midst of thirty-five minutes, he cried an ocean of tears. When at last he dried the final remnants of moisture from his eyes, he looked up, surprised to see that the vacant parking lot around him had become the staging ground of a protest. Women (and some men too) huddled with angry faces and sign-laden hands. He briefly allowed his eyes to rest on the scene, letting his mind recover for a moment before he drove to Meemaw's—*his*—home.

Without warning, a woman with a thick, dark red liquid smeared across her face and clothing appeared at his window. Russ jumped and stared, stunned by her appearance. Through the glass barrier and above the protesters who had just begun their chant, he couldn't make out her muffled voice.

"What?" he asked as he fumbled to roll down his window.

"Can you give me a ride to the dollar store?"

He blinked, bewildered by the request. But before he could answer, a truck pulled up and the driver hollered something to the woman. In reply, she shouted something unintelligible, and then she hauled off towards the crowd of protesters with a look of sheer exhilaration on her face.

Russ maneuvered his small car through the crowd slowly, careful not to cause any casualties to person or vehicle. The mob grew thicker and angrier by the second, and, as he steered through them, he came to realize that it was not one united horde but, rather, two opposing sides of some great women's interest debate. To his displeasure, the exit to the street was the dividing point between the two groups, and a number of the assembly members took out their anger at one another by beating on his car.

Nevertheless, the crowd did not prevail and, soon enough, he reached the street. But just as he pulled out and sighed relief, a paint-filled balloon, lobbed with gross miscalculation at the opposition, found its errant way to his windshield, splattering red paint in every direction.

Surprisingly for an outraged crowd of protesters, the pack proved genial assistants in getting his car cleaned up enough for Russ to drive home. In the process, he made a friend or two and acquired no less than seven pamphlets and flyers, which he threw on the floorboard of his car. In no time, he pulled into the familiar driveway, wishing it could be the one he'd shared with Katie. Sighing, he went into the house.

Per Stem's instructions (because he refused to execute the distressing task himself), Russ was to photograph Jasper and list him on eBay. It took him a couple of hours (that is, he took a nap) before he got around to it. The lighting in the living room was awful and the shag carpet camouflaged the bobcat. Nevertheless, Russ uploaded the photos and, per his friend's request, started the bidding at $50. Just before he closed the webpage, he noticed the red notifications hovering over the bell-shaped icon, but since he'd told Stem he wasn't going to babysit the bidding, he exited the page and pulled up an employment website.

The science professor came over that evening as he normally did, except this time he was carrying a load of Pad Thai. "I figured you hadn't been to the shops," he stated, though Russ suspected the real reason he had splurged on the takeout was because he aimed to cheer up his newly single friend with a plate of the greasy, spicy deliciousness.

"Actually," said Russ with a smile, which elicited a pleasantly surprised one from Stem, "I drove by the grocery store . . . but forgot to stop."

Laying out the food on the kitchen countertop, his friend replied, "Well, you drove somewhere, so that's progress." A moment of silence ensued before he followed up with, "So? News of the day?"

"Let's see," Russ said, drawing out the suspense. "Lost my home. Signed my divorce papers. And a ladies' rights activist group threw red paint at my windshield, as I was using it."

Erring on the side of optimism, Stem observed, "Look at all you've accomplished today. I'm proud of you, mate."

"Oh, and Jasper's listed."

His friend's countenance fell—yet quickly rose again. "Very good then. Now, let's pray and get something in your stomach."

Russ' weight loss was noticeable. Since that morning in Dean Scarborough's office, he'd lost eighteen pounds. If he'd been a stick like Stem, then that amount would be life-threatening. However, Russ had a bit of buffer room and he felt not in the least bit alarmed, though he could often feel Stem eyeing him in a particular way, as though visually weighing him to calculate his loss or gain. When Russ pushed back his Styrofoam tableware after only consuming half the dish, Stem protested.

"No, no. You haven't eaten enough."

"I'm full."

"No, you must eat more. Take five more bites."

"What am I, a toddler?"

"You're acting like one."

"I am not."

Glaring at his friend, Stem argued, "Your body is in a state of sur-bloody-vival. This starving yourself will lead to fatty acid depletion, impaired kidney function, compromised immunity, poor decision-making, depression, and death. Do you want to bloody *die*?"

That possibility didn't present itself as a drawback, as far as Russ could see. However, his stare down with Stem lasted only three seconds and resulted in his eating five more acceptably sized bites of his Pad Thai after which he gathered up the remnants of his meal and tossed them in the refrigerator. When Stem had finished off the last morsels of his portion, he suggested yet again that they "go to the shops."

Though he'd been a lifelong shopper at Bill's Cash Saver Grocery, Russ drove past the familiar store and headed out of town, venturing clear to the Kroger in Cabot. After all, Katie shopped at Cash Saver, and, as much as he pined to lay eyes on her, he also didn't want to chance an embarrassing run-in with his now ex. In fact, he'd done most of his shopping and errand-running of late in the surrounding communities, setting foot as rarely as possible in Searcy proper, and it had keenly been on his mind that he couldn't stay in his hometown. His home it was—nearly the only one he'd ever known—but it was Katie's now and he'd never—*never*—ask her to leave, yet he knew his presence there could cause her nothing but pain. So, he avoided all the places she might possibly go, and that was just as well because it meant he also avoided coming face to face with other people to whom he'd made himself a schmuck.

Stem didn't have to ask why his friend had driven twenty-five miles out of the way. Though as unaware an observer as he appeared to most, he often figured out life's little mysteries so quickly that his mind spent little time on the matters, and he rarely remarked upon them as they seemed mundane and uninteresting. But upon this occasion, he made one simple observation: "Kroger doesn't carry my Hot Pockets, so we'll need to stop at Cash Saver on the way back." Seeing as Katie was his friend, he saw the possibility of encountering her at the local grocery store as something of a chance he'd like to take whenever possible. Plus, he'd not gone a single week in the past ten years without a Hot Pocket and he'd prefer to die of disembowelment than break that habit.

And so it was when, on the way back to Meemaw's, Russ' car pulled into the back parking pad behind the daycare which was housed in the building next to Cash Saver.

Stem gaped. "Are you going to make me walk four hundred bloody meters just for Hot Pockets? Pull up closer, mate."

Russ shook his head. He figured even just seeing his car might bring sadness to Katie and he'd rather the Aussie walk five miles than risk that.

Stem tossed back a handful of M and M's and crunched them between his teeth as though desecrating the bones of his enemies. He was less keen on being separated from food than a black bear coming out of hibernation, and the intensity with which he slammed the passenger door underlined, as well as italicized, that fact.

Where Russ' mind went for the first few minutes, he could not say. Was he thinking of Katie? Of course. Was he thinking of all the pain he had caused her? How could he not? But the thoughts which passed through his mind were more like drops of oil flowing in the midst of a stream—distinguishable, barely, yet inseparable from the general roar and hubbub of the whole. But he became aware that time was passing, slowly, and ten minutes became twenty-five, and soon, he groaned at his friend's tardiness.

From his vantage point, he could see neither Cash Saver's parking lot nor the front door of the store. However, his frustration growing and the frozen items in his back seat thawing, he decided that the night was dark enough that he might venture around the corner and see if he could spy his friend. At the very least, he got it into his mind that he might hide behind the daycare's air conditioner units and wait for the man to return to the car, at which point he could jump out and scare him.

He might've felt lost in the darkness of the night like an astronaut drifting alone and unattached in outer space, but the hardness of the sidewalk beneath his tennis shoes gave him a much-needed sense of feeling grounded. It helped clear his head and calm his emotions. In the span of the two minutes it took to walk from his car to the front of the store, he decided he needed to take more walks under the cover of night.

What he saw did not register the moment he rounded the corner, and, before he realized what was before him, he felt a subconscious warmth flow over his body. As he leaned into the feeling, he discovered he was staring at Katie's van. It was unmistakable, with the Mercy Project Ghana bumper sticker over the accessibility modifications made to the rear that had cost such a dear penny. In his imagination, he'd expected that seeing her van would trigger a retreat to his body but, instead, all he wanted to do was go to it, stand by it, and wait for her to return to his presence. And the acknowledgement of that feeling brought about another which so contradicted the first that he felt physically ill.

Why did I do it?

That question had been asked him by Meemaw (who liked to say life was too short to not cut straight to the point), but he'd not bothered to search for the answer that day or any day since because searching for it would inevitably lead to discovering a huge flaw in himself. For he knew his affair was, in fact, caused by his own shortcomings, not any which Katie (or even Caydee) possessed.

Why did I do it?

He stood there resisting the urge to run to Katie's van, searching his heart for the answer, and, yet, at the same time, hoping he could just travel back in time and take back what had happened. If he could go back, he'd not have given into Caydee's excessive laughter at his jokes or asked her if she'd like to come to his office to borrow a book or suggested they meet in a random parking lot to discuss her issues with her boyfriend. He wouldn't have done anything but keep his eyes and mind and spirit on Katie. But even as he made himself that promise, the acknowledgment that the covenant he'd just professed was a lie and he'd do exactly as he'd done before slapped him in the face. He'd engaged in the affair because of something—some reason—and even if he did go back in time, without the knowledge of what that reason was, he'd make all the same mistakes over and over again, and he'd always end up there on the sidewalk next to Cash Saver's parking lot staring at Katie's van and wishing he could ride home with her and have her always.

He wiped the tears out of his eyes and dried his fingers on his jacket. Then, his breath caught in his lungs. There, coming out of the store, was Katie. And Stem. What, his best friend was walking his ex-wife out of the store? For the briefest of moments, he felt jealousy and anger overtaking him. But almost as soon as the emotions jumped out to gang bust him, they retreated to the darkness. How could he be angry that Stem was helping Katie carry her groceries to the car? In fact, watching this act of kindness was akin to feeling the springs of joy overflow in his heart. His friend, whom he loved, loved his ex-wife, whom he still loved. And yet, he also felt grief present because he and she had always gone to the store together and, of course, he'd always got the groceries to the van and loaded for her. And who would carry them into the house for her now? The truth was, she had no one to help her, and seeing this act of service performed by his friend brought tears to his eyes.

He wanted desperately to watch her until she was out of his sight, but he felt grief and shame wash over him and he retreated, pounding the sidewalk and struggling to see through his tears.

The moment Stem returned, Russ wanted to pounce on him with questions. But Stem volunteered without prodding.

"Saw Katie—*your* Katie," he said, and Russ was reminded that, since he'd been intimately involved with two women of that name as of late, for clarity of conversation the two men had designated Katie as *his Katie* and Caydee *as the other Caydee*.

"How's she doing?"

Stem was already ripping into a bag of candy. "Frailer and paler than usual. Care for some lollies?"

The news was the worst imaginable and Russ gripped his chest, certain for the second time that day that he was in the early stages of a heart attack. "Is she sick?"

"Don't think so."

"What—what did she say? Tell me everything."

"Sticky beak," he said with an unmistakable trace of condemnation in his voice. "I'll tell you *some* of the things she said, but the rest is confidential. She likes working at the church office but she hasn't quite figured out the copy machine yet. And she's helping plan vacation Bible school and will be teaching the fifth graders."

Russ smiled and noticed his heart attack had passed. “She loves teaching that grade.”

As though reading a bullet point list, his friend continued. “Her dishwasher is leaking and the repairman found a snakeskin behind it, but no snake.”

“What kind of snake? Poisonous?”

“Snakes are not poisonous. They are venomous.”

“Is it venomous?”

“Well, she didn’t know what kind it was, but the skin was over four feet long.” Reading the concern on Russ’ face, Stem rolled his eyes. “She’ll be apples, mate. Katie, who is a much braver bloke than her ex-husband, cut the skin up neatly and made little resin-coated necklace pendants from them which she is selling on Etsy. Said she saw it once on Pinterest and had always wanted to try it.”

“Is she—” Russ stammered, unable to finish the thought.

Stem sighed, as though bored of the conversation. “Nothing else to report.”

“But that can’t be all she said.”

Through a mouthful of Twizzlers, he confessed, “It’s not, but it’s all I’m going to tell you so bugger off.”

Chapter 7

"Have you checked your eBay listings?" Stem asked between bites of his Snicker's bar.

Exasperated from an evening spent job searching, Russ looked up from his laptop and frowned. "Nope."

"It's been two days. Don't you want to know if someone's bid?"

His friend rubbed his forehead and barked, "I told you I wasn't going to babysit the bidding!"

"Move over," ordered Stem, pushing his friend out of the spot he'd occupied on the shag carpet. A cardboard box Russ had salvaged from a shipment at American GadgetTech served as the desktop on which the laptop sat. As Stem navigated to the website, Russ went to the restroom. When he returned, Stem was engrossed in what he saw on the screen.

"Sorry for snapping at you," Russ apologized.

"Come look at this," said Stem, and the excitement in his voice was palpable.

The eBay thing had been done simply to indulge the whims of his friend and dying wishes of Meemaw, yet now, it was proving more of a pain to Russ than his job hunt. His apology forgotten, he barked again, "What?"

"Just bloody come here."

The screen, though as plain as day, did not register in Russ' tired mind. Already, he'd worked a full shift at American GadgetTech, put the first coat of paint on the living room walls, and spent two hours scanning online want ads. "Tell me what it is," he sighed. "I can't even see straight anymore."

"Look, people are bidding."

"On which item?"

"All of them. Actually, Jasper only has one bid for $50 but the sword is up to $400."

Like the blind man touched by Jesus, Russ' eyes suddenly could see clearly. He bent down and studied the screen. "That's crazy. What's the jewelry at?"

"$85, but I think it'll go higher before it's all said and done."

In unison, they glanced at the samurai sword which lay on the shag carpet in precisely the spot they'd thrown it the other day. Picking it up, Russ leaned it against the wall. Admiring his work, he then watched as it ungracefully slid down the wall and came to a thud on the carpet, leaving skid marks on the wall.

Stem smiled. "Guess you'll get to paint that wall too."

Prompted by the eBay bidding, which had risen to $700 for the sword, the Prius made its second voyage to 42B.

"Only grab valuables," Stem warned, as though the task was to his benefit.

"Like what? This?" asked Russ, reaching for a round shield. Slipping from his grasp, it crashed to the floor with a clang that echoed off the concrete walls.

"And that's why you shouldn't own nice things, Russell."

"It slipped."

"You're accident prone."

"Should we take it?"

The question bounced around in Stem's mind like a hacky sack. "The shipping on that behemoth will tank your earnings. Leave it."

There was a great debate on which items should enter the eBay market that evening, but after using food as leverage, Russ won the argument. The back seat was laid down and the rear of his car stuffed with an assortment of metallic treasures.

A short time later, as the Prius idled in the Taco Bell drive-thru, Russ spied his cousin Lance's truck driving past the restaurant.

"Shoot, he saw me," he muttered as he strained to peer around the building.

Stem was hammering away at his phone screen which was filled with falling candies, but he managed to mutter, "Who?"

A quick decision was made and Russ wheeled around the car standing between him and the pony-tailed blonde working the drive-thru window.

"What are you doing?" Stem cried. "My bean burritos!"

Ignoring him, Russ pulled up to the exit and glanced down the street in the direction Lance's truck had gone.

"Shoot!" he exclaimed. "He's turning around."

Gunning it, he peeled out in front of a yellow Mustang who proceeded to rev their engine at his tail.

"What's gotten into you?" his friend griped. "What about my dinner? You promised me."

Keeping his eyes on the rearview mirror, Russ explained, "My cousin's back there, turning around to follow me."

"So."

"So? So, he's been hounding me about selling the house. And how am I gonna explain this car loaded with Peepaw's things? Lance is gonna want to see the storage shed and then my other cousins will be on that place like butter on toast."

Stem crossed his arms. "I liked Meemaw's analogies better."

"You know what I'm saying," he grumbled as he cut onto a side street. Russ knew the roads of Searcy like a garbage truck driver, but they'd been raised in the same house so it was likely Lance knew them just as well. Taking as many twists and turns as he could, he found his way out of town and headed down a back road.

"Where are you taking me?" Stem demanded.

"Just driving around to make sure Lance doesn't find me."

"I need to eat. You know how my blood sugar gets low when I

don't." The bag of chips which he'd been munching on for the past ten minutes—and which still rested in his lap—had evidently been forgotten.

"We'll get something in Judsonia."

By the time they'd finished off their barbecue sandwiches at Good Grub BBQ, his predatory cousin had slipped Russ' mind. However, as he turned onto Walnut Street and his headlights flashed upon the large black diesel in the driveway, he suddenly felt as if chewed up bits of the slow-smoked pork might come hurdling out his mouth like a decrepit track star from the grave. As they pulled closer, the soft ember glow of Lance's cigarette indicated he was resting against the cab, awaiting his cousin's arrival.

The man was at Russ' window before he'd even shut the Prius off. Rapping on the glass, he grinned. "Knock, knock, Rusty."

Russ knew that, as soon as he opened the car door, the overhead light would come on, illuminating all his eBay cargo. To avoid this, he rolled down the window instead.

"Hey, Lance," he said, trying his best to force a smile.

"Sup, Rusty?" his cousin replied. "Noticed you in the drive-thru at Taco Bell earlier."

Something about the accusation set off Russ' anger. "Not a crime to get fast food, is it?"

"Not unless you order without paying, which it looks like you did. How come you ran away from me? Didn't think I knew where you lived?"

"No, I—" To the driver's surprise, the passenger door suddenly opened, casting an LED glow all about the car's interior.

Peering through the backseat window, Lance asked with suspicion, "What's all that?"

Russ stammered. "Oh, that's—"

"My stuff," said Stem without a trace of nerves in his voice. "Went thrifting today. Hit up Cowtown Resale, Barkin' Barn, Salvation Army. And some others. Hey, did you ever get that wedding gift for Courtney? There was a really nice 5-piece bedroom set at Fortner's. Solid bamboo. Chinoiserie. Peacock and fan motifs.

Very sexy."

Lance offered a half-smile as he considered the possibility of making love to his fiancé on such a fine bed.

"You should check it out," Stem said, tossing a wink to his friend's domineering cousin.

"Thanks, yeah, I will," Lance replied.

No longer afraid for his life, Russ exited the car. However, he was soon face-to-face (face-to-chest, anyway) with the aggression he'd been hoping to avoid. Cornered between the man and his car, Russ requested, "Please move."

"Not until you tell me how much you're getting for this house."

"I'm still doing the repairs," he explained. "You could come over and help with—"

"I ain't got time for none of that. And besides, you're living here rent free. That's basically stealing from the cousins. We're all invested in this family or don't you know?"

Russ wasn't sure exactly what the man meant by that but he figured Lance was implying that Russ was conning all the cousins out of something they were owed.

"I'll let you know as soon as the repairs have been completed and it's listed on the market."

"The sooner the better," replied his cousin coolly, though Russ knew it was conveyed as a threat.

"Of course," Russ relinquished. "Sooner the better."

Lance glared at him for another moment before stating, "Now let me in. I've gotta take a dump."

Fresh with its first coat of paint, the furnishings in the living room were sparse (nonexistent, to be exact). In the dining room which Lance passed by as he entered the house, a few cardboard boxes which served as tables and the items which had recently been listed on eBay rested haphazardly on the floor.

"See you're living the life of a king," he quipped with a smirk.

"Obviously," said Russ to be ironic, but the remark only served to elicit a grimace from his cousin.

Lance's visit to the restroom lasted so long that he almost

escaped his cousin's mind for the second time that evening. However, upon his exit from the bathroom, he made his presence known with an announcement: "The vent's broke. Fix that before you sell."

A nod from Russ seemed an adequate response. In fact, Lance's attention had, in that one second span, completely shifted to the pile of eBay items on the ground.

"What's all that stuff?" questioned the unwanted visitor.

"Mine," said Stem before his friend could reply.

"Don't you got a house of your own?"

"I do, but I don't like to keep my things there. Gets too cluttered."

Though the delivery had been convincing, Lance eyed the pair suspiciously, glancing between them and the sword. Then, walking to the weaponry, he picked it up. After a short inspection, he jumped into an attack stance, looking directly into his cousin's eyes. "Huh? How do I look?"

Evidently, the wearing day had beaten all playfulness out of Russ. "Put it down."

The remark ignored, Lance questioned, "How about a rumble? Be just like the good ole days 'cept Meemaw ain't here to save your hide."

"Put it down. I'm not gonna fight you." Everything inside him wished he'd had a gun so he could purposely accidentally shoot his cousin in the foot.

"Come on, Rusty," he chided. "Scared?"

"It's not a fair fight. You're holding a sword and I'm unarmed. I'd either end up dead or infected with tetanus."

A crazy look entered the sword-wielding man's face as he took a step closer to Russ. "Well, maybe that's fine by me."

The authenticity of Lance's threat could hardly be mistaken for play. Taking a step back, Russ warned, "Just leave."

Heeding his request didn't appear to be a consideration. As the larger man lunged forward and pretended to disembowel him, Russ flinched. This was met with uproarious laughter from Lance whose cigarette- and halitosis-riddled breath was as noxious as breathing the fumes of a rogue fire at the city dump. However, when the humor of the moment seemed to pass, Lance glared at Russ and questioned, "You visit Peepaw's storage shed yet?"

Once again, Russ was thankful for the generous pigment in his skin because he could feel his face flushing.

"I did," he said with conviction.

"And? What's there?"

Lying had never been a strength of his. A lie he had conjured had never—not once—made it past Meemaw, and he wasn't sure at all that he could muster the acting skills to pull one over his cousin.

"Come on, Rusty," Lance said, almost singing the words.

Russ could feel the sword inching closer to his gut.

"Tell the Bucker what you found."

Long ago, 'the Bucker' had been the self-designated name Lance had chosen when they were children. It represented, Lance said, his inner villain, and Russ knew from past experiences that the Bucker took villainy seriously. All in all, Russ had never quite understood how the term originated but he felt strongly that it was inspired in equal parts by Batman's nemesis and by its rhyming with America's top bad word.

Swallowing the dryness in his throat, Russ spluttered, "Put—put the sword down and I'll tell you."

If, as children, they had been in this same situation, Russ knew he'd soon be making a trip to the emergency room. The scenario playing out in adulthood, however, had a more bearable outcome. Lance hesitated but ultimately tossed the sword onto the horrible smoke-engrained shag carpet.

"Tell, tell," he said.

"I didn't find anything."

Lance didn't like the news, but at the very least, Russ could see he accepted it as the truth.

Going further into explanation/lying, Russ said, "Meemaw had evidently not made the monthly payments on the unit and management had cleared everything out. It happened years ago."

"What did they do with it all?"

"I don't know. Tossed it probably."

His cousin's disappointment was unmistakable. After uttering an expletive, Lance hiked up his pants by the belt and headed for the door. "So long, Rusty. I want top dollar for this house. It's been in the family for fifty years."

Russ stared with gaping jaw. "What are you stapling to my freshly painted wall?"

Concentrating on the task, Stem ordered, "Grab that corner. Hold it up."

Obediently, Russ picked up the corner of the white sheet.

"Lower."

"Here?"

"Higher."

"Here?"

With obvious frustration, Stem yanked the queen-sized bedsheet from Russ' hand and affixed it where he wanted. Then, he pulled the bottom part of the sheet away from the wall, draping it across the floor. Standing back, he admired his handiwork. "How's it look?"

"Like a white sheet stapled to my freshly painted wall."

"Russell, sometimes you scare me."

"The feeling is mutual."

"This is the backdrop for your eBay photos."

"Ah," said Russ, and he did actually pity himself at that moment as a slow-witted person.

Two hours later, as Russ awoke from his nap, Stem announced, "I've taken bonzer photos, mate."

"Is that . . . a good thing?"

"Of course." Handing Russ' phone back to him, he instructed, "I've downloaded the eBay app for you. Now edit these pics and get those items posted. And remember," reminded his friend as he reclined on the carpet for some shuteye. "Start the bidding low and hype up the shipping price."

Of all the steps required to list an item on eBay, Russ was certain the step of actually listing the item was his least favorite. Per his friend's instructions—and based on tips he'd verified on the internet—a seller should list every flaw, marking, identification, and detail apparent (or not) on the item. Inspecting each object as thoroughly as a law enforcement officer performing a body cavity search, Russ soon grew tired of the task. Short of listing nine items, he laid down on his makeshift pallet to sleep, noting that the first thing he'd buy when the money from the sword came in was an air mattress.

The next morning, Stem reported that the bidding for the sword had reached over $900.

A renewed surge of energy coursed through Russ. "That's insane."

"And that necklace you listed last night is already up to $400."

"For real? Let me see."

Quickly scrolling through his listings, Russ was astounded to see how high some of the bids had reached. "I didn't even think people still used eBay," he remarked as he poured himself a bowl of cereal.

Reaching for it, Stem said, "Thanks for the brekkie, mate."

Sighing, Russ got out a fresh bowl and filled it with cereal and milk. "Do you think we should clean the dust off the sword?"

Stem's palm slapped the countertop. "Are you mad? We can't alter an item once we've listed it. The buyer's bidding on a dusty old sword and that's exactly what you're gonna give them."

During his lunch break, Russ stepped out into the alley behind American GadgetTech and sat on a stack of pallets. Fiddling with his phone, he opened his newly added eBay app. His eyes could hardly believe the message he'd received—a buyer had offered him $1500 to end the listing early and sell the sword directly to him. With shaking fingers, he took a screen shot and texted it to his confidante.

Thirty seconds later, his phone rang.

"Don't do it," came Stem's voice.

"But it's $1500."

"You'll get more if you wait on the bidding."

"Or I could cash in and get $1500 right now."

"I have no doubt if some bloke is out there tossing around $1500 then others are thinking the same. A bidding war will ensue and it'll skyrocket. Just wait and see."

He sighed. "All right, I will."

As he hung up, Russ couldn't believe his luck—something of Peepaw's had value and he was going to bank on it.

"Sup, Rusty?"

Russ jumped, nearly toppling off the pallets. "Lance," he gasped.

The man tossed his cigarette butt against the building and Russ hoped the pile of trash that had accumulated in the area didn't catch fire. Sauntering towards him, the large redneck wore a stupid grin on his face like a man who'd just caught an eighteen-pound bass.

"You been lyin' to me, Rusty?"

Russ shook his head.

"You keepin' secrets, huh?"

Knowing he couldn't pull off another convincing lie, Russ maintained his silence.

"'Cause I think you are." Lance towered over his smaller cousin like Goliath. "What's that $1500 you was talkin' 'bout just then on the phone?"

"It—it was . . ."

Stem was good at lying. He spun yarns on the whim. Russ wished he was there.

"'It. It. It,'" Lance mocked. "You know what I think *it* is? Life insurance. Meemaw had a policy and you thought you was gonna keep it all for yourself, isn't that right?"

Of course this was the wrong assumption, but thinking it over quickly, Russ decided it wasn't such a bad thing for his cousin to believe.

"Yes. You're right," he confirmed. "It *is* a life insurance policy, but I wasn't going to keep it to myself. I was gonna split it ten ways between myself and the cousins. $150 each."

"$150!" Lance exclaimed, spitting on the ground. "I got three kids to feed. You think I can keep them fed for that? Yeah, that's right. Them three's gonna be skin and bones on $150. So, what're you gonna do about it?"

A vasectomy should improve the situation. Or at the very least, prevent it from becoming worse, but he kept that notion to himself. "Here's what I suggest. How's about I give you a double portion? $300."

Lance's face changed from menacing to angry. "You tryin'a cut out my sisters, huh? Thought you'd keep a little suh-em-suh-em for yourself and leave out Becky and JoAnne?"

"Just trying to be fair," Russ clarified, taking a cautious step back.

"Fair, huh?" he said, stuffing a pinch of snuff into his bottom lip. "Well, fair's fair, ain't it? How's 'bout you and I split this share 50/50? $650 each since, you know, we two are working the hardest to care for Meemaw's estate." Leaning in, he added, "And we won't tell the others."

The thought passed through Russ' mind that, given enough brain cells, Lance would make a good mastermind villain. "Fine," he agreed. "Sounds good. I'll give you your share next week when I have the money."

Lance glanced at his watch. "Next week. Same time—" he smirked like an idiot "—same alley."

Chapter 8

At first, Russ was looking forward to owning the television that a customer had returned to American GadgetTech. It might've had faulty wiring which caused the 30-minute sleep timer to always be engaged, but the diversion it would create overpowered this drawback. But the longer the narrator on the National Scientific Channel droned on about fringe medicine, the more frustrated Stem became. What had once just been a string of mutters had become full-on shouting.

"It's as if they've hired a mob of roos to script this show!" hollered the physics professor. "Is science not sacred?"

Just as Stem's blood began to boil over the narrator's claim that the term "mesmerism" was derived because of the practitioner's attempt to mesmerize his subjects, the tv shut itself off.

"Rubbish!" shouted the riled man. "The lot of ya!"

Russ gathered up the various food wrappers and takeout boxes which his friend, in his zeal, had hurled across the room at the tv, and he put them in their final and proper resting place. However, Stem's diatribe regarding the irresponsibility of the National Scientific Channel as well as their obligation to responsibly educate American youth continued ad nauseum until Russ suggested they check the eBay listings.

Monitoring the bids had become an amusement for the pair

ever since they had accepted an offer of $800 for a collection of watches a few days earlier. As a result, the gaudy necklace, which Russ had once been certain contained fake diamonds, had been withdrawn due to Stem's curiosity over their possible authenticity, and the diamond checking device was on its way over from Amazon with an expected delivery of prior to 9pm the next Tuesday. (To the vexation of Stem, who was the thriftiest person Russ had ever known, his friend had opted to delay the delivery by a day in order to receive $1 digital credit, and this was a current point of contention.)

"I've got an offer on the mask," said Russ. As he read the message, his hands began to shake.

"Well?" huffed Stem who was still sore about the inaccuracies on the evening programming.

"I can't believe this. It's a scam, right? They're offering $12,000."

"What?" Stem exclaimed as he yanked the phone from Russ' hand. All frustration at the National Scientific Channel was immediately put in the past as he scanned the message.

"Are they swindling me? What do you think?"

"I'm checking their buying history. I can't determine exactly what they've bought, but going to this seller's page, who left feedback about a purchase this buyer made a few days back, it's all high-end antiques. Rare, first printings of Charles Dickens. Steuben art glass."

"What's that?"

Stem frowned at the interruption made by his apparently uneducated friend. "And there's a Chinese silk embroidered dragon robe—authentic, from the look of it—and Niels Moller teak dining chairs. A complete set. $5500."

Russ waited impatiently as his friend scrolled through the images. "Stem, the offer. Is it legit? Should I accept it?"

"Listen to this: 'Great buyer! Fast payment! Easy transaction! A+++++++'"

"Did you really just read me seven pluses in a row?"

"Every bloody one."

"Ok, so what is that you're saying?"

"Russell, I'm saying I literally read every single plus—"

"Not that. Just what are all those pluses? A grade or something?"

"It's the feedback left for this buyer from the seller of the midcentury modern dining set."

"And it proves what?"

"Keep up, Russell. It means this buyer is legit. Accept his offer and bank cash."

Russ took a cautious step away from the phone Stem had shoved in his face. "Wait a minute. You told me not to accept the first offer on the sword, to let the bidders run the figures up. So, what makes this different?"

"A hunch."

The basis for Stem's suggestion was less than impressive for his friend. "You're the scientist who said, and I quote, 'Hunches are just a fool's wishful thinking.'"

"Fine. What's the bidding up to anyway?"

Somewhat sheepishly, Russ confessed, "$900." Before Stem could work harder to change his slow-witted mind, he added, "But it's still got two days left. The bidding will rise."

The Aussie threw his hands into the air. "Your money, not mine."

Ignoring the remark, Russ checked the bids on his other items. "They're all looking good. I think I'm gonna quit my job."

"Be reasonable, mate. $12,000? Maybe quit your job. $900? Keep kissing up to the nineteen-year-old tyrant."

"But what if . . ."

"What? Peepaw was really a collector? 42B contains a treasure trove—thousands of dollars' worth of items just waiting to be listed on eBay?"

Goosebumps rose on Russ' arms. "I was gonna say, 'What if I just went to part-time?' but, yeah. What if *that*? Just imagine."

"It's improbable but intriguing."

Russ' final trip to American GadgetTech was to purchase a bundle of top-of-the-line security cameras.

"What're you doing with these?" quizzed Dirk. With a sick chuckle, he joked, "Worried someone's gonna steal your piece of trash car?"

"Yep," replied Russ who wasn't about to disclose that they were intended to guard a cellarful of treasures bequeathed to him by his grandparents.

Powering the security cameras would've been impossible had the pair of friends not made the fortuitous discovery of an electrical box on the premises—and a sizeable one, at that.

"This outfit is legit," Stem had remarked when they found it. "Massive enough to electrify Sydney Cricket Ground."

Russ wasn't sure if the darkness skewed his vision but it had appeared his friend was drooling.

To their further rapture, they had found the cellar was outfitted with overhead light fixtures. After picking up some new bulbs and a deadbolt for the exterior door—and after convincing the lady at the electric company to turn the power back on at the property which, to Russ' astonishment, was titled in Peepaw's name—Russ and Stem headed to the storage shed where a mystery awaited them.

As the Prius neared the end of Mermaid Lane, Stem suddenly bolted up in his seat (he had been alternating between munching on Lucky Charms marshmallows and dozing). With alarm, he stated, "My teeth are chattering in my head."

"Do you have a fever?"

"No, you bogan, it's electricity. Buzzing the air."

And sure enough, as the car rolled to a stop, Russ could feel the strange sensation as if a metallic bee were trapped inside his mouth.

"Hurry," urged Stem as he snatched up three shopping bags full of munchies which he planned to stash in the storage shed.

As they passed through the grassy field, an eerie electrical hum filled the air, seizing all nature with its force like the grasp of a gigantic robot. Save for the audible electricity and the two dumbfounded visitors, the field was silent and devoid of life.

To their astonishment, as they lifted 42B, a soft blue glow emitted from the cellar.

"What the bloody heck?" Stem whispered under his breath.

"What's that light?"

"No bloody clue."

"Think someone's down there?"

"Go check," instructed Stem as he backed away from the opening.

Russ' death wish had faded somewhat, mostly due to his recent success on eBay, so he was more hesitant than usual to explore the darkened corners of the Earth. However, he couldn't risk a fatal blow to his reputation, even if the only one to witness the lapse in bravery was his pansy friend, so he grabbed a rotting plank from the board heap and descended the steps.

The peculiar blue light crept through the dark cellar like fog in a cemetery. Shadows played on the lifeless metal objects, making imps of statues and demons of menageries. As he verged deeper into the nefarious cavern, Russ remembered having seen an old Egyptian-looking relic resting innocently on one of the shelves. It had struck him as having an uncanny resemblance to the life-giving tablet in *Night at the Museum*, and, though he knew the notion was nonsense, he became gripped with fear that all the weaponry and metallic creatures and implements lurking in the depths might suddenly come to life and pulverize him.

If they had needed to make a stealthy entrance into the blue-lit cellar, Stem's call would've blown their cover. "What do you see, mate?"

Despite his friend's unhealthy need to intrude on the exploration, Russ felt all the energy inside himself channeling into one precise requirement—keeping his wits about him.

"Russell, what's down there?"

"Shhh!"

Two walls, which met in the far corner of the space, a place where he had not yet ventured, illuminated with great blue intensity, drawing Russ in like a moth. A warmth began to rush over him—something palpable, as though he stood in the exhaust of a great machine.

"Eat or be eaten," he suddenly heard his old soccer coach say.

Russ had spent an unfortunate number of years being first pick for every soccer team he'd ever signed up to join, only for the coaches to realize that a dark-skinned man does not necessarily a great soccer player make. Now, like some of those unfortunate games in which his coaches had made him a starter, would his being first pick to descend into the blue depths lead to his being masticated by some yet-unseen force?

As his eyes discovered the source of the glow, he found himself both mesmerized and frightened. It was a massive machine—of some sort—like nothing he'd ever seen. A wide, floor-to-ceiling metal casing (the weld lines of which were very neat) with tubes and wires pouring out of it like medusa's hair, gave the contraption a homemade appearance, and his first thought was that it must be an electric generator crafted by Peepaw. But as he studied it, he realized there were not one but two metallic structures. The blue light, emitting like a gas, exited the metal chamber of the barrel-chested apparatus through a clear tube and was then carried to the pinnacle of the second structure (which had the distinct insinuation of a person-sized birdcage).

"Crikey!" exclaimed Stem as he rushed past the brave explorer.

"Geez!" screamed Russ, gripping his chest. "'Bout scared the crap out of me!"

Either unaware or apathetic that he had nearly caused his friend's first toileting accident in years, the science professor indulged the object's allurement with awestruck captivation. "What is it?"

Russ, who was every bit as dumbstruck as his buddy (though much more so), felt himself equally as drawn to the blue light. "What is *that*?"

Entranced like his friend, Stem moved nearer to get a better look.

"Wait!" objected Russ, panic rushing through him. "It might be radioactive."

"Do you know nothing? Radium is colorless without the addition of phosphorus, in which case it is green."

The Simpsons episode where Homer knocked a green radioactive chemical onto himself was on Russ' mind, and he made a mental note to check the accuracy of his friend's claim against Google's wisdom later.

"Then, what is it?"

With his face six inches from the glowing tube, Stem carefully studied it.

"You're going to go blind looking at it that closely," argued the man, which was his best attempt to dissuade his friend from interacting with a radioactive substance without actually getting into an argument about its being radioactive. With his warning ignored, Russ suggested, "At least turn it off so our brain waves aren't fried by the electricity."

"I've got to study it first."

"Well, can you do it quickly? This thing is giving me a headache."

"Shhh," Stem ordered. However, a poor pupil Russ made and, upon his third interruption of the scientist's concentration, the prof suggested, "Look, mate, why don't you do something within your paygrade and check out the lightbulbs, yeah? I'll examine this machine and then, once I've made a conclusive analysis, I'll fill you in on the blanks. What say you?"

Paygrade level or not, Russ had lost interest in the glowing metal and rubber and glass contraption which enamored his friend so thoroughly, and he was developing a headache (from the radiation, he presumed). Gladly he undertook the effort of illuminating the storage space, save for one brief span between replacing the second and third bulb in which time he laid on the cool floor and dozed off.

"Bonzer!"

The cry knocked him out of a very pleasant dream in which he was walking hand in hand with Katie. It had seemed so real to the man that he had to look about him to remember where he was or what he'd been doing in real life prior to unconsciousness. The buzzing in his teeth, which had not subsided, brought him all the more quickly to the present.

"Russell, I've figured it out!"

"What?"

Stem came running around the corner. "The bloody machine! It's an interuniversal Dirac magnetic monopole transtemporal placement superconducting quantum interference device!" He giggled shamelessly. "Isn't this amazing?"

"That's . . . a mouthful," was all the enthusiasm the clueless man could muster. "Can you shut it off now?"

"Come on, mate. This is quite literally the most important discovery of all time."

To be honest, Russ had no idea what his friend's scientific jargon equated to in layman's term. With a shrug of his shoulders, he offered, "Uh . . . okay?"

Mistaking his confusion for skepticism, Stem sulked, "I see. My own mate—the man whose back I've had all these years—the bloke who cheated on his wife and didn't bother to tell his best mate, and, yet, whose side I stuck by through depression and self-loathing and gluttony—"

"Gluttony?" he interrupted. "When was I ever—"

"*My* gluttony," Stem snapped. "*Mine*. I have feelings too. It's not all about you."

"Okay, okay," Russ said, patting his friend's shoulder. "I'm sure I believe you—I just don't understand what in the world it is you've discovered. You'll have to explain it to me."

With giddiness, Stem clasped his hands together and rubbed them as one might do on a particularly brisk evening around a campfire, and Russ knew, now, that he was prisoner to his friend's rapture with science and sci-fi. However, before the scientist had time to dive into it, Russ once again voiced his petition to shut off the machine.

"All bloody right!" Stem hollered as he crossed to the breaker panel. When he'd satisfied the request, he began. "It's all got to do with magnetic monopoles." A warning briefly inserted itself in his tone. "Don't confuse a magnetic monopole with a quasi-particle."

"I would never," Russ said dryly.

"The magnetic monopoles we're working with are new elementary particles. Well, new to *us*. Peepaw clearly made the discovery years ago."

Hoping to rush things along, Russ observed, "So, Peepaw made a new scientific discovery, and, from that, he built this awesome machine."

If not for the fact that they'd known each other for going on ten years and Stem had witnessed a great number of glimpses in that time of Russ' disappointing intellectualism, Stem would've been dissatisfied with his friend's simple-mindedness. However, as it were, he just pitied the poor fellow.

"Russell. Mate. This wasn't just a Saint Valentine's Day monopole blip—Peepaw devised a machine that could detect monopoles *and* harness their power. The man was a genius."

Russ laughed. "Peepaw? You're talking about the man who used to lay on the couch, bareback under his overalls, and curse and throw beer cans at the tv when the other team scored against the Hogs?"

This actually heightened Stem's opinion of the man and he beamed with pride. "Yes, *that* man."

If Meemaw had overheard the scientist's incredible assessment of her late husband, she would've been able to caress her hairline with her eyebrows, and Russ found himself just as incredulous. "The man who, as I recall, earned a living welding machinery parts?"

"Yes!"

The futility and frustration of arguing with the stubborn foreigner was enough for Russ to call a ceasefire. "Fine. Peepaw invented this machine. So, what is it anyway?"

If he had said, "You've won a billion dollars and a horde of supermodels will be here soon to worship your body," Stem wouldn't have been more thrilled than he was at that moment.

"All right," he said, shaking with exhilaration. "So, how to explain this to a layman."

The demeaning term, though unappreciated, was both well-earned and not insulting enough to induce Russ' objection.

"For symmetry breaking to occur—no . . . The Wilson loop must pass through—no, let me start over." A rarely seen perplexity was evident on the man. "Do you want me to go back to the beginning?"

Russ had to weigh his options—spend the next thirteen hours listening to scientific jargon and theories he couldn't possibly comprehend, or risk skipping over something, leaving a dangerous amount of pulsing excitement in his friend which could lead to his spontaneous combustion right there in that cellar.

As he sunk to the floor, Russ sighed. "From the top, please."

Pointing to the long, rectangular glass cover through which the blue light emitted, he explained, "All right. First, this glass-encased piece here is a particle accelerator called a cyclotron. It's more rudimentary than the ones I worked with in college but it'll get the job done." His finger traced the path of several tubes exiting out the metal housing of the cyclotron which all eventually terminated at the pinnacle of the metal cage-like contraption. "These tubes pass the energy from colliding particles to here."

Pointing to the top of the birdcage where the light dimly shone, Russ inquired, "And what is *that* thing exactly?"

With pride and a deep breath, as if about to deliver monumental news, Stem smiled. "If my analysis is correct, this large glowing orb is a sizeable diamond, the core of which is impossibly a lodestone. The chances of that happening are likely a trillion to one."

"How do you know it's a diamond? And why is that stuff blue? And—"

"Russell!" he interrupted with exasperation. "I will answer all your questions at the end of my lecture. For now, simply take notes."

Suddenly Russ understood how it was that his sanguine friend managed to hold down a career as a tenured (and revered) professor.

Upon Russ' apology for his rude intrusion, the lecture continued.

"Even without a diamond detector device, which you so unfortunately and cheaply delayed the shipping on, it is quite simple to determine a mineral of the sort, and my explanation, which will follow, will leave you with no doubts of that certainty." Pausing, he pointed to the man whose hand had raised halfway through the sentence. "Yes, Russell?"

"So, it's a diamond, but why is that stuff glowing?"

"This is—"

"And blue?"

"I will—"

"And is it radioactive?"

Stem pointed a stern finger at the man. "I would deduct ten percent off your final for that, you know."

"*Sorry*," hissed his friend.

A glare from the scientist silenced any further obstinance from his student.

"To bed down your worries, I'll confirm that it's *not* radium," Stem assured.

"That's good news."

"It's either one of two things. First and most likely, the glow is a biproduct of the collision of atoms in the particle accelerator."

Hesitation noted, Russ pushed, "And the other thing?"

"Actinium . . . which is a *different* radioactive element."

"What the—"

"It's perfectly harmless . . . unless you inhale, ingest, or touch it . . . or stand too closely to it." Simultaneously, they each shifted a little away from the glow. "Now, back to diamonds. As you know (though Russ did not, but he appreciated Stem's confidence in him), a diamond is an electrical insulator. However, I believe this diamond is undergoing some sort of manipulation. For example, when pressure is applied to the nano-needles in a diamond, it reduces the bandgap. You do know what bandgap is, yeah?"

Hyped by Stem's assertion that he would know the electrical properties of diamonds, Russ lied, "Yes, of course."

This came as a relief to Stem who, having subbed in an undergrad chemical science class that very morning, had reached the threshold of his tolerance for explaining elementary scientific anomalies in one day. "Eventually, if the nano-needles are pressed all the way, just before the breaking point of the lattice-like structure, the diamond experiences an entire range of bandgaps from 5.6 to zero."

"Hmmm," said Russ, offering a nod to hide his confusion and disinterest.

"This means that the diamond can go instantaneously from being an electric insulator to being a semi-conductor—and back again. Another facet of this phenomenon is that a diamond under this type of treatment would be able to produce all light types, from infrared to ultraviolet. Since it has always been my esteemed theory that monopoles exist as entangled particles on constantly differing waves of light, the diamond, piggybacking off the lodestone's magnetism, can detect and be made to mimic the monopole's electromagnetic radiation vibration which, in turn, will attract it to the entangled monopole—and vice versa—and you know what that means, yeah?"

Russ wanted to come up with something clever to say but he was hopelessly drawing a blank. "Yes. But I'm sure you'll explain it better."

"A magnetic dipole is created!"

Having no clue what that was, his mate feigned surprised excitement by oohing.

"I know—it's incredible! But Russell, here's the most amazing part. If the entangled monopole is detected, either by accident or design, from another era then I believe this basically opens a temporary wormhole between the two periods which will last the length of time it takes the electrons to complete the equatorial loop. Any non-electromagnetic object within the chamber cage will be affected by the temporal effect."

The pause in dialogue prompted a verbal response from Russ. "That's great, man."

Pleased with his student's fervor (though there was none to actually note), the professor wrapped up. "This changes everything. Until now, the Dirac string was assumed to be a semi-infinite line of unphysical matter. However, this machine—*Peepaw's* machine," he emphasized, although there could be no doubt which he meant, "proves that Dirac's theory is only partially correct. It's the difference in an infinitesimal path and a finite path. The string is really, actually, impossibly physical—and yet it's possible. Isn't that bonzer?"

"So . . ." said Russ, trailing off as he tried to think of some sort of meaningful and appropriate response. The first thing which landed in his mind did not, in his friend's estimation, reveal any intelligence. "What's that birdcage thing?"

"I wonder how you ever earned your doctorate."

"Cheated."

"It shows."

"So, what's the birdcage thing?"

"First, it's not a birdcage."

"I'm *sorry,*" Russ apologized. "What's that *other* machine over there?"

"Second, it is not a separate machine at all. These two parts of the *one singular* machine work in tandem."

Exasperated, Russ barked, "And do what?"

The ruddiness of Stem's complexion deepened in direct proportion to the length of the ensuing silence until, after ten or more seconds, he burst. "Russell, haven't you heard a bloody word I've said? I've just explained to you that this is a bloody time machine!"

Chapter 9

Slowly, Russ' surprise following Stem's analysis of the machine led to skepticism which, as the scientist explained and showed and used Google as proof and then contradicted Google's asinine assumptions, turned into belief which followed with excitement. And by early morning, the out-of-work college professor found himself enamored with the possibilities that this discovery held.

"But do you think it actually works?" he questioned once again.

"What madness gets into you at times!" his exhausted friend exclaimed. "Of course it works! All the science is there and backs it up. In fact, Peepaw's disappearance, his vanishing into thin air, for that's exactly what happened, is nothing short of proof of the machine's viability."

"So can we try it out?"

"Oh, no, of course not. It's broken. Now where's that snack bag?"

Russ, who had decided that laying on the cellar floor was only bearable if one inserted an air mattress between themselves and the concrete, gaped. "What? It's broken?"

"Your slowness of thought does not affect your hearing, I see."

"But you're just now telling me this after, what, like ten hours of your explaining the mechanics of time travel to me?"

"Nine hours and thirteen minutes, actually, not counting the fifty-three minutes during my explanation of Lenz's Law when you so rudely dozed off, you bludger."

"But I don't understand."

"That's no surprise."

"If it's broken, how did Peepaw disappear in it in the first place?"

Though he had already conveyed the particulars of the machine's mechanism seizing midcycle no less than three times to his friend, Stem took a deep breath and began explaining, very slowly, using the smallest words possible.

"Peepaw got in the machine. He turned it on. He time traveled. But before he returned, the machine cactused." Realizing he erroneously used a term which his mate was likely not to know, he offered an even more succinct and simplified explanation. "It broke while he was time traveling."

This statement, though overly simplified and abridged, had a profound effect on Russ. "You mean . . . he meant to come back . . . but it quit working before he could?"

Stem patted his friend's shoulder. "You know, you appear vaguely smart when I dumb things down for you."

His mind enraptured by the news, Russ fell quiet and contemplative. Stem took this as his opportunity to sneak away to tinker with the new toy.

Quite to himself, Russ repeated, "He meant to come back," and the words, somehow, felt light on his tongue as a flutter began in his heart. Over the next several minutes, while he mindlessly performed the task of replacing the remaining lightbulbs, the flittering of some invisible force inside him (which he began to suspect was hope and happiness birthed together) gave the affect to his spirit of being as light as a butterfly. And before he knew it, he was singing.

"Oh, stop! Please!" begged Stem. "I'll Spotify you any music—even *country*—just please, cease and desist this audible torture!"

Russ discovered in that short span, between when Stem engaged his portable speaker and they walked across that sunbathed field to the car, that every note and every lyric of every song sounded more perfect than he had ever recalled. And just as they turned onto Walnut Street, a strange yet liberating thought hit him.

Is this happiness I'm feeling?

"That's preposterous," Stem declared. "A buyer has offered you $30,000 for that cheap lead-lined Mayan mask?"

The truth of Russ' claim was so plainly written upon his face that his friend snatched the phone from his hands and opened the eBay app, just so he too might lay his eyes on such a glorious sight.

"Crikey," Stem stammered, and it was more magnificent in writing than when his ears had first heard the news.

"Should I accept?"

"What? No, of course not!"

"Are you serious? But what if the bidding doesn't go that high?"

"Never question my honesty. I promise you—it will go over."

"But what if it doesn't?"

"Russell, sometimes I fear Meemaw and Peepaw's secondhand smoke must've altered the molecules in your brain when you were a child. This offer is good for the next twenty-four hours and there's only twelve hours left on the auction. If you are so worried about it then wait until the last minute and then, if the bidding isn't that high, accept the offer."

Persuaded by greed, the idea sounded reasonable enough. However, four hours later, an eBay notification devastated the seller. "The buyer's retracted the offer!" he exclaimed.

His friend licked tutti frutti ice cream off a cone. "Cheer up. At least now you won't have to worry about buying that extra shipping insurance."

Russ' fretting over the bidding, which rose steadily to $22,000 in a matter of minutes after the dreadful notification arrived, was enough for Stem to take his leave of Meemaw's house early that evening.

"Where are you going?" inquired Russ. "You can't leave me when you're the one who upset me about this."

"You're no fun right now and I have plans," Stem said simply, and he left but not before giving his friend strict instructions: "Add those pictures I took to the listings you uploaded earlier."

In the middle of the night, Stem awoke to the pleasant sound of Moonlight Sonata. Tired from a full day of tinkering with the time machine, he almost chose not to answer Russ' call. However, realizing the time and that the bidding for the mask must've just ended—and his curiosity piqued—he clicked the green button and grouched, "What?"

"Did I wake you up?"

"It's the middle of the bloody night and I'm not a nocturnal creature, so of course you did."

"You won't believe how much the mask sold for."

"That's unlikely."

Russ could hardly believe it himself and he was staring right at the screen.

"How much, Russell?"

"$47,512.34."

Had he said anything less than $45,000, Stem would've received the news with indignation. As it were, he felt inclined to counsel his friend on finances. "Your two best options are as follows. Invest in a Roth IRA, which will set you up nicely for an early retirement. Or for my sake and as a thank you for setting up your eBay account, buy out the pastry tart factory down the road and add these flavors to your line: Nutella, passion fruit, and ginger. I cast my vote for the latter."

Driving around with some arm candy in the passenger seat of a new sports car sounded like a better plan to Russ.

If the mask had been a newborn child, it could not have been handled with more care and delicacy than Russ administered to it. When touching it, he wore white gloves, newly purchased that morning at Dollar Tree just for the occasion. His discount store excursion immediately preceded his maiden voyage into a fabric retailer where he bought materials in which to wrap the mask, first in silk, secondly in felt, and thirdly in some exquisitely soft faux fur which he knew was an impulse buy but that he just couldn't pass up. The entirety of the package contents, which was quite bulkier than he'd anticipated, just fit into a large Priority Mail box.

At the post office counter, tracking, sign-upon-receival, and every form of insurance thinkable was added to the basic purchase, and, with the precious package in the capable hands of the postal employees, Russ sent the expensive specimen on its way to buyer eloimen_ia5. He was nearly giddy as he left which led to his impulsively stopping by Sonic where he upgraded his usual small vanilla Dr. Pepper to a Route 44 and added an order of cheddar peppers (which he later regretted in the restroom).

Since he and Katie's split, a new checking account had been set up in his name. To date, the balance had hovered between $3–$137, but that was about to change. Russ was not even sure that the account was FDIC approved for a deposit as large as the one heading his way in 3-7 business days, but that was really no concern on his mind. Right at that moment, he was headed to a sports car dealership in Little Rock, and the only thought he could hold was of which custom color he'd like to paint his upcoming purchase.

The options at the dealership were disappointingly lacking. José the salesman blamed it on the pandemic. He assured his customer, however, that they received new inventory twice a week and they could also search a country-wide database to locate just the vehicle Russ was after. Having never ridden in a sports car (aside from Jeremy Ruger's dad's Corvette once in middle school), the buyer wanted to test drive several options to land on one.

A second dealership with more in stock was sought, and one located in Bentonville, which was no less than three hours away, caught his eye. Deciding against driving there (because of his lack of faith in the declining health of his Prius), he instead perused their inventory online and called the dealership upwards of half a dozen times to discuss this or that. And at last, after a weary day of searching and researching, he had settled upon two possibilities: a red Tesla Model S Plaid and a yellow Corvette.

Stem despaired at the news. "You're bloody throwing your money down the gurgler for a car?"

"A sports car."

"But mate . . . what about owning the pastry tart factory?"

Stem's words brought about a movement of conscience in Russ and he decided much was owed to this friend of his for at first pressing him to clean out Peepaw's storage shed and then to list the items on eBay and then to not take less than top dollar. As a concession, he offered, "I'll buy shares in it, in your honor." Seeing this had not fully alleviated his friend's disappointment, he added, "And I'll press for new flavors like Nutella and passion fruit."

"And ginger?" questioned Stem with eyes as large and droopy as a begging dog's.

"Of course."

This happy news was followed by more: a certain metal sculpture of a half-human half-feline sphinx had reached bids up to $17,000.

"That ought to buy several hundred shares!" cheered Stem.

To save the pair the trouble of relocating each item from Peepaw's shed to Meemaw's house where appropriate eBay photos could be captured, they moved some shelves and set up a 6' x 10' photo booth in the cellar, which they deemed was a more secure location than Meemaw's house anyway.

"And it'll keep your degenerate cousins from spotting your loot," Stem pointed out.

The idea of shelling out shares of the proceeds to various cousins had crossed Russ' mind a time or two—and he had not forgotten that Lance would be coming for his $650—but each time the thought flickered through his head, he reminded himself that the lot of them was irresponsible and would most likely waste the money frivolously at casinos or on drugs or alcohol or video games. *So*, he reasoned, *better to keep it in my responsible hands.*

Obsessing over the Time Magnet, as Stem had dubbed Peepaw's incredible creation, became the Aussie's favorite pastime. To Russ' satisfaction, Stem demonstrated how to use the diamond checking apparatus and, with little effort, the authenticity of the machine's crown jewel was verified. Increasingly, the dream of time travel drew nearer to their reach, and, though unspoken, both knew their maiden voyage would take Russ back in time to undo his stupidest mistake and, thus, restore his marriage.

But to Stem's vexation, the hitch in the system was more difficult to locate than he'd expected.

"I thought for sure it was the ion injector, but now I'm thinking it's the dees."

Russ nodded—for moral support because he still had no idea how the Time Magnet worked—and his response was received as confirmation that the twin D-shaped copper electrodes should indeed be checked. While Stem returned to his work, Russ logged onto a travel website and dreamed of a European vacation which he'd put off for too long. After all, 90% of Europe was not wheelchair friendly which meant his beloved ex-bride would not have navigated the trip very well.

"You ever been to Vienna?" he called to his friend. When no response came, he added, "'Cause I found a package for $1999 that includes air, 5 nights in two different 4-star hotels, a manual transmission economy car, dinner every night including drinks and tips, and entry fees to two popular attractions. Sounds like a pretty good deal, right?"

"If you're paying," came his friend's voice just before he shouted and cursed, "These buggered dees!"

"Are they broken?"

"No! That's what's infuriating!"

Picturesque photos of Machu Picchu stole Russ' attention and he spent several minutes perusing albums of 'traveler photos' and dreaming of exploring Incan ruins.

"Is Cusco or Machu Pichu a better place to visit? Stem?"

The man appeared, his face riddled with frustration and red blotches. "Do I look like the little traveling bloody gnome? If you want recommendations, consult Travelocity!" Then he disappeared around the corner again after which Russ kept his vacation dreams mostly to himself.

An hour passed, and the dreamer had settled on a 15-day Viking Cruise down the Rhone River. He debated about whether to buy his friend passage on the ship-based vacation, but upon Stem's vehement refusal of the offer, stating there was nothing he hated worse than "a wannabe cruise ship filled with entitled hipsters traveling nigh out of sight of land" he clicked the 'single passenger fare' button. To his agitation, there was no getting around listing his passport number—without it, booking the package would be impossible.

Drat. It's at the house.

Of course, he meant by this the house which he had signed over to Katie, and he made a note on his phone to text her the following morning (when he'd for certain feel braver) and ask if he might come over to grab a few of his things. If she refused, he reasoned he could at the very least ask her to text him a photo of his passport.

Seconds from finalizing a deal online for a brand-new red Tesla Model S Plaid, a terrible thought occurred to Russ: If his cousins spotted his new wheels they would come hounding him for money quicker than the IRS on April 15th. No, he'd have to be a little more cautious with his cash flow, at least for a while. The last thing he wanted to do was get stalked by a cousin with cash lust only to have his secret hideout discovered and the top blown off his sweet moneymaking scheme.

Of course, he had chickened out texting Katie—he'd not even had the gall to ask for his passport number.

Why? she'd want to know. *Where are you going? Somewhere with your new girl?*

The news of Caydee's breakup with him had surely reached Katie's ears . . . but perhaps it had not.

If she thinks I'm still with the other Caydee then maybe that explains why she wanted the divorce. Maybe I should've explained we weren't together anymore.

The very idea that he and Caydee were ever "together" in the first place had not occurred to him until this moment. His girlfriend, he had never considered her. A lover and distracter of emotional pain was more like it. It made no difference, he knew, whether he and Caydee were still "together" or not, for his fate as a divorcee was sealed the moment he unzipped his pants for her, but it might ease some of Katie's grief to know that his errant love affair had not withstood the test of Caydee's suspension from college.

Well, now he felt like crap, so to TravelZoo.com he went and booked an autumn domestic flight to Hawaii. For a moment, he contemplated purchasing a one-way ticket, but given that wasn't an option, he pushed forth with securing the roundtrip. A decision not to return could be made at a later date. The dream of surfing on a beach in Hawaii eased some of the icky feelings which had swelled inside him, but just to be sure he'd fully eliminated the taste, he chased them down with an impulse buy for a speed motorboat tour off the Na Pali Coast of Kauai.

Chapter 10

The message from buyer pingopong69 was more troubling than the voicemail Russ had received from Katie's lawyer stating Katie wanted to meet with him face to face to read him a pre-written letter. In fact, if anything, seeing his ex-wife in person was something he longed for more and more with each new sunrise.

The eBay message, on the other hand, frightened him.

Upon reading it that evening while taking a break from tinkering with the Time Magnet, Stem stated, "It's a hoax. Ig-bloody-nore it." And he followed this up by deleting the message, an action which he felt would equally eliminate his friend's anxiety. However, to his dismay, it only heightened the man's paranoia.

"But he said there will be consequences if I don't immediately turn the sword over to him."

"You are being unreasonable," the Aussie assured between bites of a Twix bar. "You can't possibly turn it over to him—you've already sold and shipped it. Not your property, not your problem."

"But what if he's right? What if it really is the stolen sword he's talking about?"

"It might be." Seeing how his assertion of that possibility affected his friend, Stem sighed. "First of all, we have no reason to believe this pingopong69 is a legitimate person. By the sound of his letter, he's out for extortion. Second of all, you came about owning the sword by honest means. Meemaw died. She named you executor of her estate, which included Peepaw's storage shed and everything therein contained. Even if it was obtained through dishonest methods, that fact was unknown to you. Third of all, the statute of limitations on the theft of the sword in question has likely been exceeded. In essence, even if they came after you, they would have no case."

Russ hoped his friend was correct.

Nothing like the menacing eBay message reappeared in Russ' inbox, and he took this as a sign that he'd outwitted some would-be scammer. However, his meeting with Katie the Thursday afternoon of the next week loomed in his brain. He was simultaneously looking forward to seeing her and dreading the words that might come out of her mouth. One minute, he was confident she never would've wanted to meet in person if it wasn't good news she brought him. But the next he was certain that she only wanted to face him because sending her grievances in a text or email would not have been a dignified manner of communication.

She'd always been big on meeting with people face to face. Countless times, when a friend was texting her in crisis or a college student from church needed some encouragement (or whatever the situation might be), Katie insisted they get together in person.

"This is how real life happens," she'd say.

And Russ admired her for that because he, on the other hand, was always more likely to text someone encouraging words—or evade them altogether in their time of crisis—than tell it to their face. The one exception had been Caydee, and the fact that he'd used his wife's words to justify getting together with the girl in person (which had been the beginnings of their subsequent affair) only made his stomach sour.

To keep his mind occupied and sane, he performed a marathon of new eBay listings. Forty-seven, to be exact, and nearly every one of them received bids within the first twenty-four hours. He tried to stay humble, but his account, with only eighteen positive feedbacks (and no negatives) had drawn at least twice as many followers. If all went well, he'd be able to retire on the proceeds of Peepaw's hoard.

The day and hour approaching, Russ had made a last-minute decision to scrap the back-alley meeting with Lance, and, instead, he suggested a nice sit-down meal at El Almacen for the day after. The proposal not tempting enough to his cousin, Russ sweetened the deal by offering to pick up the tab, and that settled the matter.

"So?" said Lance as he pulled his chair out from the table a whole twenty minutes late for their appointment. "You got it?" As was Lance's MO, he immediately followed the question up with the parameters for an appropriate response. "And don't be thinkin' you can take this lunch outta my share, 'cause it ain't gonna be like that, ya hear?"

An envelope containing all $650 was slid across the table, and, to the satisfaction of Lance, who proceeded to lay out every bill upon the table as he counted it, every blessed dime was accounted for.

"Good," he said. "Now let's eat."

The expectation that Lance would order the most expensive meal, along with four tequila shots and a sampling of all three desserts El Almacen had to boast, should have been ever present on Russ' mind, but he found himself aggravated as he paid the $98 tab. Nevertheless, he could not find it in himself to cheat Paco out of his 20%, and he added the proportionately large tip with cheer in his heart.

A mean smile gleamed in Lance's eyes as Russ opened his own car door. "You still drivin' that corroded piece of rust?" And before his cousin could answer, the redneck followed it up with, "Guess that cripple drained you bloodless, didn't she?"

As a minority residing in White County, there were plenty of insults Russ had allowed to bounce off him over the years, but demeaning remarks about his girl weren't ones he'd easily tolerate. His lips curled into a snarl and even Meemaw would've been proud of the way he commanded his eyebrows to form a proper V across his forehead.

"What did you say?"

Receiving the response he'd hoped for, Lance spit a mouthful of baccy juice and bowed his spine.

Russ hardly heard the words as his cousin repeated them, for his ears were blocked with the fumes of rage. There was something about being the possessor of great wealth (as Russ thought he now was) that made a man feel empowered, and the insulting of one's woman (though, in this case, his ex) was liable to fill any man with rage—and the combination of the two emboldening emotions were felt deeply in Lance's gut as his cousin bull-rammed him. It was an ungraceful move but one with which Russ was satisfied, as he conveyed to the police officer who had broken up the fight when it rolled out onto Race Avenue. And what filled him with more contentment was watching the bully's arrest. After all, public intoxication is not handled lightly in the small town, especially when it threatens the good citizens driving down the main thoroughfare. With his citation for a busted headlight in bloodied hand, Russ drove home.

"What the bloody heck happened to you?" Stem gasped.

"Beat up Lance."

"That's fan-bloody-tastic! Do you have any peanut butter?"

While picking a fight with his larger and more aggressive cousin had seemed like a wonderful idea at the moment (not that Russ had actually consciously considered whether it was a good idea or not before headbutting the man), his stinging lip, scraped knuckles with specks of gravel from El Almacen's parking lot still embedded, pounding forehead, and bruised kidney (which he'd self-diagnosed after doing a Google search for 'why am I peeing blood after a fist fight') all reminded him of the futility of fighting a fool. Like it or not, Lance would be in his life for(likely)ever and he wasn't one whom you'd want to hold a beef against you.

If the sound of Stem's chewing and slurping milk had not awoken Russ from a snooze then his raging at the National Scientific Channel would've.

"Can you believe this pack of dingoes?" he spewed, along with bits of his peanut butter sandwich. "Low energy nuclear reaction is *not* a form of cold fusion! And it does *not* prove the Standard Model wrong!"

Russ weighed his options of ignoring the rant or crossing the room to switch off the television. After his friend launched into a rampage about the impossibility of overcoming the Coulomb barrier at relatively low degrees Fahrenheit, Russ wisely chose the latter.

"Why'd you do that?" Stem barked. "It was just getting good."

"You're irritating my headache."

"Well, excuse me for living," his friend pouted as he exited the room. Then, from the kitchen, he called, "Want any Cheetos? Too bad—I ate them all!"

"Then bring me an ice pack."

Seconds later, a bag of frozen french fries landed in his lap. The look of confusion Russ tossed at his friend was returned with, "Deal with it," and so he did. Though lumpy, the cold potato bits eased the pain in his left eye.

"How's it look?" he asked some minutes later through a half-opened slit. "Is it black?"

While his eye was chilling, a Snicker's bar had evidently cooled down his friend. "No," replied the scientist. "Barely pink."

"Man, it hurts."

"Quit your whining, mate. You're making an ocean of an oasis."

The next morning, however, Russ snapped a photo of his face which he struggled to text to his friend, what for bruised knuckles and one and a half eyes swollen shut. Evidently, his pathetic battered mug had pulled at his friend's heartstrings because a DoorDash arrived some hours later with a Peanut Buster Parfait from Dairy Queen and a large pepperoni and pineapple pizza, the leftovers of which Stem devoured when he came over after his two o'clock class final.

"I told my juniors," he said through bites, "that if I heard that even one of them had watched a single episode of National Scientific Channel this summer then I'd flunk the lot of them. You should have seen their faces." Like he did when something particularly clever struck him as funny, he giggled, and the sound never failed to cheer up his friend. But one moment later, he dropped his smile and grouched, "I can't believe you ate my parfait."

Running to his own defense, Russ argued, "I thought it was for me."

"Why would I buy *you* an ice cream?"

"You sent it to *my* house."

"Yeah, for *me*. To celebrate. Because my finals are over. I had to bloody walk the kilometer to Dairy Queen and back just to get my own parfait."

"It's less than half a mile," Russ corrected him.

Stem wiped his face with a paper napkin, wadded it up, and tossed it across the room. "I'm rounding bloody up! Now can you see well enough to drive or not?"

As it turned out, not, and, as the tow truck hauled the Prius away down the rural road, Russ was glad he had not been driving a brand-new Tesla Model S Plaid. That would've brought tears to his swollen eyes.

"You'll pay for an Uber," stated Stem, clicking buttons on the app on his phone.

"Me?" Russ hissed. "This is *your* fault."

"Mine? Oh, no! I asked if you could see well enough to drive and you said yes and then you drove us over an abyss."

The abyss was really just a three-foot-high drop into a drain water ditch, but it wouldn't have mattered if it had only been three inches—what Stem was angry about was missing his chance to toy with the Time Magnet.

"I can see just fine through this slit in my face, thank you very much," Russ argued. But softening his tone, he admitted, "It's just that I couldn't get my contacts in."

The idea of driving without one's vision accessories was as preposterous to Stem as if Russ had said, "Thomas Edison invented the lightbulb," and he hurled a mouthful of curse words into the wind.

"Well, I'm not as blind as a bat," said his now indignant companion, who wasn't sure what to make of the vernacular word drongo which sometimes found its way into Stem's tirades. "My eye doctor said I have 60/20 vision."

"Must've been driving with the 60, yeah? And another thing," stewed Stem, "why don't I have cell service? Give me your phone."

As though he intended to order an Uber himself, Russ yanked his cell out of Stem's reach. However, vision as it was, he had to hold it up to the slit in his eye, and, like that, he couldn't see the entire screen at once. For a minute, he staved off Stem's attempts to steal the phone from his hand until, at last, he just gave up and handed the device over along with an apology.

Stem sighed. "Oh, it's not a dog's breakfast. Are you with AT&T?"

"Verizon."

"Figures. Your service is spotty."

"Well, yours isn't working at all."

"Precisely. I've got an attack of the munchies. Got anything to eat?"

Russ wasn't even sure he'd remembered to grab his wallet, but as he patted his pockets, a blue compact SUV pulled to a stop beside them, and, as the driver rolled down the window, Stem let out a whoop.

"Hey, Professor Bik!" hollered a young man.

Stem smiled ear to ear. "Mr. Michael Shasta, my man! Good to see you!"

"Same. But what're you doing out here?"

Tossing an arm around Russ, he said, "Me and my best mate have found ourselves out in the back o' Bourke and we sure could use a ride into town. You got room for two, mate?"

"Sure, hop in!"

Mr. Michael Shasta, as it happened, had been on his way out of Searcy homebound to the Kansas City metropolitan area, though he did not mind backtracking for a few minutes with his favorite teacher. While Professor Bik took the front seat, Russ was forced to cram into the rear and make room for himself amongst the other inhabitants of the seat, namely clothing (both washed and dirty), intramural gear (definitely not washed), and bedding (wash status indeterminate). To his further displeasure, halfway to his house his former student recognized him.

Squinting into the rearview mirror, the young man gawked, "Professor Brown? Is that you?"

Flourishing a knuckle-beaten hand and a trace of sheepish disillusionment, Russ greeted him. "Hey, man."

"What in the world happened you?"

"Just, uh, living my best life. Beating up thugs and whatnot."

"That's clutch."

"Yeah, thanks for the ride, man." Adding a request to keep his unsightly appearance on the lowdown crossed the former professor's mind, but Stem quickly commandeered the convo and the thought passed.

Upon their return to Meemaw's house, Russ laid down on the living room floor and announced he needed a nap. To his pleasant surprise, Stem let himself out quietly without so much as a, "How dare you, mate?" and the battered man slept the evening away in relative peace.

At a quarter to one in the morning, however, Russ' slumber was disturbed by a familiar nightmare which had been as unbearable as it always was, like a rerun of Barney. As in all ridiculous dreams, no matter how quickly he ran, the gap between him and the object of his attention only grew farther. Try as he did, he could not stop Katie from running away, her legs pumping out one final jog as she passed the pregnant tree and vanished out of sight.

And there was, of course, the rain. Always the rain. The interminable, irritating rain. Even in his semi-consciousness he felt the deluge's effects on his skin. Reaching up to gingerly wipe his tender forehead, he realized his body was dewy with sweat. Likewise, the orange carpet beneath him displayed the effects of his perspiration, making it feel like a wet dog (and its odor only made the insinuation more pronounced).

While he contemplated whether to remain in the same spot or roll over to let the carroty patch of polyester air dry, a bass drum solo erupted on his front porch. Freezing, Russ listened, and a chill flushed over him as he realized, rather, that someone was banging on the door.

"Rusty!" came Lance's voice, and it was almost certain he was inebriated. "Open up!"

Unprepared for the dropping in of an aggressive midnight visitor, Russ held his breath, and a series of possible and disastrous outcomes from the encounter flooded his mind. Deciding his best chance of evading a second assault was to stay silent, he remained supine on the floor, his fingers worrying strands of the damp shag carpet.

Minutes later, his strategy paid off. Though Lance had done his best to peek in the windows, he had seen no evidence of his cousin's presence (presumably the idea was boosted in his mind by the absence of Russ' car in the driveway), and he left.

Russ arose with the sun and called in a claim to his car insurance company. Given the state of his vehicle, the likelihood of it being a total loss was significant, and his claims adjuster advised him to secure a rental vehicle, which was precisely as Russ had hoped. His swelling had subsided to the point that he could more or less see clearly (though the validity that his driver's license actually bore his image was speculated by no less than three employees at the car rental facility), and he found himself pulling out of the Enterprise Rent-A-Car lot at 10:15 in the morning, just in time to swing by the Burger King drive-thru for breakfast burritos.

The pair of friends—both devoid of job obligations for a minimum of three and a half months, save for eBay-related endeavors—arrived at 42B around lunchtime toting an abundance of beef jerky, dried fruits, Skittles (which were on an unpassuppable BOGO sale at Cash Saver), and malted milk balls. Russ, who loathed soft shell tacos but, given his swollen jaw, opted for them anyway at Taco Bell, surfed the internet for another red Tesla Model S Plaid while eating. To his dismay, the one available vehicle of this type which he'd found days earlier had since been sold. Searching for other options, Russ ran a possible alternative by his friend.

"What about this Lambo?"

"What's a Lambo?"

"A Lamborghini."

"No one calls them that."

"It's in the title of this video. 'Lambo versus Vette.'"

"Any idiot can slap a poorly labeled video up on YouTube. That doesn't mean it's good grammar."

"Well, I don't think it's a matter of grammar. More like preference of terms." Stem's piercing gaze silenced what remaining shreds of the argument lie inside Russ' feeble mind, and he once again asked, "So, what about this car, the Urus? It goes up to 190 miles per hour and is one of the world's fastest SUVs."

"An S-bloody-UV? Let me see that." The few seconds he took his eyes off the Time Magnet and aimed them at the image on the screen were all Stem needed to verify his suspicions. "It looks like a Ford Escape."

"It's not," argued Russ. "It's a Lamborghini."

"If you want an SUV, buy a Hyundai. Cheaper. Roomier. Better warranty."

"But it's a *Lamborghini*."

"It's a *cheap* Lamborghini, and, by the looks of it, you can't afford it anyway."

Undoubtedly, the price tag had made Russ' stomach do a somersault, but he figured with projected eBay sales what they were, he could swing the $5000 per month payment plus maintenance and insurance. However, any wishful thinking he had about owning such a pricey car was dashed upon Stem's next observation: "But with the way you drive, you ought to get an inexpensive, gas-efficient sedan that's already been banged around a little."

Deciding his search for the perfect sports car could wait until he'd received the settlement check from his insurance company, Russ put his efforts into photographing Peepaw's stash of treasures. There was something therapeutic he found in the careful handling of the ancient and rare objects, and, after a while, curiosity seized him. "Hey, why do you think all these things Peepaw had are metal?"

"What do you mean?" Stem hollered over rows of shelving.

"Like why didn't he collect, I don't know, jewels? Or bring back porcelain teacups from England or bricks from ancient Egypt or gopher wood from Noah's Ark? Why choose only metal?"

"Oh, that," said Stem dismissively. "Because grasping an electrical conductor from the second monopole era is necessary for the magnetic completion of the Wilson Loop which must be accomplished for symmetry breaking which, I'll add, Peepaw evidently knew how to pull off without causing the irreversible change of the first monopole era, at least as he experienced it."

Try as he might, Russ' bright though vastly lesser developed brain struggled to comprehend the explanation just given him. "Can you say that again but use words that I know?"

The pity Stem felt for his friend was palpable as he crossed the cellar floor to come to his aid. After giving Russ a look which conveyed his condolences, the scientist rested one machine-greased hand on the man's shoulder and explained, "Mate, it's like this. When he went into the past, he had to grab something metal or else he couldn't return to the current time. Got it?"

Relief flooded Russ. "Yes, thank you, that made perfect sense."

Stem offered a satisfied nod and turned back to tend to the Time Magnet. "But," added his friend which brought a prompt and unwelcomed halt to his retreat.

"Yes?" he replied through gritted teeth.

"*Could* he have grabbed some other material too?"

Where pity had once rested upon the Australian's face,

incredulity took residence. “Mate, it wouldn’t—”

“I mean, would it have also come back with him like the metal did?”

“There wouldn’t be any—”

“Or would it have vanished into thin air when he returned—”

“It wouldn’t have—”

“To the present?”

As though standing too close to an invisible fire, red hot color flashed on the scientist’s face. “Ten percent off your final!” he snapped, his heels kicking up clouds of dust as he stamped away.

Chapter 11

Ever since finding shelter under the caring and disciplinary wing of Meemaw, Russ had gone to church on Sunday mornings. It wasn't optional as a child even if he sometimes found it to be stodgy. Yet as a young man navigating the currents of adulthood, he'd discovered the place offered much more than just a dry religion—as his spirituality grew so did the number of his church friends. And they were good friends, loyal people he could count on, who could likewise count on him, that is, until he betrayed them all by committing a grievous and selfish sin. And just like that, he'd alienated himself from them and forced them to choose between him and Katie.

What was worse, since Harding was associated with the Churches of Christ, and since Searcy and the surrounding microscopic towns were saturated with congregations of the type, there was no pocket of his sect where he could find anonymous refuge (not that he'd even tried, but he'd surmised as much). Therefore, Russ had not been to Sunday church (or church on any other day of the week) since the holy day before that 8am meeting in Dean Scarborough's office on Valentine's Day. And despite what many were probably thinking about him (if they even still thought about him at all), he yearned to come back, to return to a large group of individuals who were more deeply connected to him than just geography, circumstances in life, or career choices. His thought processes and anxieties and aspirations—and the very jargon which he spoke—had been influenced by this wonderful forever family he'd acquired throughout his lifetime. And forever family, they were, for with them he shared a deeper and stronger relationship than that of his own biological family.

Several members of his former church family had reached out to him in the weeks following the discovery of his affair. (In fact, one man—an elder in their congregation who had welcomed Russ and Katie into his own home on countless occasions—had called or texted the errant adulterer every other day for the first month after that horrible disclosure of his sins.) But Russ had not felt worthy of any of the attention, and he often didn't answer their calls or respond to their texts, and, thus, the communications had almost entirely ceased.

Stem was Russ' one lifeline to the old life which he once had lived so comfortably and effortlessly. Even if Russ had tried to discontinue the relationship, for Stem's part it would have been impossible. The man was relentless in his efforts to connect with the grieving ex-husband, and, for that, Russ was infinitely grateful.

But even Stem had his boundaries. Sunday mornings for him looked much like Russ' past, and Russ knew that any calls or texts he sent to his friend during that time would go unanswered for several hours. (Stem also took Sunday afternoon naps very seriously, so he was often unreachable until around 5pm on the first day of the week.)

And there was one other time when the Aussie was unavailable. He'd never said so, but over the past couple of years, Russ had deduced that, for reasons unbeknownst to him, Monday evenings were a time of cellular silence for the man. Yes, Stem would never appear at Russ' door unexpectedly on Mondays after his last afternoon class. In fact, Katie and Russ had joked with one another that that was 'our night.' Not that their friend's intrusion in their home night after night was necessarily unwelcome, but maybe, they had thought, Stem leaves us be on Monday evenings for our own sanity—and perhaps even his. They found it amusing to keep a running list of possible places he went or things he did on that second night of each week.

"I figured it out," Russ had once announced triumphantly. "He's secretly a spy for the Australian government, and, on Mondays, he meets up with his superior to brief him on the week's occurrences."

"No," objected Katie, "that's too obvious."

Though he'd felt clever for thinking it up, Russ inquired what her newest hypothesis was.

"He's secretly dating an ex-circus performer—one of those fire breathing line dancing ladies—"

"Do they have those in the circus?"

"Of course they do."

"I've never seen one."

"Well, you've never been to the circus."

Russ acknowledged this fact with a shrug and a nod.

"And she's covered in head-to-toe tattoos, and he's not ashamed of her but he doesn't want anyone to see him with her because what makes their relationship magical is the fact that no one else knows about it." As though she'd solved the mystery once and for all, she wore a triumphant smile which made her green eyes sparkle.

A grin swept across his face as he offered a rebuttal. "That could never happen."

"And just why not?"

"I don't think it's possible for him to fall in love."

"What?" she guffawed. "It's perfectly possible. Why would you say that?"

"I just don't think he could fall in love with someone. He loves food too much—and science—and he's too thrifty. He doesn't have room in his heart for a woman."

"Not like you?"

"He's nothing like me."

"But you two get along so well."

"It's because I feed him and give him rides."

"And what does *he* do for *you*?"

"He amuses me, and, though he's just about as detached from humanity as anyone I know, he provides me with a constant source of human connection."

"Oh, you're too critical of him."

"Am I?"

"Yes. He's got a compassionate and caring heart—"

"About food."

"No, about *people*. He cares about others." When her husband displayed disbelief in his eyebrows, she pushed on with her point. "I watch him—I see things he does to show his care for people. It's not like you or I would show our love, but he has his ways."

Studying her with a sly grin, he questioned, "If I died, would you marry him?"

"Stem? No, of course not."

"I would."

"Oh, stop it," she giggled.

He laid a kiss on her hand, which he'd been holding for the past hour. "No, in all honesty, if you died, I'd die."

Her face grew sad and pouty. "No, don't say that."

"But I would."

"No, I don't want to think about you dying."

"But you'd be dead."

"Well, it's still an unpleasant thought." Bringing his hand to her lips, she caressed it gently. "The fact is, Russell Delacroix Brown, I don't want to be parted from you in death or ever. Got that?"

He gazed into her eyes. "Ditto."

Of all the things that had ever sat in Meemaw's driveway, Russ figured the current asphalt ornament took the cake. He'd already washed and detailed the steel gray Mazda MX-5 Miata, but as he contemplated putting on a second coat of wax (just to be sure), he heard Lance's diesel truck turn onto the street. As he was accustomed to going into the third mode of the fight, flight, freeze reaction, he stood there motionless, staring at the Mazda logo on which he noticed a small chip of the silver paint.

The first sound he heard from Lance, besides the roaring tailpipe, was a whistle. This was followed by the intelligible (though not particularly intelligent) words, “Hot dang, Rusty! What’d you do—win the Mega Millions?” And before Russ could reply (not that his tongue was currently working), Lance added, “’Cause last I heard, buyin’ lottery tickets was a sin. Course, you’re not exactly a saint, are you?”

“What do you want?” he hollered. Despite his trying to sound irritated at the uninvited guest, Russ heard a quaver in his own voice which was either from his own fear or the reverberations of Lance’s truck’s exhaust on his vocal cords.

The redneck, whose face had fared a little better in the fist fight than Russ’, hiked his belt up over his beer belly and narrowed his eyes. “Came to see what you were up to, and it looks about right.”

“Yeah?” Russ had no idea what he meant but the response seemed as good as any.

“I went to find you at that gadget store and guess what I’s told? You quit ’em, and, besides that, you had the audacity to come back and buy two or three dozen spy cameras. Now I see why that ole boy said you’d want to be keepin’ an eye on your cruise. It’s cuzza this thing!”

By ‘this thing’ Lance obviously meant the Miata, which Russ found laughable—in spite of its sporty looks, the used value of such a vehicle was less than that of a Ford Focus of the same year.

“It didn’t cost as much as you think,” he shouted over the exhaust. “Less than thirty grand.”

“Yeah? And how’d you afford that if you ain’t workin’, huh?”

For this question, Russ had already prepared an answer. “I got a job working remote—a professor at one of those online colleges.”

“Yeah? Which one?”

Though the possibility of Lance knowing the names of any online schools was slim, Russ threw out one of the more prestigious just to bolster his own self-esteem. “Purdue.”

Russ determined, by the uncomfortable shift of his cousin's weight, that Lance had no idea if he was bluffing or not. A span of six or seven seconds passed in which Russ awaited his cousin's response. At last, it came.

"Well, sounds pretty high and mighty to me! Guess they pay well enough anyway."

"Yeah, they do," said Russ, and he immediately felt like a fool for saying it.

Turning his attention to the house, Lance gestured. "Get this on the market yet?"

Though repairing Meemaw's former residence had once been at the top of Russ' to-do list, it had steadily slipped down to the double digits.

"No. I've been really busy with work." Seizing an opportunity to jab at his cousin, he added, "And no one's helped me fix it up, either!"

"Yeah, well, we've all got our obligations, don't we?"

Russ was certain that was true, but he also suspected Lance's were upside down and backwards.

"Don't you try and go runnin' off with nunnuh Meemaw's dough, ya hear? I'll be watchin' ya."

Russ simply nodded at the threat.

The redneck took a long gaze at the Miata before spitting a line of tobacco juice into the grass. "Well, I ain't got time to stand here and chitchat. I got my kids tonight."

"Tell them I said hi," said Russ, and he meant it. The apples had fallen far from the patriarchal tree, and, incomprehensibly, Lance's three kids were a pleasant sort.

Chapter 12

A stop by American GadgetTech was in order. Russ suspected business at the retailer would be slow on a Wednesday evening, and his assumptions were rewarded with an empty store.

Not that he expected a warm welcome from his ex-boss, but the silent glare verging on suspicion which he received wasn't along the lines of what was called for, and it roiled up his own feelings of suspicious alert.

"Sup?" replied the young man, his shadowy tone betraying the intimacy of his colloquialism.

Despite having prepared his speech for almost an entire day, Russ found the words did not roll off his tongue with finesse, and he finally managed to choke out, "My business is *my* business. Stay out of it, all right?"

"I don't even know what you're talking about, dude."

"You know exactly what I'm talking about. You told some guy that I'd bought cameras and quit my job here."

Narrowing his eyes, Dirk argued, "No, I didn't."

With the futility of his efforts glaring him in the eyes, Russ headed for the door.

"Hey, wait, dude," called the punk. "Those your new wheels?"

"Yeah. So?"

"Pretty sweet ride. Mind if I take a look at it?"

While the kid admired Russ' Miata, the two surprisingly found common ground in discussing what features were being added to the new Tesla Model S Plaid. By the end of their visit, they departed shaking each other's hands, and Russ got into his new coupe feeling like the situation had turned around quickly and amicably.

Two dozen items in total had been shipped via USPS Priority Mail, and Russ prepared to head to the post office with half a dozen more of varying sizes. Either from excitement or nerves, his hands shook as he loaded the packages into the passenger seat of his car. But just to double check, he ran back into the house and studied his face in the bathroom mirror.

He was wearing a new shirt he'd bought at Walmart—and it was Katie's favorite color. And he'd taken the time to comb the bedhead out and tame the waves in his hair, which his girl always appreciated him doing.

Minty fresh breath? Check. *Tied shoes?* Check. *Two black eyes?* Check. He was as good to go as he could hope.

Attempting to not speed on the way to the post office or run into the building once he arrived or rush the postal clerk—all were difficult though achievable tasks for the man, and, soon enough, he found himself parked in front of Katie's lawyer's office twenty minutes ahead of schedule. In the event that this happened, he'd brought a book to read, however, he found that none of the sentences were as amusing to his brain as worrying and trying to contain his excitement about the upcoming meeting.

Though he had purposely not parked directly in front of the building, his eyes stayed glued to the front door of the law office. But his vigilance was pointless—Katie would take the closest parking spot when she arrived, thus her van would be spotted long before her face. He did not want to go in until he'd seen her, but at three minutes past the hour, he decided he must head inside. Maybe by some strange sequence of events, she had already arrived and was expecting him, and he most certainly did not want to keep her waiting.

As he crossed the parking lot, he cursed himself for not bringing her a bouquet of flowers. Why must he be an idiot? If ever she arranged to meet with him again, he promised himself he'd have blooms in hand.

The receptionist asked him to have a seat and told him the attorney would be right with him. Evidently, the attorney was working on her own timetable because the moment of her appearance arrived, indeed, a full fifteen minutes later. Greetings were made, and he was ushered into her spacious and tastefully decorated office.

Almost as soon as she'd shut the door, she said, "I apologize—we will need to reschedule."

"Excuse me."

"We'll need to reschedule."

"May I ask why?" he said, gritting his teeth to keep the tears from stinging his eyes.

"Circumstances prevented the meeting today," she explained (without actually explaining anything).

Since he'd not seen Katie in the vicinity (and since he and the lawyer were obviously present), he surmised the rescheduling had been called for on Katie's behalf. And if she needed to reschedule, then he'd, of course, allow her that.

Calming himself, he thanked the woman for all fifty-seven seconds of her time and left.

He'd promised himself he'd not do this, not one time, but he couldn't help it—he had to drive by the house. *Their* house. *Katie's* house. If he'd still had the Prius, the bravery to perform such an audacious move would have no doubt eluded him. However, with the Miata's illegal window tint skewing the view of any onlookers, he proceeded with the hastily made plan.

His intent had been to turn onto the street and cruise by hastily, just taking a quick glance at the house. However, when the time came, he found himself almost in shock. In the yard, a real estate sign sat, proud and bold, as though the centerpiece of a prize-winning garden. Brakes were engaged, and, before he knew it, he was parked in front of the house catty-corner to what had once been his and his bride's.

He'd cried over Katie—yes, he had. But now he felt a deeper grief hit him as unsuspectingly and violently as a tsunami.

The house they had shared together. It had been *their home*. She said she didn't mind buying a different house—she'd manage—but he had built *this house* specifically for her. Had worked with the best architect in the tri-county region. Had designed every feature to suit her. After all, finding a wheelchair accessible residence was like finding a half Eastern Indian man in White County, and he couldn't live another day watching his wife struggle to maneuver through their small starter home. For months, he had poured his heart into the project and had visited the construction site every single day, good weather or not. It was perfectly designed for her and her alone.

One of the first things Katie had made known about herself was her dislike of the cold winters she had endured in her family's Boston home. The warm sunshine was her friend, so the tropical climate of Ghana came as a bonus since she'd chosen the country as the target for her medical missionary ministry. Of course, after the accident, her lifelong dream became just that—a fantasy out of her grasp. With a complete T3 spinal cord injury, her body could no longer tolerate the hotter days, and, even if she could, the third world country was not at all suited for anyone rolling around on wheels. So, she had settled down in Searcy and made home with the man who had faithfully remained by her side through her recovery.

She still managed to find joy in this new, unexpected life—and the custom-built home had played a large role in nurturing her happiness. In the summers, she'd sit by the wide bay window, just watching life happen outside on their active street. The kids in the neighborhood were always moving about, going from one kid's house to the other, running through front yard sprinklers, throwing water balloons, shooting water guns. There was fun and laughter, and all of it brought joy to his wife.

Russ had ultimately planned to sell Meemaw's house not because he needed the money but so he could simply vacate Searcy. This plan would allow Katie to continue her happy life in the town without the concern of running into the man who had broken her heart. But the realization that she was leaving (and likely moving back to cold New England) distressed him.

Stay, he silently pleaded through tears. *This is your home.*

Happy hour at Sonic, though hugely popular in the college town, was Russ' least favorite time to visit the restaurant—saving $1.18 on his vanilla Dr. Pepper was not worth fighting the crowd of soccer moms (with half the team onboard, to boot), half-broke university students, or frazzled teachers in need of their afternoon caffeine fix. However, to his thrift-conscious friend, patronizing the drive-in at any other time nearly equated to a sin.

While they sat in silence waiting for Russ' drink and Stem's M&M's Sonic Blast, footlong chili cheese coney, and large tots, the latter's phone chimed. Withdrawing it from his pocket, he questioned, "Mate, this your AirTag?"

The long wait at the inundated restaurant was getting to Russ. Irritated, he responded, "I don't know what you're talking about."

Showing his friend the notification on his phone, Stem repeated his question.

Shaking his head, Russ dismissed it with, "I think that's something to do with the Miata's navigation system."

"This car doesn't have nav assist." With the arrival of their food, the issue sat neglected until they were about half a mile from the restaurant at which point Stem revisited the issue. "You sure you didn't get an AirTag?"

Still frustrated with the 30-minute wait at Sonic, Russ didn't appreciate the interrogation. "I told you—I don't even know what that is."

"Well, that can only mean one thing."

"Which is?"

"Someone stuck an AirTag to your car and is tracking you." At Russ' speechlessness, Stem became indignant. "Hasn't your phone received notifications about this?"

"Yeah, I guess so, but I thought it was just my new car's navigation system."

"It doesn't have nav."

"I know—you said that already!" The sudden news that someone was following him elicited an odd mixture of fear and anger.

"Who'd want to know where you're going?"

"I have no idea."

But by the time they'd reached Mermaid Lane, Stem had compiled his own list of the usual suspects.

"First, there's Lance."

It didn't take a physicist to understand why Russ' cousin would want to follow him, yet Stem presented a possible explanation for the behavior.

"He thinks you're stiffing him."

Russ approved this summary with a nod.

The investigator continued. "Second, there's me."

"You?"

"Yes, I'm an obvious suspect, yeah?"

"I don't know. Do you want to track my movements?"

"No."

"But you just said—"

"I said I was a suspect, but I never said I did it."

"So . . . I'm confused. *Did* you do it?"

"No," Stem denied as though he had never been accused of anything more preposterous. "I didn't put the bloody AirTag on your car. Why would I?"

"I honestly don't have any idea."

Indignance fell short of describing Stem's mood. "Well, I wouldn't have done that."

"I didn't think you did. It's just that you said you were a suspect so I thought maybe you were sending me subliminal messages."

"Well, that's not very subliminal, yeah?"

Noticing Stem's pouty lip, Russ patted the man's shoulder. "Hey, it's okay, buddy. I didn't mean to accuse you of anything."

"All right, fine," Stem sighed. "Then, thirdly, there's Caydee."

"But why would Katie want to follow me? We're divorced now."

"Not *that* Katie. The *other* Caydee."

Russ' mind reeled.

Could Caydee be tracking me? If she is then the only reason for it is because she wants to get back together, right?

Though improbable, the idea made half-drunk butterflies take over his stomach.

As though reading his mind, Stem accused, "You like that possibility, don't you?"

"What?" Russ thundered, doing his best to hide the truth but fearing at the same time that the expression on his face had already said too much.

"I know exactly what you're thinking, mate. You *want* it to be the other Caydee."

"Don't be ridiculous."

"I'm being anything but. You like the idea that she might still have a thing for you."

Despite his dark skin, the blush on Russ' face could not be concealed. "No, I don't."

"Don't come the raw prawn with me! I can practically read your mind!"

"What? What are you accusing me of? Of entertaining the idea that my ex—" he couldn't find the right word "—female person partner that I, you know, she and I did together—and that she might still want me? Huh? Is that it?"

Stem fumed. "Not in those inelegant words, but that's exactly what I'm accusing you of!"

"Well, you're wrong! I don't care about *that* Caydee!"

"Well, you bloody should!"

Russ had had enough irritations for the day. "What does *that* mean? Why should I care about *her*?"

Crimson like lava flowed onto Stem's face. "Because you bloody ruined her life too!"

Russ wasn't sure why he did what he did next, but it was one of those actions which a person does impulsively to show how angry they are, but instead, it backfires and the action itself causes them more grief than what had originally angered them in the first place.

As the driver's foot stomped the brake, Stem's Sonic Blast slammed into the dashboard. One-tenth of a second later, the Miata fishtailed on the dirt road, and, as Russ overcorrected, it veered off to the left, plowing right through the ditch, the barb-wired fence, and some twenty feet of a cow pasture.

With the engine still idling, Stem ripped off his seatbelt and shouted, "That's it! And you're buying me a new Sonic Blast!" After scrambling out of the car, he slammed the door shut and screamed into the air, "Blood-sucking leeches on a crocodile's tit!"

A cow lowed in response, and, soon, he'd put the whole herd in an uproar.

As Russ remained in the driver's seat contemplating what had just happened, two moods vied for his attention—anger and frustration, both of which were directed at himself. Bouncing between the two like a tennis ball on a court, his head began to ache, and he found he hated himself more than ever. But then, he realized that what he'd just wrecked—both his new car and his friend's dessert—were fixable, and his mind began to calm. Five minutes after his impulsive decision to hammer the brakes, Russ shut off the car and went to sit on the dirt-covered hood beside his friend. Neither said anything, and, for a span of minutes, they watched the cows (who were staring them down because they were obviously the most interesting thing in the entire field).

At last, Russ broke the silence with a heavy sigh and a greeting. "Hey."

"Hey," Stem replied, as lackluster as his friend.

"Sorry about that. I'll buy you a new Sonic Blast."

He nodded and they were silent again until Stem said, "I want extra M&M's this time. And a cherry."

"Done," promised Russ.

"A *few* cherries. You owe me at least five or six."

Russ nodded but his expression was more akin to an offer of condolence than confirmation. "I'm sorry I didn't tell you."

"About what?"

"That I was having an affair."

"If you had, I would've told Katie."

"I know, and that's why I didn't tell you. But still, I feel like I betrayed you."

"You did. But not because you didn't tell me."

Uncertain what his friend meant, Russ silently regarded him, beckoning him to explain.

Ignoring the man's gaze, Stem fixed his eyes on a particularly nosy cow who had waddled up near them. The physics prof instinctively kicked at the animal though she was a good ten feet away. "We were like a family. You, me, and Katie. I was like your—" for lack of a better word he completed the thought with "—child."

That wasn't precisely how Russ had seen the three's relationship, but now that Stem said it, it made since.

"My parents are divorced and my mum . . ."

Remembering that Stem's mother had passed, Russ nodded.

"And I'm not close to my father. But you two—you and Katie—you mates were steady and stable like parents should be and I was just this drifter like a fart in the wind, and, somehow, I landed on you two."

Though Russ felt the analogy was lacking, he appreciated the underlying sentiment.

"You two adopted me and welcomed me into your family. I had a place to belong. I could come over for dinner or go on holidays with you. Katie always made me a birthday cake." Tears filled his eyes, and, try as he might to resist, his lip began quivering. "Who's gonna make me a birthday cake now, mate?"

Russ touched the man's shoulder. "I'll buy you one."

"Can I pick it?"

"Sure."

"Thanks, mate," Stem replied with a smile which was followed up with a giggle and the wiping of many tears.

"I'm really sorry," apologized Russ. "I know I messed up. A lot. Not just my life, but yours and Katie's, obviously, and . . . you're right. I messed up the other Caydee's life too." He gritted his teeth because, though he'd known how his actions had hurt others, it now ached his bones to acknowledge the pain he'd inflicted. "I know her expulsion from school was humiliating for her, and I'm sure that caused issues with her family and community."

"She from Denver?"

"Boulder."

"Aren't many Christians up there."

The statement, like a punch to his gut, brought tears to Russ' eyes. When he'd first been offered the job at Harding University, a place where students from all over the world had chosen to come for their higher education in a Christ-centered environment, he had felt a holy calling of sorts. In a way, he'd seen himself as a minister, leading these young people towards a deepening relationship with Jesus.

"I veered off track," Russ confessed.

Turning to examine the ruts in the pasture, Stem asserted, "I'd say you redefined it."

"No, I mean as a professor. As a Christian." He bit his bottom lip, hoping the pain would keep the tears from streaming down his face, but it didn't work, and, next, he discovered that his throat felt a little tight like he'd gobbled down a buttery warm bread roll from the cafeteria a little too quickly.

"We've all lost our way at one point or another, mate."

"I don't know who I've become," he confessed as he mopped up with his shirt tail what his eyes had spilled onto his cheeks. "And I don't know how I got where I am. How did I go from a husband of fidelity and devotion, and a spiritual leader for dozens of young people, to . . . this?"

That was the question he'd been asking himself for the past few months, and he had yet to figure out the answer.

"I don't know, mate. But you're not so bad to be around. That is, if you're not driving."

They shared a chuckle which spooked the curious heifer who'd been inching closer. The speed and agility with which she bounded off impressed the pair.

"Guess I need to call a wrecker," Russ observed.

"The ground's fairly dry. Try turning her around and heading back the way you came. Just gun it through that ditch. Couldn't hurt. Might save you another bill."

With his friend's help, Russ maneuvered the Miata out of the cow pasture, but the sporty coupe wouldn't budge up the ditch. While waiting for the tow truck, they remembered the AirTag.

Russ inquired, "What's it look like?"

"Small and round, like a button."

In minutes, the nefarious little device was located in the trunk wedged in a gap between two panels.

"Let me see it," said Stem, taking charge. Scanning it with his phone, he soon pulled up its registration information. "Ah," he said. "It's the little wanker from GadgetTech."

"Dirk? Why the heck is *he* stalking me?"

"Don't know, mate, but you should report this. Tracking someone with an AirTag is illegal."

"Will that thing send him a message and tell him where I've been?"

"Sure will."

"It's just so bizarre, unless—" Russ could feel hot flames rising inside him. "I'll bet Lance coerced him to do it. That twerp. I knew this had to do with him somehow. Shoot! I've been driving around with that thing for days."

Hoping the answer was no, Stem inquired, "You taken it clear to 42B?"

With a sigh, Russ verified, "Yep. And now Lance may figure out what I'm up to."

Chapter 13

Minutes after the tow truck pulled the Miata safely back onto the dirt road, Russ and Stem trudged across the field at the end of Mermaid Lane and disappeared into the depths of the earth. While Stem recorded on his Notes app some measurements which he was taking of the Time Magnet, Russ checked his eBay messages. Right away, his hands began to shake.

"Hey, remember that message I got from that pingopong69?"

"He contact you again, yeah?"

"No, but I got another message from some user named nunzchet77. He says that that mask I sold—you know, that golden-colored one—that it looks just like a *real* gold one that used to be a part of a collection that belongs to—or maybe it's now at, I'm not sure—"

"Where?"

"San Antonio Abad National University of Cusco in Peru."

"I know where Cusco is."

"But he says the mask I sold looks just like one which was stolen from there."

Stem's head popped up. "When?"

"Around the beginning of World War 1."

"Could be true. I thought it might be dinky-di."

"What the heck does that mean?"

"That it looked like real gold."

"But you never said that!" Russ hissed. "I even asked you if it could be real gold and you said it was an 'implausible assertion.'"

"Well, it was, but even implausible assertions can be proven true."

Russ' heart pounded. "Crud! What if it *was* real gold?"

"Then you were undoubtedly cheated."

"This isn't about money now! If it's real then what'll happen?"

There was no doubt that the news Stem was about to deliver was bad. "In that case, you may have some trouble on your hands."

"What do you mean?"

"That it's perfectly plausible Peepaw may have been a bower bird. In fact, he likely stole all these little treasures which now fund your lifestyle."

"But you—you're the one who said I should sell them. Remember?"

"Yes, I have not forgotten my sage advice to a man who didn't have a brass razoo to his name, whose career had been suddenly thrust into the dunny, and who owed his ex-wife alimony which was beyond his means to pay. But that doesn't mean it was good advice."

"You just called it sage."

Stem shoved a greasy hand through his unruly curls. "Well, that's also the name of a herb! Are you going to hold that against me too?"

Irritation flared inside Russ and he stormed off. He needed something to do with his hands to get his mind off the troubling message he'd received.

At first, he set up in the onsite photo booth something which looked akin to an inkwell. However, since they had designed the photography area for larger objects, the lighting didn't quite sit right on the small item in question. After several attempts to correct the issue, he decided to take pictures of a metal footstool instead. But as he turned it and clicked his phone and turned it and snapped another shot, he decided the whole process of photographing the eBay items was tedious and boring and not at all the distraction from the eBay message which he had hoped it'd be.

Almost upon first descent into the basement, he had spotted a random sock on the floor. For weeks now, the men had stepped over it as though it didn't exist. Now going to it, he whacked it several times against one of the shelves, beating the grime out of it like some gladiator, and he took to dusting everything in his path.

Some minutes later, he found that the task had eased the worry in his mind, and, soon, he was thinking about entirely different things, like if the Miata would beat a Mustang (the car salesman had claimed it would but, then again, he had also said that Covid was a hoax). Then, he began thinking about Katie and what she would think if she saw him driving the Miata with the top down.

Would she want to ride with me?

"Russell, I need you."

Irritation and sweat dripped from the scientist. He'd clocked hours tinkering with the machine and had yet to come to any solid conclusions as to why it wasn't properly functioning.

"Stand here and hold this," Stem instructed. As Russ lightly rested one hand in the indicated location, his pal frowned in disapproval. Pointing to the large glass case on which Russ had his hands, he explained, "You have to hold this very steady—with both hands. This is the vacuum chamber where the charged subatomic particles are accelerated. This part (he touched the glass, pointing to a metal plate inside the chamber) creates the magnetic field which allows the particles to pass through several times during acceleration." Pausing to bend and point to a series of rudimentary knobs which protruded from the metal upon which the glass sat, he explained, "One or more of these transits has become uncalibrated. Without them all working in perfect harmony, the particles will not reach the gap at the same point in the RF cycle." Russ looked as dumbfounded as he felt. To summarize, Stem growled, "It's broken, and, until I repair it, there's not enough energy to get the bloody Time Magnet running!"

The simplified explanation sufficed, as far as Russ was

concerned. "Do you think messing with this thing is safe?"

"No, of course not!" Stem grouched. "It's nuclear technology! Now hold that glass in place while I calibrate these."

The process of calibrating a nuclear perpendicular magnetic field was tedious and heightened Stem's frustration at every opportunity. For Russ, the length of time doing a mindless activity (that is, pressing his hands against a glass case to steady the machine as Stem pulled it this way and that) enabled him to return to his thoughts.

I wonder what Katie was going to say at her attorney's office.

Foremost, he wished she'd offer her forgiveness and express her desire to reunify the marriage. Every new day without her felt like the longest day he'd lived. If Stem ever got this contraption working properly, Russ swore he'd go back in time and fix his pointless, mindless, heartless mistake.

Why did I ever get mixed up with the other Caydee?

He still could not say. Why had he cheated on his kind, sweet, spirited, gentle wife? He would never spend another birthday with her. Already, she'd turned another year older without him by her side. And what other special occasions would he miss? Their anniversary, no doubt, for the holiday didn't even exist anymore. And then there'd be the Fourth of July spent out at his uncle's farm shooting off fireworks. And their yearly Labor Day trip to a quaint bed and breakfast in Eureka Springs. And every Thanksgiving and Christmas and New Years would pass him by without his best friend within arm's reach, sharing his life, making more joyful memories.

As this realization struck him, it felt unbearable. His chest tightened and ached. Like a fountain, tears sprang forth. Pausing his ordered job, Russ wiped his eyes quickly and returned his hands to the glass cover.

"Apply pressure," Stem growled.

No more New Year's kisses. No more admiring her in her new Easter dress. No more creative Halloween costumes to impress their friends' kids when they stopped by for candy.

Tears breeched the dams in his eyes a second time and he

turned his head this way and that, wiping moisture on his shirt sleeves.

Katie, please don't leave me.

The rainstorm pouring forth from his face staunched his ability to see straight.

"Hold still!" Stem demanded. "This is precise instrumentation!"

Russ tried. And he struggled. And he repressed sobs. Though, if he was making any sound, Stem didn't let on that he'd heard. Likely, the scientist was in his own world, completely aloof to his friend's mourning.

"Bugger! Hold the bloody thing still!"

His hands braced and wiped and braced and slipped on the glass as the rain shower of tears fell upon the Time Magnet. For seconds—maybe minutes—Russ felt he was in agony. His wife, his sweet, dear, beloved bride. Gone.

God, give her back to me. Please.

Despite the possibility that they might at last repair the Time Magnet and, thus, he might one day hold her again, a fracture had already formed in his heart like a thawing icy lake, and he had fallen straight through the ice into a cold bath of buried tears.

The belligerence of his irritable friend grew to a climax with a spew of words Russ could not interpret, but he was certain by the tone with which they were delivered they meant (in some Australian backwoods jargon), "Keep your bloody hands on that glass, or so help me, I will cut them off!"

So, obeying, Russ wiped his hands on his shirt and pressed with all his might.

And immediately, he heard an awful crack.

That was it. Although Russ found himself still blind from tear shed, he could sense Stem's head drawing up slowly. In an unnaturally calm voice, the outraged man slowly questioned, "What the bloody devil of the underworld was that?"

Because Stem could see clearly with his eyes that the glass top had cracked, Russ need not answer (not that he fully comprehended in his state of grief the disaster he'd just caused).

A haze of insults—words which Stem himself had never dared utter—permeated the cellar like tear gas, drifted behind him as he made his exit up the stairs, through the shed, across the pasture, and two miles down moonlit Mermaid Lane. All Russ had to do once his episode of blinding anguish had passed was follow the foggy trail of f-bombs and the like, and stomping the ground like a bull, he found his buddy.

Russ pulled up alongside the irate man and rolled down the passenger window. "I'm sorry," he offered meekly. However, it was not immediately evident if his friend had heard his words or not, so after having waited a good ten seconds, he repeated the phrase.

"I bloody heard you!" Stem shouted.

"Can you fix it?"

Those words, there was no doubt Stem had heard.

"Can I fix it?" he barked. "Can I *fix it*?" The irate physicist halted his pace, his chest heaving in anger. "The type of glass—the curvature of it—it's almost impossible to replicate without detailed—*highly* detailed—drawings of the machine. I can't just run to Walmart and fetch one off the shelf. Do you understand?"

"Well," Russ thought aloud, and a little tremble of breath like an infant exhausted from crying shook his lips and lungs. "You said to push."

Hearing the shaky tone in his friend's voice, the pedestrian bent down, reached in through the car window, and clicked on the overhead light. After a quick inspection of his friend's face, he rolled his eyes and clicked it off. "Get out," he ordered.

As he cautiously reached for the door handle, Russ questioned, "Are you going to punch me?" But it wouldn't have made any difference if Stem had said yes—he would still obey the order to exit the car.

His friend made no reply, which caused Russ to brace for impact as he neared the angered man. As Stem raised an arm, Russ shut his eyes and tried to think of bunnies at a playground, which is, for some reason, the same thing he'd make himself think when he was younger and Lance was practicing his boxing moves on him.

However, to Russ' pleasant surprise, he felt a warm embrace engulf his shoulders.

"What are you doing?"

"Hugging you."

The pair stood in the Miata's slightly askew high beams for a few seconds. Though Russ didn't exactly return the affection, he felt it deeply and soothingly to his core, like a cool shower after a hard football practice.

Upon releasing his friend, Stem said, "Better now, mate?"

"Thanks for not punching me."

"Well, you looked about as happy as a bastard on Father's Day, and I figured making you blubber was more punishment than you deserved."

"*You* didn't make me cry."

"Oh, well then, I guess I'll have to punch you."

And he did, but not very hard—and only to the gut. It was probably for the best that Russ hadn't seen it coming, for he knew all too well that bracing for impact always leads to more extensive injuries than not.

The pair returned shortly afterwards to 42B and surveyed the extent of the damage.

"So, is it fixable?" Russ inquired, desperately hoping he'd say yes.

"Not in the least bit. But that's okay. I'm not sure if I'd be able to take snacks with me through time travel anyway, and I'd rather eat here in plenty than starve in the past."

Russ spent a moment contemplating the possibility of time travel, of going back to the day when he'd first thought of having an affair and warning himself of the disastrous consequences of such a heartless action. Then, he imagined life with Katie as it would've been today if he had not made that horrible decision, and it slowly dawned on him that, had he made other choices, they would've been leaving soon for sunny Orlando for a belated eighth wedding anniversary vacation. His eyes, still black and blue from his run-in with Lance, stung, and a fresh wave of tears issued forth.

Suddenly, he felt Stem's hand on his shoulder, that comforting embrace of a friend who understands the troubles of your heart, and a quiet whisper reached his ear. "Mate?"

His friend's concern for him warmed his soul, and he longed to hear what words of comfort the man would speak.

"Mate, hand me your keys. I think I left my Skittles in the car."

While the man ran out to the Miata to search for his lost candy like the widow with the mite, Russ took a seat on the floor and rested his weary head against the wall. Spending his newly acquired money had been fun and had helped deaden the pain he felt, but unless he planned to start doing crystal meth or staying hammered every moment of every day, he would find no thrill quite potent enough to fully ease his misery. Life without Katie was just not a life he wanted to live. Not that he wanted to take his own life, but he desperately wanted the Time Magnet fixed so he could go back and correct the error of his ways.

"Have you found them?" called Stem.

"What?"

"My Skittles. Haven't you been looking for them?"

"No."

The man was incredulous. "Then get off your bum and start searching. I can't work without sustenance."

Given Russ wanted the Time Magnet fixed (likely more than his friend, if that was possible), he helped in the search and rescue efforts. However, what he found minutes later was intriguing enough to distract both friends from the hunt.

"What is that?" asked Stem.

"Don't know. Notes of some sort. A bunch of numbers."

Taking the journal from his friend, Stem examined it for a moment. "Crikey! This is a list of all Peepaw's time travel journeys."

"Really?"

"Yeah, look here. This column is the date and this one is the time in coordinated universal time."

"What's that?"

"Russell, there are times when I feel absolutely certain you cheated your way through your doctorate."

"I never said I didn't."

"True. Moving on, I'll have to study this documentation more but I'll venture a guess that these columns are coordinates of some fashion indicating where he traveled to in space and time."

"Do you mean, when he went back in time, he could travel to some other place on the globe—like Europe or something—and not just end up right here in this field?"

Stem smiled and patted his friend's back. "I'm very proud of you for deducing that without my simplifying it for you."

"Thank you."

Gazing at the journal in awe, Stem further explained, "To achieve transtemporal location displacement in such an experimental contrivance is beyond impressive. I'll have to study these notations to make sense of his array, but look here—he's listed the precise metallic article which he retrieved from each second monopole era."

"Oh, like an inventory. Neat." From the expression his remark immediately provoked upon his friend's face, Russ could see his simplistic mind was, at the moment, disturbing Stem's more complex sensibilities. "I'll just go . . . do . . . something else," he suggested.

"Greatly appreciated."

Some hours later, Russ awoke to his friend gently smacking his face. "What? What?" he grouched. "Quit that."

"Sorry, I was thoroughly enjoying it," Stem apologized. "Got carried away. Listen, I've cracked Peepaw's algorithm for these arrays and I've identified several of the locations and dates and times to which he traveled."

"Okay."

"Is that all you've got to say? I've spent the past six and a quarter bloody hours calculating—with not one scrap of food, mind you—"

Russ conveyed suspicion through his eyebrows, an expression he had perfected in childhood.

"Oh, all right," confessed his friend. "I ate a bag or two of beef jerky, but they were basically sample packs. Okay, and I had a pudding pack, but that hardly counts. Anyway, my point is that I crunched my brain very hard to decipher this code, and your condescension is not appreciated."

"I wasn't patronizing you. I just thought you were going to say more, so I was waiting."

"Well, in that case, thank you, because I do have plenty more to say."

To Russ' elation, Stem spared him the explanation of the analytics which enabled him to determine the cypher, and, instead, chose to point out a curious notation that he found written in the margin.

"I think it says, 'Hank.'"

"Or 'Honk,'" interjected Russ.

Looking up from the journal, Stem said flatly, "Let's see if that makes sense. 'Send links to Honk. Have him shave to 0.23 inches.'"

"Well, when you say it that way . . ."

"So, who do you think this *Hank* is? It seems he may have helped Peepaw design the device. I covet a discussion with the man, if he is to be found."

"I don't remember Peepaw knowing anyone named Hank."

Grinning, Stem questioned, "And what about Honk? That ring a bell, yeah?"

"Shut up."

"Thus far, I've mostly focused just on deciphering the algorithm for the coordinates, so now, I'm going to scour the pages and see if there are any more interesting remarks which might yield helpful information."

"What should I do?"

"Go back to sleep, mate. I can handle this without you."

Chapter 14

"There's another message," Russ hollered the moment he heard Stem open the front door.

As he quickly scanned the message on his friend's eBay app, Stem mumbled to himself, "Honjo Masamune sword . . . 13th century . . . national treasure . . . unique hamon—"

"That's the edge pattern on a sword created during the hardening process."

"I know what a hamon is, thank you . . . see drawing for reference . . . disappeared during World War 2 American occupation . . . send at once for inspection . . . Tokugawa Memorial Foundation." Handing the phone back to his friend, he said, "Awesome. You got any of those string cheese sticks? Meemaw always kept some in the refrigerator for me."

"Awesome? That's all you have to say? The Japanese government is coming after me and you think that's awesome?"

"Look," Stem huffed, "I've just walked through the bloody door and I haven't eaten in almost an hour, so expecting me to be able to focus on anything is an error on your part. Now, do you have string cheeses or do I need to run to Cash Saver for some?"

With the particular snack item in question being in short supply, Russ finally convinced Stem to settle for peanut butter crackers and a glass of milk. As the number of crackers dwindled away, so did

Stem's foul mood. At last, he stretched and said, "Here's what I think. Peepaw stole the sword sometime around when it was taken from the Japanese."

"Christmas, 1945. And the family surrendered it."

"Fine. When they *surrendered* the sword."

"So, you think I actually sold the legendary Honjo Masamune sword for $1800?"

"It's only natural for you to feel taken advantage of."

"That's not what I'm talking about! I may be in some real trouble here. And what about the other items I've sold? That mask, for example. Someone's hounding me about it too."

"I think you're getting all worked up about things which may prove to be nothing."

"Well, you said the mask wasn't real gold even though it was crazy heavy."

"Could've been painted lead."

"Well, I know we didn't even bother to clean up the sword, but I'm telling you, when Lance nearly plunged it into my gut, it felt legit sharp, like it could've disemboweled me."

"You just used a twelve-letter word. I'm mildly impressed."

"So, what if I've really been hawking priceless ancient treasures on eBay like they're used college books? What's gonna happen, because I'm starting to freak out."

"Russell, sit down." When his friend had obeyed his orders, Stem said slowly, "Now, listen carefully to me and I'll tell you what's going on. This is textbook. The paranoia you're experiencing is a common phenomenon amongst poor people who unexpectedly come into big bickies. First, they put up security cameras everywhere."

"But those were your idea."

"Hey, I'm just as susceptible to new money fever as the next guy. But after that, they stow away their valuables in some kind of vault or cellar, something hidden from the naked eye." The way Stem's eyebrows rose to indicate Russ was guilty of this accusation would've made Meemaw proud.

"But 42B was Peepaw's idea."

"You're his grandson and paranoia is proven to be genetic. And lastly, individuals handling new money become reclusive curmudgeons."

"I—I get out," Russ lied. "I do stuff. At places. With people."

"No, Russell, you're like a bandicoot on a burnt ridge. You wait around your dead grandmother's house until I show up and *make* you leave the house."

"Well, I did go . . . somewhere . . . without you."

"Where?"

"To the shops," he replied, repeating his friend's phrasing.

Narrowing his eyes, Stem protested, "That's a lie, and you and I both know it! You've been sitting in this stuffy old house having your bloody groceries delivered through the Walmart app."

"That's just to save gas."

"You tip the driver $10 to deliver them! That's twice what it would cost you to do the job yourself."

With no viable argument, Russ sat in silence.

"Mate, what you need is to get out of your house and out of your head. And first and foremost, you need to get back to church."

At those words, Russ' heart began pounding and sweat broke out upon his body like humidity in July. "I can't go back. That's Katie's church now."

Stem's patience had been exasperated. "You live in White bloody County, Arkansas, one and a half miles from a Christian bloody university, at the apex of the American bloody Bible Belt! Do you think there's a shortage of churches that your ex-wife doesn't attend?"

"Well, I—" Russ wanted to argue his point but he had to stop for a moment to figure out what it was. "I can't go anywhere around here. I ruined my reputation and made a mockery of myself!"

The expression upon his friend's face was so serious and stern that Russ suddenly felt like he was in the principal's office. Leaning in, Stem declared, "Mate, the only place for a man like you is in a church, and, if those people really are following in the footsteps of their Savior then they'll welcome you like the prodigal son you are. Now, are you gonna give me your bloody keys or drive me to Cash Saver yourself?"

The fact that Russ' first venture back into civilization (at least, in his hometown) had been uneventful—and more importantly, not humiliating—filled him with a small measure of hope that, perhaps by the time he was geriatric, he'd be able to reintegrate into society without fearing any stigma associated with his transgressions. However, that was hardly good enough for Stem who, unbeknownst to Russ, had already made arrangements for his second outing.

After a few hours spent at 42B, the science prof suggested they grab some McDonald's. Afterwards, he directed the driver on the particulars of which turns to take and which on and off ramps not to use. Soon they found themselves in the insignificant town of Pangburn. The Miata's wheels turned into an unfamiliar parking lot beside which sat an aluminum-sided building which looked very much like one of those inexpensive gyms a church erects next to its more esteemed sanctuary building.

Tossing his friend a glance, Russ questioned, "Are you taking me to church or something?"

"Something," said Stem, who was being uncomfortably hush hush about the whole thing. As the pair slunk towards the entrance, he added, "We're a few minutes late."

Right away, his mate recognized the sound of worship music, and his eyes begged for Stem to tell him what was going on. However, the Aussie maintained his silence on the matter.

They entered through an aluminum door into a rudimentary basketball gym turned makeshift auditorium. Folding chairs filled with warm bodies sat in several neatly organized rows facing a screen upon which was projected the music video of a Christian band whose name Russ could not at the moment remember. Low lighting gave the effect of intimacy, and, yet, also promoted a sense of anonymity among the crowd. Following Stem (actually, dragged by him), Russ soon found himself occupying a seat third row from the front. Due to apprehension of the unknown, his mind had more or less shut down when they'd exited the car, and, now, he found himself staring blankly at a man standing on a short stage, holding a mic.

"I'm a grateful believer in Jesus," said the speaker. "I celebrate recovery over alcoholism and drug abuse, and I struggle with lust, pornography, self-worth, and co-dependency, and my name is Jack."

As though scripted, the inhabitants of the gym replied in unison, "Hi, Jack!"

Caught off guard by the rote response, Russ glanced around nervously and struggled to peel his dry tongue off the roof of his mouth. He hardly heard a word the speaker said as he extended a welcome to everyone present and reminded all that, "What is heard here, what is said here, who is seen here, stays here."

"Here, here!" the crowd boasted.

Wearing a triumphant expression, Stem leaned over and whispered, "Like Fight Club, only better."

"What is this?" Russ whispered. "I feel like I've walked into 1984."

"Just watch and listen."

Stem's cool manner gave off the vibe that he'd been to something like this before and knew what to expect. Russ, on the other hand, was taken unawares at every turn.

A young woman probably no older than Caydee took the mic next, and, with nervous quivering in her voice, introduced herself. "I'm a faithful believer in Jesus Christ and I struggle with anxiety and an eating disorder and my name is Rosie."

"Hi, Rosie!" chimed the crowd.

"Step one: We admitted we were powerless over our addictions and compulsive behaviors, that our lives had become unmanageable."

Russ leaned over and hissed, "You brought me to an addiction—" But his voice was drowned out by the crowd who, like one body, began reciting a Bible verse. Irritated by the lot of it, Russ grimaced at his friend and stood to make his quick exit. By the time he reached the parking lot, Stem was right on his heels.

"Where are you going?" questioned the Aussie, but when his friend huffed silently to his car, he hollered, "So you're just leaving me here, then? Running out on me because I brought you to a strange place, yeah?"

Russ' irritation verging on betrayal came lashing back at his friend. "What is this? You bring me to some drug addiction group and expect me to, what—thank you for it? I'm not one of *those* people. I'm going home."

As he ripped open his car door, Stem voiced a most unexpected protest. "Well, I'm one of them! I'm one of *those* people!"

"What are you talking about? You don't do drugs!"

"How do you know? All you can see is your own issues. Well, I'm not immune to temptations. I'm susceptible to corruptions of the soul just like any man."

Russ' heart had not stopped pounding since the second he'd first stepped foot onto that parking lot, but now there was a discomforting pulsating of blood rushing through his ears. "Then what are you saying? You brought me here for *you*?"

"No! I brought you here for *you*!"

For a moment, Russ contemplated standing there and arguing, however, he decided it would be a waste of his efforts. "I'm leaving. Stay if you want but—"

He was interrupted by a man who furtively poked his head out the door like a prairie dog. "Stem!" he whisper-shouted. "You're on in about a minute. Everything hunky-dory?"

Russ had never seen his friend transform so quickly from agitation to calm. After one slow deep breath, the scientist turned to the man. "It's fine, Grant. Just give me one second, yeah?"

"Sure thing," said the man, looking from Stem to Russ and back. "I'll stall for ya."

When Grant had left them, Stem ran a hand through his tangled mess of curls. "Russell, I won't force you to return inside—but if you leave right now, you'll never know the real me . . . and you may never discover the real you."

Russ watched his friend's lanky figure leap across the parking lot, and, in three long strides and a yank of the door, he disappeared into the building.

The confused man hesitated and huffed angry breaths into the air. This whole evening seemed to be one big set up, and he didn't like to be left in the dark. But slowly, his mind regained rationality. He knew he'd kept secrets from his friend—namely, Caydee—however, it suddenly dawned on him that maybe his best friend had some secrets of his own.

Chapter 15

Russ pulled the gym door open and saw his friend stepping onto the stage. All of a sudden, it dawned on him that today was Monday. Conversations with Katie about where Stem went on the second day of the week flooded his mind, and as Russ crept back to his seat, he felt his palms begin sweating.

As the crowd watched, Stem quickly tapped a few buttons on his phone, which Russ figured meant the man would be reading from some notes he'd jotted down. Clearing his throat, the speaker began.

"I'm a grateful believer in Christ. I celebrate recovery over a gambling addiction, and I'm working on anger, swearing, and—" his cringe was unmistakable "—a junk food addiction. And my name is Stem."

Russ' knee nervously bobbed up and down as he quickly glanced around the room. At least fifty pairs of eyes were laser focused on his friend, whom he feared was committing social and career suicide before them all. Silently, he begged the man to shut his mouth and come sit down. However, Stem had no impulse of the sort, and he proceeded to deliver his message with immense liberality.

"My first dirty little secret is that while my mother *is* Australian, I'm technically not—by birth, I'm a Kiwi. I was born in Wellington,

New Zealand."

This was news to his best mate of nearly ten years.

"And Stem's just my nickname. I was born Ura'astema Bik the fourth, son of Ura'astema Bik the third, son of, well, you get the idea. On my father's side, I come from a long and proud line of Māori, the indigenous people of New Zealand, but my mother's family is Pākehā—or white, for you blokes. Clearly, my coloring favors her.

"I was always a precocious child, and, at a young age, I desired to be a ballerina dancer like my mum. However, my father didn't see that as a fitting career for his son so he pushed me into academics. I attended a private school in Melbourne for several years. At age nine, my father was appointed governor-general of the Realm of New Zealand. For you Americans, that means he was chosen by her majesty, Queen Elizabeth, to represent her as viceregal for a five-year term in my home country."

Russ had never heard a hint of the information which Stem had just conveyed, and it was so startling to the speaker's closest friend that the man began to doubt the truth of it altogether. Yet fascinated by the words falling from his friend's mouth, Russ silently listened, as captivated by the story as the rest of the crowd.

"My father unfortunately did not view marriage as a relationship for which fidelity was required. As you can imagine, his affairs and my parents' subsequent divorce were fodder for every tabloid in the southern hemisphere. At age fourteen, I found myself caught in the midst of a scandal about which I knew practically nothing. And at home, with my now disgraced mum, I quickly gained a new role—caretaker to her debilitating depression. She had a son from her first marriage, from which she was widowed, and very little help was this older brother of mine. As often as his financial legacy from his father's death allowed, he indulged himself in every whim that could distract him from responsibilities, thus causing my mum more grief.

"The summer I turned fifteen, my father invited me to stay with him in his new home in Queenstown Lakes, which is one of the most exclusive neighborhoods in New Zealand. I don't tell you this to brag but to convey how high-profile my awkward teenage years were. Often, paparazzi swarmed our house, and, as my father's dalliances intensified, so did the public's interest in our family. That summer with my father was madness and hell. What had first begun for me as an entertaining amusement living at his lavish private estate became more akin to a hostage situation. My father soon prohibited me from any contact with my mum, whom I knew was suffering greatly.

"As a side note, I spent years convinced that he did this out of spite for her. However, as I've retrospectively examined his actions over recent years, I've concluded that he likely had no such malice, and, instead, merely intended to redirect my life and possibly protect me from her mental illness. He was a caring father even if he was a womanizer. Nevertheless, I wanted to speak with my mum, to hear how she was handling life, but my father always had an excuse why that wasn't possible.

"Eventually, I ran away from my father's house and hitched my way to my mum's apartment some seventy-five kilometers away, or just under fifty miles. However, when I arrived, I discovered that, just days before, my mum had attempted suicide, and, upon her recovery, she had checked into a facility for the mentally unstable. So, my father sent a car for me and brought me back to his house.

"Her suicide attempt left me feeling very upset—I thought she didn't care enough about me to want to live. And what I perceived as my father's growing coldness and distance towards me made me feel both unwanted and controlled. Soon, anger filled me.

"I remember the first time I indulged in the feeling of wrath. It was overwhelming and made me feel powerful. I went into my father's office while he was out for the evening and took out my anger on the room, on his prized possessions, his fancy artwork, and anything I could get my hands on. When he came home and discovered what had happened, he questioned me. I denied having a part in it. No doubt, he knew it was I who had wrecked his office, but he reported it to the press as vandalism by an unknown party. I believe he did it to protect me in some way, as the press was having a heyday with my having run away. But his lie just angered me more, I think because I wanted him to have it out with me, to have a battle of words about what was happening with him and with my mum, and to let me know, too, what the future held for me. Would I continue to live with him? Could I go back home to Mum? But even when I had outbursts at him, shouting fits and breaking things, he was silent on all matters."

The heaviness of his pal's story weighed on Russ' heart like an anchor. In all the years he'd known the man, they'd never discussed any of the events which were unfolding before an audience of strangers. In some way, his transparency comforted Russ, but in other ways, Russ began to feel betrayed himself, as if he'd been friends with an imposter all these years.

"At summer's end, I returned to Mum's But, soon, she started feeling sick and she sent me to live with my brother. I think she hoped it would help settle him down, but I had no such power over the man. He grew wilder, seemingly by the day, and, eventually, my father, who had previously adopted him, formally denounced him as his son. My brother was, after all, bad press, and my father's reputation had already suffered enough at his own hand and, also, because of my bad behavior and my mum's suicide attempt.

"When I was sixteen, my mum died unexpectedly." He paused to take a deep breath. "As I mentioned, she'd felt ill but her doctors had not known what was wrong. They suggested her depression had physically manifested symptoms in her body. However, upon her autopsy we discovered cancer had inundated her stomach and core organs. I was angry at her doctors for not more thoroughly examining her, and I was angry at her for not insisting they look into her illness further. Giving into my anger, I trashed my brother's apartment and ran away. While living on the street, I vandalized people's properties, smashing house windows and vehicle windshields with bricks. I got arrested and my father left me in jail for a few days before the press caught wind of it, at which point he bailed me out.

"I completed school a few months later and began university. At some point in my earlier teens, I had taught myself how to count cards and cheat at card games, so I used this to my advantage at uni and scammed a lot of classmates out of a lot of money. It wasn't that I needed the money—my father still provided for me—but it was simply an amusement, something to make me feel good amidst the pain I carried. However, it got me on probation and, eventually, expelled. But this was no big deal, I thought. I had high marks and enrolled in another university right away. Stupidly, however, I followed the same path I'd trudged before and was expelled again.

"My father wasn't as forgiving of my antics this go around. He warned me this was the last time he'd pay for me to attend uni. If I was kicked out again, he'd cut me off. I heeded his warning—sort of. This time, instead of wheeling my classmates, I hustled my professors. At one point, a professor owed me over $50,000 New Zealand. Using that as leverage, I told him I'd forgive his debt if he'd pass me in his class, which he did. A similar scenario worked with another professor. But somehow the university caught wind of that and I was expelled a third time."

A smile formed on Russ' face, and, despite the man's despicable blackmailing ploys, Russ was humored by his esteemed friend's boyhood antics.

"My gambling days were far from over. My brother's entire existence revolved around partying, often with famous young celebrities who liked to flaunt fists full of cash. Conning the intoxicated socialites out of several thousand dollars in one night was no difficult task, and it kept me more than afloat for a couple of years without my father's support.

"After his stent as the Viceregal, my father had begun his career as the Lead Minister for the Department of Internal Affairs. A division of his office enforced gambling laws and oversaw the general profitability of casinos in the country. Given my success with gambling and my father's disapproval of my current means of income, he offered me a job as a slot machine tester. As the name indicates, I was to select slot machines at random and track their monetary growth or decline over a series of plays, ensuring they were within the stipulations of the department. It required complex mathematical calculations, which sounded interesting at first, but the job quickly plummeted into boredom.

"Casinos were and *are* exceedingly tempting for me. Though my job prohibited me from gambling, I soon found my way over to a dark corner of a card table, earned a large sum of cash, and made a special friend named Yan. Yan was a goliath-sized bouncer who was not actually my friend. The casino I'd scammed wanted him to send me a message—cheat us again and you'll disappear forever. Wisdom would've said to stay away from the card games, but I listened to folly and went right back for another taste of the win. It didn't take long at all and there was Yan standing behind me. He yanked me out of my seat and dragged me off the casino floor via a hidden door. I figured that was probably the end of my short and pitiful life. However, someone who'd been watching me had a better proposition—I could work for the casino as a kat . . . or else Yan would kill me.

"Now, the term kat is derived from the New Zealand katipō spider and I'll save you the unpleasantries but will tell you the name was dubbed because of the female's uncouth mating habits. As a kat, I was to pose as a gambler and win by a small margin to keep the other gamblers at my table bidding higher and higher until, in the end, I bore down and won all their money. The catch is that the kat doesn't get to keep any of their earnings—the casino keeps it, but it's done under the table so it doesn't go on *their* books. Therefore, the casino doesn't have to report the money to my father's office and, thereby, they can evade taxes.

"So here I was, twenty years old, helping a casino cheat the office I worked for just so a human hammer named Yan didn't pound me to death. For a while, I felt like a character out of an Ian Fleming novel, living a high stakes life, but the novel effects of the job, pardon my pun, wore off as the fatigue set in. I got about three to four hours of sleep a night, between the time when the casino let off and the division office opened. And I couldn't snooze without dreaming of cards and slot machines. I began to desperately want a way out and I also began to fear that the Department would catch on and I'd be in some serious trouble.

"Then God provided a way out."

Having never heard Stem's conversion story (or really any of his backstory), Russ sat intrigued by his friend's confession.

"One morning as I was getting around in a drowsy haze, I tripped and fell and hit my head on the footboard of my bed. I didn't think much of it, and I got up and went to work. A headache started up about mid-morning, but I just took it to mean that I needed some caffeine. As I walked to the snack shop in the casino, I suddenly felt as if my head was splitting open. In fact, I actually reached up and pressed my head together between my hands because I thought I must've been shot and I didn't want my brain to fall out. Then, I blacked out.

"I awoke in a hospital bed with my head wrapped up and gauze taped over both of my eyes. The fall I'd had that morning had caused a subdural hematoma, or a brain bleed. But while I was unconscious, as the medical team prepared my body for brain surgery, they discovered a tumor behind my eyes which was wrapped around my optic nerves. So while I was out, I underwent extensive brain surgery to repair both issues. However, due to damage done to my optic nerves by the tumor, they concluded I would likely be blind. I'd have to wear the gauze over my eyes for six weeks to completely allow my optic nerves to heal, and then they could remove the gauze to see if my sight had come back or not.

"This unanticipated health complication was an inestimable blessing in disguise. The Department of Internal Affairs had been cracking down on widespread casino corruption. The very evening I was undergoing emergency brain surgery, they initiated a choreographed sting operation in six casinos across the country in which they arrested over fifty people who were central to the corruption. Had I not fallen that morning, I would've been one of the ones arrested. Every person taken into custody that evening was prosecuted and sentenced to no less than three years in prison. My mate, Yan, was amongst the convicts. When I heard about all this a few days after I woke up, I felt certain that some sort of power beyond myself had been watching out for me. I felt I'd been given a second chance, only, I didn't know why.

"A second miracle happened which also convinced me I'd been given another opportunity to straighten out my life. When the ambo I was riding in was en route to the hospital, their radio suddenly cactused. They assumed I should be taken to one hospital, however, come to find out, another hospital was being prepped for me. There at the wrong hospital, the country's best brain surgeon just happened to be visiting his nephew, an intern at the emergency surgery department. When I arrived there unexpectedly, the intern told his uncle about my condition, and the brain surgeon, knowing the surgery would be complex, volunteered to assist with it. His expertise and special knowledge of my type of brain tumor, called intra-orbital meningioma, helped save my vision and possibly my life.

"A third miracle also took place, further convincing me of a supernatural provision over me. Benjo Portier volunteered part-time as a chaplain at the hospital where I was taken by accident. The day I had surgery, he was scheduled to leave on a cruise with his wife, Nan. However, the ship they were to sail on experienced unexpected electrical issues and had to be docked for repairs. Though he was scheduled off duty for two weeks, he came into the hospital anyway, and prompted by God, he brought his suitcase along which he'd already packed for their holiday so he could stay at the hospital for a length of time if need be. When I came out of surgery, he sat by my bed praying over me specifically that God would restore my sight. Hours later when I awoke, he was there still, in his words, 'Bathing me in prayer.' My father was inundated with business related to the casino sting, so he didn't come to visit me at all. Instead, Benjo sat by my side for a week, acting as my support system and becoming one of my dearest friends."

With those words, Stem glanced up from his notes and his eyes met Russ'. Though he'd mentioned the name of the chaplain once or twice, Russ had no idea how close he and Stem had been.

"Benjo's quiet yet faithful nature was like an anchor I'd never had. When bad news came in for me, he remained calm and hopeful. The way he spoke of God was unlike anything I'd ever heard, and I soaked up his words like dry ground. Never had anyone told me that there was a God in Heaven who cared about me, who had purposefully created me to be just who I am. Up to that point, I'd really bought into atheism and science's sterile explanation of human existence and life on Earth, and I realized while listening to Benjo's retelling of the Genesis creation story that nature created in a logical order by an exceptional scientist actually fit all the scientific evidence I'd studied. The Big Bang was true, only, it hadn't been the result of incalculably random forces—it was *God* who had orchestrated this rapid development of life.

"When I was released from the hospital, Benjo invited me to stay at his home. He and Nan cared for me and made me feel more welcome than I'd ever felt aside from living with my mum. I felt like I'd come home."

His words reminded Russ of what Stem had said regarding he and Katie—he was like their child, and they were a steady home he'd always wished for.

"When my six weeks of blindness was up, I returned to the hospital to get the gauzes removed. I'd been nervous about permanent blindness, however, Benjo and Nan and their care for me and their faith in God had given me a great measure of peace. I knew that, no matter what happened to my vision, I would be all right. When the gauze was removed, I could see. Upon an eye exam, it was determined that my sight was better than it had been since I was a child. Beyond any doubt, I saw this as a testimony of God's miraculous healing powers, for which Benjo and Nan had been interceding in prayer. It was then that I fully came to believe in God and I gave myself to my Higher Power that day.

"But I still had an armory full of questions, some of which Benjo and Nan had no answers for other than to say, 'You'll know in time.' Being reassured that it was all right to not have all the answers I wanted today gave me the courage to keep seeking answers to other questions I had. Every answer I gained strengthened my belief in God and also made me more voracious to study science.

"I had not gone back to work for the Department, nor had I returned to casinos. But the draw to gamble was undeniable. I knew that, if I stayed where I was, I'd end up going back to that folly. So, I decided to return to college—only, for the diversion, I sought colleges in other countries. The pieces came together and I soon enrolled at Oklahoma Christian University. I'd previously been to America twice but had never visited Oklahoma. Let me just say that, upon arrival, I was disappointed to discover that Native Americans did not still freely roam the countryside on horseback and buffalos were constrained to wildlife refuges."

His remark elicited chuckles from a number of individuals in the crowd, including Russ.

"At the time, gambling in Oklahoma was limited to horse racing, and I was aware there was a horse track near the campus. However, with God's help, I never ventured through those gates. Unfortunately, while I was finishing up my undergraduate work there, legislature approved the operation of casinos in the state. When I graduated, ground was being broken for the first gambling houses. No doubt, I knew I had to leave.

"I chose the University of Hawaii for my masters. Not only was gambling illegal in the state but the climate was superb—plus the surfing was amazing.

"When my time there ended, I was accepted into Texas A & M's nuclear physics doctorate program. Only two and a half hours from the beach, I thought life in College Station would be exactly what I wanted. But then I discovered that, in addition to dolphin tours and an innocuous if not annoying Rainforest Café, Galveston boasts a floating casino. I'd like to say that I had the strength to stay far from it, but I didn't. In fact, it became a larger-than-life problem for me. I wanted to just be able to enjoy gambling like it seems people do on commercials or movies, but I found that, while it wasn't even fun anymore, I still could not help but go back to it time and again. My studies suffered and I was on the brink of being expelled from the program. I wanted to stop gambling, but it felt impossible. Every time I left the casino, I'd tell myself I wasn't coming back . . . but I always did.

"Then, one day, my old friends Benjo and Nan stopped by to see me on their holiday. They planned to stay with me at my apartment for a week. I didn't want to leave them and go to the casino, but the desire to gamble pulled me so hard that I left in the night and told myself I'd be back before morning. Well, I binged hard and night turned into day. When Benjo found me at the games table, I'd won about half a million dollars—and lost more than that. When I saw my friend, I thought, 'I must not have made it back before sunrise.' Then he informed me that I had left my house almost three days earlier. Ashamed, I left with him and promised God I'd never return to that casino.

"It took some begging and quite a lot of make-up work, but the dean allowed me to continue with my current studies. At the end of the semester, I had improved enough that he let me stay on the program. A year later, with God's grace and help, I completed the program and earned my doctorate."

At this, the crowd erupted in cheers. Russ had been so lost in his friend's life story that he'd almost completely forgotten where he was, but he soon joined in the applause, celebrating Stem's achievement.

"I returned to New Zealand for what was supposed to be a brief monthlong stay so I could attend both my brother's and my father's weddings. Shortly after visiting me in Texas, Benjo had been diagnosed with cancer, and his health had declined steadily. I had a job lined up teaching physics at Oklahoma Christian, my alma mater, however I decided to decline the position and stay in New Zealand to help Nan with Benjo. After all, he'd been there for me in my sickness. He was like a father to me and I was honored to spend his last several months with him before he passed away. Remembering how fragile my mum had been after she and my father's divorce, I feared Nan would be crippled by grief. No doubt, she grieved, but with the help of our Lord, she was not defeated. Assured of her strength and wellbeing, I once again sought employment.

"Another job at Oklahoma Christian opened up in the science department, and, though it wasn't really my specialty, I applied for it. But I had fears, now, because of how saturated Oklahoma had become with casinos. I was offered the job, and, with no other solid prospects, I accepted. But there would be over a dozen casinos within 100 miles of me. Doubt and fear began to plague me as the time drew nearer for my return to the United States, and I spent many sleepless nights lying in bed worrying about if I'd be able to resist the temptations that lay ahead. But God stepped in again.

"One week before I was to leave, I received an email from the dean of science at Harding University. She had heard about me from a friend who knew I'd been job searching, and that friend recommended she contact me. I already had a job and I knew that Arkansas, too, had casinos, but I called her the next day anyway. It was 9am for her but 2am the next morning for me. Sleep deprived and nervous, I attempted the interview, certain that I was botching it at every turn. However, God can accomplish what man can't, and, within a few hours, she emailed me making an official offer of employment."

Drawn in by the win of the underdog, Stem's audience burst into applause once more.

"I'd actually been to Arkansas once before. When I was about eight, my parents and brother and I dug for diamonds in Murfreesboro. I had gone there hoping to find treasures but, unfortunately, we left with nothing but the sweat on our backs and the dirt on our knees. I'd never been on Harding's campus until that first day when I was given a tour and the keys to my new office. As I was settling in, I dropped by the local coffee shop. It was there that I met a man who would become a dear friend."

He gestured towards Russ, who was pleased his own darker complexion mixed with the dim lighting would disguise the blush he felt rising on his face.

"This fellow sitting right here is my best mate, Russell. He's a year younger than me but he and his wife, Katie, became my second set of surrogate parents." Turning towards Russ, he added, "I really look up to you, mate. You're the brother I always wanted."

A man in the back of the gym sporting a leather jacket and a long, shaggy gray beard cupped his hands around his mouth and jeered with obvious humor, "That's crosstalk!"

"Sorry, mate," Stem apologized with a laugh. "Won't happen again."

"You're doing it again!" teased a woman with a voice so like Meemaw's that Russ turned to see what she looked like.

Her appearance was like any other woman who'd had a harder life that had been turned around in her later years. Younger than Meemaw, she was dressed in outdated but decent secondhand garb, with long faux black hair, false eyelashes and nails, and crooked yellow teeth. For reasons he couldn't first say, the sight of her brought a smile to his eyes. Then, it hit him: This might be what his mother would look like today if she were still alive.

Stuck in his own thoughts for a time, Russ missed his friend's next words. But his daze soon faded and he heard Stem say, "My relationship with my father is still rocky, but God is making progress there. And it's been over a year since I gambled and that won't happen again, at least not in Arkansas—and not just because the Arkansas Racing Commission has banned me from returning. But I've got a support group now who I can be open and honest with, who keeps me accountable, and reminds me to go to God for the strength I need.

"I'm not perfect—I mess up like anyone else. I still struggle with my anger and I let it control me at times. And I am still working on eliminating certain words from my vocabulary. And junk food . . . that's an addiction that'll take many years and a lot of God's power to overcome. But what I've learned is that I've got a God who always outshows me. When I make a little mistake, he's there with bigger grace. When I make a huge mistake, he hits me over the head—sometimes literally—and gets me back on the right track, and I don't mean the horse races. And I think my time is up now so I thank you for listening."

The sound of applause drew Russ from his seat to his feet. A strange reverent awe filled him as he watched his friend return to his seat. If Meemaw were there, she'd throw her arms around the young whippersnapper's neck and convey (especially with her eyebrows) how proud of him she was. Inspired, Russ even found himself pulling his friend in for a hug.

Chapter 16

Driving home in the dark and drizzling rain, it was difficult to perceive Stem's thoughts, and Russ somehow felt that, even though he had just learned a whole heck of a lot about the man, he somehow knew him even less than he had at the beginning of the evening.

Clearing his throat, Russ eased into a conversation with him as one might wade into a cold swimming pool. "Hey, man," he began, but the words were hollow and shallow. Trying again, he attempted something a little more heartfelt. "So, you ever go pro with that ballerina thing?"

"Danced in The Nutcracker once. Basically should've won an Oscar but the judging was rigged."

His mate chuckled.

And then there was silence, and Russ really wanted to say something—he almost wanted to burst with so many things at once that he couldn't think of just one to say—but he found the right words elusive. "You know," he began, except he had no clue what he was about to say.

"What?"

Going with the first thought that popped into his head, Russ continued, "Katie and I knew you were up to something on Monday nights."

"Yeah? When did you two figure it out?"

"Probably two summers ago."

"Makes sense. I've only been going to this Celebrate Recovery for about four years, and I know you're slow to figure things out."

"Thanks."

Silence again—almost awkwardly—and Russ hated that because he and Stem had been so comfortable with one another that they'd not experienced a moment of awkwardness in twice as many years as Stem had been sneaking off to the recovery meeting.

"So," said Russ. The wipers needed adjusting and he was grateful to have something to do with his hands, and he also hoped the motion would somehow make Stem forget that he was about to say something but was halted without completing the thought.

"Got something on your mind?" quizzed his friend.

"I just—I'm not sure what to say, is all. Everything you said—I knew almost none of that."

"I'm sorry."

"No, don't be."

"Okay, then I'm not."

After waiting nearly ten seconds, Russ inquired, "Okay, but what were you going to apologize for anyway?"

"I just wanted to tell you that I have wished over the years that I'd been more upfront with you and Katie at first because it seemed, somehow, the longer I hid myself from you two then the harder it was to confess who I really am."

"I definitely get that."

"Are you hurt that I kept so many things from you?"

"Oh, no. Well, maybe a little, but I have no room to judge you. I obviously kept my own secrets too."

"It upset Katie."

"What did? Wait, you told Katie what you said tonight?"

"Sure. Weeks ago, after I finished writing my testimony. She helped me polish it, make it a little more 'personable.' I wanted her to be there tonight too but I knew you'd be the one to go with me."

"I'm sure she was surprised."

"Nevertheless, she was grateful that I was honest with her."

"I am too, man. And getting up there in front of all those people and just laying it all out there—wow. I'm amazed you had the guts to do that."

"Doing that tonight with the group wasn't difficult. They already knew most of it anyway."

"What? Really?"

"Yeah, that's what we do there. Openly communicate with one another about what's going on in our lives. It's therapeutic."

"But aren't you afraid they'll tell what they heard?"

"Tell who?"

"Oh, come on. You know how much the university puts on us professors, morally speaking. We have to sign contracts that we won't do this or that. There's all this pressure to be perfect because people are always watching and our jobs could be in limbo."

"First of all, Harding holds its professors to a high level of conduct. I respect them for not just being a Christian university on paper but, also, implementing, monitoring, and enforcing the proper behavior of their employees."

"Touché."

"Secondly, the recovery meeting is confidential and anonymous." Repeating his earlier sentiments, he added, "Like Fight Club, only better."

"So, you don't think anyone will tell?"

"Exactly what is there to tell, mate? That I've repented of my sins and changed my ways? That I'm human and make mistakes like any other person on this planet? Or maybe that I intermingle with drug users and porn addicts?"

Feeling the pressure to choose the correct multiple choice, Russ replied, "Maybe that last one?"

"Isn't that what Jesus did?"

"Okay, then maybe that one about you making mistakes?"

"As in, I'm a human who needs God's grace? Pretty sure even the dean of the Bible department is in that same boat, yeah?"

"Okay, true, but it just worries me is all. Sometimes people hear things and then they get it twisted and turned and then you've got a mess on your hands."

Resting his hand on the man's shoulder, Stem said, "I appreciate your concern for me, but it's not necessary, I promise. That place back there with Jack, the former alcoholic, and Rosie, the young lady with the eating disorder—it's one of the best things that's ever happened in my life. In fact, I . . ."

"What?"

"I wish I'd told you about it a long time ago, back before Caydee. The *other* Caydee, that is, not *your* Katie. She's great. Love her. But if I'd been honest with you then maybe you wouldn't have, you know, done what you did and screwed your life up."

Russ had to take a break from the conversation for a second to accept and subsequently digest what his passenger had just told him. No doubt, some part of his words had agitated the emotional pain that Russ constantly felt as keenly as needles in his back, but it took him a while to accept that, though they hurt, the words might've actually contained the truth.

"Wait," Russ said at length, "why would that have changed anything, for you to have told me about that group?"

"Because then you could've come with me and worked on your own recovery."

"My *own* recovery? What does that mean? Recovery from *what*? I didn't have any issues until I had an affair."

Stem bellowed out an uncharacteristic guffaw.

"Why are you laughing? You think I've got issues?"

"Mate, everyone has issues. *Everybody.* But some people don't realize it until they've got bigger issues."

"Like me?"

"Precisely."

The accusation didn't sit right with Russ, and he felt his face growing hotter and his seatbelt becoming too tight. Readjusting it, he growled, "Just what do you mean by that?"

After eyeing his friend for a moment, Stem said, "If you really want to know, I'll tell you."

"Yeah!" Russ roared. "Since you're so smart, tell me all the ways I'm flawed! Tell me how your little support group has enlightened you about me!" The silence drew out for almost a mile before Russ said, "Well, what's the matter? You too chicken to say it?"

"No," his friend replied, and his voice was filled with an unusual calmness. "I just needed a minute to cool down so I didn't punch you."

"Cool enough?" Russ goaded. "Or care to punch me?"

"Still thinking it over."

"Yeah, well let me say a few things while you give it a think. Number one: I know I've got issues and I know you've pulled your life together from a lot of crap you've done, but that doesn't make you an expert on what all's wrong with me. Secondly, my life was great until I—"

Months had passed and Russ still couldn't decide what terminology most appropriately defined the commencement of his sexual relationship with Caydee. He'd once tried 'unzipped my pants' but it sounded too crass, and, just for the record, he'd always met up with her at times when he'd told his Katie he was going to the gym so, for every encounter, he'd shown up wearing athletic shorts with an elastic waistband (and he also now admitted to himself that there were well over six occurrences, so Stem definitely would've called it a pattern). But now that Russ had put himself on the spot to define how their relationship began, he froze because, at that exact moment when his mind was stretching back in time to sort out dark places it had roamed in the past, he remembered something he'd either forgotten or stifled—and it filled him with shame.

While his friend was coming to grips with reality, Stem ripped open a bag of licorice and chewed away.

An interminable length of time passed, and, soon enough, they'd reached Stem's house where Russ planned to drop the man off for the night. However, instead of getting out, Russ' friend sat in relative silence save for moments when the sound of his teeth masticating the chewy candy wafted through his thin cheeks.

At last, Russ spoke, and his voice came out quietly, like a shamed boy confessing he'd thrown a baseball through a window. "So . . . maybe I didn't have the perfect life before the other Caydee entered into the picture."

Choosing silence as his form of response, Stem slipped another Twizzler into his mouth.

"So, that day last summer when I found out about Meemaw having a spot on her lungs that they were biopsying for cancer . . . Well, I did something I haven't done in a really long time, since, like, undergrad. Katie was out of town, you remember? She had just left on a weekend trip to Memphis with some of her friends. I'd got the news about Meemaw, and I felt really down. Worried, more like it. And upset. And disappointed, I think. But not in Meemaw, but in myself because I hadn't been taking care of her as well as I had in the past. I'd let her yard grow long. Well, you remember—you even mowed it a time or two for her."

Though he'd actually cut her grass no less than two dozen times, Stem didn't correct his errant friend.

"I should've spent more time helping her. She was getting older, and she started to get that cough, and I'd thought about making her go to the doctor, but honestly, I worried they'd tell her she had lung cancer because you know she smoked like a chimney stack all my childhood. So, I was feeling guilty—guilty when I found out she had a spot on her lungs because I knew . . . I knew she had lung cancer. I just knew it and I hated it and I hated myself for not being there for her, for not driving her to her doctor's appointments and for not filling up her car with gas and taking her out to eat on Sundays after church. I mean, I should've done so much more for her than I had been doing."

If the Miata had not been parked in Stem's driveway, then the two men would've been in a dangerous situation, for tears were running from Russ' eyeballs faster than the rain fell on the windshield. Instinctively knowing they might be sitting there for a while as his friend sorted through his thoughts, Stem reclined his seat and stared up at the black soft top.

"So, like I said, I wasn't feeling great. I felt guilty, plain and simple, for not having been there more for Meemaw. But then, somehow, the thought entered my mind that it was because of my Katie. Yeah, I blamed my not helping Meemaw on Katie because, of course, Katie needed my attention. Well, *you* know—she just needed me more than a lot of wives need their husbands. You know, I liked that, actually, that she needed me to do all these things for her like put away the dishes and carry in the groceries and do the yardwork. All those same things I used to do for Meemaw before I met Katie—and so I blamed my neglect of Meemaw on Katie. And that was wrong. Katie couldn't help—"

As his bottom lip quivered, Stem offered him a strip of licorice which he politely refused, and, instead, he requested his buddy hand him a napkin from his McDonald's bag so he could staunch his tear flow.

"It wasn't Katie's fault that she was hit by that truck, that she was paralyzed." The urge to confess the whole truth about her accident—that is, what *really* happened that day—vied for airspace, but because of the burdensome guilt he constantly carried around, Russ still could not bear to tell a soul even if the soul was his best mate. "But I got this crazy idea in my head after I got off the phone with you that night I found out about Meemaw. I blamed Meemaw's sickness on Katie's need for me to care for her, and, like that one Bible verse says, 'I despised her in my heart.'"

"That's not verbatim."

"I know but it's something like that."

"That was King David's wife, Michal, and she was barren afterwards."

"Was she? That sucks."

"Sure does."

Russ took a deep breath. "So, as if blaming my grandma's cancer on my wife wasn't bad enough, getting back to what I said earlier, I did something that night that I haven't done since undergrad."

"Watched a porno?"

Surprised, he gaped and turned towards his friend. "Yeah, how'd you know?"

"Good guess."

Russ sighed. "That just made me hate myself more, and hate Katie more, since she was out of town and not there to comfort me like she always did so well. And, so, I think I just spiraled downhill after that. I basically binged on porn all weekend, and, after Katie got back, I promised myself I'd never do that again. But kind of like what you said about the casino, that was a lie."

"As almost all white-knuckling promises are."

"What's that mean, white-knuckling?"

"Like you're trying to conquer your problems using only your willpower."

"I guess that's what I was doing. I didn't even want to confess to God what I'd done."

"As if he didn't already know."

"I know—it was dumb. I'm an idiot. And porn led me into thinking that I might want a steamier relationship. Not that there was anything ever wrong with Katie. She was . . . perfect in every way, in that regard, even despite her limited mobility and whatnot. She could still—"

Stem put out his hand to stop his friend. "Don't need details, mate."

"Sure. So, I just started feeling really selfish and kept going back and forth from loving to hating Katie when, really, it was *my* fault Meemaw got cancer. I should've been there and done more for her. I should've made her go to the doctor sooner and not listened to her telling me that the coughing and wheezing were nothing. But the guilt didn't feel good and the porn made it feel better for a time but then it just ended up adding more guilt and shame and confusing me about how I felt about Katie. Do you—do you think she knew?"

"About?"

"That I had blamed her? That I'd talked myself into believing a lie?"

Slowly, Stem processed his thoughts aloud. "I don't know that she ever felt like you had blamed Meemaw's cancer on her, no."

Russ had known the man long enough to know when he was holding something back. Curious what it was, he prodded, "And?"

As he did when he was under emotional duress, Stem devoured whatever food was within sight. The last few Twizzlers went down in record time. "Mate . . . I take my vow of confidentiality very seriously and I would not easily be coerced to break it but . . . searching Katie's words and the circumstances in which she conveyed this particular piece of information to me, and, as I played a role in it myself, I see no reason why it would not be pertinent to share with you what I know, from my own firsthand account."

Bracing himself for the news, Russ felt every muscle in his body tense up.

"Katie discovered your pornography use when you were in Washington, D.C."

His heart rate shot up like a rocket. "She knew about it since last October? But that—that was *before* the other Caydee, well, before the physical part of the affair began, anyway."

"While you were away, she had been planning to renovate your office at work. I was going to help her. She wanted it to be a big surprise, said you'd seemed off lately, since Meemaw's diagnosis, and she wanted to cheer you up and she thought a simple 'spruce up,' as she called it, might have that effect. I didn't bother telling her that you couldn't care less about the color of the walls in your office because the idea made her feel good and I was game to be a part of that. So, right after you left for the airport, she went in to tidy the place up. I was to help her following my afternoon Molecular Physics class."

Seeing the drawn-out story had his friend in agony, he cut to the chase.

"She found your old iPhone in your desk drawer and she logged in and saw what was on the open webpage. She was upset and she begged me to do some additional snooping and discover exactly what it was you'd been looking at. I told her that was a bad idea for both she and me, as I didn't want those images to be stuck in either of our heads. She was, however, insistent that I make certain there was no child pornography."

"I would never look at that," Russ hissed in disgust.

"I know, mate, but the amygdala puts crazy ideas into distraught people's heads sometimes, and she needed the confirmation that you weren't a pedophile, which I did indeed confirm and assure her of."

"Thank you."

"Of course. So, needless to say, the little spruce up didn't occur. She left your office as it was."

"Why didn't you tell me this?"

"The question you should be asking is, 'Why didn't *she*?'"

"I don't know."

"Maybe it was because she was waiting for you to tell her."

"That I'd been jacking off?"

"No, mate," Stem said, sighing mildly to disguise his utter disappointment in his friend's intellect. "That was explicitly obvious to the both of us, I assure you. What she wanted to hear from you was that your heart had changed and you were repentant."

"Crap. I messed that up, didn't I?"

"An understatement, but yes, you did."

"I can't believe—" What he couldn't believe, he actually didn't know, but it sounded like a good enough way to express his profound disappointment in himself. "And then, instead of my heartfelt apology, she heard me confess I'd been having an affair."

"I'm sorry, mate."

Crestfallen, Russ' voice was barely louder than the patter of the rain. "It's not your fault. It's mine."

"True, but I still hate that you're having to undergo the consequences of your own actions. I know from experience how much that sucks. You want to have a cry about it?"

Searching inside his heart, Russ realized he was beyond sadness and grief, for any tears he released now would only be for his own self-pity, and those weren't worth shedding. "No," he said in a pitifully defeated tone. "I just wish you could fix the Time Magnet so I could go back and change the past."

The hand on his shoulder, Stem's gesture of sincerity, felt comforting. "Mate, I've got to poop so I'm going inside. G'night."

Chapter 17

While waiting for the first coat of paint to dry in the extra bedroom, Russ and Stem sat on the hallway floor eating their microwave dinners and wasting time on their phones. Following Stem's request for Russ to add Cheetos to his Walmart delivery order, he pointed to the phone in his friend's hand.

"What the bloody heck are you looking at?"

"Nothing."

"That's Katie's Etsy store, yeah? Mate, you can't stalk the woman. She isn't your wife anymore."

Clutching the phone protectively to his chest, Russ argued, "This isn't stalking. I'm just shopping online." He didn't have to look at Stem to feel the glare the man shot in his direction. Defending himself, he added, "And it's not pornography, anyway, so mind your own business."

"And I suppose you're planning to order something from her, yeah?"

"I'm thinking about it."

"And just where will you have it shipped?" The simple brain inside his mate's head hadn't thought that far into the future. While he searched for an answer, Stem launched another missile into his plan. "And to whom will she address it?"

"I don't know," griped Russ as he crammed his phone into his pocket and stirred congealed gravy into his powdered mashed potatoes. "You're the smart one. Why don't you tell me?"

"Let me see it," he said, waving his fingers.

Though reluctant, Russ handed over his device and pretended to focus on his meal.

"You don't have an Etsy account yet, yeah?"

"Haven't set it up. Do I need one?"

Following several taps and clicks, Stem thrust Russ' phone in his face. "Enter your credit card number."

As he retrieved his wallet from his bedroom, he called, "What'd you do?"

"You're purchasing an oval snakeskin pendant with 16" silver chain and shipping it to a Ms. Heather Hendricks in St. Paul, Minnesota."

"Who's that?"

"Just some random person I found on Google just now."

"Is that even legal?"

"What, to buy jewelry for a perfect stranger? Of course it's legal, and, with luck, Ms. Heather Hendricks will be thrilled when she opens the package."

Russ gaped. "But what if Katie finds out I'm the one who bought the necklace and when she sees I had it sent to some other lady, then she thinks I have another woman?"

A heavy sigh filled the air, and Stem squeezed his eyes shut and breathed slowly and deeply. "First of all, she will never know you purchased it. Secondly—well, that's really all there is to this. All other points are unnecessary."

Minutes later, while Russ poured more paint into the roller pan, Stem reclined in the hallway just outside the bedroom. Within arm's reach was a bag of Fritos, and, as he scanned his social media, a chuckle erupted from him that first sent Fritos spewing across the shag carpet and then had him coughing in fits.

"What's so funny?" quizzed Russ as he worked his roller brush through the paint.

Gripping his chest, Stem sputtered between coughs, "It's just a video AnnaLyn posted of her kids."

"My AnnaLyn?"

"Yeah, mate."

Shortly after light was shed on his infidelity, Russ thought it pertinent to delete all his social media accounts. Partially this severing of ties with online society served to prevent the hate slingers from getting to him. But it also functioned as a form of self-denial which Russ believed he deserved.

"I didn't know you were friends with her."

A guffaw was hurled from his friend's chest (and along with it, moistened bits of Fritos). "Of course I'm friends with her. She's lovely. And her kids' antics are a riot—another reason to love her."

Holding out his hand, Russ requested, "Let me see what they did."

Stem shrunk away from him. "No."

"What? Just let me see."

"I'm not giving you my phone."

"Really? Because wasn't it just ten minutes ago that you took mine and bought something with my credit card and sent it to some lady I don't even know?"

Relenting, he sighed, "Oh, fine. Here."

The video likewise brought a chuckle to Russ, who dutifully relinquished the phone the second it ended. "Funny kids," he remarked. "Crazy how fast they grow. And I didn't even realize she had four now."

"Mate, the baby's three years old."

Russ tossed up a shrug as he lifted the roller. A few drops of paint trickled onto the floor.

"Watch the carpet!" Stem exclaimed.

"Afraid I'll drip paint on the Fritos you coughed all over it?"

"Who'll buy a house with painted carpet?"

"I'm gonna replace it before I list the house."

"What?" The devastation in his friend's tone filled the room. "You're getting rid of Meemaw's special rug? But she handpicked this herself in the '70s."

"Which is exactly why it needs replaced." As the argument clearly didn't live up to Stem's standards, Russ added, "You think some couple's gonna want their babies crawling around on this nasty old wool shag?"

"But *you* lie on it."

"That's because I'm used to it. I've lived with it for thirty years. But I wouldn't put *my* baby on it."

"What baby?"

"Just a hypothetical baby."

Relieved, Stem sighed. "Bugger. I thought maybe you hadn't told me something."

The possibility of getting the other Caydee pregnant had never crossed his mind—until now.

"Well, crap," uttered Russ. "Thanks for giving me something *else* to worry about."

"Don't give me that look. I'm not the one who got her up the duff."

As he mindlessly worked the light gray color into the grooves between the wood paneling strips, the possibility of producing a child with his mistress rekindled a source of grief for Russ.

When Katie had the accident—when the truck struck her and nearly took her life—her body was left never the same. Though a skilled nurse, she would never walk another rotation on her feet. And her reproductive parts had not fared any better—to save her life and prevent her from bleeding to death, surgeons performed a hysterectomy. In that one single, horrible moment, her life completely changed.

She and Russ had considered adoption, but Katie always came back to one point. Would she make a good mother? More specifically, could a child depend on her to care for them? Sure, she could teach piano lessons to a dozen young students each week in their home. And she could cook and clean and perform most tasks any mother could. But the tragic accident which stole her previous mobility had also permanently affected her endurance level. Whereas before the accident she could work a 12-hour shift and then go for a six-mile jog around town, now an outing to the grocery store or church sometimes left her wilted for hours. She'd never said so to Russ but he knew she feared that their adopting a child would put too much pressure on him. As it was, he already spent an abundance of his time caring for his wife. Though Russ had assured Katie that he wanted to raise children with her, she'd always concluded it was a blessing not meant for them . . . not meant for her, anyway.

But what if he'd gotten the other Caydee pregnant? When his Katie found out . . . The news would be heartbreaking.

"Mate?" Stem called from across the room.

"Huh?" said Russ. In his hands, the roller brush caressed the pan of paint, and he repeated the motions absentmindedly. Easing down into the thick, gray liquid. Rolling. Slowly pulling up. Pressing against the grooves in the pan floor. Gliding down again.

"Mate, we're done with the second coat."

The aloof expression on Russ' face was akin to some Stem had witnessed years ago in his brother's care—Hollywood's best and brightest upcoming stars, mellow from intoxicating substances.

"Russell?"

"Huh?"

Reaching out, Stem took the roller from the man's hand. "Fumes have got to you, yeah? Why don't you take a break outside for a few minutes? I'll cover the paint and brushes."

A few minutes later, he found Russ sitting on the steps of the back stoop, slouched, his elbows resting on his thighs. Beneath him, the concrete revealed its age through cracks and chips. Finding his own spot amongst them, Stem sat beside his friend, the feet on the end of his lanky legs resting one step lower than Russ'.

"What's on your mind?" he inquired as he handed over an icy cold water bottle.

"Nothing," Russ lied. Then, under his friend's glare, he confessed. "It's just that stupid thing you said."

"Must have me confused with some other bloke."

"About me getting the other Caydee pregnant."

His friend sighed. “You can hardly afford alimony. Poor baby will have to get on food stamps.”

“She’s not pregnant. At least, I think she would’ve told me if she was.”

“Text her and ask.”

“I can’t do that.”

“Why not?”

He shrugged. “Guess I could.”

“Well, go on, then,” goaded Stem. “Text your baby mama.”

Russ pulled out his phone and quickly thumbed a message: *Are you pregnant?*

Glancing over his shoulder, Stem disparaged, “That’s it? This shamed girl may be secretly carrying your lovechild and *that’s* what you’re going to send to her?”

“What, do you have something better?”

For a moment, Stem gave off the vibe that his mate was nothing but a fool. At length, however, he relinquished. “Not really. Just send it.”

Russ executed the command, irrevocably delivering the message.

“Says she got it,” he said, almost fretting. “What am I gonna do if she *is* pregnant?”

“I guess, name the thing and slap a nappy on it.”

“I’m serious.”

“So am I. Have you seen how much babies pee and poo? And that tarlike substance which newborns defecate liberally—it’s no joke. They don’t care if you’re wearing an Armani suit, not that you would be. They’ll mark it faster than a dog.”

The chiming phone in Russ’ pocket made his eyebrows raise in alarm. “That’s her text tone. Check it. Check it for me, please.”

“I’m not gonna fish the thing out of your pants like some pickpocket. Hand it to me then.”

Like a game of hot potato, Russ quickly withdrew the device and threw it in his friend’s lap.

“Bugger!” Stem exclaimed.

Jumping to his feet, Russ cried, "What?"

Turning the phone around for the man to see, he chided, "You still haven't fixed your bloody screen!"

"Quit jacking around and read me the text!"

Clearing his throat, Stem paused to read the message to himself.

Agonizing, Russ gnawed a fingernail between his teeth. "Is it bad?"

Stem cast him a sideways glance and confessed, "Well, it's not good."

"Crap! What'd she say?"

"She said . . . 'Is this Dan?'"

"What?" Russ roared. Ripping the phone from the man's hands, he read the words himself.

"Who's Dan?" inquired Stem.

"I have no idea!"

"All I'm saying is you need to get a verified paternity test before you pay any child support."

A few seconds later, Russ shot a reply back. Then, shoving the phone in Stem's hands, he instructed, "Here, hold this. Let me know the minute she responds."

Within thirty seconds, his agony was turned to joy. "Oh, thank you, Lord!" he cried with hands lifted to the dimming sky.

Handing him the phone, Stem asked, "You figure out who Dan was?"

"No, and I don't care. I'm done. All ties are broken."

"You apologized to her, yeah?"

Diverting his eyes, Russ admitted, "Well, no, not yet. But I will."

Stem shook his head. "Do it now, mate. I'm telling you—the longer an amends is put off, the harder it is to make." Rising to his feet, he announced, "I'll go check on the second coat, see if it's ready for the third. You, take your time wording that apology."

Thirty minutes later, as the moon rose over Searcy, Russ returned to the house.

"Get that text sent?" questioned Stem, and there was an

unmistakable trace of warning in his tone.

"No, I called her. And apologized. She spoke her peace and that's that."

As a smile swept across his face, the physicist found himself speechless.

"Proud of me?"

Stem rested a confident hand on the man's shoulder. "I'm beaming with so much pride for you, mate . . . that I'm going to let you do the last coat yourself."

Russ feigned offense as his buddy shoved the roller brush into his hand. "No way—you're gonna help me with it."

Backing slowly out of the bedroom doorway, Stem teased, "No, you're a big boy now, mate, what with a pregnancy scare and all. I'll just get out of your way and let you take charge."

"Oh, yeah?" Russ challenged.

Seeing that the playful side of his friend had been roused, Stem could not hold back a grin. "You can manage this simple task without me breathing down your neck. I've got all confidence in you."

Just as Stem bolted down the hallway, Russ took off after him, roller in hand. "Get back here!"

"You've got this, mate!" Stem hollered as he thrust open the sliding door. Though his strides were longer, Russ' shorter, more athletic legs pumped quicker. Jumping off the back stoop, the pursuer attacked the chased, and, for a couple of minutes, the pair wrestled in the yard like ten-year-old brothers. Out of breath, they rolled onto their backs and heaved deeply.

"I'm getting too old for that," Russ sighed between breaths.

"You painted my hair, you egg!"

The laughter emanating from his mate spurred a second wave of friendly attacks, this time with the Aussie in pursuit.

Ten minutes later, the pair sat, shag under bottom, their backs leaned against the living room wall. Stem sported a bag of frozen hashbrowns on his right shoulder while Russ doctored a busted lip.

"We should do that more often," stated the latter.

"Definitely," agreed Stem.

"You ready to knock out that last coat?"

Climbing to his feet, he shook his head. "No, I'm heading home."

"Yeah, well, go home and wash your hair. This is a job for men anyway."

When he reached the front door, Stem shrugged. "Sling mud all you want, but while you're up painting past midnight, I'll be asleep."

By pulling the door shut quickly, he just managed to miss the bag of frozen hashbrowns which Russ hurled in his direction along with the warning, "Keep an ice pack handy! You're gonna need it!"

Chapter 18

The occasional sporadic birthday card notwithstanding (especially since it usually arrived in January rather than July), Russ could count on one hand the number of times his father had reached out to him since he passed the threshold into manhood. As best he could remember, it had been seven years since he had seen the man. The last time, he had met Russ and Katie in Memphis at Bass Pro Shop, where he spent the majority of their hour together snapping photos of the captive alligators and ogling a young female employee who worked in the fishing section. However, besides that one-hour interruption in their trip, Russ and Katie had thoroughly enjoyed the weekend getaway to one of their favorite cities. In fact, Katie's presence was more or less what had eased the pain of another disappointing encounter with the man who had had a brief relationship with Russ' mother so many years ago. With his wife's help, Russ had concluded that he had made it this far in life without his father's help or support, and, though he could've used some of the man's intervention in the earlier years of his life, he was now well above the need.

Nevertheless, on those extremely rare occasions when Pat Khurana contacted his oldest child, Russ suddenly felt a garden of butterflies soar in his stomach, and his mind became seized with silly thoughts of tossing a football in the yard or sitting up late playing a game of Risk with the man—and thus he found himself on that Monday morning when he received a text from his dad which read, "Passing through Little Rock this evening. Wanna meet up for dinner?"

Russ agonized over his response for nearly an hour. That he'd reply in the positive, there was no doubt, however he found his ability to type a satisfactory message (at least by his own standards) a thing of great difficulty. At last, with trembling hands, he dashed off the luminous words: "Sounds good. What time and place?"

Texts from his dad, who claimed he was driving his family across the country on a road trip, trickled in slowly throughout the day. News that Russ' two younger half-brothers would be in tow nearly thrilled him. He'd never met the boys in person, and, yet, he at once envisioned the three brothers and their father in matching sports gear all rooting on the Razorbacks from the grandstands (which he knew was completely absurd since the three were from Washington state, but he indulged the fantasy nevertheless).

Hoping to keep his nerves in check by occupying his hands, he spent the afternoon washing and waxing the Miata. All the while, his mind reeled with ridiculous notions of how pleased his father would be with the way he'd polished up his car, and he strained his brain to concoct funny things to casually throw into their upcoming conversation.

When the hour arrived, Russ ventured forty-five minutes south and pulled into the Capital Hotel's parking lot where he shoveled out $25 for valet parking. Soon, he stepped into the Capital Bar and Grill and spied his father upon a barstool with a martini glass in hand.

"Russell!" the man crowed with outstretched arms. "My boy! Come here!"

The long-awaited embrace was warm enough to make Russ feel slightly boozy. Beaming, he greeted, "Hi, Dad. Good to see you again."

"Have a seat, son!" said his father, and he patted the stool beside his. "You want a drink? I'm just getting started with a little espresso martini myself."

To the attentive bartender, Russ requested, "Just a vanilla Dr. Pepper, thanks."

"Ah," said his dad, poking his side. "Come on, son. You're my only child who's a *real* man. Throw one back with me. Bartender, give my boy, here, a screwdriver. Grey Goose and fresh squeezed."

Though Harding's strict teetotaler rule for profs and their households had occasionally irked Katie, who liked to celebrate special occasions with a glass of champagne, Russ had never been miffed by it. By his own account, he hated consuming alcohol because it always left him with a headache. His father, however, overrode his polite refusal, stating, "No son of mine is gonna snub my hospitality. Now, let's drink up!"

Giving in (and figuring one glass wouldn't work up any aches), Russ threw back the orangey concoction and winced as the sour bite slid down his throat.

"Pretty good, huh?" his dad grinned. Surmising his son's expression indicated an aversion to citrusy drinks, he snapped his fingers and called, "Bartender, give my boy a Brandy Alexander, heavy on the cream. It'll go down smoother that way. You'll like this one better, son."

"I really shouldn't have any more," Russ declined.

"You know, everywhere I go, I always tell people how proud I am of my son. 'Did you know my son's a college professor?' I tell people that. Yes, I brag about you all the time. 'Here's a picture of my son, the spitting image of me,' and it's right here on my phone. Of course, people can see right away you're my boy. You always have favored me." Taking the Brandy Alexander from the bartender, the man slid it across to his companion. "Now, let's drink up. This time to your career. My son, Dr. Khurana!"

Russ' face flushed, both from the alcohol and from his father's erroneous assumption that he shared his last name (though his son had been a Brown since birth, Pat always conveniently overlooked this fact). But instead of correcting the man, Russ bore a second assault to his throat, noting that this time the concoction was actually quite smoother than the first.

"Where're the boys?" he questioned as he glanced around.

"Oh," said his father, tossing a dismissive wave of his hand. "Sam and Philip stayed behind at the hotel to swim. You know teenage boys—always wanting to have fun."

To hide his disappointment, Russ asked the first question which popped into his brain. "So, you're not staying here?"

"At the Capital?" said his father, glancing around. "No, too high and mighty, if you ask me. We're cozied up for the night at the Holiday Inn Express down the road." Disdainfully, he added, "And you know how cheap women are—Pamela refuses to stay at any hotel that doesn't serve free breakfast."

Russ nodded as though he knew that all women were cheapskates—and he immediately felt riddled with remorse, as if he'd betrayed all womankind by the churlish gesture. Just as he was about to ask how his father's wife was doing, his dad interrupted.

"You really won't believe when I tell you what's happened," chirped Pat. "I'm the president."

"Of?"

"My own company, of course. Yes, your father—me—I'm running a company now."

"Wow, Dad. That's great."

"DenForce! I presume you've heard about it?" As Russ was contemplating whether to lie and say he had or to confess that he was completely in the dark about the business, his father continued. "Come on, son. We're the newest on the stock exchange. Don't you keep up with the times? No, I suppose you don't since all you study is history!" The man laughed at his own joke. "But I'll fill you in on what you've missed. We are set right now to overtake Sysware. Can you believe that? You ought to because you're looking at the man leading the pack in software technology. I'm telling you—buy a hefty share now and you'll thank me later."

With the way his father commanded his one raised eyebrow as he stared down his son, Russ suddenly wondered if he'd inherited malleable eyebrows from both his parentals.

"What do you say, my boy? Are you in?"

"Into what?"

"Aren't you going to invest in your old man? Here, pull it up on your phone." Taking the device from his son, he guffawed at the cracked screen. "Clumsy, I see, just like your brother, Sam!"

The discovery of his similarity to his younger half-brother filled Russ with enough joy to overlook the insult.

"Now, look here," said his dad, pulling a pair of bifocals from the breast pocket of his Polo. "DENF. That's my company." Flashing the screen at his son, he fished for compliments. "Not bad, huh? Stock rose three points today. You see, this company is practically running itself. Never been a more secure stock—or a better time to invest. What do you say? Best decision you'll ever make!" Reading the hesitation on his son's face, Pat called, "Bartender, another round for the both of us, please."

Russ' mind was already spinning a little with the alcohol he'd consumed, and he silently prayed a headache would not ensue. But as he tossed back another Brandy Alexander, he felt the familiar ache setting in. "No more," he said, pushing the empty glass away. "I'm finished."

Pat gave his son a sideways glance, almost disdainfully. "Can't hold the alcohol like your old man, though, huh? Well, your mother never could either. She was no fun to take to bars. Always left droopy and drab—crying, usually. Guess alcohol has that effect on you too, huh? Makes you all teary-eyed and blubbery?"

Russ shook his aching head. "Just gives me a migraine."

"Oh, nothing a little hair of the dog won't cure," Pat dismissed. "Try an espresso martini. The caffeine will zap that in no time."

Resting his temple on his fist, Russ murmured, "I need something to eat." After perusing a menu through fuzzy vision, he ordered a plateful of french fries because he'd once been told in college that the starch would help absorb the alcohol more quickly. "And a glass of water, please," he tossed at the waitress as she headed out of sight.

Calling his son's attention back to the cracked screen, Pat ordered, "Now, here—download this app. Schwab Mobile. That's it. Click that button. Okay, now get your account set up."

Russ rubbed his eyes but the fuzziness remained. "I can't do it right now."

"Oh, nonsense," the man laughed. "Here, I'll type it for you." After creating a login and password, Pat said, "Now, I'm setting up facial recognition."

At that moment, the waitress arrived with a heaping plate of steak fries and a bottle of Heinz.

"Water?" Russ requested, taking the plate. "Can I get some, please?"

The distraction of the food was enough to get his father's nerves a pinch riled up. Forcing a chuckle, he said, "Okay, enough with the dilly-dallying. Look at your phone." Though bleary-eyed and sporting ketchup on his lip, Russ' image was recognized by the device. "Good, now let's set up your funds. You know your banking account number, I presume."

As he devoured the end of a french fry, the inebriated man reached for his phone and questioned, "Wait, what are you doing?"

"Son, trust this old, wise man—this'll be the best decision you make for your future. Investing in DenForce is a fail-safe plan. A return on your investment in spades. All you've got to do is fill in a few little blanks."

Russ squinted to read the small words on the phone.

"Right there," said Pat, his finger hovering over the screen. "Banking account and then you're connected."

"I don't know—"

"Gosh, it's good to see you again!" interrupted his dad, gazing at him with affection. "Being with you makes me happier than a bulldog in heat. Let's drink to this moment, son." Raising his glass, Pat downed another espresso martini. Seeing his son's hesitation to imbibe another drink, he chided, "Now, don't be a wet blanket. Tonight's all about us celebrating. Our bond. Our careers. Our dashing good looks. Caution has no place at this table, I assure you that."

Though stone-cold drunk, Russ still felt suspicions creep into his head. Investing in a company he knew nothing about didn't seem prudent. However, his drunken mind played tricks on him. Didn't Stem recently ask him to type his credit card number into his phone? And didn't Stem also ask him to buy shares in the pastry tart factory? Russ wasn't even sure the pastry tart factory traded in shares but he'd promised his friend he'd buy some. So, why was he hesitant to trust his dad?

As if reading his mind, Pat said, "Son, I'm your own flesh and blood, the man who supplied half your DNA. If you can't trust me then who *can* you trust? I'm only looking out for your good here. I only want what's best for you, my boy."

That little part of Russ that had always longed for his father's approval suddenly jumped behind the wheel.

"Yeah," he said with a smile.

The man rested a proud hand on his son's back. "That's my boy! A spitting image of me, you are. Let's have another drink to celebrate! We're just two wise businessmen making solid financial choices for our futures. Now, enter your account number here."

Though Russ could not remember his account number, his phone remembered his face and that was enough for his dad to walk him through the steps of accessing the information he required for the task.

"Excellent!" Pat exclaimed. "Now, I know this may seem like a big number, but you're a strong young man with many years ahead of you, no children, nothing holding you back. But I'll bet you'd like to retire young, am I right? Who wants to be old like me and still working, huh? So, let's get you invested for $50,000. Surely an economical man like you has such a meager amount at his disposal."

"I've got some money," Russ assured his father.

The man's eyes sparkled as he chuckled. "Good sense of humor too. Spitting image of me, you are!"

In a few short minutes, both Russ' plate of fries and his bank account were depleted.

"Best decision you've ever made," his father assured him. Then, glancing at his phone, the man rose from his barstool. "Nice seeing you, son. I've got some business to tend to."

The pair walked to the hotel lobby, though for Russ it felt more like finding his way through a maze of mirrors.

"Better call your DD, son," warned Pat. "Don't want my boy getting himself in a twist."

"You can drive me?"

"I'm gonna sober up here for a couple of hours with a little friend of mine I'm meeting upstairs." His wink conveyed more than Russ' brain could comprehend at the moment. "See you later, son." After a quick hug, the man disappeared into an elevator.

A sofa in the lobby caught Russ' derriere as he sunk down into a woozy, headaching mess. Pulling out his phone, he struggled to find Stem's number. With some persistence, the man at last answered.

"Mate, the fact that you know I'm in my recovery meeting and yet you've rang me *six times* in a row can only mean one of two things: you're in a dire situation and need me to rescue you or you're sitting on your phone. Now which is it?"

"Just wondering if you could carry me home," Russ slurred.

"Well, that doesn't sound good," remarked his compadre with a sigh. "You somewhere safe for the moment, mate?"

"At the hotel. The big old one."

"All right, just let me just put that into my GPS. 'The big old hotel.' Welp, sorry, mate. Google can't identify those search parameters, so you'll have to give me more to go on."

Glancing around, Russ struggled to remember the name of the building. Calling out to the lady working at the front desk, he hollered, "Where is this place?"

Stem could hear some dialogue being conversed between the drunken man and others in the vicinity.

"Markham," Russ said at last. "West Street. Of the Markham."

Searching Safari, Stem murmured, "West Street of the Markham. Big old hotel."

"Little Rock!" interjected his friend.

"What are you doing there?"

"My dad was here. He's upstairs getting laid."

"All right," Stem said slowly. "And you went on a bender, yeah?"

"I had one or two of 'em."

"That was an interesting decision you made, mate, considering you hate drinking."

"My dad ordered. I got french fries."

"I see. And what did he want to meet you about?"

"Some . . . well, my brothers didn't come. They're—they're swimming . . ."

"Hmmm . . ." said Stem contemplatively. "Well, let me see if I can find you. Now, we've got Markham House Suites, but that's neither old nor particularly big. And Little Rock Marriott. Oh, wait! You there at Capital Hotel, mate?"

"At the Capital," Russ concurred. "In the bar."

"Okay, pay your tab and leave the bar. Go to the hotel lobby. Fall asleep in a chair. I'll come find you."

An hour later, Stem located his friend on the mezzanine, curled up on the carpet in a corner behind a baby grand piano.

"Up with you, mate," said the DD as he pulled on the drunk's arm.

Droopy-eyed and wincing, Russ offered a small complaint. "My head hurts."

"It's because ethanol is a diuretic," Stem said with a sigh. "And as it breaks down inside your body, it releases acetaldehyde which is a highly toxic carcinogen."

"But it's hurting," whined Russ.

"I'll bet it is. Have something hard? Rum? Red wine?"

"All the brandy."

"All of it, yeah? Then it's no wonder you've got a splitting headache, mate. That dark liquor has a very high congener content." As he walked the man to the elevator, he explained, "Those little toxins produced during the fermentation of the alcohol stimulate your body to release epinephrine and norepinephrine. That nasty little duo will make you feel like crap, not to mention the fact that both congeners and ethanol must be broken down in the body which creates a very unfriendly competition in your liver."

"Does that happen?"

Tossing him a wink, he assured, "It's happening right now."

"Can I pee?"

"You want to go to jail, yeah?"

"Am I going to jail?"

"Probably are, if you pee in this elevator."

As they stepped out, Russ glanced around. "Where are we? Is this church?"

"This is the Capital Hotel, mate."

"Meemaw said we can't go to church drunk."

Stem patted his friend's cheek. "A wise woman, she was."

As they shuffled across the lobby, Russ pointed. "In that plant?"

"Can't pee there either."

In the lobby restroom, Stem assisted his friend as far as he dared.

"I'm not holding it for you," he objected. "You do that yourself. Aim it. Higher." Sensing his directions would go disastrously ignored, Stem pointed at the deodorizing tablet in the urinal and instructed, "See that green thing in there? Pee on it."

His mate wore an expression which conveyed his confusion. "What if they're mad about it?"

"Oh, they won't be."

"They'll like that?"

"Yes, they'll be very happy with you. They'll erect statues in your honor. Now pee on it."

For following directions, Stem would've given Russ a B+, noting that while his aim was quite accurate, ten percent was deducted from the final grade because the drunken man led his appendage into retreat before the job was quite finished.

"Now zip up and wash your hands," Stem said with disgust. "And do you need to vomit before we get in the car?"

An hour later, Stem pulled the Miata into Russ' driveway. Shutting off the engine, he contemplated whether to leave the sleeping drunk in the car or haul him into the house. Because summer was already getting on quite well and he knew the car would be hot enough to bake his poor friend by as early as 10:00 in the morning, he opted for the latter (though some passive aggressiveness vied for him to ignore conventional wisdom and let the man suffer his own consequences).

"Okay, out we go," he said, dragging Russ from the car. The three steps leading up to the front stoop were the hardest challenge he'd faced that evening, and he was grateful he'd had the foresight to unlock the deadbolt and prop the screen door open before hoisting his friend across the yard.

"Here's your bed, mate," sighed Stem as he lowered the man onto it.

"Am I home?" mumbled Russ.

"Yeah, you're home."

"Where's Katie? Is she all right?"

"She's okay."

"I wanna kiss her."

Stem pulled the blanket up over his friend. Then, with a sigh, he assured, "I'm working on it, mate."

Chapter 19

Russ spent several hours the next morning beating himself up for all the stupidity he'd indulged in (both the evening before as well as upon countless other occasions). His visit with his father had gone disastrously, and he blamed himself for even agreeing to meet up with the man. Why must he always feel compelled to jump when Pat Khurana calls? Why did he covet the attention of a man who had spent the better part of his life ignoring his existence? The one thing in the whole of the encounter that he did not regret was that he had sobered up soon enough to stop the money transfer from his bank account. The DenForce president would have to find another chump to fund his endeavors.

The pounding on the front door only aggravated Russ' headache.

"Coming!" he shouted at the top of his lungs, which he immediately and acutely regretted as it sent waves of pulsating pressure through his temples.

"Bloody heck," Stem exclaimed the second he was permitted to enter the house. "What have you been doing?"

"Sleeping," Russ snapped.

"I instructed you in my text to call me in the morning, and we are decidedly well into the second half of the day."

"No, you said to call when I got around. Well, guess what? I'm not around yet!"

Stem was hot on Russ' heels which stomped the shag carpet with a vengeance as he retreated to his bedroom. Amazon had come in clutch with the replacement air mattress for the first one that had a hole in it, and Russ plopped down on his new bed like a walrus in winter.

"So, you're going to waste the day away in bed, yeah?" When his friend covered his head with his pillow, Stem scoffed. "Is this because of your hangover or the fact that you made an idiot of yourself last night?"

"Both."

"I take it dinner with Daddy didn't go well."

Russ took a full ten seconds before answering. "It went fine if you exclude the fact that he almost suckered me for $50,000."

Stem whistled. "So, you got hammered to celebrate the occasion of an enormously foolish financial decision, yeah?"

"No," Russ grouched. "I got hammered because, once again, I was seeking the approval of a ghost."

"A useless endeavor, if ever there was one." Though he understood the pain his friend experienced because of daddy issues, he wasn't one to indulge self-pity. "Fine, then. I won't tell you the shocking discovery I made this morning about Peepaw's not particularly cryptic notation in the margins of his time travel log."

Though he'd calculated that the sharing of this clickbait would draw Russ out of the grave he so clearly was digging for himself, Stem was disappointed to discover that the man had no intention of leaving the bed—ever. However, it was to his further disappointment that he never got the chance that afternoon to initiate his hastily concocted 'get Russ out of bed' plan, which was to begin with a drop elbow move right onto his mate's stomach. Just as he was bracing his elbow for maximum impact, the pillow rolled off the face of the dejected ex-husband and he said rather gravely, "Leave me here to die. But first tell me what you found."

With a frown and a disappointed sigh, Stem lowered his arm.

"All right. I did some research and located a man who worked in the same machine shop as Peepaw, and you'll never guess his name."

"Hank?"

"No. Unthinkably, it's Honk."

A smile appeared on his friend's face.

"Don't look so triumphant," said Stem with noted bitterness. "I am, after all, the one who located said individual."

"Yeah, and how'd you find ole Honk?"

"I paid a visit to an exclusive, members-only edifice boasting an incredible collection of lucrative information." In response to his friend's expression of confusion, he clarified, "The library. They had microfiche of old newspapers dating back to Peepaw's disappearance. In one of the last articles written about him, a man named Honk—which, in all likelihood, is his *nick*name—was quoted as saying, 'I doubt Larry is ever coming back. He was smart enough to disappear for good.' From that succinct statement alone, I've identified at least half a dozen supporting elements to indicate he was a close cohort of one Larry Brown, aka Peepaw."

"So, is he still alive?"

"I can't be certain, but I may have located his current or possibly former address. If you'll tart yourself up and take some Tylenol, then we can drive over there and see for ourselves."

Less than an hour later, the two paused at a four-way stop. Smiling at the homegrown feed supply store on the corner which had been planted in a rustic downtown building decades earlier, Stem observed with noted cheer, "Bradford seems like a pleasant community to visit."

Two eyebrows shot up as Russ mumbled, "If you're looking for meth."

Casting him a sideways glance, Stem assessed, "You seem suspiciously self-assured on that fact, mate."

A few seconds passed before he confided, "It's where my mom got hers. Well, the last place she got it, anyway." Ignoring the map app on Stem's phone, Russ took a brief detour. Soon, slowing for a moment, he pointed at a cluster of dilapidated trailer houses sitting amidst tetanus-laiden debris. "See those? My mom and I lived there once. With her boyfriend, a meth dealer. He was . . . a really bad guy."

Stem offered a pat on his friend's shoulder, and this time it was to convey his sympathy. "Sorry, mate. Sometimes life sucks."

"Yep," was Russ' only reply.

Five minutes later, the Miata pulled down a gravel drive that headed off blindly into a wooded area which emitted an aura of questionable safety.

"You sure this is it?" quizzed the driver.

"This is what was listed online."

Gently pressing the gas, Russ proceeded with caution down the winding trail. Soon, the gravel fizzled out and the car bobbed across a series of deep ruts that seemed strategically placed to cause maximum damage to a trespassing vehicle. At last, they emerged into a small clearing surrounded by a chain link fence. In the enclosure were an older but decent looking double wide trailer and five dogs of varying breeds and sizes who guarded the place with ferocious vigilance.

At Russ' shutting off the engine, Stem bore a look of surprise. "What are you doing?"

"Parking."

"But what about the dogs? How will we get to the house to see if he's home?"

"Trust me—if anyone's home, they already know we're here."

Weighing his options, Russ decided the safest, should the dogs manage to pull a Houdini maneuver, was to remain in the car. Rolling the window down, he cupped his hands around his mouth and hollered, "Hello? Anybody home?"

For a stretch of time, it appeared that their venture to the backwoods of Bradford had been in vain. However, barreling down the dusty trail behind the Miata came a rusty battered farm truck sporting a cattle grille. Though Russ was in the process of getting his car out of the way, the pickup whipped around them and parked alongside the fence.

"Are we safe?" whispered Stem.

"No clue."

Exiting the driver's door of the truck first came an orthopedic tennis shoe followed by an overall-clad man who qualified as both bariatric and geriatric. While his audience watched, awed by his impossible agility, the truck's occupant waddled over to the Miata. Through the open window, Russ gaped at the fellow. The voice which exited his mouth was winded and perplexingly high pitched. Between breaths, he rasped, "You lost, boy?"

"Yes, sir," replied Russ, who had not yet recovered his wits.

"Then, y'all git on outta here."

"Wait!" called Russ as he jumped out and hustled after the man who was already in retreat. "Wait, we—my friend and I—" and he pointed at Stem "—we're looking for a guy named Honk. Are you him or do you know him? It's important we find him."

Russ' approach had not shaken the man's determination to return to the comfort of his memory foam gel-cooled seat cushion liner. After he'd got into position, he questioned, "Why's that?" and it came out sounding almost like he'd whistled it.

"Because, sir, I think he may have worked with my Peepaw."

"Peepaw? What's that?"

"My grandpa. Larry Brown."

At the sound of the name, an unmistakable darkness shadowed the man's face. "Got the wrong fella, boy."

Now, beyond a doubt, Russ knew this was the man they were seeking, and, with thoughts of how the Time Magnet could save his marriage, he desperately searched his brain to solve the dilemma. At last, he exclaimed, "42B!"

Having just put the truck into reverse, the man pressed the brake and slowly turned to face the irritating nosybody at his window.

Russ half expected the man to ask, "What did you say?" however, no words exited his mouth.

"We've found it," explained Russ. "My friend—he's a scientist. He's working to repair it but we've ran into some issues and would like your advice or help on solving them. Please, sir."

Honk (for that's who Russ was dealing with) lifted the farmers co-op ballcap with two fingers and scratched his balding head with the other three. Then, resetting it upon his crown, he leaned towards the open window and sent a line of skoal whizzing past Russ, narrowly missing his shoulder by an inch. Russ had seen men chew tobacco, but the way Honk masticated the dip, he would have thought the man was trying to win a jerky eating contest.

Throwing his thumb over his shoulder, Honk instructed, "Open that fence, son."

Given the ferocious dogs on the other side of the chain length, it took no small amount of bravery to enable Russ to obey the order, and he had to keep reminding himself that this would all end well and the Time Magnet would get fixed and he'd soon have Katie back in his arms and he'd not be mauled in the backwoods of Arkansas by a rabid pack of dogs.

Remarkably, all went well. The dogs, though overly curious about the smell of Russ' posterior, proved amiable hosts. To Stem, they were less friendly but perfectly genial, nonetheless. The two men endured the body sniffing and wagging tails beating against their legs while Honk pulled his truck as near to the front steps as was possible according to what was currently known about modern physics.

As Honk teetered up the wooden steps which led to the door of his trailer, anxiety rose in his guests. While one was certain he'd topple backwards and they'd have to hire a crane to right him, the other feared he'd bust through the deck boards, which would also require a crane. However, the octogenarian who had ambled on those legs for many years was perfectly aware of their limits, as well as those of the wooden planks. Alas, the guests soon followed their host into his living room, and, while Honk cranked on the window air conditioner unit, Russ and Stem were subjected to a second full body sniff, this time by the house dog, an elderly Great Pyrenees who took the job as seriously as a TSA officer.

The second Honk plopped into a heavy-duty recliner, he gave

the order, “Sit!” and, though it was meant for the dog, both men acceded his request and promptly planted their rear ends on the worn love seat across the coffee table.

“Y’all’s a funny bunch,” said their host as he reached for a mini-fridge which had been strategically located at arm’s length from his easy chair. “Mr. Pibb?”

Still ailing from a headache, Russ accepted the caffeine boost and chugged the drink like an underage boy at a frat party.

His friend, however, refused all forms of caffeinated beverage unless it was V Energy Drink or high-quality coffee, and he replied with a polite, “No, thank you.” However, sensing some kind of unspoken disapproval from both his buddy and host, Stem changed his mind. Taking the cooled can from the man, Stem indulged as ascetically as a puritan in the sack.

Pleased at their actions, Honk folded his hands and rested them on his chest. “Don’t get many guests,” he whistled between breaths. “Most folks won’t brave my dogs. Ain’t gonna hurt nobody. Just a bunch of sissies.”

“Who?” questioned Stem. “Your guests or the dogs?”

Sizing up the lanky man who, though tall, gave off no intimidating vibes, Honk replied, “Reckon both.” Turning his eyes to Russ, the man questioned, “You really Larry’s boy?”

“His grandson, yes,” he corrected. “Russell Brown.”

Honk had a slow way of conversing that almost made it appear as though he’d entirely forgotten he was entertaining guests. At length, he rasped out another question. “You adopted?”

“No, sir. I’m his daughter’s biological son. But I’m a spitting image of my father, evidently, and his parents are from India, so that’s why I look like I do.”

After a long draw on his soda, the large man asked, “He had a few daughters. Which’uns your mama?”

Despite the subject’s unpleasantries, Russ indulged the man’s wishes to carry it forth. “His middle one, Lisa.”

“That the one that died young?”

Russ gave a nod and threw back the rest of his soda, hoping it would wash down the lump in his throat.

"D'you grow up 'round these parts?"

"Yes, sir."

"Where 'bouts?

Speaking of his childhood was exasperating, and Russ took a long deep breath before replying, "All over."

"That so?" he questioned, and there was something in the man's tone and countenance that indicated Russ was obligated to offer up more details.

Acquiescing, he produced a list. "Here in Bradford. Bald Knob. Hickory Flat. Pangburn. Beebe. Cabot. Searcy . . . And probably some places around here I've blocked from my memory."

Honk seemed to ponder this information for quite some time, which allowed Russ and Stem to exchange several glances. Just as Russ was going to ask Honk the name of the dog which sat at his feet, Stem interjected, "Sir, it's our hope that you can tell us—"

"Where're you from, son?" interrupted the man whose eye keenly studied Stem.

"New Zealand. Now, what I've discovered about the Time Magnet—"

"You're not Australian?"

"No, sir, I'm not. If you don't mind, can we now discuss the—"

"'Cause I been to Sydney once. With my folks as a boy and—"

"I hardly think this pertains—"

Without any warning signs, Russ jumped to his feet, drawing all eyes upon him. "Sir!" he began. "May I use your restroom, please?"

With an action akin to a sloth, Honk slowly raised a finger as thick as a sausage and pointed towards the hallway which ran along the length of the ceiling joint where the two halves of the trailer met. "First door on the right. Give the handle a jiggle when you're done."

A polite nod was given to his host before he turned to Stem. "Care to join me?"

Stem's face expressed surprised suspicion. However, he commanded coolness in his tone and replied, "Sure, mate. I'll . . .

come too."

The anomalous actions of his houseguests prompted Honk to lift the hat's brim and scratch his forehead. As his eyes examined one man and then the other, his high-toned voice pierced the air. "Ya boys been drinkin'?"

Stem pointed at his mate. "Only him."

Russ, however, objected to the accusation. "That's not true. *He* got hammered on the way over."

"It's the only way I can tolerate riding with *you*."

Their host kept his eyes glued to the dubious pair until they had disappeared down the hallway.

The second the bathroom door closed, Stem fired, "Why'd you want me to come with you to the dunny? Wasn't last night humiliating enough?"

"I didn't want you to join me for a pee—I just needed to talk with you for a sec."

"Then, why didn't you just say that?"

"I don't know," barked the exasperated man.

"Well, get on with it, then."

"Listen, this fella's a good ole boy. You can't rush the convo to the Time Magnet—we've got to go at it at *his* pace or we're gonna tick him off and he's gonna refuse to be of any help to us."

Keeping his voice down, Stem hissed as loudly as possible, "We've already wasted twenty minutes here! At this rate, he'll have a coronary in his La-Z-Boy before we get one helpful word out of him. And besides, he most certainly does *not* strike me as a man who has anything of value to convey to us about that complex machine. I assure you, we are wasting our time here!"

"You're the one who dragged us out here to the middle of Deliverance."

"Oh, and if you followed me off a bridge would you blame me for that too?"

"You don't know—this might be the man who helped Peepaw build it."

"That's so improbable I won't even bother calculating the

odds."

"All I'm saying is that my grandpa is a very unlikely candidate for having built that machine yet, implausibly, he did. Now, you may judge this man's appearance, but he could very well be the one we're looking for. So, let's give it a little while longer and see what he has to say."

Checking his phone, Stem said, "I'll give you fifteen more minutes to work your redneck magic on this guy."

"Oh, what are you in such a hurry to do anyway, huh? Throw gummy wrappers at the National Scientific Channel?"

"That was a cheap shot."

"That was an honest assumption which you've not yet repudiated."

"Mate, you used another ten-letter word. Proud of you."

"Thanks. But you can't rush this guy. Promise me you won't or else my chances of repairing my marriage—and your chances of repairing that machine—are as good as the chances that Honk's gonna do a CrossFit workout after we leave."

Like a runner winded after a marathon, Stem clasped his raised hands behind his head and took several deep, oxygenated breaths. At last, he relinquished, "All right."

"You calm?"

"Yes."

"And you promise to let me ease him into the conversation?"

"As much as it pains me, you have my word," Stem swore before tacking on a disclaimer. "But if this thing drags out into the bloody night, I call the love seat."

"Deal."

"And do you have any snacks?"

"I thought you brought a whole bagful."

"I ate it on the bloody way over here!"

Chapter 20

Stem could only tolerate so much talk about the Hogs' summer training, and he excused himself to the kitchen, stating he'd whip up a meal for the party of three. Some minutes later as Honk examined the unfamiliar contents of his fork, he inquired, "What is this, son?"

"It's a steak and cheese pie," explained the cook who, with half a pie in his belly now, had a more positive outlook on life. "First meal my mum taught me to make."

"Pretty good."

They finished their food in relative silence, aside from the dog whose rhythmic snores palpitated the air like a slow and steady bass drum. Honk appeared quite content in his recliner as he licked his plate clean. When he was finished, Russ took the dishes and even offered to wash them. Though Stem was utterly certain the man sitting before him had absolutely no involvement whatsoever in the creation of the Time Magnet, he took Russ' leave of absence as a sign that their host had been smoothed over enough to now be prodded about the matter.

Stem led with, "So, how did you meet Larry Brown?"

"MIT nuclear physics lab, second year."

No doubt, Stem's eyebrows were buried somewhere in the tangle of curls upon his head. "Come again?"

"We was both students there in Massachusetts. I didn't switch majors 'til sophomore year. Had been chemical engineering, but it bored me."

For a span of twenty seconds, no sound exited Stem's mouth. He blinked—and blinked again—and at last, he managed to exhale, "Well, bloody heck."

"'Spect you's 'bout ready to hear 'bout that machine we built, ain't ya?"

Stem gaped and nodded.

"Must've come up with the idea in about '57. Can't take credit, though. It was Larry's brainchild. He drew up the schematics and we showed them to a professor." All the talking had evidently parched Honk's mouth, and he reached for, opened, and drained an entire can of Mr. Pibb before continuing. "That professor offered up his lab for prototypes. Wanted to take credit for it hisself. Tried stealing it from Larry. So, we left."

"You dropped out of MIT?"

"Came here. We was both from Arkansas anyway."

The span of silence which followed probably lasted around seven and a half seconds, but to Stem, it felt like an hour. "And then?" he begged to know. "Please, tell me the *entire* story."

Honk chuckled. "Couldn't do that, even if I had all night," to which Stem thought, *You could if you'd speak faster than you walk*, only, out of his promise to Russ, he bit his tongue. "Built a little lab outta my family's homestead," continued the host. "Did some testing. Perfected the prototype." With a shake of his head, Honk confessed, "Didn't work."

The lull which followed agonized Stem to the point that he nearly shouted, "Bloody heck, man! Spit it out!"

After a time, however, Honk carried on. "S'pose we both ran outta money. Transferred my homestead property to his name 'n we lived off the loan for a while 'til we both had to git jobs. Larry found him a girl 'n got settled down. Project sat on hold for nigh . . ." he contemplated the span of time, and, then at length, added, "fifteen years."

At this point in the conversation, Russ had already washed up the dishes, and he returned to the living room with half a watermelon which he'd sliced into strips on the rind. Needing something to do with his hands and mouth while he waited the interminable length of time the man would take to convey the story, Stem gnawed away several slices of the juicy fruit.

"Larry'd rebuilt the lab sometime in the '70s. Underground. Said the nuclear energy needed to be contained in case of a 'splosion. Guess it was 'bout '80 when we finally had the thing goin'. Added a third magnet. Refocused the beams." Seeing as he'd swallowed and spit the lump of chew he'd put in after dinner, Honk paused to fill his bottom lip with another generous pinch. "Larry was first to go. I didn't have the guts. Tried something easy. Maybe five years back. Knew the time rebound would be short. But we didn't guess how short."

With the watermelon devoured, Stem had taken to torturing his fingernails, a habit of stress he'd not engaged in since his casino days. "How long was it?"

"'Bout five minutes. A minute per year. Half the time we 'spected."

"And where did he go?" As the length of time it took Honk to answer the question dragged out, Stem, realizing it really made no difference where Peepaw had gone on that first journey, shifted to a new thought. "As you know, it's stuck in loop, but I haven't concluded where the issue lies. I thought if you and I put our heads together on this then we could correct the Time Magnet."

Honk scratched his head. "That what you call it?"

Stem nodded but didn't venture down the path of semantics, as he was sure neither he nor Honk were up to walking that trail. "Just to jog your memory, the time loop—it's a little over halfway through the cycle. When we turned on the electricity, the machinery reengaged, however, it just kept spinning through the RF cycle. I tried recalibrating the transits but before I could finish—" he glanced over at Russ who had dozed off ten minutes earlier "—we broke the glass."

Another Mr. Pibb was consumed—by both men, in fact—and then Honk said, "Weld was always coming loose during that time rebound. I'd just J-B Weld it back on 'fore he got back. When he disappeared, I figured it'd got him stuck."

"So, you—" Stem began. Then, glancing at his friend to ensure he really was asleep, he lowered his voice and questioned, "You weren't there when Larry traveled the last time?"

Honk shook his head, and the yawn he released increased Stem's anxiety.

I've got to get the info out before this bloke falls asleep.

"Tell me about the loose weld. Where is it?"

He'd anticipated Honk might need a customary minute or two before responding, but Stem did not foresee that the fellow would suddenly activate a button on his chair which would slowly evacuate him from his recliner. Thus far, they'd sat in the living room for four hours and the man had not moved one inch.

The mechanical lift struggled under the weight of its occupant, emitting a low yet strident whir which aroused Russ from his slumber.

"We leaving?" he asked as he rubbed his eyes.

Neither of the young men had any knowledge of where their host was going, so they followed him out the back door which exited onto a deck where the guard dogs evidently resided. All at once, a commotion of howls, barks, and whines ensued. Ignoring the lot of them, Honk staggered along, hand on rail, descending the stairs to the yard where he fought and shifted and, at last, squeezed into the seat of a UTV like a cat in a Kleenex box.

"Keep up," he told them.

What speed he lacked on foot the man made up for on his travel aide. Stem and Russ were out of breath by the time they reached a haybarn some quarter mile from the house. Having no intention of getting off the thing, Honk directed the men to open the barn door and in he drove, accompanied by a company of canines.

All actions in the barn were choreographed by Honk in precisely a way which required nothing more of him than a voice and, occasionally, a pointy finger.

"This one?" asked Stem as he stood near the top of a ladder which Russ had carried over to the location and was currently holding for the man.

"Left," said Honk, and, as improbable as it was, he sounded as though the entire ordeal had completely winded him.

"This one?" Stem once again questioned. When he received a nod, he retrieved the box of interest and carefully descended the ladder with it in hand. Laying it on the hood of the UTV, Stem took the pocketknife which Honk had extended and, with terrific caution, slid it along the taped flaps. There was no knowing what would be in the box, and, for all Stem knew, a raccoon was just as likely to appear as a tube of J-B Weld.

One by one, Stem withdrew the box's contents (which to his relief consisted almost exclusively of paperwork) while Honk slowly evaluated each item and declared (with a dismissing wave of his hand) that Stem should proceed to the next item. At last, a folder of papers was pulled forth and Honk's hands alighted on it with tenacity.

"This is it," he whistled through his trachea. Briefly, he thumbed through the papers there within until the proper one was located. "Larry's schematics," said the man, handing it over to Stem.

The once white paper was browned like the macrame which had adorned Meemaw and Peepaw's entryway. Creases resisted the unfolding of the document like mossbacks to change, but Stem accomplished the task with as much care and gentleness as a brand-new father.

In contrast, Honk reached out and pulled the schematics from his hands, wrinkling the edges beneath his sausage fingers. Additional lighting was required, and Russ made use of his phone's flashlight. As he eyed the drawing, drafted with his own grandfather's hands, Russ felt an unexpected rush of moisture flooding his eyes.

"Right there," said Honk, pointing rather unspecifically to the diagram. "Beam shutter."

"Of course!" exclaimed Stem, planting his palm on his forehead. "The shutter's been closed this whole time."

Honk offered a quick nod and made a hazardous attempt to refold the paper with new crease lines. Fearing for the document, Stem snatched it from his hands with a polite, "Let me do that for you," and he carefully laid it across the top of the box.

To Russ, Stem said, "Shine your light on it. A little further back. There, hold still." With his own phone, he snapped several photos.

"See that propagator?" Honk said, pointing to a darkened corner of the barn. "Over yonder?"

As Stem had occupied himself with the task of preserving the existing creases, Russ was chosen for the job. Following the landowner's directions, he undug the object in question (and undigging it did require for a leg was missing, and, as it had watched the passing of several decades from its askew position on the floor, it had been buried haphazardly beneath an assortment of farming equipment parts, gardening tools, and corn feed bags). At last, the propagation table was unearthed, and, though Russ stared dumbly at the thing as he wiped his filthy hands on his cargo shorts, Stem's face lit up like a streetlamp.

"Is that?" he dared gasp, to which Honk gave a nod of affirmation. With this, Stem was on the thing like a moth. In a short time, he'd disassembled the apparatus, and, with great triumph, he lifted the grimy top and held it above his head like a trophy and declared, "We're in business!"

Russ squinted at it. "What is that thing?"

Stem gave his friend a pitying look. "Russell. Mate. This is the glass."

"From the Time Magnet?"

A sigh was heaved from his friend's chest, and he took a moment of silence to keep his tongue from tossing garbage out his lips.

The successful treasure hunt had brought a cheerful glow to Honk's face. "Larry and I didn't fabricate glass. Used the humidity dome off a propagator. Bought a couple in case we broke one. Wife used it for seedlings."

In a span of ten minutes, tears filled Russ' eyes for a second time (or a fifth, if you count his dust allergy besting him). "I can't believe this," he crooned, leaving streaks of grime on his cheeks as he wiped away tears of joy. "I'm gonna get my wife back."

Touched by the statement, Honk stared at him, as though in awe. "Wish I could have mine. Gone two years ago last March. Hold 'er tight, son. Life's too short."

Chapter 21

After some more slow conversation and a pot of Folgers (which Stem dutifully choked down), Honk finally sent them on their way back down Highway 367. A general spirit of merriment, coupled with a late-night caffeine high, filled the car.

Russ chuckled. "How crazy was that, that we found the guy who helped Peepaw invent a time machine or that Honk was that guy?"

"If you're asking which is more absurd, definitely the latter."

"Dude, Honk doesn't look like much now but they were like bandits back in the day, breaking into their college's lab and running off with the schematics."

"And the door."

"42B!" Russ roared. "I can't believe they got away with that."

"No wonder it's bloody heavy—it's a lead-lined nuclear lab door."

"I'm just so stoked that we found him—"

"*I* found him."

"That *you* found him."

Stem cleared his throat. "I have to confess something. When we first discovered that Peepaw had a silent partner in the time traveling endeavor, I wondered if, perhaps, said partner had intentionally broken the machine midcycle."

"I hadn't even thought about that."

"I figured as much, and, as I wasn't sure you'd handle the theory in a constructive manner, I purposely didn't mention the possibility to you."

"So, is that what happened? Did Honk have some beef with Peepaw and trap him in the Time Magnet?"

"You must've been asleep when we discussed that. No, according to Honk the two had a falling out over Peepaw's kleptomania. I guess, originally, the theft of valuable items had been agreeable to both and had funded the payments on Peepaw's loan to buy the land from Honk. However, once the loan had been satisfied, Honk wanted to focus on scientific discovery whereas Peepaw preferred thievery."

"So, he was stealing things on purpose."

"And Honk feared this might lead to their discovery and subsequent prosecution for the thefts. So, he parted ways with Peepaw, evidently only days before he vanished."

For a minute, Russ worked through his feelings on the matter. Like a gambler, Peepaw had taken risks. And like many who wager, he had lost.

However, Russ didn't feel particularly let down. What Peepaw had created and unintentionally left to his posterity would now be used for good, to repair that which Russ had so carelessly broken. Whether it was that thought or the caffeine or both, Russ felt his spirits soar.

"Even so," he remarked, "we got everything out of this visit that we were hoping to. The glass. The solution to the Time Magnet's issue. Even the schematics which we didn't know existed. Can you believe our luck?"

Stem lightly stroked the large glass piece, freshly smelling of Windex. "Not luck, mate."

"No doubt," he agreed. "God's been watching out for us."

"Do you ever wonder what God thinks about us possessing the technology to time travel?"

Heavy thoughts of the sort rarely found their way into Russ' brain without the insinuation of an outside influence.

"No," he replied. "Haven't actually thought about that."

Stem gazed out the window at the stars. "I've been wondering about it myself, and, to be honest, I'm not sure mankind was meant to command such power."

The only purpose Russ had ever considered using the Time Magnet for was going back and preventing himself from ruining his marriage. Was having that kind of opportunity powerful? Maybe, but who wouldn't take advantage of it if they were wearing his shoes.

"I'm still doing it," Russ said, somewhat more defiantly than he had meant to.

"I'm not saying I'll stop you," clarified his friend, "but I just wanted to know if you'd ever pondered the implications—and *consequences*—of time travel."

"Well, it's not like I'm gonna go back in time just for the thrill of stealing some precious metal object of antiquity."

"True, your cause is more noble than that. But there will undoubtedly be unpredictable outcomes."

"What are you saying? That I'm gonna go back and try to fix my marriage but somehow screw it all up and, what, the world's going to end or something?"

"No, mate, not what I'm suggesting. I have all confidence in you." Russ tossed him a look of disbelief. "All right, maybe not *all* confidence, but I am rooting for the success of your journey. After all, I benefit from the reparation of your marriage as well. But can you imagine the pandemonium if this technology got out to the whole world? Our planet would not last 20 minutes before the lot of us wrecked it."

"That's a little pessimistic for a scientist, isn't it? I mean, you told me yourself that you had studied the idea of time magnets before we'd ever found one. Why would you do that if you thought it was wrong?"

"Not wrong, just dangerous. Okay, and maybe wrong too. The idea of time travel intrigued me in a sci-fi, Star Trekkie kind of way. But to come face to face with this kind of discovery—this manmade creation that defies God's natural laws—it makes one step back and take a more thoughtful look at what could happen if mankind embraced it, if we tried to put ourselves in the role of God."

Russ huffed and squared his shoulders. "I'm not trying to play God. I just want to undo a few stupid decisions I made and have my life come out the better for it."

"All right, don't get your nappy in a wad. I'm perfectly aware you only want to correct the error of your ways."

"Yeah, and who wouldn't if given the chance? Don't you have regrets? Things you'd like to go back and change?"

"Plenty of regrets, but not many I'd change."

"So, you wouldn't go back in time and change *any* of the aspects of your life, not one?"

"I didn't say that."

"Do tell, then. What's the thing you'd change? Your mom's death?"

The idea of preventing his own mother's death had not entered Russ' mind. Now, as he spoke those words to his friend, the shocking possibility stunned him.

Stem spent a moment contemplating his feelings before responding. "No. I miss her but she's at peace, and only God should raise the dead."

His reasoning seemed wise enough, though Russ needed more time to consider his feelings about his *own* mother.

"All right, then what?" questioned Russ.

"Well, if we're strictly speaking of decisions I've made—and not bigger world issues like 9-11 or the Oklahoma City bombing—then there's one thing I can think of that I'd change. That is, if I could."

"Well? The suspense is killing me."

"Olive."

Russ scoffed. "I should've known it would have to do with food."

"No, not food. Olive Cartwright. The girl I dated."

"Oh, Tropical Smoothie girl?"

Stem glared at the driver. "If by that you mean the

exceptionally intelligent and exquisitely designed woman who moonlighted as an assistant manager at the fruitery while obtaining her highly specialized law degree in copyright and trademark infringement, then, yes. She's Tropical Smoothie girl."

"Okay, but didn't she have a kid?"

"She had a lovely daughter, Ruby, who, like her mother, was very bright and delightful. She relished a good board game, although I love Chutes and Ladders as much as anyone enjoys Chinese water torture. And she showed me how to do backflips on her trampoline."

"Olive or Ruby?"

"Ruby. And we caught a turtle once which her mother said she couldn't keep at her house, so I kept it at mine."

"Oh, I remember him! What was his name?"

"Chewy. And living up to the title, the little devil chewed right through his cardboard box and escaped out the back door. But that was after I broke up with Olive, so Ruby never knew."

"Why don't you just call her up and ask her out again?"

"Russell, if it were that easy, I would've already executed that plan, yeah? What you don't know about Olive is that she was badly burned—"

"Literally?"

"Figuratively—by Ruby's father. She took a risk on me and I failed her. I doubt she'll ever trust a man again, especially if that man is me."

"So, if you're crazy about her, why'd you break it off?"

Before he gave the explanation, Stem had to perform no less than three cycles of deep breathing to prepare himself for what he was about to say, and, even after that, he had second thoughts about making the confession. "It's going to sound really dumb."

"Let's hear it. I need some more material to ridicule you."

He chuckled. "All right, here it is. Olive liked Starbuck's." At Russ' incredulous glance, Stem shrugged.

"You broke up with the love of your life because she liked what is, in your opinion, subpar coffee?"

"Charbuck's, and it lives up to its nickname."

"Well, I like their coffee."

"I rest my case. However, her infatuation with the place in and of itself would not have persuaded me to end the relationship."

"Then why'd you dump her?"

"Because she had an unhealthy addiction to it."

Exasperation filled Russ like a bloated helium balloon. "What! You, a self-proclaimed junk food addict, judged someone else for having an unhealthy food addiction?"

"All right, shut up and let me explain. She bought no less than six beverages there per week—that's over three hundred every calendar cycle! And since her yearly debt to the place, which I'll calculate for you, was pushing $2000, I surmised she would be a drain on my salary which at the time eight years ago was quite low."

"You are so petty."

"Parsimonious."

"Cheap."

"Well, I wouldn't have minded so much if it had been good coffee!"

"Ah-ha! I knew it! You're judging her cheap taste in coffee while you're sitting over there munching on Smarties!"

Clutching the tiny crinkly wrappers to his chest, Stem defended himself. "Honk said I could take them!" Turning towards his window, he murmured, "After all, his great-grandkids don't like them."

"*Nobody* likes them."

To prove some kind of point, though Russ could not determine exactly what it was, Stem stuffed a handful of the candies into his mouth and bobbed his jaw with vivacious energy. Through the powdery dust, he started to say something which he no doubt felt would defend his position. However, some rocky bits slid down his throat, making him choke and sputter and, soon, all the candy had been coughed out onto his palm (as well as the dashboard and glass dome which was nestled between his legs for safekeeping).

"Like them now?" Russ asked dryly.

"No," Stem choked out. "I hate them."

"That's not what it looked like thirty seconds ago."

Snatching up Russ' bottle of water, Stem spun off the cap, letting it bounce off the glass before getting lost forever in the crack between the seat and center console. After chugging liberally and coughing up some of the liquid, he spent a few seconds gasping for air. Then, through his now-scratchy throat, he eked out, "I've never mentioned this because it makes me feel like an idiot."

Russ was all ears to listen to his friend self-deprecate.

"I often buy snacks that I despise in the hopes that I won't eat them or, at the very least, won't enjoy eating them."

"You are so sick."

"I know," Stem agreed, tossing back another gulp of the refreshment. Then, clearing his throat, he said, "I suspect it's a form of an eating disorder, but I've been in denial about it until recently so I've yet to research it."

"There's something wrong with you."

"I just bloody admitted that. Have some bloody tact."

"All right, sorry. Don't choke on your Smarties."

Glaring at the driver, he huffed, "Are you trying to dig at me for telling you not to get your nappy in a wad, because that was pretty lame."

"Oh, go choke on your Smarties!"

"Ugh," groaned Stem. "I don't ever want Smarties again. They disgust me. And licorice. And pineapples."

"But you always get pineapple on your pizza."

"A bloody testimony as to how sick I am!"

"Buddy, I've got to admit—I'm seeing an entirely new side of you with this recent uptick in transparency."

"Twelve letters. Good."

"Thanks."

"I suppose, now that you know my dirty little secret, you can hold me accountable."

"Like how?"

"You know, bloody call me out if you see me eating something I don't like."

"How would I know—you eat everything."

The man's guffaw was staunched by little bits of Smarties clinging to his throat like cat's claws. "For starters, I never want another Mr. Pibb again in all my life, nor do I want to consume any form of coffee made from crystals which dissolve in water. Hospitality or not, that verged on torturous."

"I'll admit—the coffee was stale."

"See, even you noticed that, and that's saying something."

"What about M&M's? You like those?"

"Are you bloody crazy? They're like God's angels pooped little drops of heaven on Earth."

"So . . . is that a good thing?"

"Yes, it bloody well is!"

The conversation which followed was rife with such immature commentary that it is not worthy of documenting. However, some five minutes later, just as they simultaneously broke down into childish laughter and crested a hill, Russ caught a glimpse of an 11-point buck out of the corner of his eye. At once, he slammed the brakes, only, it was too late. What to Honk's truck would've been a collision of inconvenience was to Russ' Miata like a child on training wheels trying to hop a curb at full speed.

Chapter 22

"Mr. Brown, do have a preference which hospital we take you to?" asked the emergency medical technician as she shined a small flashlight into his eyes.

Given Russ' slurred response, they transported him to Unity Health in his hometown where he was admitted to the emergency room. Seven hours later, they released him with a diagnosis of a minor concussion and with the order to refrain from driving or operating heavy equipment for the next forty-eight hours. As he had managed to total his second car in a month, Russ decided the warning was worth heeding, but before he ordered an Uber, he stopped by Stem's room on the third floor of the hospital.

The sight of his friend sleeping, reclined and slightly askew on the bed, was pitiable. Beside him sat an untouched breakfast of powdered eggs, manufactured bacon, and some sort of substance that fell along the consistency scale between pudding and cottage cheese. The bruises on the man's face were the least of his worries. Shattered bits of glass, pieces of the trophy he'd so proudly clutched in his hands in Honk's barn only three hours before the accident, had embedded into his skin, and he'd spent the entire early morning hours sedated as nurses plucked shards out of his face and lips, neck and chest.

Pulling up a chair, Russ waited for the man to awaken. When

twenty minutes of slumber had passed, the visitor snatched one of the bacons strips and crammed it into his mouth. It was far from stellar but not the worst piece of meat-like substance he'd ever eaten. There had been that one time after Peepaw disappeared when the budget ran thin and Meemaw had fed all the grands pan-fried chicken feet. That was a meal he'd never forget.

As Russ reached for the other bacon strip, he noticed Stem's head slowly turn in his direction. The patient's slightly buggy eyes, now tinged red and purple, drooped heavily, as did his jaw, which was entirely cloaked in a bandage. The natural brown curls, now a disheveled mess upon his head, gave the impression he'd just spent the night in the year 800,000AD trying to fight off an invasion of cannibalistic Morlocks.

Following southern hospitality, Russ led the convo with, "Hey, man. How's it going?"

Besides blinking, Stem's face remained unchanged and he gave off not a sound, yet Russ got the distinct impression that the man was mocking him for spouting off such an asinine greeting.

"Sorry," Russ apologized. "You look like crap."

That was material Stem could work with. "So you do."

"You look worse."

"You nearly killed me."

"Sorry about that. If it makes you feel any better, my car's totaled—again."

"Good. Without a danger like you on the road, everyone else's car insurance rates are sure to drop at least ten percent."

Stem let out a half-hearted laugh at his own joke, and, as he reached out a feeble hand towards the plastic hospital cup which sat at his bedside, Russ kindly completed the task for him. Sipping through the straw with lacerated lips was not a task which appeared easy or comfortable, and Russ cringed as he watched.

"Sorry the glass broke," said Russ as he set the cup down.

"I should say the same to you."

"Yeah, but you, well, you know."

They both knew, although the man in the hospital bed was the only one who fully understood the extent of the physical pain.

"Go home and sleep," said Stem. "I'm gonna crash, myself."

"I already did that for you." His lame jest was once again met only with a gaping, droopy-eyed stare. "Right," said Russ. "I'll call you later."

A couple of Stem's fingers bobbed up and fell back down to his lap, the only farewell Russ would receive from the man.

When Russ had arrived home from the hospital, a shiny black Chevy Tahoe had pulled up his street directly behind the Uber. He wouldn't have noticed it except his neighbor, Fran, who had lived in the house next door for as long as he had recollection, struck up a conversation with him from her porch. In the span of the eight minutes they spoke across the lawns, the Tahoe drove by three times. At last, it parked two doors down on the other side of the street. And as if that weren't suspicious enough, Fran pointed at the vehicle and remarked, "Seen that truck driving by here a lot lately. No one ever gets out—they just set there a while and then go on their way. I think they're eyeing your granny's place but Earl says them's real estate developers and gonna tear down the whole block."

Several times each day, Russ peeked out between the yellowed miniblinds in the dining room. Sure enough, at nearly all hours of the day and night, the Tahoe was parked somewhere on the street—and always within sight of the house. Anxiety struck so hard and abruptly that Russ had not even had time to fully process how his hopes and dreams of repairing his marriage had shattered when that glass did.

"They're watching me," he whispered into his phone.

"Who?"

"I don't know. Maybe eBay." Stem's incredulity flowed so clearly through the cell towers that Russ quickly added, "Or the FBI. Or maybe a foreign government. Maybe Japan."

Stem had only been home from the hospital for about three

hours and he wasn't in the mood to sympathize with the man's paranoia. "You know what activities are beneficial for a perfectly healthy man like you, who isn't battered and bruised and cut up all over his body?"

"What?"

"Quit staring out the bloody window and go for a walk. Or jog. Or bike ride."

"I don't have a bike."

"What are you, a beggar? Walk to the bloody store and buy one."

"This is serious," Russ fretted. "I keep getting these eBay messages from random people that say I'm selling stolen goods. And now that SUV's been following me everywhere. And I'm pretty sure someone was in my backyard last night."

"It was probably Fran's cat."

"No, it wasn't. He got run over."

"If only someone had warned the poor feline that you're a menace on the road."

"I didn't do it!"

"All right, calm down. Let's just examine the facts."

With slight indignance, Russ acquiesced.

"Number one: You live at 213 Walnut Street. Number two: The little sweet woman at 211 Walnut Street is mourning her precious kitten. I'd say that's enough evidence right there to prove something."

"Like what?"

"That you murdered her cat."

"Shut up."

"Any court of law would convict you."

"I didn't kill Sprinkles!"

"I'd testify of your recklessness myself."

Russ sighed. "Are you going to help me or not?"

"Yes, I will, mate. You're obviously at substantial risk of losing your source of income—for the second time this year—not to mention that filing your taxes next year will be a nightmare. My advice to you is to put away your money wisely. Invest in something which can't be stolen from you, something which will benefit you down the road."

"What do you suggest?"

"Enroll in a driver's course. Better yet, sign up for them all. Every bloody one."

"Okay, I'm hanging up."

The weekend (which was agonizingly long since his one friend refused to come over, citing the need to rest and recuperate from his near-death experience), Russ endeavored to keep tabs on his tailer. Taking Stem's advice, he strategically planned walks and pointless outings at varying times during the day. On his iPhone, he kept notes of where he went and when, but most importantly, he tracked the whereabouts of the Tahoe.

The plan proved more difficult than he could have imagined. One minute, the Tahoe was in sight. The next minute, it was as if the two were playing hide and seek. Overall, he came to no solid conclusions, yet his suspicions remained.

He sought advice from Google on what to do if accused of a crime, and he concluded that his best option was to remain silent. Nevertheless, as the number of messages and emails grew, so did his anxiety. The walks and middle-of-the-night jogs around town were a welcome distraction.

On top of all this, the possibility of using the Time Magnet seemed to be slipping farther from his fingertips. In order to repair his marriage, he first must repair the broken machine, but without the glass, this plan was utterly, completely, totally, incomprehensibly impossible.

As the sun rose on Monday morning, Russ laid on his air mattress, wide awake, sleep deprived, and munching on Tums by the handful.

"God, help me," he whispered. "I'm in a mess."

The spot on the particular blind—at his eye level where he

always parted the shades with his forefinger and middle finger when spying out the window—it was now cleaner and noticeably whiter than the rest of the lot. That morning as the man gazed out, he was astonished at what he saw, or rather, didn't see. Nowhere in sight was the nefarious black vehicle, and his mind began playing tricks on him.

Maybe it belonged to a friend who was just spending the week at one of the neighbor's houses.

Maybe it hadn't been there at all.

Maybe I'm losing my mind.

Seeking a reality check, he phoned Stem.

"So, it's gone, yeah?" asked the man.

"It's not there anymore."

"So, what's the issue?"

"I don't know. I'm just worried now that I don't see it."

"Mate, let me see if I understand your neurosis. Its presence made you paranoid, and its absence now fills you with dread, yeah?" Though hesitating a second, Russ at last agreed with the analysis. "You need a therapist, mate."

"You think I'm crazy?"

"Never doubted it, but I expect stress is also contributing to your newly developed paranoia. You lost your wife and Meemaw within a couple of months of each other. You suddenly have excess cash you don't know what to do with while also trying to hide it from your cousins. You're wrecking your cars. You smashed the one irreplaceable part for the machine. Mate, that load is enough to mess with anyone's head. Don't let the paranoia get to you, yeah?"

"All of these troubles would just go away if we could get the machine up and running."

Stem sighed. "Well, pray for a miracle because it'll take one."

Chapter 23

Giving the recovery meeting a second try had been Stem's idea—and not one that Russ was too keen on. He could name no less than half a dozen reasons why he didn't want to attend, including the fact that Stem was still on the mend—but each objection was deemed invalid. Thus, on that Monday evening, Russ walked through the doors of a (sort of) church for the third time since that Sunday before his infidelity was revealed to the world.

Once again, they arrived a few minutes late, and, as they took their seats, Stem whispered with a distinctively giddy tone, "It's testimony night."

For clarification, Russ asked, "So someone else is gonna do what you did and tell everybody all their crap?"

Stem couldn't have been less impressed with his friend's summary of a testimony. "No, they will testify how God bloody changed their crappy life."

"Well, forgive me," hissed Russ, "for not knowing all the secret handshakes to your little club."

As the meeting proceeded—and more or less followed the same order of events as the previous one he'd attended—Russ began to feel both comforted by the familiarity as well as apprehensive (that it might, in fact, be a cult).

At length, a man who looked remarkably normal and well-kempt took the stage. "I love Jesus and I'm grateful he rescued me from dishonesty, selfishness, and resentment, and I'm dealing with grief right now, and my name is Chaz."

During his former visit, Russ had not participated in reciting the Bible verses following Rosie's reading of each step. However, tonight as the majority of the gym's occupants read them aloud in unison, he quietly mumbled the scriptures. It wasn't that God's word displeased him—he was just a little out of his element and still on his guard. When the reading of the 12 steps was completed, Russ leaned over and whispered, "Do they do all this same stuff every week?"

"Same framework—alternating content."

Jack, the leader apparent, took the stage. After a brief introduction of himself, he then offered a warm welcome to another gentleman, who Russ noticed was one of only three people present with darker-than-beige skin. As he clutched a passel of papers in his hand, Russ presumed he was to be the speaker for the evening.

"Hi," he began. "I'm a child of the one true king who has enabled me to celebrate recovery over drug and sexual addiction, wild living, anger, and thievery, and I'm Campo."

The name immediately struck Russ as unusual—and for an unknown reason, he felt a rush of icy water pour over his soul. Part of him felt like fleeing, but another part of him told him the feeling was irrational, that he only felt this way because he'd walked out two weeks earlier when he'd come with Stem for the first time.

The man's testimony started with a recap of his childhood which, for the son of illegal Mexican immigrants evading the law in southern Texas in the early 1970s, was poverty riddled. Eventually, Campo ended up in west Tennessee where he learned that he could earn more money running drugs as a mule than working an honest job. A run-in with the law landed him in jail for two years, but when his sentence and probation ended, he relocated with a girlfriend to central Arkansas.

For a while, he made a living transporting salvage vehicles to the auction block. But soon, his old way of life called him back. While trying to hold down his job and support his girlfriend and their baby girl, Campo moonlighted as a drug dealer as well as a user. Eventually, he lost everything. For the next several years, he lived a wild and dangerous life. Only by God's protection did he survive those years of servitude to violence, drugs, sex, and selfishness.

Clearing his throat, Campo continued. "A rival drove me out of Pangburn so I got a place in Bradford and opened shop. A woman who'd been buying from me owed me a lot of money so I told her she could pay it out by doing favors for me. At first, I kept her for myself, but then I started pimping her out to other buyers. I didn't do her right—didn't treat her well at all—and I regret that I supplied her with the drugs which ultimately led to her overdose and death."

Russ didn't have to hear another word of Campo's testimony to know the truth—the woman was his mother. Everything inside him raced with intensity. His thoughts, his heartrate, his breaths—none were under his control. Like a sinking boat, his mind suddenly flooded with awful memories he'd repressed. They flashed before him as if taking place in real time, blinding his eyes to all reality. How he managed to find his way out of the gym, he couldn't say, but, soon, he found himself doubled over in the parking lot.

"Russell!" hollered Stem as he followed his friend out the gym doors. However, the feral look in Russ' eyes made him cautiously keep his distance. In a lowered voice, he suggested, "Mate, let's talk about this."

Words were beyond Russ' capability at the moment, and he oscillated between near hyperventilation and vomiting. At one point, Stem reached towards him, suggesting they go sit down, but Russ clawed at him like a wild beast being caged.

Jumping out of his way, Stem said, "All right, Wolverine. No need to bring out the blades. I'm backing up." He could do nothing but wait out his friend's violent fit, and, long before Russ said so, Stem understood exactly what had brought on his savagery.

After screaming obscenities at the top of his lungs and tossing handfuls of rocks at a dumpster as well as beating it senseless with a stray metal pipe, Russ sunk to the ground, panting as heavily as a rabid dog.

Stem approached with caution. "Nice smash, Hulk. You really put that rubbish bin to work." When he saw his lighthearted remark had not elicited a response, he requested, "If you don't mind, may I please speak to Dr. Banner now?"

Mouth agape, Russ nodded slowly.

The wild look in his eyes had not yet subsided so Stem took slow, small steps toward the man. Reaching out, he eased the metal pipe from Russ' grasp, saying, "Let me take care of that for you, mate," before hurling it off into the grass. Then offering a hand, he said, "How about we find a nice, padded room to hang out in for a while, yeah?"

Russ accepted the hand up and rose to his feet. His body suddenly felt heavy and his mouth parched. "I need a drink," he declared.

"Water or tequila?"

With a slow nod, Russ headed for the street, Stem close on his heels. Meandering, he eventually entered T-Ricks gas station two blocks away. Like a zombie, he crossed to the cooler and tore the lid off a gallon water jug. While he chugged, Stem warned away any unaware passersby.

One woman paused to question the situation. "Is he all right?"

"Oh, him?" replied Stem, tossing a thumb at the sweaty man. "Yeah, of course. He's just got rabies so we like to keep him well hydrated. But you might want to stay back a ways. He can be a little volatile when he's thirsty like this."

Eyeing the multiple lacerations on Stem's face and neck which were obviously a result of his motor vehicle accident the week before (though this fact was not obvious to her), she remarked, "Looks like he got you pretty good."

"Indeed."

Before the woman could say another word, Russ abruptly

lowered the jug. Streams of water poured out of his mouth as he stared off through dazed eyes. Slowly, replacing the lid on the half-empty jug, he returned it to the cooler and headed for the exit.

Chasing his friend out the door, Stem paused to toss a five-dollar bill at the vexed clerk. "That's very common where he comes from," he lied. "They just drink what they want and then put the bottle back for the next person. They're just really hospitable like that."

Stem caught up with Russ just as he jaywalked a second time across the main thoroughfare.

"Where you headed, mate?" When he received only a shrug, Stem asked, "Want me to call you a car?" Again, Russ tossed his shoulders up. "Okay, let's just take a walk. It's a lovely day, after all. Only a hundred and fifty-seven degrees out here with two hundred percent humidity."

They neared a park where a line of eager kids stood, waiting for their snow cones. Seeing it, Russ beelined for the food truck.

A few minutes later, the pair sat on a bench in the shade, silently munching on their frozen treats, watching kids fish tadpoles from a small stream. Stem knew better than to bring up the obvious, that Campo had directly contributed to Russ' mom's death. However, by and by, Russ spoke and the subject rolled off his tongue like water on a duck's back.

"We lived with him in that trailer I showed you, the one on the way to Honk's."

In response, Stem simply nodded.

"I had forgot his face. And his name. I can just remember his voice, him yelling at my mom and me." As though they were at a theme park discussing which ride to hop on next, Russ coolly sipped clear syrup through his straw and bit off the top of his silver fox cone. "Sometimes he'd get in a rage and just shoot." He made the shape of a gun with his hand. "Through the walls. Or ceiling. Or furniture." For a moment, his mouth gaped like he was in a faraway place. Then, rousing himself, he downed a couple spoonful's of ice, pausing to remark, "This is a good flavor. How's yours?"

"Great, mate. Always been a fan of tutti frutti."

They sat in silence, finishing their treats. Then, setting his Styrofoam cup and spoon on the ground near his feet, Russ sighed. "That was good. I could almost have gotten a large."

"We can go back for a second."

"No, I should cut back on sugar. So should you." Poking Stem's side, he added, "Felt a little soft when we wrestled."

"Yeah?" said Stem. Pinching his own side, he concurred, "Guess you're right. So, you okay now? Back in your right mind, yeah?"

Russ nodded.

"Planning to try out your Hulk smash again? Park's not the place, though, what with the ankle biters around."

"Nah, I'm good now."

"Wanna go home?"

He rolled the question over in his mind for a while. At last, however, he said, "I want to talk to Campo."

Stem let out a nervous chuckle. "Why don't we save that for another time, yeah? I can get his number from Jack and we can call him up when you're ready—"

"I'm ready now."

After biting his bottom lip, Stem confessed, "Mate, I hear Mondays are a really bad day to get arrested for assault and battery—"

"I'm not gonna hurt him," Russ objected. "I'm half terrified of him anyway." His chest rose and fell with a sigh. "I just want to know if . . ."

"If what?"

Tears glistened in his eyes. "If anyone was with her when she died."

Chapter 24

Like the joy on Baby's face when Mommy picks her up, the sky glowed under the watchful eye of the full moon. Fireflies danced in the backyard, twinkling here and there like pinpricks in a blackout drape. Sandy dirt clung to Russ and Stem's sweaty bare feet, and the glasses of ice water in the lawn chair cupholders gave off an infinitesimal—but welcomed—amount of coolness.

Pointing at the flying bugs, Russ reminisced, "We used to catch them and put them in Meemaw's old butter tubs. They'd always die by morning, but it was fun anyway."

Stem shared, "In New Zealand, we have these caves that are filled with glowworms. They make their home on the ceilings and walls, and they light up the whole place with their bluish green glow."

"That sounds magical."

"Actually, the bioluminescence is just an enzymic reaction in their kidney."

"Well, when you say it that way, it . . . doesn't sound appealing at all." They shared a mutual chuckle before Russ added, "You'll have to take me there sometime."

"Yeah, mate, we'd have a blast. I'd take you out for the best pie and coffee you ever had. I could teach you to surf. And I'd show you all the coolest sights my motherland has to offer."

"If you're so proud of New Zealand, how come you always tell people you're Australian?"

"Mainly just to hide my identity. Not that I'm a celebrity, but my family can easily be looked up if one knows I'm a Kiwi. I have my own Wikipedia page, you know. But I didn't want anybody to think the less of me just because they could find images of pimple-faced, gangly-legged little Ura'astema getting sloshed at a party at his brother's flat."

"You gonna keep up the façade?"

"You know," he said, offering a contemplative pause. "I won't lie anymore. If someone wants to think badly of me just because of poor choices I made in my adolescence, then that reflects on their character, not mine. Besides, my openness about my past may help someone who's struggling with their own demons."

Liking that response, Russ nodded and took a sip of his water.

The crickets strummed their loud chords as frogs in the drainage creek behind Stem's house kept the rhythm with their mating calls.

At length, Russ remarked, "Finding out she didn't die alone—that she died in the hospital . . ."

"A relief?"

"Yeah. I always felt so guilty that I wasn't there with her. One day, I'd just gone to school—and then, DHS picked me up and dropped me off at Meemaw's. And I never saw my mom again. But you know, as bad as life with her got, I never once wanted to leave her and I hated that I wasn't with her when she died."

"Same here with my mum."

"I think, every Mother's Day, that I'll go put flowers on her grave, but I never do."

"That was her buried beside Meemaw, yeah?"

Russ gave a nod. "I think that's why Meemaw's cancer hit me so hard."

"Because you'd already lost your mum?"

"And Meemaw was like a mother to me. I didn't want to lose her too."

"It's like you began grieving for her before she was gone."

"That's not a bad way to put it. And I didn't want to deal with those feelings so I tried to cover them up or erase them or something stupid and irrational like that."

"Avoiding pain is a natural instinct—that's what prevents people from doing dumb things in the first place. But there are times when the pain comes on against our wishes, and how we handle it determines our ignorance."

"So, you're saying I'm an idiot?"

"That's putting it mildly." When his friend punched his shoulder, he added, "You were married to a one in a million girl—and you blew it."

"Well, thanks to you, I'm gonna fix that mistake."

"Let's hope so."

"So, if I go back and change things and then return to the present, will I remember any of this, any of what we've done with the Time Magnet?"

"You will, but I won't."

Russ' body tensed. "What? You're going to forget?"

"I have a positive outlook on it. Honestly, mate, these past few months of your and Katie's separation has sucked. I'd be happy to go back to the blissful existence we all led prior to your screw-up. So, do us all a favor and don't mess it up a second time, yeah?"

Now, it's strange how one can be so physically and mentally exhausted, yet they find sleep as elusive as a lost sock. It was in precisely this fashion that Russ 'slept' that Monday night. On his air mattress, beneath the whirring ceiling fan, he laid motionless—but that coveted rest would not enter his body, and his mind ran and leaped and jumped through thoughts like an obstacle course.

More than ever, his mother was on his mind. And Meemaw. And Katie. The three special women he no longer had in his life. The losses were undoubtedly sources of grief, but there was something different in his thoughts about his mother now, almost like a little sweetness had found its way into his memories. Knowing she had died with someone by her side (even if it was just a random nurse in the hospital) gave him a measure of relief he'd simply not expected. And it revealed a simple truth to him: He'd spent the past thirtyish years of his life feeling responsible for her death. But now, seeing little nine-year-old Rusty for the helpless and weak little boy he was, he became convicted that he'd been powerless to change the outcome of her life. Nothing he could have done thirty years ago could've changed the actions his mother had taken. She chose drugs and they consumed her.

And with that realization came a startling new one—he couldn't have prevented Meemaw's lung cancer any more than he could've prevented his mother's drug overdose. Before he was ever conceived, Meemaw was a two-pack-a-day smoker. Granted, she probably didn't realize the damage the cigarettes were doing to her lungs when she began smoking at age thirteen, but that was a decision she'd made, nonetheless, and Russ couldn't change that either. At best, he maybe could've prolonged her life by a few years by encouraging her to be screened regularly for the disease. Releasing his guilt over her death, he sighed and his mind wandered to his third woman.

No doubt, Katie was moving on. This side of the Wilson Loop or time rebound or whatever anyone wanted to call it, there was no hope for mending their once happy marriage. They'd both signed the divorce papers—she with her maiden name, no less. The for-sale sign in her yard had spoken for itself. He no longer had any influence upon her decisions. Relocating and every future decision she made was her prerogative now, and he at last accepted it.

This train of thought naturally led the man to once again wish that he could reverse the past. Yet he was so keenly aware that, without a propagator dome, he had zero chances of accomplishing such a momentous feat. And as much as he wanted to fix the Time Magnet, Russ acknowledged he had made choices and now he'd have to live with them, just as his mother and grandmother had.

As he lay on the air mattress staring at the ceiling, he wished he'd had some sleeping pills or lavender tea. Reaching for his phone to check the time, he noticed the image on his home screen. That snapshot had captured beams of joy radiating from Katie's face. How happy she'd looked before he broke her heart.

I wish I could make her happy again. She deserves so much better.

And so it was that, all at once, an unexpected yet brilliant thought entered the mind of Russell Delacroix Brown. It was so singularly perfect—how could he have been so slow to grasp the epiphany! Without a doubt, it was the most amazing thing his feeble mind had ever conjured, a thought so marvelous that, if he could but pull it off, it would not only remove all traces of unhappiness from Katie's heart but would also fill him with immeasurable joy.

Chapter 25

"I changed my mind about going back to stop my affair," Russ announced.

Stem immediately froze, and Russ couldn't tell if his gaping mouth was attributable to his shock or if it was because he was making way for a potato chip. At last, he dropped the chip back in the bag and requested, "Can you repeat that, mate?"

"I'm not going back to talk myself out of the affair. I've decided that's not the right thing to do."

"Okay," his friend said slowly. "I'm waiting for this to turn into some kind of material I can use to crack a joke. Only, I can't be funny if you keep saying ridiculously absurd things like that."

"Just hear me out. First off, to go back to prevent the affair is not a bad idea. I mean, my marriage could go back to how it'd been before, and you and I and Katie would all be happy."

"Which is precisely why you should do that. Go back in time, slap yourself around—" he swung a cheap shot at Russ for demonstration "—tell yourself what a wanker you'd be for cheating on her, and then return to the altered first monopole era where we all can live in harmonious bliss. Great idea, yeah?"

Russ sighed. "Yes, but I have a better one."

In the past minute, Stem's expression had grown shades darker. "Spit it out before I choke it out of you because, thus far, I don't like where this conversation is going!"

"I—" Russ' head fell in shame. "I have to confess something to you first."

Stem jumped out of his seat, sending potato chips flying in all directions. "Bloody heck, you egg!"

Sensing his friend's rising anger, Russ leapt to his feet. "What?"

"I can't believe you'd do this!"

"Do what? I thought you'd be all supportive of me making a confession!"

"Oh, yeah, I'm about to support you—with my fists!"

A wild look flashed in Stem's eyes. As he reared back a clenched hand, Russ bolted to refuge at the end of the hallway. Half a second after he was safely locked in the bathroom, Stem's angry fist pounded the door.

"Hey, stop that!" Russ shouted. "You're gonna break it!"

"I'll beat this bloody door down and your dead body with it!"

The heat of Stem's rage radiated through the barrier, leaving Russ in a stupor. "Why are you suddenly so angry?"

"Because I've lost my temper!"

"But—what did I say?"

"It's what you were *going* to say!"

Russ gripped the door handle on his side as Stem violently shook it from the other end.

"Hang on!" called Russ. "What do you think it is I'm confessing?"

"That the other Caydee wasn't the first girl you cheated with!"

"No!" Russ objected.

For a moment, all was quiet. Then came Stem's voice, heaving but calming. "No?"

Relieved, Russ threw his hands in the air and triumphantly concurred. "Yes!"

"Yes?!" Stem's raging assault on the door handle began again, and Russ grasped it as tightly as he could and pressed his shoulder into the effort with all his might to keep the lock from bursting under the pressure.

"I mean, no!" shouted Russ. "No, no, no! The other Caydee was the first—and only!"

All was silent on the other side of the door.

"Stem?" Russ said softly. Leaning his ear onto the door to listen, he heard nothing until suddenly there came a loud *BAM!* as Stem took out his anger on the door one last time.

"Geez! Stop that!"

"Sorry," came Stem's muffled voice. "Sorry about that."

"Is it safe for me to come out?"

"You might give me a minute."

Accepting his friend's volatility for what it was, Russ conveyed, "What I was going to tell you before you so *rudely tried to kill me*—"

"I said I was sorry," he hissed.

"Was that I want to go back further in time and prevent something else first."

"Wait, is this the confession?"

"Oh, I forgot about that." Taking a deep breath, he began. "That day Katie was in the accident. You remember that?"

"It's not like anger affects my memory. Of course I remember."

"So . . . I could've stopped it from happening."

"Mate, unless you're Superman, which you're obviously not because you don't wear glasses, then you couldn't have prevented that truck from smashing into her."

"No, just listen. You know how I'd . . . *noticed* Katie before then."

"Understatement. You stalked the poor girl."

Coming to his own defense, he stated, "I think *enamored* is a better term for my level of interest."

"Mate, you anonymously sent her flowers—"

"I know."

"Everyday—"

"Yeah, I remember."

"For an entire week."

"It was Valentine's week, okay, and Theta club was trying to raise money for their spring break mission trip. I bought the flowers to support their cause . . . I just got a little carried away."

"It was creepy."

"It was *romantic*."

"That only works if the other person knows you exist."

"That's not true," he argued with a shake of his head. "Well, she knew who I was anyway. She'd seen me before at the coffee shop and chapel. She even smiled at me . . . once."

"This is pathetic. I'm going back to the kitchen."

Exiting, Russ examined the door for signs of abuse.

"It's fine," Stem said, dismissing his concern.

As they crossed through the house, Russ explained, "So, you know I'd sent her anonymous little messages everyday attached to the bouquet."

"Tawdry, disingenuous hogwash—"

"Love notes."

"Senseless lumbering of forests, if you ask me."

"Which is why I didn't. But what I never told you was that on that last day, the day before her accident, I'd attached a message to her bouquet revealing that her secret admirer was a fellow member of faculty—and single—and I asked her to meet me at 1:15 under the pregnant tree."

"The bloody pregnant tree!" Stem exclaimed in disgust. "Of all the places you could've met her on campus—the coffee shop—"

"That's technically not on campus."

"Then the forum, the fountain, after chapel, the caf—and you chose the *pregnant tree*!"

"It was a centralized location point between our two buildings, all right?"

To show his repugnance for the gesture, Stem spit in the sink.

Russ huffed, "Well, I don't think anything was weird about it."

"Then why didn't you tell me all this back then?"

"Because telling you about it didn't seem very romantic, and I wanted it to be. So, I—"

"Hang on, mate," he said, putting out his hand to stop the

fellow. "I just need a minute for my stomach to settle. This is too much sappiness to imbibe at once." After spending a moment doubled over, Stem finally uprighted himself and announced, "You may proceed."

"I was planning to get there a few minutes early and be waiting with another bouquet."

"As if the *seven* she'd already received weren't enough punishment to her sinuses."

"But it was rainy and, just before I stepped out of the humanities building, it started downpouring. I didn't have an umbrella and didn't want the flowers to wilt."

"Why not just leave them behind?"

"I thought about that, but I wanted to give them to her. But I also figured she wouldn't come out in the deluge, not to meet someone she didn't even know. And I started to feel all nervous about it. What if she didn't like me? Or she didn't show up? What if she had some boyfriend I didn't know about? So . . ." His head fell in shame. "I chickened out."

Stem spent a moment massaging the headache out of his forehead. Then, looking at his friend, he opened his mouth—however, it was consumed with speechlessness.

"Say something," urged Russ.

The man's mouth gaped for a full twenty seconds before words poured forth. "You spent $400 and an entire week of your life—probably lumbered half a forest with all the hogwash you wrote. You did all this for charming a girl you'd never met, only to leave her standing outside in a monsoon?"

A sheepish expression adorned Russ' face as he offered up a half-hearted nod.

Stem shook his head. "Mate, that is the dumbest thing you have ever done . . . and I don't say that lightly."

"Wasn't my best moment—which is why I've never said a word about it."

"So, I'm guessing that, after waiting a few minutes under the pregnant tree, she then walked down the sidewalk, and, as she was crossing that drive just before the parking lot . . ."

"She was hit by the truck."

"And she never discovered it was you who stood her up, yeah?"

Russ affirmed this deduction with a nod. "The accident affected her memory and she forgot that last note I'd sent. Didn't even remember the meeting under the pregnant tree, not that she would've known I'd sent it anyway."

Stem shook his head. "You're an idiot."

"All right, fine, I know I am. It was the stupidest thing I've ever done, which is why I want to go back and change it."

His friend hesitated to speak. At last, with a sigh, he conveyed, "Really noble of you but, mate, let me put it like this. The accident completely changed the trajectory of her life."

"I'm aware."

"Her future before it was clear—at the end of that semester, she was leaving her adjunct position, quitting her job at the hospital, moving to Africa to serve on a medical mission, and she was *not* coming back."

"Which had been her dream since she was a little girl. But because of that day, her dreams were crushed, and she's lived with horrible, agonizing pain that physically and mentally tortures her—and *I'm responsible for that*."

"Mate—"

"No, I can't change the decisions my mom or Meemaw made that led to their deaths, but I can change *my* decision."

"But mate, just because you played a role in it doesn't mean you have to—"

"No," Russ objected. "I realize now that guilt has eaten me up. I've spent years with it. And when I said I was mad at Katie for needing me so much and that I blamed her for Meemaw's cancer, I was wrong. It wasn't Katie at all. What finally got to me was that I'd let this happen to her, that I'd brought about her paralysis and failing health." Stem opened his mouth, but Russ cut him off. "Not only was I losing Meemaw but all the signs were there—Katie would die young. She *will* die young if I don't do something about this." As Stem started to make another objection, Russ silenced him. "And even if I wasn't responsible for it, I love her too much to allow it to happen. Now go ahead and say what you're going to, but I've already made up my mind."

Placing a hand on his shoulder, Stem lowered his voice. "Mate, this is the most admirable and self-sacrificial decision you've ever made, but I just want to make it abso-bloody-lutely crystal clear to you what's at stake if you follow through with this plan. If she had never been struck by that truck . . . she never would've chosen you."

Chapter 26

Russ' determination to go back and change the trajectory of his ex-wife's life was more resolute than ever, however whereas he'd envisioned he'd have all the time he needed to accomplish this task, he was soon compelled to admit that perhaps his timeline might be shorter than expected.

What had begun with just the one alarming eBay message had grown to twenty-two, and added to their count were five emails. It mattered not to Russ whether he could confirm that the two communications claiming to be from the Japanese government were, in fact, genuine, for he surmised that the sheer quantity of overall messages and diversity of their contents and origins testified to their authenticity.

"We've got to fix this machine," he fretted. "Or else I'm gonna end up in jail, and it's going to be discovered, and the world's basically gonna end."

"That's a little overdramatic, yeah?"

"You're the one who said pandemonium would break out."

"Yeah, well I also said last Tuesday that I'd never eat Cheetos again." Stem glared at his friend as he shoved a handful of the orange puffs into his mouth.

"So, is the original glass repairable?"

After chasing down the cheesy snack with a gulp of milk, he

explained, "Look, it's got to be vacuum sealed, all right? To accomplish that with a crack like the one you put in it would be nearly impossible."

"Then we find another glass."

"Where? We've already scoured the internet with no luck."

"Check the feed stores. Call the farmers' co-ops. Advertise it in the rodeo pamphlet."

Charmed by the idea, Stem confessed, "I've never been to the rodeo before."

"They're overrated. But surely some good ole boy around here has one of these ancient commercial seed propagators in some barn somewhere."

"The chances of that are high, however, locating it with unblemished glass intact will be the biggest obstacle."

"Then we'd better get started."

Working with farmers proved more difficult than they'd anticipated. What was to Russ and Stem a matter of urgency was to the people they encountered a minor issue at best.

"Why don't ya just git yerself a new one?" asked one fellow. "Be a lot cheaper."

As Stem had reached his maximum tolerance for the question, Russ intervened. "Yes, you're right—that *would* save us money. But I've got very sentimental attachments to this particular propagation table."

The man sympathized. "I know how it is when ya git attached to a piece of equipment. Just can't let it go. But son, one thing I learned a long time ago is that some of them ole things ain't worth the grief. Always breakin' on ya. Ya end up spendin' more than you're earnin'. Take my advice 'n jus' buy yerself a new one."

Extending a handshake, Russ said, "I appreciate you. Thank you for your time."

"Been my pleasure."

Snatching up an irate Stem by the shirt sleeve, Russ dragged him out of the feed store. As they sat in the front seat of a rental car, Russ searched Google for more options.

"This is pointless," griped Stem. "We'd be better off ordering a new piece of glass."

"The glass and mirror store said it would take them months to reproduce it."

"I guarantee if you offered them $50,000, they'd have it done in a week."

Russ sighed. "You may be right about that, but in case you've forgotten, eBay is shutting down my account effective 9am Monday morning. And I have no doubt that those other email threats will soon result in an investigation."

"Let's go underground," suggested Stem.

"What does that mean?"

"It means we fake them out. We get false identities and hide in plain sight."

"Look at us," fumed Russ. "A half East Indian man and a crossbreed Aussie-Kiwi . . . in the middle of flipping Arkansas! Neither of us belong here, so what exactly is your plan for hiding either of us in plain sight?"

"I can fake an American accent," he said, horribly botching his attempt at the thing. "And you just speak in that voice you do. You know, that Indian gas station guy."

Russ chortled. "Imitating Apu from the Simpson's will likely draw more attention to me than just speaking like a regular hick."

"Your freshmen enjoy it every year when you teach the first class in the accent."

"*Enjoy* is a strong word. More like they spend the hour stressed, straining to understand the words coming out of my mouth."

"Then why do you do it?"

"For the same reason you teach an entire lecture every year pronouncing every word backwards."

Giggling, Stem confessed, "That's just fun for me."

Turning his attention to his cracked phone screen, Russ pulled up the address of the next feed store.

"Well, you know, you could say *y'all* more often."

Russ shook his head.

"I'm just saying, it's weird that you're from here but you don't sound like it."

"Okay, so now you want me to talk like that farmer in there?" Laying on the southern drawl, he said, "'You done need da git yerself a new propagator if'n yer to grow any of them seedlin's, son.' Huh? How's that?"

"Impeccable, actually. Why don't you normally speak like that?"

"*Why don't I normally*—Why in the heck would I want to sound like a dumb hick?"

"Because it identifies you as a native of this land."

"Look, when I need to lay the hick on thick, I can. But if that's not required of the sit-chee-ay-shun, then I prefer to sound intelligent."

Stem guffawed. "You? Sound intelligent?"

"Shut up."

"You know, mate, it's not all about the accent. A person's word choice is like a window into their IQ."

"That explains why a moment ago you said, 'That Indian gas station guy.'"

Stem guffawed. "I simply couldn't remember his name, and, with your excessive knowledge of the Simpson's, I knew you'd know about whom I spoke."

"Who cares. We could sit here and argue about semantics all day long, or we could get to work and search for a way to fix this dilemma."

Stem nodded in silence. However, as Russ turned his attention back to his phone, he tacked another argument onto his case. "See, you could've said right there, 'We could sit and argue semantics or find a resolution to our predicament.' Not only would it have been more *con*cise, but it would've been more *pre*cise."

"And you know what else I can say?"

"What?"

"Shut up."

The knock on Russ' door Friday morning startled him from a deep sleep. Rolling off the air mattress, he stumbled across the house, yawning all the way to the entryway. Believing the caller was Stem, he opened the door without caution. However, the hair on his neck stood up as he gazed upon two men in black suits. Behind them, idling in his driveway, sat the SUV which had shadowed him for almost a week.

"Russell Delacroix Brown?" one questioned.

"Yes," he responded slowly. "What do you want?"

"We're with the FBI. You are hereby summoned for questioning."

"Like right now?"

One nod from the man shattered Russ' plans for the day.

After quickly dressing, he texted Stem. "SOS! FBI at my house, taking me in for questioning!"

Silently fretting in the rear seat of the Tahoe, Russ was halfway to Little Rock when his pal replied, "That sucks."

"That's all you have to say? Call this guy—he's a grain broker. See if he can find the glass. Sweeten the deal for him."

Just as Russ sent the man's contact to his buddy's phone, Stem texted back, "What's a bloody grain broker???"

"He's the middleman between farmers. Buys feed from one, sells to another. Coordinates the transportation logistics too."

"There are so many things I don't know about redneck culture."

As the vehicle crossed over the Presidential Clinton Park Bridge into downtown Little Rock, Russ replied, "Just call the guy!"

"Ok. Are you arrested?"

"Not by this conversation."

The message had not been sent a moment too soon—just then, Russ and his chaperones pulled into an underground parking garage. Immediately, the four bars on Russ' phone were replaced with the words, "No signal."

Chapter 27

Stem glanced over Russ' shoulder as he admitted him entrance to his house. "They follow you?"

"Yeah, I asked them to drop me off here."

"Cool!"

Russ had hardly begun rehashing the events of the day before Stem put up his hands to stop him.

"Wait," he interrupted. "They bought you breakfast *and* lunch?"

"I knew that part would distract you."

"Offended is more like it."

"Because they didn't let me starve?"

"Hey, I'm as much a part of this as you are, and I'm just wondering why they didn't ask *me* some questions. For a couple of good meals, I'd have coughed up some really valuable info."

"Yeah, well you might get that chance. They wanted to know all about you."

Like a child gazing at presents on Christmas morning, his eyes lit up. "Tell me everything, but start with the part where they interrogated you about me."

"It wasn't much," said Russ, plopping onto the couch. "But thanks to your testimony the other day, I could at least answer them honestly. Told them your real name, although I have no idea how to spell it. And I told them where you're from and what your dad does."

"Did," he corrected. "He's retired."

"Then I probably wasn't much help in that realm."

Waving a hand, he dismissed the concern. "They can just Google him. What else?"

"Beyond that, they asked about my getting fired, which was embarrassing to disclose. And they wanted to know about Lance, of all things. I don't know why they think he's involved. But most of all, they were curious about what I sold on eBay."

"And you told them everything?"

"Well, I didn't deny that I have or have had possession of or have sold what may or may not have been stolen items."

Stem squinted and cocked his head to the side. "I'm definitely not convinced by that statement that you're not going to prison for a really long time."

"Well, it didn't matter what I said anyway. They had documented proof—copies of some of the messages I've received and printouts of my eBay transactions. Plus, they showed me all these documents I've never seen, proof that some of the things I sold really were stolen."

"We already knew they were."

"Yeah, but I didn't know *they* knew."

"Well, you know now. So, how did you explain that these objects came into your possession?"

"I just told them the truth—Meemaw died and left me a key to Peepaw's storage shed. When I went to clean it out, I found all these metal things which I assumed had belonged to Peepaw."

Stem's eyebrows shot up to his hairline and he ran a hand through his mess of curls. "I'm sure that piqued their curiosity, yeah?"

"Don't worry—I didn't say a thing about the Time Magnet, just that I assumed, because Peepaw was a welder, that he had created the items, which, as you'll recall, was indeed my first thought."

"True."

"So, I told them I had no knowledge of the items being stolen before I hawked them on eBay."

Shaking his head, Stem sighed. "See, Russell, this is what I mean."

"What?"

"Did you actually use that word, *hawked*?"

"Probably."

Stem gave a disapproving glare.

"What's wrong with saying it?"

"I'm aware that you know how to navigate the finer points of the English language, but I'm perplexed about why you choose to command it as though you're a teenage skateboarder."

"I'm colloquial."

Light flooded Stem's eyes and a smile swept across his face. "That was a satisfying, succinct and yet informative choice of words."

"Thank you."

"There's more praise where that came from—you simply must earn it. Now, where were we? Ah, yes, you were just displaying your idiomatic ability to converse with the everyday man through the use of the mono-syllabic expression *hawked*."

A noted glare emitted from Russ' pupils. "So, as I was saying before you flaunted your ego in my face, I denied knowing about the thefts. And then they wanted to know what else was in Peepaw's storage shed."

"And did you tell them?"

"Well . . . I told them there were other items which may or may not have been stolen as well."

"And?"

"And I offered to hand them over if they wanted them. I mean, if it'll buy us enough time to get this machine repaired, what's it matter if I turn over the rest of the stolen goods to the feds? The entire outcome of this current time and date—What do you call it?"

"The first monopole era."

"Yes. *That* will be new and improved."

"Altered."

"Same thing."

"Not really."

Russ cast the man another scowl.

Shrugging, Stem questioned, "So, did they want to know anything else?"

"Probably, but my brain's kind of shot. And my nerves, a little. I could use a nap."

Stooping beside his couch where Russ lay dozing, Stem lightly touched Russ' arm. "Wake up, mate."

Drowsiness seized Russ like a vise.

Stem grinned as he realized the situation called for a more violent force to fully awaken his friend. Grabbing the man's shoulders, he shook him as hard as he could.

"Stop!" roared Russ, squirming away. "I'm awake. What the heck do you want?"

Flashing his phone screen at the guy, Stem instructed, "Look at this."

"What am I looking at?"

"It's the app I downloaded for the security cameras."

"I didn't know there was an app for that."

"How else should we know who's snooping around the place?"

A yawn the size of the Grand Canyon emitted from Russ' lungs. Through it, he managed to reply, "I don't know."

"Look!" Stem ordered. Pointing to his phone screen, he said, "Watch. This footage is from seven minutes ago."

Russ squinted as he stared at the dark screen. To make out any shapes or movement definitively was difficult. "I can't see a thing."

"See that?"

"What, that gray blob?"

"Right here." Stem's finger hovered over the screen.

Suddenly, his brain picked up on what his eyes were seeing. Taking the phone, Russ replayed the footage again. "Wait, is that a person?"

"Yes! Someone's poking around 42B."

Russ' heart pounded. "Did they get inside?"

"No, looks like they're just examining the exterior."

"Do you recognize them?"

"I was going to ask you the same."

"I can't tell anything about them except that it's a man—I think."

While Russ poured over footage from other camera angles, Stem warmed up two frozen dinners.

"Find anything?" the cook hollered from his kitchen.

"Not really. I could see headlights from when they pulled up, but I couldn't make out the type of vehicle. And it looks like they sat in their car for about five minutes before they drove away. But that's all I could tell."

Stem returned to the living room, warm chicken pot pies in hand. Setting one on the coffee table for Russ, he took his phone back. After viewing the other videos, he concluded, "This is getting too serious. We must find a replacement glass soon."

"Yep," agreed Russ. "Looks like it's just a matter of time before we're both screwed."

Sophia, the bank manager, had once been Russ' junior high love interest, though, standing before her now, he could not at all imagine why he'd been infatuated with the girl. Not that she was ugly or unpleasant, but she had an annoying way about how she spoke (both the movement of her lips and the snap of her tongue against the roof of her mouth like a leather whip), and this irritated his nerves like wearing a pair of wet jeans. For her part, however, she remained professional as she counted out his cash.

"Now, sweetie, since you have the *free* checking account," she conveyed, "you can only withdraw a maximum of $10,000 a day. You'll have to come back *on Monday* if you need any more."

Noting this with a nod, he crammed the bulging stack of $100 bills into his athletic shorts and ordered an Uber. As he sat waiting on the curb, he tossed a wave at his pals in the black Tahoe who had resumed their observations of him. While their presence had at first been alarming, it now just rankled his nerves.

For some reason, he had expected that riding in a taxi which was being tailed by another vehicle would be more exhilarating. Kendall, the Uber driver with whom he grew more familiar by the day (and who Stem raved was White County's top driver for hire), also seemed to be under the impression that the ride should feel more akin to a James Bond movie, but given his testy driving record, he lamented he couldn't go past three over the speed limit. In the hopes of shaking the Tahoe, Russ impulsively suggested Kendall pretend to pull into a car wash which he could then whip through and exit into the alley behind the building, thus shaking their pursuers. To their utter disappointment, they realized all too late that it was a track-guided wash with which you must align your tires so it can pull you along. As the driver contemplated maneuvering around the obstacle, two more people pulled up in line behind them. Three minutes and $15 later, the glistening silver Kia exited the car wash into the alley where the Tahoe awaited them.

When they reached Stem's house, Russ ordered, "Wait here," before jumping out. Welcoming the chance, Kendall pulled out his phone to pass the time with TikTok videos. To his chagrin, his passengers returned within the minute.

Half an hour later, the three pulled to the end of Mermaid Lane. Eyeing the field suspiciously, Kendall questioned, "This?"

"Wait here," said Stem. "We may be a while."

"Like, how long?" questioned the driver.

The two men looked at each other, neither knowing the precise answer.

"A while," replied Russ.

"I charge by the minute not the mile," their driver explained.

"That's fine."

"Not that I care," remarked Kendall as the men slid out of their seats, "but wouldn't it just be cheaper to rent a car?"

Stem guffawed. "Not with this bloke's driving record."

Putting the brittle caulking to work with a box knife and a letter opener Russ had found on one of the shelves, the pair carefully removed the cracked glass from the apparatus.

"Gently," Russ reminded as he watched Stem carefully pull on the fragile piece.

"You think that remark's necessary?" quizzed the man. "As if I'm not already aware that I'm removing a fractured protective barrier from a non-professionally crafted volatile nuclear device."

About an hour after they arrived, Stem triumphantly exited the storage shed with the glass intact in his hands. Calling back to his friend, he ordered, "Lock it up tightly!"

"You think that remark's necessary?" Russ barked. "As if I'm not already aware that I'm being investigated by the FBI for crimes I committed!"

As they headed back to town, Kendall glanced nervously at the Tahoe in his rearview mirror. "Hey, guys? Why are we being followed again?"

"No reason," said Stem, and Russ affirmed this with a nod.

Forcing a nervous chuckle, he questioned, "I'm not helping y'all do anything illegal, am I?"

"No," they quickly replied in unison.

"Perfectly legit," Russ added.

"We are law abiding American citizens," assured Stem.

Two sets of eyes fell upon him.

"Well," he backpedaled. "He is. And you are. And I have a visa. So, everything's on the up and up."

Their first stop at Arkansas Glass and Mirror proved disappointing.

"I told y'all already," spoke the manager through his droopy frown, "I'd love to help you fellas out, but the fact is, it'll take months and will cost more than it's worth."

Glancing around, Russ withdrew the cash from his pocket and slid it across the man's desk. "$10,000 deposit today. Another 10K when we pick up the glass. How soon can you have it ready?"

The man scoffed. "Same timeframe."

"What?" Stem exclaimed. "We're offering you $20,000 cash, mate, under the table, and you're unwilling to budge a centimeter?"

"Look, fellas, I'd love it if cold hard cash could magically make custom-ordered glass appear, but the truth is, the lady who does my specialty orders is on maternity leave, and she's the only one who can take complex measurements like what you're needing for this fabrication."

Challenging the man, Stem said, "I'm sure she wouldn't mind to set that bub down for a few minutes to put a bit of padding in her nappy bag, yeah?"

If his goal was to bristle the manager's feathers, he would've won a gold medal.

"Gentlemen!" the man boomed. "This is not how professional businesses are run!"

"Ran."

Stem's murmur received a glare from his friend, who intervened in the matter.

"All right, sir, we understand," Russ said calmly. "You're right—we are being unprofessional demanding this type of request from you." Taking the slow dissipation of the redness in the man's face as a good sign, he continued. "However, I'm sure you have *many* capable employees working for you who are overly qualified to assist in the fabrication of a custom order such as this. And cash under the table is *not* our only option of payment—we are perfectly happy to charge it on a credit card, write you a check, Venmo you some dough, send a Western Union transaction, or compensate you in *whatever* method you prefer. And we hope our willingness to pay a premium for your services conveys to you the urgency and importance of the matter."

Though this response appeased his anger, it further aroused the manager's skepticism. Crossing his arms over his potbelly, he declared, "Son, you're evidently a well-spoken young man who knows how to get what he wants. But I'm no fool, and any two fellas willing to pay $20,000 for what's basically a cake stand dome are up to no good, and I ain't gonna be a part of it. So, you two best leave this business establishment before I call the chief of police down here, you understand?"

Fumes could almost be seen emitting from Stem's nostrils as Russ dragged him out of the building, and a calming distraction was called for.

"Hey, Stem, what'd you hear from that grain broker?"

"Abso-bloody-nothing!" he barked. "Left a voicemail yesterday morning and haven't heard a word from the bludger."

Handing the glass to Stem, he instructed, "Here, you go put this up and I'll try him." Pulling out his phone, Russ dialed the man's number.

"Y'hello!" came a voice on the other end.

Russ cleared his throat. "Is this Wade Dodger?"

"Sure is. What can I do for ya?"

Hearing the southern drawl in the man's tone, Russ engaged his colloquial accent. "Mr. Dodger, my name is Russ Brown. I'm in a bind, 'n someone said you might could help me."

"Don't know if I can, son, but I'll try. What's ailin' ya?"

"I've got this commercial propagation table—a real relic which belonged to my granddad. I'm needin' to replace the glass humidity dome on it. However, I haven't been able to find such a piece, 'n I thought maybe, given your connections, you might be the fella to call."

"A humidity dome?" Mr. Dodger laughed. "I've helped a lot of people find a lot of things they need but I ain't never done one of them. What's this here dome look like exactly?"

"I'll text you a pit'ture, if that's all right? It's a real dinosaur 'n fairly large." Glancing over at Stem who was carefully loading the piece in the back of the Kia, Russ described, "Maybe one by two by three feet rectangular. I'll have to measure it to be sure. The sides curve up to a flattened top, 'n it's hinged to the propagation table so it lifts up easy like. Might've been made by a local farm equipment company that used to be in these parts."

"FarmGrow?"

"You've heard of it."

"Sure, but can't say I seen much of their equipment in use these days."

Seeing Russ' shoulders slump, Stem sported a frown.

"But I do know a fella at the U of A Agri Experiment Station who might know somethin' 'bout how to track down that propagation table. I'll giv'im a jingle."

A relieved, "Thank you very much," flowed out of Russ.

"Say, how much you willin' to spend on such a thang? Ballpark?"

"Much as they want."

"Thousand bucks?"

"Ten times that if that's what it takes."

"Well, all righty." Though never harsh, Mr. Dodger's voice took on a pleasanter tone. "I'll call you soon as I know somethin'."

When Russ got into the car, Stem questioned, "Bad news?"

Russ' accent returned to normal. "No news except that he'll look into it."

"Well, I've got news," announced his pal. "I'm buying lunch."

Chapter 28

The three men in the Kia found it amusing that their tailers seized the liberty to order their own meals at the fast-food establishment.

"He got the banana cream blast," Stem gawked. "I should've ordered one of those."

Leaning towards the front seat, Russ questioned, "So, Kendall, what's our bill at for the day?"

Checking his app, he declared, "$417.32."

"Bugger!" exclaimed Stem.

Kendall came to his own defense. "Hey, man, there was a surge today. I don't make the prices."

"It's all right," Russ assured, offering his buddy a pacifying pat on the shoulder. "I've got the dough."

"You know," said Kendall, "just spitballing here but for *that* price you probably could've made the monthly payment on a brand-new Mustang."

Stem grinned. "While you may be correct, my mate here cannot afford the insurance payment."

As the driver took a bite of his burger, he tossed out, "So, why don't *you* drive?"

Enjoying the interrogation, Russ filled the air with a sardonic laugh.

After glaring at his mate for a moment, Stem explained, “The reason is . . . personal.”

Vanilla Dr. Pepper coupled with the laughter rising in his belly nearly choked Russ.

Turning around to face the heckler, Stem barked, “The bludger in the backseat has something to say, yeah?”

While Russ dabbed a paper napkin at the drops of soda he’d expelled onto the back of Kendall’s seat, he accused, “It’s because you’re a cheapskate.”

Stem crossed his arms. “I will not deny that accusation, however, I feel it’s a shallow analysis of my resolution.”

“Oh, no!” roared his friend. “I know you’ve calculated the costs of owning a car versus bumming rides off people—” When Stem opened his mouth to object, Russ quickly added, “And *occasionally* paying for hired transportation—and you’ve concluded it’s more cost effective—for *your* pocket, mind you—to choose the latter.”

He could almost see a blush rise in Stem’s face.

“Oversimplified, once again,” objected the man in question.

“But true nonetheless.”

“All right, I’ll grant you that. However, there’s more to it.”

“Care to share?” Russ challenged.

“Okay, I will. I have nothing to hide. Possessing my own vehicle would provide me with limitless access to any number of casinos within the septuple-state area which would no doubt be detrimental to my gambling sobriety.”

“Oof,” Kendall chuckled. “He got you.”

Russ shoved a tater tot in his mouth and glared out the window.

“Satisfied?” Stem asked.

“Here’s a suggestion,” snapped his mate. “*You* buy a car and get the insurance and *I* drive it. Then we’d both be happy.”

“Not a bad idea—if I wanted to throw thirty thousand dollars down the dunny!”

“Oof!” their driver roared. “You guys are great!”

On Monday morning, bad news arrived on Russ' doorstep. Upon its delivery, he took a moment to steady his nerves before questioning, "And what if I refuse to let you inspect the storage shed?"

"Then we will issue a search warrant."

"How quickly can you get one of those?"

Sizing up the man standing before him in his boxer shorts, the FBI agent squared his jaw. "There's *nothing* preventing us from issuing a warrant *this very minute* . . . but we would like to give you the opportunity to accede to our request before we take extreme measures. Your cooperation will, after all, cast you in a more favorable light *in court*."

Russ laced his fingers behind his head and took a deep breath. "Okay, I understand. Can you just please give me twenty-four hours?"

The man glanced at his watch. "If you don't cooperate by 8:15 tomorrow morning, we will take measures into our own hands."

Right away, Russ called Stem.

"Bloody heck!" the Kiwi exclaimed. "Even *I'm* getting paranoid now."

"We've got to do something about that glass."

"All right, I've been thinking about it and I have a really irresponsible idea."

"Perfect. Let's do it."

Though he had once again driven Russ to the bank, the presence of an additional black Tahoe on their tail as they headed out of town caused Kendall an intolerable amount of anxiety. At Tanner's One Stop just outside Searcy, he dropped his occupants. As Russ watched their driver speed away, Stem took off in the other direction.

"Where are you going?" Russ questioned.

Stem pointed at the gas station. "Into the servo to get some lollies, mate. Want anything?"

He kicked at a rock and pouted, "No." However, rethinking the decision, he hollered, "Well, maybe a box of Hot Tamales!"

"Got it!"

The two SUVs trailing them had parked in front of the tire air pressure machine. After contemplating a crazy idea for a moment, a desperate Russ ambled over and knocked on the window. As it rolled down, he spied a muscular man behind the wheel.

"Hi," Russ greeted. "Uh, since you guys are gonna follow us everywhere, we were just wondering if maybe you could give us a ride?"

The driver snickered. However, turning his head, he deferred to his teammate.

"Where ya headed?" the passenger asked.

"Mermaid Lane." As the two agents exchanged a look, Russ quickly added, "Come on, guys. You know you'll end up there sooner or later anyway."

Along with a nod, the agent in the passenger seat issued a pat down for the tagalongs. Stem exited the gas station, two full plastic bags in tow, just in time to see Russ spread his feet apart and place his hands on the Tahoe's rear window. As Stem strolled over, slightly amused but mostly horrified, an agent in the second SUV got out to see what the situation was. Hearing their suspects wanted a lift, he laughed, shook his head in slight disbelief, and returned to his own vehicle.

The only break in the silence as they rode to Mermaid Lane occurred when Stem offered some Starbursts to the agents. While the driver declined, the passenger accepted a couple of the boxy chews with gladness. Russ feared the agents might try to follow them into the storage shed, but the men appeared uninterested in exiting their vehicles, save for one who stepped out to take a phone call.

Once they were securely locked inside 42B, Russ whipped out his phone.

"Hi, I need a windshield repairman to come to me," he said, waving away a bag of chips Stem insisted on offering him. "I'm in

Rose Bud, all the way down Mermaid Lane. At the very end. How soon can someone be here? Oh, really? Well, it's really important and I'm willing to pay extra for them—yes, I have a credit card number. Just a sec."

Forty-five minutes later, a white 15-passenger van with whited out rear windows pulled to a stop at the end of Mermaid Lane. Having tracked the repairman on his newly added app, Russ stood near the cattle gate awaiting his arrival.

"Howdy," greeted the visitor who, though a few years past his prime, carried himself with the energy of a young man. "Which of these SUVs needs fixed?"

"Actually," said Russ, "it's not either of them."

Turning, the repairman glanced around for a third vehicle.

Russ explained, "So, we've got a little situation, you see. We have a large piece of glass—it's a humidity dome for a propagation table—"

"Oh yeah?" questioned the man as he squinted the sun out of his eyes.

"It's cracked a little and we would like you to fix it."

"Sorry, son. I'm only insured to do windshields."

Glancing around, Russ lowered his voice. Withdrawing a few hundreds from his pocket, he promised, "I can pay you $1000 and I'll never tell a soul."

The repairman took a nervous glance around, his eyes running over the field and Tahoes and prairie home all at once. "Son, now, I'm assuming this is all legal, that you're on the up and up, am I right?"

"Yes, sir."

"'Cause I don't want this to be no setup, what you calling me out here in the middle of nothing."

"No, sir, I completely understand your concern. This is not a setup. I'm just a guy who needs this propagation dome repaired immediately."

As though he'd suddenly figured it out, a light of recognition flashed in the man's eyes.

"This one of them CBD farms?" asked the man. "'Cause I always been curious about them but never knew nobody who had one."

"Oh," uttered Russ. "Um, well, in that case, how about we keep this just between us then, huh?"

"Yes, sir," he said with a smile. "Where's your glass? Let me see what I can do with it."

Leading him just inside the storage shed where Stem waited nervously with the item in question, Russ explained, "We'd really like it to be as sturdy as possible."

"Completely solid," added Stem.

The repairman's head snapped up and a toothy smile formed on his face. "Say, you're not from around here, are ya, pal?"

"I'm a Kiwi," Stem replied.

"I thought that was a fruit."

After explaining the finer points of the nuanced title, Stem questioned, "How strong will this be when you're done with it?"

"Why? You gonna throw baseballs at it?"

"That had not crossed my mind, but I guess if this goes south, we just might."

"Well, I wouldn't do that if I was you, pal. But if you're planning to grow, well, *you know what* under it then I'd say it'll last you for years to come, know what I mean?"

"Certainly," he replied with a trace of uncertainty in his voice. "But let's assume my mate, Russ, decided to press with all his might against this glass. Would it withstand such an attack?"

After sizing up the man in question, the repairman stated, "If it's him, yes. If it's me, no."

In less than thirty minutes, their venerated guest made his departure. And as soon as the doors were locked again, the pair got to work installing the new piece of glass.

Admiring it, Stem remarked, "He did a good job, yeah? I can't even see where the crack was."

"How long does the caulk have to cure for?"

Not eager to break the bad news, Stem muttered, "Twenty-four hours."

"What? But they're gonna bust in here in less than twenty!"

"I'm aware. We'll just have to test it first."

After thirty-eight minutes of waiting, Russ was ready to test it.

"Turn it on," he urged.

"No."

"Come on, let's just see."

"It's not been long enough."

Frustrated, Russ demanded to know, "How long are you gonna wait?"

"At least three hours."

"Three hours?" he whined.

"What are you in such a hurry for? You've still got over three-quarters of a day."

"Yeah, but what if it doesn't work?"

"Our chances of it working are greater the longer we let it cure."

Stem's refusal to activate the machine even one minute before the three-hour mark nearly drove Russ mad. At last, Stem's phone timer sounded and Russ jumped into action.

"Turn it on."

"I'm working on it," grouched the scientist. "Just stand back."

"But when do I get in it. When do you send me back in time?"

"You cannot go back in time until the previous Wilson Loop has been completed."

"How long will that take?"

"Hopefully only a matter of seconds." With no idea of what to expect, Stem suggested Russ stand as far back as possible. "That way if the gamma rays incinerate me, you might be spared."

Heeding the warning, Russ grabbed a metal shield off one of the shelves and went to the far corner where he hid behind it. "Tell me when it's over," he called.

Stem's chest rose and fell with a deep, slow breath. Then, in his noblest voice, he announced, "Initiating Time Magnet."

The first thing Russ noticed was the vibration in his teeth—the electricity was palpable enough to put one in need of a dental plan, and it suddenly occurred to him that this may have been the reason all of Peepaw's teeth were chipped or broken. Keeping his jaw slack, he hoped his chompers would fare better.

"It's working!" called Stem, and his voice shook to the rhythm of the pulsations in the air.

Testing his own voice, Russ tried holding out a note. It tickled his lips, and the sound reminded him of sitting on the floor in front of Meemaw's box fan, laughing with his cousins as their choruses vibrated.

Driving away the good memory came a sudden flash of blue light, and a loud boom, like the shattering of glass, filled the air. Then, inexplicably, as though all sound and energy were sucked out of the room, the air fell silent and dark.

"Stem?" he said, almost in a whisper. The passing moment brought about a feeling of concern. Raising his voice, he called, "Stem?"

"I'm all right," said the man, although he hardly sounded so. "Just stay put until I get the breaker flipped on."

Fumbling for his phone, Russ dropped the shield.

"What the bloody heck was that?" hollered Stem.

"Sorry!"

In the light of his flashlight, Russ slowly made his way across the basement. However, an earsplitting scream sent him dashing past rows of shelves, crying, "What is it?" As Stem soiled the air with his profligate vocabulary, Russ took comfort in knowing the gamma rays had not killed his friend.

"Just look!" shrieked the scientist.

Unable to see well enough from his vantage point, Russ ran past the man towards the birdcage-shaped contraption. His phone light fell across the startling discovery, but his brain could hardly believe what his visual synapses told him. Gazing down at the putrescent, lifeless creature, Russ at last gasped.

"It's Peepaw."

Chapter 29

As Russ came to grips with the fact that Searcy's longest running missing person's case had just been solved, Stem restored electricity to the building.

"I can't believe it," Russ said, gaping as he hovered over the lifeless body. "Peepaw's . . . well, he's not come back to life, but he's come back from the dead."

Putting a hand on Russ' shoulder, Stem offered him a box of Milk Duds.

"No, thank you," he muttered. "Don't have much of an appetite at the moment."

Shrugging, Stem ripped the top off the box and poured a fourth of it into his mouth.

Russ stooped down, and, with a brave finger, he touched the corpse. "Seems like he's petrified."

"If you ask me," his buddy said through a mouthful of chocolate and caramel, "he's been freeze dried."

Beaming an expression of horror, Russ stared up at the man.

"Don't worry, mate. I'm sure it wasn't *too* painful."

For a moment, Russ took up vigil beside the man, resting his back against the birdcage bars. When the wave of lightheadedness passed, he lifted his face and looked around—and a second wave of bad news hit him. The sound of shattering glass had not solely been an auditory anomaly—the final leg of the Wilson Loop had obliterated their precious humidity dome.

"Sorry, mate," Stem sympathized. "But the good news is that we know for sure you won't end up like Peepaw."

At that moment, Russ' last ounce of hope drained from him like blood from a stab wound.

"I'm going to jail," he said slowly.

"There's always the chance you won't, although it's highly improbable. But hey, sunny side up here: The machine is officially broken so the powers at be will . . . have to fix it themselves."

"I'm going to jail."

"Now, now," said Stem. "You've got to stay positive. Reason number one: There is free food in jail. Reason number two: You won't have to go back to work for Dirk. And there are probably other reasons which escape me at this point since I'm basically as petrified in spirit as Peepaw is in body."

What at first felt like nausea in Russ' stomach began bubbling up as a giggle. Stem seemed to have the same sensation, and, soon, both men roared simultaneously with laughter.

"I can't believe this!" Russ chortled. "We've got less than sixteen hours until the feds bust in here—and we've got a cellar full of stolen goods *and* a dead body!"

The pair snorted and hooted until their lungs hurt. As the moment died down, Stem said, "Mate, we are so screwed."

At this, Russ erupted in laughter and they giggled together and cut jokes until their sides ached.

"Aw," said Russ, struggling to catch his breath. "That was the best laugh I've had in so long."

"It was great, mate." Reaching out to help his friend to his feet, Stem said, "I've got to give you an honest apology for helping get you into this mess."

"Don't worry about it," he said with a shake of his head. "It's been a pleasure having you at my side these ten or so years. Heck, maybe one day we can build our own Time Magnet and just go back and watch ourselves screw it all up like a rerun."

Inspirational posters featuring kittens and rainbows graffitied the walls of the room. As the men took their seats in chairs meant for tiny people, Russ couldn't help but smile and inwardly laugh at the situation. His last night as a free man and he chose to attend a recovery meeting held in a children's Bible classroom.

"Welcome to small group," began their leader. "I celebrate recovery over alcoholism and drug abuse, and I struggle with lust, pornography, self-worth, and co-dependency, and my name is Jack."

In unison, the other nine men in the room greeted, "Hi, Jack!"

"Hi, everybody. Let me just remind y'all: Keep your language clean. Stem, that means you too."

The scientist acknowledged the warning with a nod.

"So, let's go around and introduce ourselves."

As his time neared, Russ felt surprisingly calm. When the man to his right had wrapped up his intro, Russ adjusted his back in the seat. "My turn? All right. Uh, I'm Russ. I've never been to a small group meeting like this, but it sounded fun. So, yeah, I'm a thankful believer in God, and I don't think I qualify as having an alcohol addiction, but I did get hammered a couple weeks back and almost gave my bum dad fifty grand. And I totaled my second car in a month, but those two incidents were actually unrelated. And, uh, let's see. Oh, the FBI's been following me everywhere. Nice fellows actually. Gave me a lift over here, and they're waiting in the parking lot to drive me back to my cellar and arrest me. Uh, just out of curiosity, any of you fellows work for the FBI? Don't want to incriminate myself."

When he'd been assured that no members of the bureau had infiltrated the room, he continued.

"Cool. So, I was previously a history professor at Harding University until I had an affair with a student and was fired. And then I found a hidden basement full of stolen treasures which I sold on eBay. And I tried to fix this time machine that my friend and I found so I could go back and prevent all this stuff from happening, but I broke it on accident and it's not repairable. Oh, and my dead grandpa just showed up tonight but we still haven't buried him yet but I think we'll have time before we get arrested. So, yeah, I think that's about it. Thanks for listening."

The group gave him an enthusiastic, "Hi, Russ," before turning their attention to Stem.

"Hey, mates. I'm a grateful believer in Christ. I celebrate recovery over gambling and I'm working on swearing and junk food addiction, although I jumped off that band wagon headfirst, but I'll get back on it once I'm in prison tomorrow. Oh, and I need to take a chip for my anger because I tried to kill my best mate, Russ, last week. And I need to add another thing that I was struggling with but I guess I'm not really anymore, but maybe I still am. This is kind of existential, I suppose, but back when I was fixing the time machine for Russ, I felt uneasy with the idea that as soon as I sent him back to the past I, as I am now, would cease to exist. So, maybe that was grief. Or just selfishness. I'm not sure, but I'll take a chip for that too. And my name is Stem."

"Hi, Stem!" chorused the men.

The next fellow to introduce himself had a twinkle in his eyes as he glanced over at the two men who had gone before him.

"I believe in Jesus and all that," he began, "and I too suffer from paranoid schizophrenia and I just want to say that I've struggled for years to find a place where I fit in, but brothers—" he reached out a hand and rested it lightly on Stem's shoulder "—tonight I've finally found where I belong."

"Your name, mate?" asked Stem.

"It's Yancey."

"Hi, Yancey," said the group.

"Glad to meet you," said Stem, extending his hand for a shake. But when tears filled the man's eyes, the Aussie opened his arms wide and offered, "Come here. Lean in, mate."

As the crowd of men stacked the preschool chairs and slowly filed out of the room, Russ felt his phone vibrating in his pocket. Extracting it and seeing the name on the screen, his heart began racing. Quickly stepping out of the room, he answered, "Hello?"

"Mr. Brown?"

"Yes."

"Hi, there, this is Wade Dodger."

"Hello, Mr. Dodger."

"Say, I've got good news for you. I found a fella out in Dewey who's got just what you're looking for."

As hope rushed into Russ' soul, the blood drained from his head. Sliding slowly down the wall, he gasped, "You're serious?"

"Sure. 'N he says he can deliver as many as three in as early as tomorrow mornin'."

His heart was beating so quickly he could hardly hear a word the man said much less hold a solid thought.

"I'll come get them," proposed Russ. "I'll meet him somewhere—anywhere—as long as it's tonight."

"All right, let me check with the fella."

"I'll give him $19,000 cash on the spot."

"Well, now, hang on just a sec and I'll three-way him right in."

The 'sec' felt like an eternity until, at last, Russ heard Mr. Dodger's voice again.

"Mr. Brown? You there, son?"

"Yes, sir, I'm here."

"Good, now I've got Elias Whorlton here on the line. He's the fella with those humidity domes."

"Hello, Mr. Brown," came a drawled southerner's voice.

"Hi, Mr. Whorlton," Russ beamed. "I need those domes tonight. What'll I have to do to get them from you? I can pay as much as $19,000 cash."

Mr. Whorlton laughed. "You must sure be in a bind, son, to pay top dollar for such a relic as these. I reckon I can meet you halfway. Where are you now, son?"

"I'm in Pangburn."

"Pangburn? Why, that's just ten minutes or so down the road from me. How's about I meet you there at T-Ricks in about thirty minutes? Sound good?"

Tears filled his eyes. "Yes, sir!" he exclaimed. "I'll be there!"

In a daze, with shaking hands, Russ hung up the phone. His legs glided over the carpet as he headed for the kitten-postered classroom. Stem, who had been chatting with Yancey about time travel, greeted him. "Ready for prison, mate?"

"Stem." Russ spoke in such a commanding voice that both men turned their heads towards him.

"Why do you look like that?" questioned his pal.

"Because we're about to fix all of this."

Chapter 30

Of the three domes, Stem concluded only one was viable.

"Can't use that one because of the crack," he said, pointing out the obvious. "And this one has a chip on the top of the curve."

Examining their options, Russ felt doubtful about the man's conclusion. "Is that chip really more detrimental than the huge chip on the rim of this one?"

"Russell, am I the scientist or the ex-history professor?"

Rolling his eyes, he verified, "Scientist."

"Then trust my bloody analysis!"

They set to work removing the fresh caulk, and, in the midst of the laborious process they discovered that half-dried caulk is loads more resilient than its forty-year-old counterpart. After a while of fighting the devious sealant, their backs ached.

"I've got to rest a minute," said Stem. "Sustenance. I need a snack. Chips. Lollies. Anything."

Russ opened a snack-sized bag of Doritos, extracted a handful which he ate, and then tossed the remainder to the man.

"I'm gonna look online for some kind of caulk dissolver," announced Russ who had spent the past half hour stripping the same four-inch section.

"What will you do when you find it? Order it snailmail on Amazon and bank the digital download dollars?"

"I'll just go to Walmart for it."

"Mate, since Covid they've closed at eleven every night. If you haven't noticed, it's nearly 1am."

Stem wiped sweat off his forehead and wadded up his shirt as a pad beneath his knees.

Russ' feet would no longer stay planted in one spot, and, despite his attempts to work on the caulk, he found himself pacing the floor. As a wave of anxiety hit, he cupped his hands over his mouth, stifling the hyperventilation coming on.

"Go up for some air," Stem barked, "before you suck all the oxygen out of this bloody stuffy basement!"

The night air felt muggy, but the skies were clear enough to reveal a sea of stars beyond the atmosphere. As Russ peed behind the homestead-turned-storage shed, a gentle wind blew the stench of cattle across the open field, and he suddenly felt parched. Without any facilities or water at the end of Mermaid Lane, he dreaded the night lagging on any further. Soaking up his last night as a free man, he closed his eyes and let the wind caress his cheeks.

"Hello, Rusty."

At the sound of the familiar voice, Russ stumbled backwards. "What the crap, Lance! What are you doing here?"

"Should ask you the same. Seems like you've spent a lot of time here lately. And guess what I know?"

A whole bunch of nothing, thought his cousin.

"I know this land here you've been hanging out on belongs to Peepaw. And if I had my say, I'd guess this buildin' here was his storage shed, am I right?" Before Russ could respond, he added, "And don't try to lie to the Bucker or ya know what he'll do."

"All right," Russ said, steadying his breathing. "This *is* Peepaw's storage shed. But the reason I've been hanging around here is because my friend and I are working on an experimental project of his and he needed a secret laboratory in which to do it."

"That so? Then, ya won't mind showing the Bucker around, will ya."

As it was not posed as an inquiry, Russ had no other option but to acquiesce the rude intrusion.

"Sure," he said. "Just follow me."

As Russ descended the steps with Lance in tow, he called out, "Stem, we've got company."

"Bloody heck!" shouted the man. "You said they wouldn't be here until eight bloody fifteen in the morning!"

"It's not our pals in the Tahoes," his friend conveyed in a not so cheerful voice.

Almost as quickly as Stem's head popped around the corner of a shelving unit, deep red streaks colored his neck and face. "What the bloody heck do *you* want!"

"Nice way to treat a guest!" Lance hollered. "And I seen all this stuff you've been hoardin' down here, Rusty!" Pulling out his phone, he shouted, "I'm 'bout ta call in the infantry! Let's see what Haley and Gemini think 'bout all this, shall we?"

"Lance, hang on," said Russ, putting up his hands. "Before you do that, you need to see something."

"Yeah? And just what is it?"

"We found Peepaw."

A stream of tobacco juice piggybacked off a curse word which was hurled from his cousin's lips.

"It's no joke," Russ assured. "Just follow me. And brace yourself—it's gruesome."

Wearing a serious expression and taking a long gander at both men, Lance finally gave a small nod.

"He's this way," said his cousin somberly, ushering with his hand.

After Lance passed slowly between the two men, Russ made eye contact with his friend and tossed a nod towards a shelf. Having never liked his mate's domineering cousin, Stem was on the plan like cheese on mac. Snatching up some implements, he handed a couple to Russ and kept a sizable one for himself.

Quietly and quickly, they approached Lance, who stood captivated by the sight of his dead grandfather. Just as the same expletive from a moment earlier was spit from his lips, Stem heaved a thirty-five-pound copper diving helmet onto the man's head. A brief struggle ensued. However, within seconds, Russ had a pair of handcuffs linked around his cousin's outstretched wrists. As riled up as a bull in the arena, Lance raised his tandem hands to pull off the helmet, but his two rivals were already halfway into the next phase of their plan to subdue him. A metal baseball bat to the gut knocked the wind out of him long enough for them to hogtie him with ankle shackles. With his hands linked in front of his body and chained to his legs, which were splayed out like a frog's, the front-heavy man rolled onto his side and was rendered almost completely immobile by the restraints.

"Bloody heck!" Stem exclaimed, resting his hands on his knees to catch his breath.

Still sporting the diving helmet, Lance rolled around on the floor like an upside turtle. "Let me go! Rusty, you're gonna pay for this!"

As he strained to reach his phone which had landed a few feet from him, Russ kicked it across the room and hollered, "Shut up, or I'll fry you like Peepaw!"

The threat silenced the man, and the helmet, which rested against the floor, stayed in one spot as Lance turned his head this way and that like a ball in a joint.

"What should we do with him?" asked Stem, who figured Russ' barrage of redneckery skills might include some sort of protocol for hogtied intruders.

"Let's drag him to the corner under the stairs."

By the time the man's posterior was slid across the concrete floor, his pants were halfway to his knees and he sported a raspberry on his left butt cheek the size of a mango.

Pointing at the blubbering man, Stem questioned, "Should we, you know, pull them up, mate?"

Wiping sweat from his brow, he opposed the suggestion. "Nah, just leave 'em. If we get this machine up and running, he won't remember any of this anyway."

"Good enough for me. How about we get Peepaw dragged over here too?"

"Sounds good."

Though the dead body looked rather icky, the effects of the time-space vacuum coupled with the freeze drying had actually preserved it in a more or less solid state. After they moved the body, they removed the diving helmet from Lance's head. Seeing his dead grandfather lying next to him, he whimpered, "Don't leave me here with him, please, Rusty."

Ignoring him, they turned their attention back to the propagator dome.

"I've made progress on the caulk," Stem announced.

Squinting, Russ remarked, "Like an inch, maybe."

"Well, it's more than the help you've been the last twenty bloody minutes!"

"All right!" he shouted. "I'm just a little stressed is all. And thirsty. And sleepy. And buzzed on those sugar bombs you gave me earlier. What the heck were those?"

"Nerds clusters. You've had them before."

"No, I haven't!" he snapped. Then to himself, he muttered, "But they are addicting."

"I told you they're fair dinkum!"

In silence, they scraped and pulled and peeled away the new caulk, cursing the fact that they'd applied it so liberally only hours earlier.

"There," Stem at last stated. "It's clean."

Glancing at his phone, Russ announced with a yawn, "It's 3:30. Let's get this glass installed so we can take a short nap."

"It must cure for three hours *minimum*," warned the physicist.

As Russ pumped out the bead of caulk around the lip of the glass, Stem smoothed it and filled in any gaps between the glass and its base. All seemed to be going well until Russ muttered, "Oh, crap."

"Why do you say that?"

"Because it's a lot less offensive than the S word."

"Fair enough," he conceded, touching up a section of caulk. "But I should clarify what I meant by my question: What provoked you to say that?"

Holding up the caulk gun, he squeezed the handle. To Stem's horror, nothing came out. "Did you make it all the way around?" he shrilled.

"No. There's still at least six to eight inches left."

"But you bought more, yeah?"

"No. I only got the one tube."

Stem's scowl could've pierced his mate's heart.

"How was I to know we'd be installing two glass pieces today? I thought the other was one and done."

"Uh, guys," called Lance. "I need to pee."

"Don't let us stop you!" barked his cousin.

Stem rose to his feet and dusted off his knees, rather roughly too, hoping the action would keep the harshness out of his voice. "Firstly, one should always overprepare when scarcity may become an issue. Secondly, you're an idiot so let me see that gun for myself." Despite his efforts, his buddy's conclusion was correct. "Well, crap," he repeated. "Let me see what I can do."

While Stem reworked and resmoothed beads of caulk which he'd already doctored, Russ sat on the metal floor of the birdcage.

"Is this really gonna work?" he fretted more than inquired.

"It bloody well better now, or else you and I will spend the next twenty to thirty years in solitary confinement."

With a sigh, he professed, "I hope it does. And I hope I can prevent Katie's accident. I can't even remember what it was like to see her walk on her own feet."

The thought brought a smile and small chuckle to Stem's lips. "She had really nice legs, mate."

"She was a runner."

"And you remember she used to play intramurals sometimes?"

"Oh, yeah!" Russ exclaimed. "I used to come to the soccer games just to watch her run around on the field."

"And she did Ultimate. I played her team a few times. And I might've more or less sort of tackled her once or twice."

"What? But Ultimate's no-contact."

Stem sported a grin. "I know."

"Wait, you're saying you had the hots for my wife."

"She wasn't your wife—*yet*."

"Fair enough."

"In all honesty and platonicness—"

"That's not a word."

"Shut up. It's four in the bloody morning. And I am overjoyed at the thought of her having the full use of all her appendages again."

"You gonna marry her?"

"Are *you*?"

Russ scoffed. "You were right when you said it—she wouldn't marry me if she wasn't injured in that accident. She was . . ."

"Leagues above you?"

"And she still is," he added with a yawn. Reclining, he sighed, "Unfortunately, this guy has no future with that woman and . . . I'm just happy she'll be able to pursue her dream."

As he dabbed at a line of caulk with his finger, Stem inquired, "She the first girl you ever loved?"

Russ contemplated the question for a moment before responding, "I think so. There were other girls before her with whom I was infatuated, but I didn't really love any of them. Not like Katie."

"So, Russell Brown was a player, huh?"

"No," his friend objected with a slight blush. "I was never the type of guy that girls were really into, at least not at first appearance anyway. But there always were those girls who seemed to have a thing for foreign-looking guys and I might have taken advantage of that a time or two." Upon Stem's request for an amusing story, Russ shared, "All right, so there was this girl in undergrad. Stacy. She loved movies and I had to take this classic films course for some random humanities credit. Not that I hate movies, but I just really didn't care to spend the time watching all these weird retro ones like *American Graffiti* and *The Graduate* and stuff like that."

"Those are great shows, mate."

Shrugging Russ confessed, “Well, I never watched ’em. But Stacy had seen them all, and each week we were supposed to watch one of these movies and then write this essay about it answering all these random questions our prof came up with. And I wasn’t really that into Stacy but she offered to write my papers for me, so . . .”

“I always knew you cheated your way through college.”

“Never said I didn’t. But that was actually the only time.”

“So, how’d you break it off?”

“Well, she went back home for the summer and I just never answered her phone calls after that.” To Stem’s look of absolute disdain, Russ replied, “Not that I’m proud of it. Geez, I’ve known you ten years and I’m just now confessing this. Cut me some slack.”

“All right,” said Stem, “while we’re on the subject of confessions regarding women, I’ve never told anyone this. Not a soul.”

A grin spread across his friend’s face. “Lay it on me.”

“All right, also not my proudest moment but . . . I pashed with Britney Spears once.”

“What the—” Russ bolted upright. “You made out with *the* Britney Spears?”

Stem confirmed with a nod. As though recalling a casual Saturday afternoon game of pickup football, he nonchalantly conveyed, “It was in the early days of her first tour in Europe. My brother had backstage passes and she came to the after party. Anyway, it didn’t go beyond the couch but we pashed for like an hour.”

From under the stairwell, Lance hollered, “You’re the man!”

“Appreciate that, mate,” Stem called out. “Anyway, not my proudest moment either.”

“Wow,” said Russ as he shook his head and laid back down. “Just wow.”

“Anything else you’d like to get off your chest before you possibly die in a time traveling catastrophe?”

“Let me think about it for a sec.” Staring up at the birdcage’s pinnacle, he remarked, “That’s a really big diamond. Wonder where he got that."

"Who knows? Maybe he had better luck at the diamond mine than my family did."

"Wouldn't it have been weird if I'd been there at the same time you were and our paths had crossed, like, when we were kids?"

"No. The chances of two people's paths crossing prior to their official first meeting are actually higher than being killed in a car crash."

"Really?"

"That is, unless you're driving. Then the odds are switched."

Russ scoffed. "Did I ever tell you about the first time I drove, when I stole Peepaw's old truck when I was, like, twelve?"

"I remember that!" Lance hollered. "You drove that thang to—"

Russ silenced him with a shout. "Are you telling this story or am I?"

"Sorry. You tell it."

"So, the reason I took it in the first place was because I was going to run away. It seems like I was mad because Meemaw said I couldn't get a skateboard."

Lance interjected, "I thought it was 'cause she whooped your butt?"

"No!" his cousin objected. "She did that all the time. I remember now—this was specifically because she wouldn't let me buy this skateboard at the store because it had a skull and crossbones on it. And I wanted to buy it with my *own* money, but she said it was demonic and no grandson of hers was gonna become a devil worshiper."

Stem stood up and stretched.

"Finished it?" Russ asked with hopefulness in his voice.

"Solid seal, best as I could get it." After grabbing a bag of lollies, he plopped down in the birdcage beside his friend, exhausted. "Gummy worm?" he offered.

"No, thank you."

"I'll take one!" called Lance.

Though Stem tossed a frown at his best mate, he lumbered

across the room, stepped over Peepaw's dead body, and dropped one of the gelatin fruits in the captive's mouth. Then, returning to Russ' side, he laid back and said, "Continue your story of childhood rebellion."

"Oh, yeah, so I'd seen this video, maybe on MTV. All these kids were skating around San Francisco, like on the hills and down the streets and sidewalks and in these cool skateparks. And I know this probably sounds dumb but they were all different skin colors and I just felt like maybe I'd finally fit in somewhere for once, so I decided to run away and become a SoCal skate rat—"

"San Francisco's not in southern California."

"I'm aware." In response to Stem's dubious gaze, Russ defended himself. "Though I was not well-versed in California geography as a naïve twelve-year-old, you'll no doubt recall that my doctoral thesis some fifteen years later was on the monumental impact of the California Gold Rush on the development of numismatics in the United States as well as abroad."

His friend's doubtful expression remained unaltered.

Slightly offended, Russ stated with noted smugness, "In fact, as you're aware, I've become somewhat of an *expert* on American coinage. Case in point, I was recently invited by the curator of the National Numismatic Collection to give a lecture on my thesis at the National Museum of American History in Washington, D.C. at the commemoration of the 50th anniversary of President Nixon's authorization of a series of new images on the reverse of our coinage to symbolize, for the *first time in American history*, the anniversary of our country's independence."

Through a yawn, Stem quipped, "Yet you could not distinguish spray-painted lead from authentic gold."

"Well, anyway," Russ huffed. "Never lived out my skate rat dream."

"What happened? Conscience get the better of you?"

"No, ran out of gas on the interstate. Got a good whooping for it too."

"I'll bet," Stem said as he dangled a gummy word over his

mouth.

"So, you ever run away? Oh, wait, you said you did in your testimony. That the only time?"

"No, I took off loads of times. Made it all the way to Tokyo once."

"For real?"

"Yeah, stowed away on a cruise ship. Did not expect the bloody thing to go that far."

"Wow, you've lived a much more exciting life than I have."

The man chuckled. "You kidding? My life would be drab and boring without you in it. Just think, if it weren't for you, I wouldn't be heading to prison in approximately three and a half hours nor would I also be potentially disappearing from existence in roughly the timeframe."

Russ glanced over at his friend. "I don't have to go," he said quietly. "I can stay so you can keep, like, existing."

"No, mate," he replied with a resolute shake of his head, though Russ saw tears glisten in his eyes. "I want this for Katie. Like you said, I've lived a full life—the life I wanted for myself. But she hasn't, and I want that for her."

"What if I don't fix it? Like, what if I go back in time and try to stop the accident but it's just cosmically destined to happen and nothing I can do changes that? And then I come back to era one—"

"First monopole era."

"Yeah, and the FBI's here and they arrest us both and Katie's still paralyzed?"

"Guess I'd ask them if I could take some lollies with me in the Tahoe."

A hearty laugh escaped Russ' chest. "I'm gonna miss you."

"It's not like you'll never see me again . . . unless the machine breaks and you're trapped in the Wilson Loop. But if my estimations are correct, you'd black out in less than twenty seconds in which case you wouldn't have time to truly miss me anyway."

"But what if it works? Then what'll happen? Will you be here when I get back? Like *you* you, or will it be a different you? How does that work?"

Stem took a moment to consider the question. "I believe, if you succeed, then it would be a different me. Still me, just different—and not *me* me."

"Okay, so like an altered you or just a regular you?"

"Like a me without my memories but with different memories."

"But you won't, like, have three heads or anything weird like that, right?"

Stem gave the man a look of grave pity. "You're not bloody altering the molecular and biological construction of all living existence, mate. You're just stopping a truck from slamming into your ex-wife."

"Okay," Russ said defensively. "Just checking. Didn't want it to be weird when I got back."

"Oh, it'll be a little weird, I'm sure. You are, after all, altering your entire future as well as Katie's and possibly mine. So, that being said, if you succeed then you'll enter an altered first monopole era, and, thus, have no knowledge of what's occurred in your life in the past ten years."

"Dang, they're gonna think I've got amnesia." Russ' mind reeled. "And what if I'm married to someone else? And what if she's ugly or annoying? Or what if I did something really stupid and accidentally died between then and now? Would I still, like, respawn? Or would I just be dead and go straight to Heaven?"

"Don't have a bloody clue. You sure you don't want a gummy worm?"

"No. You have any water? Or soda?"

Lifting his head slightly, Stem pointed. "Got a pinch of lemonade left in that bottle over there."

Jumping on the opportunity to whet his whistle, Russ downed the drink. However, the aftertaste was akin to drinking limoncello. "Yuck! How old is this?"

"Probably a couple weeks—or more."

Russ laid down again, flat on his back. "You set a timer for that caulk?"

"Yeah. A little over two hours left."
"Okay, because I'm probably gonna fall asleep."
"Go for it, mate."

Chapter 31

"Get up, Russell," ordered Stem.

At the smell of caulk wafting into his nostrils, he gasped. "What time is it? Are they here?"

"We've got thirty minutes."

In a flash, Russ got to his feet. "Is the caulk cured? Is it ready?"

"Curing time has been fudged a bit, however, I do not think it's prudent to delay any longer."

"I'm ready. Let's get this going."

"Okay, so listen abso-bloody-closely."

"That's not a word."

"I'm going on 12 minutes of sleep, so bloody shut up, you drongo. There are several numbers which you must memorize, and then, when you go into the past, you must tell me—the younger me—what they are. You must precisely convey this information, do you understand, so that younger me can send younger you back in time at the same moment and location where I send you—"

"Why?"

"So, you won't be stuck in the bloody Wilson Loop like Peepaw!"

Whipping out his phone, Russ clicked on the notes app. "Okay, just type them in here."

"No, Russell, you cannot take your phone. In fact, you can't take anything metal at all."

"How come?"

"Just trust me!" he snapped. Then, recovering his composure, Stem said, "Now, I searched this entire basement and there is not one bloody writing utensil unless you count that collection of antiquated nib pens which Peepaw stole, but without inkwells, they are a moot point. So, Russell, if there was ever a moment in time you needed to use your brain power to its utmost capacity, it is now."

"Wait! I've got an idea! Prick your finger and write it in blood."

"Yes!" Stem declared, as if enraptured by the idea. "And then I'll prick *your* finger. And then your head. And then your heart. Just bloody listen! I know you are deficient when it comes to numbers so I'll skip to plan B. I've converted the coordinates to Herigone's mnemonic major system so you can remember words instead. Then, when you tell them to the younger me, I can translate them back into numbers. Good?"

"Yeah, good. Tell me."

"Okay, listen closely. You must abso-bloody-lutely remember everything as I tell you. This *cannot* be altered or changed. *You must remember this verbatim*." He paused for a gummy worm. "This is the coordinate where I must send you . . . Draw. Whitish. Honeybee. Haram. Jam. Fussy. Ovum. Lorry. Unite. Hairy. Itchy. Now repeat them back."

"Draw. Whitish. Honeycomb . . . Touchy . . ."

"Crap," Stem muttered. "Okay, to plan C. Forget everything I just told you."

"Done."

"For this, we'll try the Dominic System. It aided in my ability to count cards. Listen to this phrase: 'A detonated arrow soared behind ninety dogs, catching straw, catching hay (old hay)—catching every darn barn ablaze,' Duke said . . . Now, repeat."

"No, *you* repeat it. I missed something."

"Russell, there's not a plan D! You must focus!"

"Just say it again!"

Stem rubbed his stressed temples and took a slow deep breath before walking Russ through the memorization exercise again. After four attempts, the man at last had the mnemonic set stowed in his memory.

Triumphantly, he exclaimed, "I got it! Now, anything else?"

"Yes, and this is perhaps even more important than the other, for it's the exact time today I'm sending you back which, by the way, is in about two minutes. Listen: One happy octopus ate crunchy eels. Now, repeat."

"One happy octopus ate crunchy eels."

Relief spread across Stem's face, smoothing his wrinkled brow like an iron. "Sometimes you make me so proud. Now say them both again." When Russ had satisfied the request, his friend instructed, "Now, quickly, answer these questions. Do you have any metal on your clothing or person?"

The man's phone, wallet, and house keys sailed across the basement. "That's all."

"Do you have any tattoos or body piercings?"

Indicating the redneck bicep barb tat which he got the day he turned eighteen, Russ declared, "Only this one."

Dismissively, Stem replied, "No, that one doesn't matter."

"Why not?"

"It just bloody doesn't!" Taking a deep breath, Stem calmly questioned, "Now, have you ever had any shrapnel or bullets removed from your body or metal removed from your eyes?"

Confused and exasperated, Russ barked, "Are you kidding me?"

"Just answer the bloody question!"

"Fine! No!"

After staring him down for a few seconds, Stem replied, "Good. Now repeat the phrases. You've got ninety-five seconds."

Russ spit the words out as quickly as his tongue could move.

"Excellent, mate."

Through his friend's smile, Russ could see a trace of sadness written on his face. Suddenly remembering Stem's confession of his existential conundrum, Russ flew out of the birdcage and embraced the man, wrapping him tightly in his arms, declaring, "I love you, brother."

"I know," said Stem with a devious smile. Then, pushing the man away, he ordered, "Now, go fix everything! And maybe we'll see each other again in Heaven."

Just as Russ' feet hit the metal floor of the birdcage, he felt the electrical jittering in his teeth and lips and cheeks and nose—his whole face and body. Suddenly, he felt overwhelmed with emotions. Sadness, joy, fear, peace—they consumed his soul.

"Hooroo, mate!" hollered Stem in that weird vibrating voice.

Russ forced a brave smile and tossed the man a thumb's up. However, just before the flash of blue filled the air, he saw fear sweep over his friend's face.

"Wait, Russell! Don't forget—"

But it was too late.

Chapter 32

Russ indeed passed through a vacuum, and, all around him, lights whizzed by like shooting stars. The only difference from this and space traveling at lightspeed was that he found himself free soaring without a spaceship with only his basketball shorts and t-shirt for protection from the elements. It all happened in a split second, yet with the oxygen being sucked out of his lungs and the saliva on his tongue beginning to boil, it felt like an eternity.

His chest hit something hard and it would've knocked the breath out of him had he had any.

Rolling over, he panted and stared up at a bright light, and, for a brief moment, he couldn't remember where he was or what he was supposed to do. However, all at once, reality struck him. Jumping to his feet, he glanced around and took notice of his surroundings.

The hallway in which he stood reminded him of Harding's science building.

Of course! I've gotta find Stem!

Taking off down the hall, he shouted, "Stem Bik! Professor Bik, where are you!" Pausing at a water fountain, he gulped liberally. Then, resuming his search, he flew past science labs and theater-style lecture halls, calling his friend's name. As the seconds ticked and the remaining length of hallway grew shorter, terror filled his heart.

What if I fail this mission? What if I go back to the future and nothing's changed?

"Stem Bik!" he screamed.

"What the bloody heck is going on?"

Though the voice was angry, hearing it brought immeasurable comfort to the time traveler.

"Stem!"

"What the bloody heck are you—"

"Shut up and listen!" Russ said, running up to him, panting. "I've got to tell you something and you must believe me." Catching his breath, he continued. "I'm not me. Well, I'm *me* but I'm not the me you know—I'm the me from the future."

Clearly not humored, Stem requested, "Mate, could this prank wait until after my senior physics class is over?"

"No! Listen! You—the you of the future—sent me back to this day in the Time Magnet because this is the most important day of my future ex-wife's life and I need you to write down what I'm gonna tell you so that you can send me—well, not *me* me but the me you know—you have to send him back in time on the same day and hour and to the same place where you—future you—sent me, as in, *me*."

"Lovely," said Stem with a dry stare. "A Time Magnet, you say?"

"Yes! A monopolar transmemberish . . . something."

"I see. And so because it's Valentine's Day today, someone, presumably one of my humorless colleagues, dared you to pretend that you're from the future and this is some kind of St. Valentine's Day monopole blip."

"No, listen to me!"

Irritated, Stem took off towards his classroom.

Stomping his foot, Russ hollered, "Ura'astema Bik the fourth! You Kiwi from Wellington!"

Dead in his tracks, Stem turned around, his expression a shade darker. "You've been searching the internet, I see."

"No, I'm telling the truth. I'm from the future and I need you to believe me. I've only got like eight more minutes."

"Then tell me something the internet doesn't know!"

Russ straightened up and dug deep. "You don't even like Smarties! And you're addicted to gambling and you have a terrible temper!"

"Any amateur sleuth could figure those out!" The familiar red streaks began taking over his complexion. "Russell, you've got three seconds to make me believe you!"

His mind raced. "I know what it is! You made out with Britney Spears on a couch in Europe!"

Stem's expression changed as quickly as a comet. The gaping of his mouth was soon crammed with uncontrollable giggles.

"I did it!" he exclaimed. "I created a time machine!"

"No, you didn't," Russ corrected. "My Peepaw did and it's hidden in a basement in an old shack in Rose Bud at the end of Mermaid Lane. Are you writing this all down?"

The scientist frantically patted the pockets of his lab coat. Then, tossing up his pointer finger, he quickly retreated to his classroom, and, before a crowd of senior physics majors, he exclaimed, "Ten percent bonus on their final to the first person who tosses me a pen and paper!" The professor had no way of knowing he had put his life in danger. Every manner of writing utensil soared at him like poisoned darts. Taking cover amidst a shower of writing implements, Stem stooped and grasped, retrieving a pink notepad and sparkly red ink pen. Returning to Russ, he furiously scribbled as he murmured, "Rose Bud. Mermaid Lane. Old shack."

"42B. Get the key from Meemaw. And find a man named Honk."

"You mean Hank?"

"No! Honk. H-O-N-K. He's in Bradford. He'll tell you how to repair the Time Magnet."

"All right," he said with a note of skepticism. "Anything else?"

"Yes. One happy octopus ate crunchy eels. That's my timestamp."

"Is that masticated or the number?"

Russ' eyebrows dove into a V, and, exasperated, he snapped,

"What?"

"Ate or eight? Like dinnertime or counting?"

"A-T-E . . . I think."

"Mate, why would you choose such an ambiguous word when there's an ocean of more appropriate options like 'admired' or 'accompanied'?"

"You chose it, not me!"

Raising his eyebrows, he remarked, "That's not likely. Now, what else? Coordinates?"

"Yes, thank you for remembering. A, let's see, how did it go? A detonated arrow soared behind ninety . . . dogs, catching straw, catching hay—old hay . . . catching . . . something else."

"Is that part of it, the 'something else'?"

"No. Catching straw, catching hay—old hay—catching . . . every darn barn ablaze! Duke said!"

Stem scribbled furiously. "What else?"

"What time is it?"

"1:11."

"Crap! You sent me to come back at precisely 1:06 today. Write that down. Oh, and you need to find a 12-step recovery meeting for your temper and gambling and junk food. Oh, and take me with you so I don't have an affair with my student!"

The pen paused in Stem's hand and his eyes slowly raised to meet Russ'. Dripping with disdain, he questioned, "You *did that*?"

"No. Well, yes, *I* did that, but the me you're about to stop didn't. Not yet . . . anyway." Under Stem's judgmental gaze, he exclaimed, "Oh, just write it down!"

"Recovery meeting," Stem murmured as he jotted down the note. "Russell is an idiot. Got it."

"But you've got to go right now. I'm—*the other me*—is in Kendall Hall. Keep me in there for another six or seven minutes. Do whatever you have to to keep me from leaving!"

"Yes!" Stem exclaimed as he took off with thoughts of brute force in mind.

Running after him, Russ called, "Wait! Stem!"

"Why are you bloody following me?"

"I'm headed to the pregnant tree! But I forgot to tell you something *really* important!"

Together, they rounded a corner and burst into the stairwell.

"Olive. She's a girl you'll meet. She has a sweet daughter. Marry her."

"Who? Olive or her daughter?"

"Olive. And let her buy *all* the Starbuck's coffee she wants."

Repulsed, Stem cried, "Charbuck's!"

"Do as I say! Buy her Starbuck's and marry her, you drongo!"

The insult clearly had a startling effect on the man. Pausing mid-step, he turned to read the expression on his mate's face. Russ stared him down with a hard glare. Accepting his fate, Stem gave a terse nod and hurried off.

Russ' feet picked up faster than they had in years. He had a mission and he would not fail. Exploding out the science building doors, he was immediately reminded of the deluge pouring from the sky. With his parched mouth wide open, he hustled as hard as he could past the Bible building. Taking a shortcut, he rounded the corner of the art building. Through the freezing rain, he could hardly see where his feet were taking him, yet his blood pumped so quickly he didn't feel the icy sting on his bare skin.

Cutting across the muddy front lawn, his feet splashed bucketfuls of cold sludge onto his legs. He caught a glimpse of Stem hustling as fast as lightning and it filled Russ' heart with unspeakable joy and hope. Then, the pregnant tree was in sight, the oddity of its round trunk protruding like the belly of a woman in her 40th week.

He flew so quickly that he almost missed her, but the moment his eyes spotted Katie, he slid to a stop on the soaked grass.

There she stood—on her own two legs, to his astonishment—perched beneath a yellow umbrella like a little bird. He wanted to go to her and scoop her up in his arms and hold her forever, but he suddenly felt petrified. If he did, if he stopped her from walking away in one minute and running towards her car in the northeast parking lot, then he'd never get to experience life with her. He'd return to the future and she'd not be the wife he had once had. All he had to do was *not stop her.*

Only, she looked so strong, so healthy. An exuberance—the very thing which had drawn him to her in the first place—emitted from her body like rays of sunlight. She had plans and dreams and a long life ahead of her. In spite of the rain, she lit the whole front lawn with her radiance.

There she was, glancing at her watch. He knew now what he didn't know then. She had to leave at 1:15 or she'd be late to a Valentine's luncheon with her girlfriends. She didn't have a minute to spare, but hoping to meet her secret admirer, she waited until 1:15 on the dot.

But she was turning north now. Her feet hesitated to take flight, but any moment, her runner's legs would carry her away and her destiny would be forever sealed.

His heart pumped, and, along with her legs, his flew.

"Wait!" he hollered. "Stop!"

His voice was drowned out by thunder, and she was halfway to East Center Avenue, the street the drunk was currently careening down. He knew he could still turn back and not stop it . . . only, he couldn't.

"Katie!" he shouted with all his might. "Katherine Margaret Henshaw! Stop!"

And she did, just thirty feet from the street. She turned and saw him—their eyes locked on each other as he closed the last few feet between them.

"Katie!" he gasped, grabbing her arm. "Wait! The truck—"

Just then came a terrible sound he'd never forget. Tires squealing and people screaming. The crunching of metal and smashing of bricks filled the air as the diesel struck the corner of the American Heritage Building, the very two objects between which Katie's body had once been pinned. Her survival had been a miracle.

"Oh, my goodness!" she cried. "I'm a nurse. I've got to see if anyone was hurt!"

"Wait!" he pleaded, tears filling his eyes. "Please, just stand here with me until—"

But he could already feel something odd inside himself, something not right, like falling through a hole while standing still. And that's when he remembered Stem's last warning.

Katie turned to leave—she couldn't *not* run to help—and as Russ' fingers wrapped around the stem of her umbrella, he saw a bright flash before his eyes.

The whooshing lights and deoxygenation and burning lungs gripped Russ like a vise. In his hand, clutched tightly in his fist, the umbrella remained. He simultaneously felt as if he were flying and being crushed by an elephant. And then the strangest thing happened. In the distance, shooting through the stars, he saw himself. And himself saw him. They saw each other and neither knew what to think, but both knew they were on a trajectory path of collision. And then, bam! The two Russes collided like Katie and that truck, and everything went dark.

Chapter 33

"Russ?"

The man felt as if his body had been smashed beneath a steamroller.

"Russell, mate, are you in there?"

"I can't see him."

There was a shuffling and a flash as a small beam of light quickly swept across his face. Was Russ dead? He might've been, but he hadn't expected Heaven to be so dark.

All at once, the room was lit. The rainy day nine years ago in February had been gray, and his eyes took a moment to adjust to the bright illumination.

"Oh, that's a nasty gash."

"It looks fairly superficial."

"Mate, you all right, yeah?"

Above his head, Stem hovered.

"Open your eyes, mate. Let me see your pupils."

"They're not dilated so I think he's all good."

With trembling arms dripping with rainwater, Russ tried pushing himself upright.

Stem stooped beside the man. "Whoa, let me help, mate. Easy now." He held onto the disoriented man until his back was steadily resting against the birdcage bars. "Good, yeah?"

"What happened?" mumbled Russ, and, as he brought his hand up to his aching head, he realized his fingers were still tightly wound around the wet umbrella. Dropping it, he wondered aloud, "Did I do it? Did I save Katie?"

Gesturing with his hand, Stem said, "Ask her yourself."

The confusion in Russ' head only grew as he turned it and saw Katie—*his* Katie—standing on her own two legs. Gaping, he stared at her, soaking her up like a parched desert plant.

"Katie?" he gasped.

Her gentle hand took his as she dropped to his side. "How you feeling, honey?"

His eyes tossed a questioning look from her to Stem and back to the woman at his side.

"Looks like you hit your head," she said, pushing back his damp hair. "Does it hurt?"

If his hand had been cut off, he wouldn't have felt the pain—being in her presence, the object of her affectionate gaze, filled Russ with elation. "You can stand? Katie, your legs are okay?"

Her sweet laughter echoed in the hollow, cavernous space. "Yes, sweetie. I'm just fine."

Pulling her hand to his lips, he bowed his head and pressed tears out of his eyes. Then, lifting his face, he said barely above a whisper, "You called me sweetie. What are we, you and I?"

Cozying up beside him, facing him, she cupped his cheek in her palm. "Honey, you don't remember?"

Evidently, he didn't—only, at that moment, a memory he never knew came to his mind like an epiphany.

"Wait," he said, shifting his head, reviving a little. "Wait. You came back from Ghana."

She smiled and nodded. "See, you remember."

"That's right. I do remember—somehow. It was because you got sick."

"Bilharzia," she confirmed.

"You were *really* sick and I visited you in the hospital."

"And I was curious about the man who had saved my life."

"And then we dated." As if rejoicing over his true love for the first time, he cried with joy, "We got married too, right? And we're *still* married? You didn't leave me and I didn't . . . Oh, Katie, I didn't hurt you, did I? I'm so sorry. Please tell me I didn't hurt you."

She flashed him her hand which wore a sparkling bejeweled ring. "Proof that I'm still yours." Taking his hand in hers, she slid a black metallic ring on his finger and added, "And proof that you still belong to me."

He could do nothing more than lean into her body and weep tears of joy.

"All bloody right," griped Stem. "Enough of this sappy stuff. Up with you, Russell."

As his friend pulled him to his feet, Russ noticed that, save for the machine, the entire cellar was empty. "Where is everything?" But the moment he spoke the words, he knew the answer. "We gave it all back, didn't we?"

Stem nodded. "Thanks to your sharp history skills and my ability to decode Peepaw's travel logs, we found most of the owners. The rest we donated to museums."

"And we buried Peepaw, right?"

With a nod, Stem confirmed, "Beside your mum."

Glancing around, Russ inquired, "And Lance isn't still tied up down here somewhere, is he?" Upon his friend's blank stare, he further questioned, "And the FBI didn't arrest us? eBay didn't shut me down?"

Squinting and gazing at the man, Stem said, "Mate, let me see your pupils again."

Russ chuckled. "No, I'm fine. It's just that the craziest thing happened. I saw myself in the time loop—the other me that you sent back—and we collided." Reaching up, he gently felt the gash on his forehead. "It's like we somehow meshed together and became one person, and I'm remembering his memories."

His friend's head tilted, and he stared at the man like a ghost. "Mate, you're saying you're the *other* Russell, yeah? The one who dropped out of nowhere nine years ago and vanished without a trace?"

"Yes, but that was only like ten minutes ago to me. But now it's like I'm the other Russ too, the one you sent back because I have his memories too. Is that even possible?"

"It's implausible . . . but intriguing."

Katie gazed into her husband's eyes, studying them like a book. Then, with a smile and a shrug, she announced, "You look like the Russ *I* know."

Slowly, he pulled her close and begged, "May I kiss you? Please, Katie? It's been so long."

Rising to her tippy toes, she welcomed the intimacy. Russ leaned down, savoring the long-awaited moment.

When he'd endured enough of their sappiness, Stem cleared his throat. "All right, enough of the pashing. Like I said, we've got to move this party along. Ruby's babysitting the ankle biters in the van while they watch Bluey, and she's charging me by the hour, so let's push on towards the exit, mates, before I'm a destitute man."

Russ' eyebrows commanded a smile. "Ankle biters?" Seeing his friend's nod, he questioned, "But wait—are they yours or mine?"

"I can double check with Olive, mate, but I'm pretty sure they're mine."

As they climbed the stairs, Russ inquired, "And how many kids do you have again?"

"Three, of course. Ruby, Jade, and Benjo." Locking up 42B behind them, he questioned, "And while we're on the topic of children—and because of your suspicious amnesia, outrageous suppositions, and oozing laceration which may require a copious number of stitches—may I ask how many little ones *you* have?"

"Me?" Russ squealed. "I don't—" But with a mirthful chuckle, he exclaimed, "Two! Stem, I have two kids!"

The science professor glanced from Russ to Katie and back again. "I'm aware of that fact, mate. Glad to know you are too."

"I can't believe it," laughed the elated man. Lifting his wife off the ground, he sang, "Katie, we have children!"

Her giggles filled the old storage shed, and, glancing at her watch, she chuckled, "And we'd better get them picked up before they drive Meemaw bonkers."

"Meemaw? But she died."

"No, honey. She didn't."

"But the cancer . . ."

"We caught it early, remember? She's in remission and doing great."

As they exited the storage shed, sunlight and tears filled Russ' eyes. Noticing it, his bride placed a protective arm around his waist and whispered, "Is everything ok? Does your head hurt?"

"Not a bit."

She gazed into his eyes, and, though he was certain she was just checking again to see if his pupils were dilated, he felt as if the elation in his body might suddenly lift him off the ground.

"Well," she conceded, "it's not bleeding too much now. You think you'll be ok?"

Wrapping her gently in his arms, Russ sighed contentedly and declared, "Katie, my dear, I'm superb. I cannot imagine a better life to wake up to."

THE END

Epilogue

Outside his office window, autumn leaves fell to the rhythm of the students' energetic feet. The fall semester was underway and it had never felt so good to return to campus.

Russ reached for a book he had never seen before. Plucking it off his shelf, he thumbed through the index. "Looks interesting," he chuckled to himself. "Guess the other me had good taste."

A knock on the door drew him out of his thoughts.

"Professor Brown?"

The familiar voice made the hairs on his neck rise. Turning, he saw an attractive young brunette, her eyes glistening with tears.

"Caydee," he gasped. "What are you doing here?"

Her chin quivered as she crossed the office. "Professor Brown, can you help me? I really need someone to talk to."

Closing the book, he cautiously questioned, "Is this about your boyfriend?"

Her frown quickly turned to a smile. "You're so smart. Of course, you'd know why I'm crying."

"Have a seat," he said, motioning to an armchair. Setting the book on the dark woodgrain, he settled in behind his desk.

As her book bag dropped to the floor, so did tears from her eyes. "I just don't know what to do," she cried. "All I wanted was a guy who liked me, who could really see me for me. Is that too much to ask, Professor Brown? Don't I deserve that?"

He listened and scribbled something down on a sticky note.

"Professor Brown?" she said, summoning his attention. "Do you think I deserve a better man?"

Looking up, he stated, "Absolutely."

She grinned. "So, will you help me?"

"Yes." Ripping off the sticky note, he extended it to her. "Call this number."

"Oh!" she rejoiced. "And let me give you *my* number!"

"That's not mine," he said with a shake of his head. "That's for Mandy Morgan. She owns a therapy office down the street and she offers free counseling to Harding students. You really should call her. She can help you."

The girl stuck out a pouty lip. However, seeing his resolve, she reached for her bag and muttered, "Thanks."

"You're welcome." But as he watched her head for the door, he called out, "Hang on just a sec."

Turning, she flashed him a winning smile. "You wanted me?"

He hesitated but pushed forth. "Who is . . . Dan?"

A look of confusion spread across her face. "Dan?"

"Yeah," he said, feeling somewhat stupid for having asked. "Don't you know someone named Dan? Maybe? Well, I just wondered who he was."

"Oh, Dan's not a boy! She's my roommate—Danielle."

"Oh," he gaped. "I did not see that coming."

She lingered in the doorway, resting her head against the trim, gazing at him with soft eyes.

Reaching for his phone, he checked the time. "Well, thank you for stopping by," he said politely, "but I need to head out."

As he pulled on his jacket, she perked up. "Where ya going?"

"To lunch."

At the notion, she seemed almost giddy. "Can I come too?"

"No," he said, shaking his head. "I've already got a date with a Katie—and she's the only one for me."

Accolades and Thanks

A special thank you to:

- My husband, Kent, who knows no more about writing books than I do riding bikes. You and I are tandem rhymes, fitting together like a burr and a sock, so dissimilar but attached to one another while we perform our own mysterious functions and occasionally irritate one another. I love you and am grateful I found inspiration for this story in the resurrection of our marriage (though a time machine would've made ours a lot easier and probably funnier).
- My oldest brother, Andrew, who was first to read my book and did so with the keen eye of a gifted storyteller and sci-fi enthusiast. Your bedtime stories are the things of legend (and occasionally nightmares).
- My next oldest brother, Peter, whose expertise on the inner world of Harding University, Searcy, and the like kept those parts of my story authentic. You've never steered me wrong (except when you and Andrew convinced me I was a robot—still in recovery for that, thanks).

- My part-Aussie brother-in-law, Travis, who made certain my funniest character was believable to Americans and Aussies alike. You've kept me straight on course and aligned my goal with my outcome (and I'm not just saying that because you're a stellar chiropractor, although it's the backbone of my accolade). {Check out Cowin Chiropractic Clinic if you'rc in Wollongong!}
- My feral children—Brian, Melton, and Emleigh—whose love of storytelling has not only refined but also demanded my craft. Y'all are my greatest reason for making up new stories (largely because it was my only strategy for preventing coup d'états during long car rides, especially after y'all cut your molars and figured out how to gnaw your way out of your car seats).
- And my amazing readers. Your faithfulness and exuberance propels me towards my writing destiny (which is turning out to be improbably spectacular).

If you think this novel is a gem, please leave a review! Thank you!

R. M. Snider

www.ingramcontent.com/pod-product-compliance
Lightning Source LLC
Chambersburg PA
CBHW061650190726
48289CB00006B/1815
9781736038017